# Praise for the novels of Deirdre Martin

## *With a Twist*

"Funny, energetic, and loads of fun, *With A Twist* is a tale readers shouldn't miss . . . Once you start reading *With A Twist*, you won't want to put it down."     —*Romance Reviews Today*

"A refreshing contemporary romance that shows just how much work and effort goes into making true love more than just a phrase."     —*A Romance Review*

"Don't miss this latest heartwarming romance by Ms. Martin. I never miss anything she writes. It's always a gift."

—*Fresh Fiction*

## *Power Play*

"Martin's latest hockey romance is no exception to the game plan . . . Hot and romantic."     —*Romantic Times*

"A sheer delight from the first page till the last . . . Contemporary romance doesn't get much better than this."

—*All About Romance*

"Pure bliss. It's a winning story that skates to victory, melting your heart along the way."     —*Fresh Fiction*

## *Just a Taste*

"Another victory for Martin."     —*Booklist*

"A warmhearted romance with in-depth characters, this story will leave you satisfied, salivating and ready to try one of the recipes included. Martin serves up a real treat."

—*Romantic Times* (four stars)

"Be prepared to get a li            or a tempting read you won'

day

## Chasing Stanley

"Martin has created an enjoyable sports community with quirky characters and lots of humorous dialogue."  —*Romantic Times*

"Martin has a way of bringing her dissimilar characters together that rings true, and fans and curious new readers won't want to miss her latest hockey-themed romance."  —*Booklist*

## The Penalty Box

"[Martin] can touch the heart and the funny bone."
—*Romance Junkies*

"Martin scores another goal with another witty, emotionally true-to-life, and charming hockey romance."  —*Booklist*

"Fun, fast rink-side contemporary romance . . . Martin scores with this witty blend of romance and family dynamics."
—*Publishers Weekly*

"Ms. Martin always delivers heat and romance, with a very strong conflict to keep the reader engaged. *The Penalty Box* should be added to your 'must-read list.' "
—*Contemporary Romance Writers*

## Total Rush

"*Total Rush* is just that—a total rush, an absolute delight. Deirdre Martin is the reason I read romance novels. This contemporary romance is so well written [and] has a hero to die for and a romance that turns you into a puddle. It fills your heart to overflowing with love, acceptance, and the beauty of uniqueness. I laughed, I cried, I celebrated. It's more than a read, it is a reread. Brava, Ms. Martin, you're the greatest!"  —*The Best Reviews*

"Well written . . . Makes you want to keep turning the pages to see what happens next."  —*The Columbia (SC) State*

"Martin's inventive take on opposites attracting is funny and poignant."  —*Booklist*

"A heartwarming story of passion, acceptance, and most importantly, love, this book is definitely a *Total Rush*."
—*Romance Reviews Today*

## Fair Play

"Martin depicts the worlds of both professional hockey and ethnic Brooklyn with deftness and smart detail. She has an unerring eye for humorous family dynamics [and] sweet buoyancy."
—*Publishers Weekly*

"Fast paced, wisecracking, and an enjoyable story . . . Makes you feel like you're flying."
—*Rendezvous*

## Body Check

"Heartwarming."
—*Booklist*

"Combines sports and romance in a way that reminded me of Susan Elizabeth Phillips's *It Had to Be You*, but Deirdre Martin has her own style and voice. *Body Check* is one of the best first novels I have read in a long time."
—*All About Romance* (Desert Isle Keeper)

"Deirdre Martin aims for the net and scores with *Body Check*."
—*The Romance Reader* (four hearts)

"You don't have to be a hockey fan to cheer for *Body Check*. Deirdre Martin brings readers a story that scores."
—*The Word on Romance*

"Fun, fast paced, and sexy, *Body Check* is a dazzling debut."
—*USA Today* bestselling author Millie Criswell

"Fun, delightful, emotional, and sexy, *Body Check* is an utterly enthralling, fast-paced novel. This is one author I eagerly look forward to reading more from."
—*Romance Reviews Today*

"An engaging romance that scores a hat trick [with] a fine supporting cast."
—*The Best Reviews*

Titles by Deirdre Martin

BODY CHECK
FAIR PLAY
TOTAL RUSH
THE PENALTY BOX
CHASING STANLEY
JUST A TASTE
POWER PLAY
WITH A TWIST
STRAIGHT UP

Anthologies

HOT TICKET
*(with Julia London, Annette Blair, and Geri Buckley)*

DOUBLE THE PLEASURE
*(with Lori Foster, Jacquie D'Alessandro, and Penny McCall)*

DOUBLE THE HEAT
*(with Lori Foster, Elizabeth Bevarly, and Christie Ridgway)*

# Straight Up

## Deirdre Martin

**B**

BERKLEY SENSATION, NEW YORK

**THE BERKLEY PUBLISHING GROUP**
**Published by the Penguin Group**
**Penguin Group (USA) Inc.**
**375 Hudson Street, New York, New York 10014, USA**
Penguin Group (Canada), 90 Eglinton Avenue East, Suite 700, Toronto, Ontario M4P 2Y3, Canada
(a division of Pearson Penguin Canada Inc.)
Penguin Books Ltd., 80 Strand, London WC2R 0RL, England
Penguin Group Ireland, 25 St. Stephen's Green, Dublin 2, Ireland (a division of Penguin Books Ltd.)
Penguin Group (Australia), 250 Camberwell Road, Camberwell, Victoria 3124, Australia
(a division of Pearson Australia Group Pty. Ltd.)
Penguin Books India Pvt. Ltd., 11 Community Centre, Panchsheel Park, New Delhi—110 017, India
Penguin Group (NZ), 67 Apollo Drive, Rosedale, North Shore 0632, New Zealand
(a division of Pearson New Zealand Ltd.)
Penguin Books (South Africa) (Pty.) Ltd., 24 Sturdee Avenue, Rosebank, Johannesburg 2196,
South Africa

Penguin Books Ltd., Registered Offices: 80 Strand, London WC2R 0RL, England

This is a work of fiction. Names, characters, places, and incidents either are the product of the author's imagination or are used fictitiously, and any resemblance to actual persons, living or dead, business establishments, events, or locales is entirely coincidental. The publisher does not have any control over and does not assume any responsibility for author or third-party websites or their content.

STRAIGHT UP

A Berkley Sensation Book / published by arrangement with the author

PRINTING HISTORY
Berkley Sensation mass-market edition / May 2010

Copyright © 2010 by Deirdre Martin.
Cover art and design by Laura Drew.

ISBN: 978-0-425-23466-2

BERKLEY® SENSATION
Berkley Sensation Books are published by The Berkley Publishing Group,
a division of Penguin Group (USA) Inc.,
375 Hudson Street, New York, New York 10014.
BERKLEY® SENSATION and the "B" design are trademarks of Penguin Group (USA) Inc.

PRINTED IN THE UNITED STATES OF AMERICA

10  9  8  7  6  5  4  3  2  1

*In memory of Pat O'Shea,*
*the best Irish storyteller I ever knew.*

# Acknowledgments

Mark and Rocky, my main men.

Jane, for making our trip to Ireland fabulous fun.

My wonderful agent, Miriam Kriss, and my equally wonderful editor, Kate Seaver.

Binnie Braunstein, Dee Tenorio, Eileen Buchholtz, and Jeff Schwartzenberg.

The Actors Workshop of Ithaca and Wingspace Theatre Company for helping to keep me sane.

Mom, Dad, Bill, Allison, Beth, Dave, Tom, Ken, and Brak.

# 1

*The Yank, the* Yank, the Yank. For the past two weeks, all Aislinn heard every time she ventured into Ballycraig from the farm was that there was a handsome American in town, working as a bartender at the Royal Oak. They said he was the nephew of Bridget and Paul O'Brien, two of the nicest people in town, and the dirt was that he was from New York City and was supposedly on the lam from the Irish Mob. The Yank, the Yank, the Yank. Aislinn decided it was time to check out the specimen herself.

She took her battered old truck into town rather than ride her bike, since a gentle rain was falling. Last time she'd chanced a bike ride in a light rain, the drizzle had turned into an all-out, pelting downpour. She was in no mood to find herself cycling back home drenched to the bone, clothes pasted to her like a cold second skin. No mood at all.

Aislinn had to park down Kennealy Way, one of Ballycraig's narrow, cobbled back alleys, since all the parking spots on the high street were taken. There may have been only three thousand people in the village, but from the looks of it, all of them were crammed into the Oak tonight. There was no other place to go for a pint, unless you wanted to drive the twenty miles to Crosshaven. But none of the pubs there were as nice as the Oak, and besides, who wanted to bend the elbow with strangers— not that Aislinn had any intention of lingering. No. It would be in for a quick whiskey and then home for a good night's sleep. Tomorrow was going to be a busy day, checking the fence lines to make sure none of her flock could escape.

Aislinn entered the pub, hanging her barn jacket on the row of pegs immediately inside the door. As she'd expected, every seat and table were taken. The flickering glow of the fireplace created a sense of intimacy, and as always, the mood was jovial, thick with the feel of kinship and a shared need to relax. She checked her watch: it was still a bit too early for everyone to be in their cups or for the singing to begin. A few of the other farmers sitting round a knotted old table near the fire nodded to her, and she nodded back. That was the extent of farmer conversation, which was fine with her.

Aislinn walked the wide, battered wooden planks of the floor and made her way to the bar, ignoring Fergus Purcell, David Shiels, and Teague Daly, Ballycraig's Holy Trinity of Arseholes. As boys, they'd made her school years hell, always teasing her about being a tomboy and for wanting to be a sheep farmer just like her dad. It took years before she realized it was anger that drove their taunting. She could outplay any of them in football, and when God doled out brains, she'd been miles ahead of them in line. Anyway, from the time she'd started giving boys the time of day, she'd only had eyes for Connor McCarthy. More fool her.

"Well, well," said Fergus, a slip of a man who fancied himself a comedian. "Look who's here. Lady Muck has decided to grace us with her presence."

"You're not joking when you say the word *muck*," David added. "Look at them wellies. Caked with mud, they are." The threesome laughed.

Aislinn chuckled along with them, even as she fantasized running the three of them down when the eejits staggered home after closing.

"God, you lot have me laughing so hard my sides are about to split!" she exclaimed. She cocked her head in mock wonder. "I was wondering, Fergus and David: how's your construction business going? I was reading in the *Independent* just the other day that building is down over sixty percent. That Celtic Tiger you've been riding has keeled over and died, aye? Bad luck." Their faces fell as she turned on a charming smile for Teague. "And you, Teague Daly, you great, fat, balding thing. Have you found a job yet? Or are you planning to live at home and mooch off your poor ailing parents for the rest of your life?"

"Feckin' bitch," Teague muttered under his breath, hunching his shoulders as he pointedly turned his back on her. The other two goony-faced fools were still staring at her, but all it took was one good glare, and they shrank, knowing to keep their mouths shut unless they wanted her to dish up another heap of the brutal truth. Gutless twits. Always had been, always would be.

"Evening."

Aislinn turned her attention to the man behind the bar. So, this was the Yank. Well, the tales were dead-on: he was fine-looking, with slate gray eyes and a great tousle of dark brown hair. Nice build, which he apparently was proud of if the tightness of his T-shirt was any indication. Charming smile.

"Evening," Aislinn replied curtly.

He extended his hand. "Liam."

She ignored the gesture. "Aislinn."

"Call her the McCafferty; that's her true name," she heard Fergus mutter.

Old Jack, the balding, potbellied owner of the bar, jumped in before Aislinn got a chance to shoot back at him. "Shut your pie hole, Fergus." He smiled at Aislinn. "What can I get you, love? The usual?"

"Yes, please."

She gave Liam the once-over. "So, you're the Yank everyone's blathering about."

"I prefer to think of myself as American."

"Really? I thought all you Irish Americans preferred to think of yourselves as Irish."

Jack handed her her whiskey.

"Thanks." She threw the dram down her throat and immediately asked for another. Liam was studying her, and not in a passive way, either. She didn't like it. "Quit eyeballing me."

Liam laughed. "Can't I look at the person I'm having a conversation with?"

"Since when are we having a conversation?"

David leaned over to Liam. "I'd avert my gaze if I were you, lest you want to burst into flames."

"Enough!" Jack snapped. He put another whiskey down in front of Aislinn. "Hard day?"

Aislinn nodded, appreciative of his asking. "I had to set up the creep for the lambs today."

"Did Padraig not help?"

"Padraig has been a bit off his game lately," she replied, a little more disgruntled than she intended. Padraig was part of the reason she was in a bad mood. A hired hand who'd helped her parents with the sheep farm for as long as she could remember, he was closing in on seventy-five now and was getting forgetful, sometimes doing the same chore twice, sometimes forgetting a chore entirely. Even so, she couldn't bear to let him go. Never married, he lived alone in a small cottage on her property. All he had was the farm and her.

Old Jack had moved down to the other end of the bar to take orders, leaving her with the Yank.

"I gather you work on a sheep farm," Liam said with a friendly smile.

"I own the farm, thank you very much." Work on it. Of course a man would assume that. "I hear you're on the lam from the Mob."

Liam blinked, looking at her like he couldn't quite believe she'd said that.

"Some of the ladies in the town are impressed by that, you know," she continued.

"Fine with me," he replied, a swagger in his voice. Oh, this one was full of himself, all right.

"I can't see what's so impressive about it," said Aislinn, sipping her whiskey. "Seems to me only a fool would get mixed up in such things."

"It's complicated," Liam said tersely. She smiled, seeing she'd gotten under his skin and punctured his cool.

"Why'd you come to Ballycraig to hide out?" she continued. "You're from New York City, no? Why not disappear in Dublin?"

"My people are here."

Aislinn snorted. "'My people'! God, you plastic Paddys! I suppose you'll be reconnecting with your roots while you're here, too."

Liam just smiled, which was maddening. "Stop flirting with me. You're making me uncomfortable."

Aislinn's jaw dropped. "I most certainly am not flirting with you!"

"I think you are."

"And I think you're soft in the head." She drained her whiskey glass and plunked it down on the bar, adding a glare for good measure. Flirting with him. Ha! Didn't he just wish!

She strode to the door. "Leaving so soon?" Liam called after her teasingly. She ignored him.

"Don't forget your broomstick!" Teague added cheerily. She ignored that, too.

She stomped back to her truck, fuming. First the idiocy of the Trinity, then the Yank with his flirting rubbish. Addlepated fool. She'd no patience for him, or for any of the men in this town with their big egos and big talk and not a damn bit of character to back it up. She'd learned the hard way when it came to the men of Ballycraig. Useless bunch—and now there was one more to contend with, and a Yank to boot.

Flirting with him. She snorted loudly as she started up her truck and roared out of town in the now teeming rain. *In your dreams, Yank. In your dreams.*

*   *   *

*"Anyone care to* explain to me what just happened here?" Liam asked, watching Aislinn storm out into the night. He'd noticed her the second she'd walked through the door. How could he not? She was tall, with a regal bearing, her long, red hair tangled wildly around her head like some kind of Celtic Medusa. She had porcelain skin and sparkling green eyes, as well as a seeming devil-may-care attitude when it came to clothing: a barn jacket, a plain red T-shirt, faded, ripped jeans, and mud-caked wellies. A real country girl. A *beautiful* country girl.

"What happened is you've had your first encounter with the McCafferty," said Fergus as his pals sniggered.

"The McCafferty?"

"Ay, that's her nickname around town," Old Jack explained.

"That's her last name?"

Jack nodded.

"Why the nickname?" Liam asked as he handed a pint of Harp to Grace Finnegan, who owned and operated the small grocery store on the high street.

"It's nicer than calling her the Bitch," explained Teague.

"Did you not feel your balls shriveling as you talked to her?" asked Jack.

"She seemed a little abrasive," Liam admitted. "But I didn't feel emasculated."

"She's just warming up," Jack continued with a grimace. "Wait till the next time you meet her. You'll have to check yourself to make sure your goolies aren't in shreds."

"Why was she here alone? Doesn't she have any friends?"

"Used to." David sniffed. "Drove 'em all away with that sharp tongue of hers."

"She's fierce," said Jack. "And mad independent. Used to be a nice girl, but . . ." He shook his head sadly.

"But what?" Liam pushed. He was completely intrigued.

"Got her heart broken badly," said Jack.

"She was crazy about this jackass, Connor McCarthy—" David began.

Old Jack interrupted with a snort. "He was no jackass. You're just upset she'd never give you the time of day in the romance department."

"That's not true."

"It is true." Jack took over the story. "She was seeing this fellow, Connor, for years and years. Lovely guy, gentle. Worked as a mechanic. They finally got engaged. A big, lovely wedding was planned up at her family's farm." He took a sip of his beer. "Well, the day rolled around, and didn't he confess right up there at the altar that he was gay as the day is long?"

"Jesus! That's terrible!" said Liam.

"Oh, it was, it was. The poor girl was humiliated, not to mention heartbroken and furious. And rightfully so." He lowered his voice. "But ever since that day, she's had no use for the male sex. No use for anyone, really. It changed her into a hard thing. She'd as soon eat you alive as look at you." He shuddered.

"Don't you think something like that would change you, too?" Liam asked.

"Probably," Jack admitted after a long pause. "But I'd like to think if it were me, I'd reach out to others, rather than drive them away."

"Doesn't she have any family?" Liam asked.

"One sister, Nora, who skedaddled out of town as soon as she turned eighteen. She went to England to go to university in London. Married to some richy rich stock-broker. She and Aislinn aren't close. As for her parents, Doris and Bert"—he shook his head sadly—"they were killed about six months ago in a car crash. Awful, it was, God rest their souls."

Liam wasn't surprised to hear it. The Irish were luna-tics behind the wheel, even on small, winding country roads where two cars could barely pass each other. Com-bine that with some people driving drunk, and the fatality rate from auto accidents was unbelievable.

"Drunk driver?"

"Of course," said Jack. He drained his beer. "Well, that just added another devastation for her, didn't it? She was dead close to her old man. They worked the farm together. Now she runs it with Padraig."

Teague laughed meanly. "A right coffin dodger, he is. Old as dirt and losing his wits, at least that's what I hear. Grace Finnegan told me he came into her shop the other day asking for tinned peaches, and when she handed them to him, he insisted he'd asked for pears and then wound up going home with three packets of crisps and some fags instead."

"Sad," said Jack. "He's a lovely oul fella."

Liam couldn't imagine the double blow of being left at the altar, followed by the death of both parents. He might have handled it differently, but that she handled it at all was proof in his eyes that she was strong. A lesser soul would have been demolished.

"How far out of town is the farm?"

David narrowed his eyes suspiciously. "Seems to me you're asking a helluva lot of questions about the McCafferty."

"Just curious."

"A bit too much," said Jack, beginning to look alarmed. "You fancy her, don't you?"

"Maybe."

"Like she'd have you," David sneered. "She won't even

give the time of day to an Irishman. What makes you think she'd soften her heart for a Yank?"

Liam just rolled his eyes. From the minute he'd arrived in town, he'd had to deal with animosity from these three clowns who seemed to think they were Ballycraig's cocks of the walk.

"Yeah," Fergus chimed in. "You heard her: you're a plastic Paddy. We all know it. On the lam from the Irish Mob, my arse. You're one of them rich Yanks over here looking for your roots."

"A rich Yank depriving an Irishman of a job," added Teague, gesturing at the bar.

"I hate to tell you, but Liam has years of bartending experience," said Jack, coming to his defense. "His parents own a pub in New York City."

"So that's a reason to install him here at the Oak before giving me a shot?" Teague shot back heatedly.

"Teague Daly, it's no secret to anyone in this town that you've got about as much drive as a Brit," Jack said bluntly. "I've no doubt that if I'd hired you in this job, within a fortnight you'd be moaning on day and night about how hard it is."

His friends laughed.

"Feck you, Jack," Teague hissed.

"The truth hurts, aye?" Jack teased.

Teague gave him the old two-fingered salute.

Jack put a hand on Liam's shoulder. "Listen to me. I know that under all the mud the McCafferty is a gorgeous piece of womanhood, but if you're thinkin' of trying to tame her, don't waste your time."

"You make her sound like a horse!"

"A horse would have more luck with her," Teague muttered.

"Truly, I wouldn't waste your time," Old Jack repeated solemnly. "She'll chew you up and spit you out—assuming she'd even let you close to her."

"I bet you're wrong."

Old Jack thrust his head forward as if he hadn't heard Liam correctly. "What did you just say?"

"I said, I bet you're wrong. I bet I can break down her defenses and get her to go out with me."

David, Fergus, and Teague howled with laughter.

"Christ, will you listen to the ego on it!" said David. "You Yanks! You all think you're superheroes!"

"It'll never happen," said Fergus, shaking his head. "Never in a million years."

Liam flashed a confident grin. "Wanna bet?"

Old Jack's eyes lit up. "What are we betting?"

"If I win, you double my wages. If I lose, you don't have to pay me for a year."

"You're on." They shook on it.

"See, what did I tell you?" said Fergus disgustedly. "No wages for a year? He's a rich Yank! He's hiding from the tax man, not the Mob."

"You're going to lose this wager," Teague said to Liam. "You wait and see. And then you're gonna come crawlin' back here with your tail between your legs—and believe me, that's all you'll have between your legs after the McCafferty finishes with you."

"We'll see. Now: anyone need a refill?"

# 2

*Early the next* afternoon, Liam set out to walk the two miles to Aislinn's farm. It was a beautiful day, sunny and clear, with white clouds trailing lazily across the pale blue sky that seemed to stretch on forever. A light breeze was blowing, carrying on it the smell of fresh green grass. He could smell a peat fire burning far off.

Liam took his time walking the narrow roads lined with low gray stone walls and hawthorn bushes. Rolling emerald fields stretched out before him, the color so vivid they almost looked like they'd been touched up for a post-card. He heard birdsong, and in the distance, the bleating of sheep. There was no denying it: the Irish countryside was beautiful. And yet, he missed home.

He missed the hustle of Manhattan, its quick rhythm and frenetic energy. But most of all, he missed his family. He and his brother Quinn e-mailed each other daily, and Quinn's vivid writing sometimes made Liam feel as if he were actually there witnessing life unfold at the Wild Hart. But it wasn't the same. He wasn't there in person to hug his sister Maggie and congratulate her about expecting her first child. He wasn't there to see his sister

Sinead relaxed and happy now that her horrible, prolonged divorce was through. Not there to see Quinn and his wife Natalie tease each other or to witness the affection between his parents that he and his sibs all aspired to in their own relationships. He even missed the patrons of the bar. But he couldn't go back lest he risk his life.

Thanks to his childhood friend Tommy, who was a runner for the Irish Mafia in Manhattan, he'd been set up, tricked into aiding and abetting Tommy in the torching of a video store. Whitey Connors, the head of the Irish Mob, could now drop a dime on Liam if he wanted to. Of course, Liam was just a pawn, a way for Whitey to try to stop his brother, Quinn, from working on his newspaper exposé about the Mob. At first Whitey played nice; but one day, he arranged a meeting with Quinn and made it clear that if Quinn didn't drop the story, he just might kill Liam. Whitey dare not go after Quinn directly; as Quinn had once told Liam, the Mafia were stupid, but they weren't stupid enough to kill a journalist.

Fortunately for Liam, one of the longtime patrons at his parents' bar, an elderly man known as the Major, had been an officer in the Irish Republican Army in its fight for independence. The Major was respected and still feared, even by the likes of Whitey. It was the Major who arranged for Liam to go to Ireland, believing Whitey wouldn't dare touch him if he knew it was the Major, and perhaps his shadowy old friends, behind sending him away. So Liam went, even though Quinn's article resulted in Whitey and a bunch of other goons being jailed. But Quinn's sources at the FBI told him it wasn't safe for Liam to come home yet. And now here he was, not knowing when he'd be able to go back to New York, if ever.

He yawned, walking on. He hadn't gotten much sleep. The official closing time for the Royal Oak was twelve thirty, but once the musicians started playing, there was no getting them out of there until at least two o'clock, not that anyone minded. It never failed to amaze Liam that when Old Jack finally did close, everyone stood and sang the Irish national anthem in Gaelic. He tried to picture the patrons of the Hart rising to sing "The Star-Spangled Banner" and laughed out loud.

Once in bed, he'd found himself unable to stop thinking about Aislinn. The McCafferty. How hysterical was it that a pack of men actually seemed scared of her? It might be understandable if she was an ax-wielding maniac, but she wasn't. Okay, she did come across as a spitfire, but it was obviously some kind of defense mechanism. He had no doubt he'd win his bet. All he had to do was break through, and given his track record, he had every confidence it could be achieved.

He'd never met any woman who'd been able to resist his charms for long. Part of it was his looks, but another part of it was his undeniable moodiness. Women found him deep and mysterious, and he saw no reason to disabuse them of the notion.

But it wasn't just ego that told him he'd be able to "tame" Aislinn. He was a bartender, for chrissakes. He knew how to read people, get them to talk and open up. All he had to do was gain her trust. It was going to be a cakewalk.

Liam's walk came to an end when he spotted a large stone farmhouse atop a hill. There were two barns and two small outbuildings nearby. The surrounding pastures on both sides of the road were bisected by stone walls and wire fences. The big tip-off he'd arrived were the sheep spilling across the road, being herded along by a border collie.

He dutifully waited for the herd to pass, then continued walking until he came to the long, winding, deeply rutted road leading up to the house. Hard as it was for him to believe, his heartbeat was actually picking up pace. He was *nervous*.

Liam picked his way around the potholes, pissed that he hadn't had the foresight to wear his hiking boots rather than his running shoes, which were rapidly becoming covered in oozing mud.

Now atop the hill, he turned and looked below. The view was spectacular. Open land as far as the eye could see; ancient, twisted trees; hedgerows. He closed his eyes and took a deep breath, fully experiencing the momentary sense of peace and wonder overtaking him. He opened his eyes. He could hear someone rustling around in the nearest outbuilding. He stuck his head in. "Hello?"

An ancient, hunched old man looked up from hosing out a green plastic trough. Old Jack was right: Padraig was older than God, but there was still a spark in his crinkled blue eyes. He turned off the hose, put it down, and approached Liam.

"Can I help you? Here to buy some wool?"

"Actually, I'm here to see Aislinn."

"Aislinn?" The old man looked mildly alarmed. "Who are you?"

"Liam O'Brien. I tend bar down at the Royal Oak."

Padraig relaxed as his eyes lit up with recognition. "Bridget and Paul's nephew? The Yank?"

Liam chuckled. "Yes, the Yank. Couldn't you tell from my accent?"

"Didn't really notice it, to tell the truth. I'm Padraig."

"Nice to meet you," said Liam, shaking his hand.

"They're good people, Bridget and Paul."

"They are. Maybe you remember my parents, Charlie and Kathleen O'Brien?"

"Of course I do! Moved to New York!"

"That's them."

"Lovely, lovely. Send them my regards, will you?"

"Of course."

Padraig started back toward the troughs.

"I'm here to see Aislinn, remember?" Liam called after him.

Padraig stopped and turned. "Oh, sure, sure, right enough. If you go up to the top of the hill behind the house and turn left, you'll see her far off in the high north meadow, tending to the fences. Ask her if she wants a cuppa soon. She's been up at it for hours."

"Will do. And thanks."

"My pleasure, son."

Liam resisted the urge to peer into the windows of the house, and started up the hill. *Son of a bitch*, he thought as his sneakers sank farther and farther into muddy grass. *You're an idiot. Something I'm sure Aislinn will confirm.*

He made it to the top of the hill and turned left, as Padraig instructed. There, off in the distance, no bigger than a speck on the horizon, was Aislinn. Coming closer, he saw that she was on her knees with her back to him, mending a wire fence. She was wearing a baseball cap, her dark auburn hair pulled back in a ponytail. It didn't seem to bother her to be kneeling in mud. He decided that he'd call to her from a short distance away; that way, it wouldn't look like he was creeping up on her.

"Hey!"

She turned around, and he waved to her with a big smile. When he finally was close to enough to see her expression, there was no mistaking the displeasure on her face.

She rose to her feet. "What on earth are you doing here?"

Liam shrugged affably. "I thought I'd just stop by to say hi."

She frowned. "Oh you did, did you?"

"All right, I'll be honest. I felt bad about that comment I made to you last night about your flirting with me. I'm sorry it drove you out of the pub early."

"You didn't drive me out early," Aislinn replied gruffly. "My intent was to go in, have a few quick drams to warm myself up, and then head back here—which is exactly what I did. Some of us have to get up early, you know."

"And some of us work till the early hours of the morning."

"Fair enough."

"I still wish we'd gotten off on a better foot." He held out a hand. "Friends?"

Aislinn eyed him warily. "Try acquaintances, and barely

that." She took his hand, shaking it brusquely before turning back to the fence. "I'm busy, as you can see."

"Can I help?"

She whirled to face him. "Is that your idea of a joke?"

"No."

"Well, it's funny all the same, believe me. Of course you can't help," she scoffed. "What in God's name would the likes of you know about mending fences, city boy?"

"Well, nothing," Liam admitted, "but I understand the concept behind it, and—"

Aislinn snorted. "I understand the concept behind making an atomic bomb, but that doesn't mean I can do it."

"Eejit," he heard her say under his breath. She was right. He was an idiot.

But he wasn't giving up. "Maybe if you show me . . ."

*"What?"* She pointed her pliers at him with narrowed eyes. "What's your game? Coming up here uninvited and offering to help me mend fences?"

"I told you: I came here to apologize."

"Right: apology accepted. Off with you, then. And don't ever just show up here again uninvited. It's rude."

Liam smiled roguishly. "Does that mean I might get *invited* up here sometime and you can show me then?"

Aislinn wiped a bead of sweat off her forehead and just stared at him. "You know, I'm starting to think you truly are a little soft in the head. Why in the name of Jesus would I ever invite you up here?"

"To get to know me better."

"You're mad. You truly are. *Go away.*"

"For now," Liam returned lightly. "Oh, I almost forgot: Padraig wants to know if you want a cup of tea soon."

"Tell him I'll be down in an hour or so."

"Will do."

Liam winked, starting back down the hill with a jaunty whistle. He could feel Aislinn's eyes burning smoking holes into his back. He was going to win this bet. All it would take was time.

* * *

*What in the name of hell was that all about?* Aislinn wondered as she watched Liam disappear out of sight. First he had the gall to show up unannounced, then he asked to help her out with a chore he knew nothing about, and to top it all off, he flashed an "I can charm the pants off you" smile while hinting about her inviting him over sometime. The cheek of him!

She had to admit, he did seem sincere in his apology. Even so, he could have just waited until the next time she stopped into the pub. Making a special trip up to see her didn't make sense.

She'd had a very productive day so far, and that pleased her. She turned her face up to the bright, glorious sun. Why would anyone ever want to live in a city? All that noise and people hurrying about. The country was the place that fed her soul. The land, the songs of the blackbirds and the robins, the clean, clean air, and of course, her beloved flock. She couldn't imagine living anywhere else. Ever.

She made her way down the hill. Padraig was sitting on the small bench outside the tool shed with Aislinn's border collie, Deenie, at his feet. Deenie jumped up at the sight of her.

"There's my girl," said Aislinn, crouching down to give the dog's belly a good rub and let Deenie cover her face in kisses. She rose, patting her on the head as she looked across the road. Her flock was grazing right where they were supposed to be. "Good job, Deenie. As always."

She approached Padraig. "Did you finish rinsing out the troughs, old man?"

"Of course I did. Ages ago. Shall we have some tea?"

"In a minute. That guy who was just here? If he ever comes round again, tell him to go away, all right?"

Padraig looked relieved. "I'm dead happy to hear you say that, I must confess. I thought maybe you were wantin' to hire someone else to help us out."

Aislinn patted his shoulder. "Why should I need help when I've got you, eh?"

"Too true. Now tell me: why is it you don't want the likes of him here? He seemed a nice enough lad."

"He's a pain in the arse, that's what he is. I mean it, Padraig: if he comes sniffing round again, I want you to send him on his Yankee way."

"Is he sweet on you?" Padraig asked slyly.

"Don't be daft! And even if he were, he's barking up the wrong tree. Are we clear?"

"As a pane of glass, girl." He took a deep breath, rising slowly with the grimace of someone who'd acquired a lifetime of aches and pains. "Now let's put the kettle on."

*   *   *

*Even though it* was a bit of a walk, they took their morning tea break in Padraig's cottage. It hadn't always been this way; before Aislinn's parents were killed, breaks were usually taken in the farmhouse kitchen or else out in the fields when her mother would bring her, her father, and Padraig a vacuum flask of tea. But ever since their deaths, Padraig had insisted she come to his place. Perhaps it was his way of comforting her or trying to give something back to her for keeping him on (as if that were even an issue). At any rate, Aislinn was glad of it. Change was good. At least that's what she told herself whenever she felt the old black dog of depression nipping at her heels.

She sat down at the kitchen table, watching as Padraig filled his battered old kettle before putting it on the stove.

"Padraig," Aislinn said gently. "You've lit the wrong burner."

"Ah, right, right." He turned off the flame and lit the right one. *God, he could burn down the cottage one night,* Aislinn thought worriedly. She toyed with the idea of asking him to move into the house with her, then quickly came to her senses: he'd drive her mad with his untidiness and tales of the old days.

He opened a tin of biscuits, arranging them on a small, floral patterned plate before her. "Are you excited about your sister coming tomorrow night?"

Aislinn sighed. "I guess."

A professor of economics at the University of London, Nora was on sabbatical and coming home to "spend some time with Aislinn," as well as work on an article for an esteemed economic journal that she hoped would result in tenure. Aislinn was mystified: for years, all Nora had ever talked about was how glad she was to have "escaped" Ireland, as if the whole country was Maze prison. Aislinn had gone once to visit her and her husband, Donald, a stockbroker. She didn't like Donald much—he had a stick up his arse that reached clear up to his throat—but he doted on Nora, and that's all that mattered. As for London, it wasn't her cup of tea, but unlike her sister, she didn't feel compelled to put it down the way Nora did Ballycraig.

That trip had been seven years ago. As for Nora, she returned home only once a year. To her credit, she had flown their parents to London to see her every fall, but like Aislinn, they didn't care much for city life. "Don't feel like I can breathe there," her father always said when he got home.

God, those three days of their wake. Even now, the memories felt surreal to Aislinn, the blur of mourners, their voices sympathetic yet indistinct. Condolences and casserole after casserole appearing in the kitchen. The overpowering scent of flower arrangements. The heartbreaking, lost look on Padraig's face. Sadness interspersed with toasts of whiskey and fond reminiscences.

She had to admit, she *was* glad Nora was there. She was an immense help, and it was the closest Aislinn had ever felt to her. Her sister stayed for a whole week, the two of them staying up nights talking, sometimes laughing, sometimes crying. Nora offered to stay longer, but

Aislinn didn't see the point. They both had to get back to their own lives.

That was six months ago. Since then, they had talked on the phone a bit more than in previous years. And now Nora was coming for a prolonged visit, without Donald, thank God. What would she do all day while Aislinn worked the farm? God knew, Nora's notion of hell was being out in the fields shepherding.

"I wonder what she'll do with her days," Padraig mused as if he read Aislinn's thoughts.

"She says she'll be working on her article."

"She can help clean the house, I suppose."

Aislinn laughed loudly. "You must be joking! Mum was always after her to keep her room tidy, and Nora turned a deaf ear. Her bedroom always looked like a rubbish tip."

"Does she not keep a clean house?"

"She's got someone who comes in weekly."

"Well, la-di-da," said Padraig. "We could send her into town on errands. Or into Moneygall to that big supermarket."

Aislinn bit into a stale tea biscuit. "Let's see what the lay of the land is first before we start telling her what to do."

"Too right." Padraig reached for a biscuit. "Well, it'll be interesting having her about."

"Truer words were never spoken."

# 3

*"I hear you're* wooing the McCafferty."

There was no mistaking the amused glint in his uncle Paul's eyes as he passed Liam the plate of streaky bacon and sausages. Since Liam was the one responsible for opening the pub at twelve thirty on Sunday, he usually stopped by his aunt and uncle's house for breakfast on Sunday mornings, especially since he knew his cousins Erin and Brian would be there, too. It was a chance for everyone to catch up.

Liam speared a piece of sausage. "Who told you?"

"Jack, of course."

"Actually, it's the talk of the town," said his cousin Erin. She paused thoughtfully. "I like the McCafferty."

"Do you?" her mother asked, intrigued. "And why's that?"

"I was at school with her, remember? And she was always very nice to me. I always felt bad for her, with those stupid eejits Teague, Fergus, and David giving her stick all the time. She gave it back to them good, though, I'll give her that."

Aunt Bridget poured herself a cup of tea. "You have to admit, it's a bit odd she always wanted to be a shepherd."

"Not odd at all," Erin maintained. "What are you, Ma, in the Dark Ages? Women can do what they like."

"She's right, Ma," Brian chimed in. "And I think it's great the farm is staying in the family."

"She's going to have to get some help up there soon, though, I hear," said Uncle Paul, shaking his head sadly. "I hear Padraig's losing his wits."

"He does seem a bit forgetful," said Liam.

His aunt raised an eyebrow. "And how would we know that?"

"I was up there yesterday—"

"You were up there yesterday?" Erin interrupted with a splutter. "Did Aislinn invite you?"

"Of course not."

"Did she bite your head off, then?" Uncle Paul asked.

"Basically," Liam said nonchalantly. "But I'm sure she'll come around in time."

"Right, and the Second Coming is nigh," Brian said dryly.

"What was her fiancé like?" Liam continued casually.

Erin sighed dreamily. "He was dead sweet. And good-looking, too. They were a very striking couple."

Liam was irritated. "Really."

"*And* he worshipped the ground she walked on," added Aunt Bridget.

"Too bad he didn't worship her enough to tell her the truth about himself before humiliating her in front of the whole town," Liam pointed out.

"He was a tormented soul," Uncle Paul said sympathetically.

*And now she is.*

"What's your strategy going to be, then?" Brian asked eagerly. "Overpower her with your natural charm and good looks?"

"Do I detect a note of sarcasm?" Liam asked.

"Never."

He and Liam laughed.

"Seriously," said Erin, wide-eyed with curiosity as she gulped her tea. "How on earth do you plan to win her over?"

"I have my ways," Liam said with a wink.

"You're gonna need supernatural powers with that one," said Uncle Paul, gobbling down a piece of sausage.

"Nope," Liam said confidently. "Mark my words. It's gonna happen. Just wait and see."

* * *

*Aislinn sat at* the nicked old Parsons table in the kitchen, anxiously drumming her fingers as she waited for Nora's cab to arrive. Aislinn had offered to pick her sister up at the airport, but Nora claimed Aislinn drove like a madwoman, and she didn't want to take her own life in her hands. Aislinn disagreed, but she was in no mood to dispute her sister. Better to let Nora do things the way she wanted, at least at first.

Though Aislinn knew it would probably go unnoticed, she'd cleaned the house from top to bottom. She made sure there were fresh sheets on Nora's bed, fresh soap and towels in the loo, and had even taken the time to pick some wildflowers to put in a vase on her dresser. Nora told her not to bother with supper, so she hadn't, though the refrigerator was stocked just in case she changed her mind.

Aislinn had no idea how long Nora was planning to visit, and she found that unnerving. She had her own way of running the household, and Nora could be a real bossy boots. She wondered if Nora wasn't having troubles in her marriage and that's why she was really coming, to get some distance from Donald so she could sort things out. Well, she'd find out soon enough.

She heard the cab pull up and got up from the table to peek out from behind the curtain for a moment before backing away. *What are you, a sheltered bumpkin,* she chided herself, *acting like you've never seen a bloody car pull up in the drive?*

She heard the door to the mudroom open and smiled to herself. Only company came through the front door.

"Hello? Aislinn?" Nora called out.

"In the kitchen, as if you didn't know." Aislinn was still smiling, feeling more excited than she'd been giving herself credit for. It took all her might to hang on to it, however, when Nora appeared with the cabdriver behind her, cursing and muttering to himself as he hauled in two large suitcases and put them down on the floor with a grunt. "I'll just go get the others, missus."

"Wow," said Aislinn uneasily, eyeing the bags. "There's probably enough in there to clothe the whole town!"

Nora laughed lightly. "Some of it's books. And my laptop. Don't think I've forgotten how changeable the weather can be here. I've brought enough clothing to cover every season."

"Ah."

The cabbie lurched back inside, depositing the final two bags on the kitchen floor. Nora handed him a wad of bills. "Keep the change."

"Thank you," he said. "Have a nice evening, ladies."

"You, too," said Aislinn. She turned to her sister, licking her lips nervously. "So."

"So I'm here!"

"Yes." Aislinn embraced her and found herself enveloped in a cloud of perfume. She fought not to cough as she asked, "How was your flight?"

"Oh, you know, short," said Nora, peeling off her very stylish black leather trench coat. She looked around the kitchen. "Where's Deenie?"

"She got too tired to wait up for you and went to bed," Aislinn teased.

Nora hung up her coat on the back of the mudroom door, flinging her arms open wide. "It's so nice to be home!"

*This is my home now, not yours,* Aislinn thought possessively. As always, Nora was exquisitely put together: lovely tan trousers, a deep burgundy cashmere sweater, gold earrings, and flawless makeup. Her black hair was chic and short. Aislinn wondered if Nora was going to dress like that every day. It made little sense if you lived on a farm.

"Do you want some tea?"

"Of course."

"I do have coffee if you'd prefer."

"I'm in the mood for tea, thanks."

"Tea it is."

Nora sat down, an elbow on the table as she rested her chin in the palm of her hand. "Catch me up on all the Ballycraig gossip."

"Padraig's slipping a bit, Teague Daly is still a great, lazy lummox, Erin O'Brien is going to university online, and there's a Yank working at the Oak who claims to be on the lam from the Irish Mob in New York. He's a royal eejit."

"Why do you say that?"

"Full of himself. All the women in town are gaga over him; they think he's some kind of sexy outlaw or something."

"But you haven't succumbed to his charm?" Nora asked dryly.

"I've no use for him. Like I said, full of himself, and thick as two short planks. We didn't get on too well the first time we met the other night. So he comes up here yesterday to apologize and then asks if he can help me mend the fences. As if he knows a damn thing about mending fences!"

"You're the one who's thick as two short planks, Aislinn."

Aislinn sniffed. "Oh? And why would that be?"

"He obviously fancies you. Why else would he make a special effort to come up here?"

"He's an eejit, like I said." She put the kettle on the stove and spooned some loose tea into the pot. "Even if he does fancy me, fat lot of good it's going to do him."

"Aislinn," Nora said carefully. "Have you dated anyone since—"

"No. That's the last thing I'm interested in."

"But maybe it's time," Nora wheedled gently. "It might be good for you—"

"Listen here, Nora McCafferty," Aislinn chided affectionately, "I know you're just trying to be helpful, but you cannot come marching in here and within two minutes start giving me advice about how to live my life. I'm a big girl."

"It just seems obvious to me—"

"Leave off, okay?"

Nora held up her hands in surrender. "Okay, okay."

"Thank you. I appreciate it. You sure I can't get you anything to eat?"

"I'm fine. Food's the last thing I need! Look how fat I am!"

Aislinn looked at her sister like she was mad. "You're crazy. You're an assless wonder."

Nora laughed. "Unfortunately, I'm not a tummyless wonder. Or a thighless wonder."

Aislinn shrugged. "You look fine to me."

"You're the one who looks skinny," Nora noted with a thin strain of envy in her voice.

"I'm all right. Probably from working the farm and riding my bike around when I can. I've no need of a gym."

"Speaking of the farm, you said Padraig is slipping a bit?"

"Just a bit," Aislinn said defensively.

"Maybe you should encourage him to retire."

"Not yet."

"But—"

"There you go again, offering up suggestions when you haven't lived here in years," Aislinn said, trying to keep her tone light. "Leave Padraig to me, all right?"

"I know you. You'll never let him go."

Aislinn said nothing as she poured the boiling water from the kettle into the teapot. "How long are you staying for?"

"I'm leaving it open-ended. If that's all right with you."

"Of course it is," Aislinn lied. She turned around to face Nora. "I hope you don't think I'm prying, but I can't help but wonder: have you come here to take a break from Donald? Are you two having problems?"

"God, no," said Nora, looking shocked that Aislinn could even suggest such a thing. "I wanted to see you, and I wanted a change of scenery while I worked on my article. I figured it might help jolt the creative process, you know?"

"I don't know anything about creativity, but I'll take your word for it."

"Donald will pop over on the occasional weekend," Nora continued.

*Feck,* thought Aislinn. "What's your article about?" she asked.

"Economic development in South Africa."

"You should pop up to Dublin one day and see if you can talk to Saint Bono. God knows he never shuts his yap when it comes to that subject."

Nora laughed. "True." She sighed. "Probably sounds boring to you."

"Yup," said Aislinn. "But I imagine deworming the ewes after their lambs are born sounds boring to you."

Nora shuddered. "Boring and awful."

Aislinn took the tea strainer and poured it into the first mug. "I take it you've no intention of helping me and Padraig around the farm, then?" She saw the flash of terror in Nora's eyes and burst out laughing. "I'm *kidding*!"

Nora looked relieved. "Thank *God*."

"You'll just stay in the house and write?" Aislinn asked, pouring a cup of tea for herself.

"Pretty much. I might head up to Dublin a few times to use the library at Trinity. You could come along if you like. You could sightsee while I work."

"No thank you." Aislinn handed a mug of tea to her

sister. "I might put you to work around here in some way, just so you know."

"Oh yes? Do tell."

"Maybe run errands sometimes. Cook the occasional meal."

"I can handle that." Nora took a sip of tea. "Perfect, as always." She looked amused. "I'm not totally averse to being outside, you know! I haven't walked the whole property in a long time. Maybe we could do that one afternoon."

"That would be nice."

"And I'd like to go with you to the Royal Oak to check out this Yank who's got the hots for my baby sister."

"Put a sock in it, please."

"It's going to feel odd, being back for a prolonged period of time."

"You'll get used to it soon enough," said Aislinn, more to assure herself than Nora.

"I hope so."

# 4

*"That was bloody* hair-raising. You're as bad as every other driver in this country."

Aislinn shot Nora a dirty look as they walked into the pub with Padraig. They'd driven in Aislinn's truck, the three of them crushed into the front seat. Padraig had wanted to drive, but Aislinn wouldn't let him. He tended to turn his head to look at you when he talked, taking his eyes off the road for long periods of time. Aislinn had no desire to find herself in a ditch.

Nora had been at the farm a week, and so far, so good. She wasn't getting underfoot, and really, the only time she plucked on Aislinn's nerves was when she complained about having to drive all the way into Moneygall to shop. She came home moaning about all the things she couldn't find, like sun-dried tomatoes, bruschetta, and fresh pasta. "You're not in London anymore," Aislinn reminded her patiently. *Can't get bloody bruschetta. Boo-hoo,* Aislinn thought.

"My driving is fine," Aislinn insisted as she held the door open, preparing for the onslaught. The locals would be surrounding Nora to welcome her back to Ballycraig, even though all of them knew that when she'd left years ago, she'd termed it an "escape."

"God, this place never changes," Nora marveled as they stepped inside. Padraig didn't even bother to take his coat off as he made a beeline to the bar. Aislinn's eyes cut surreptitiously to the left; of course the Yank was there, along with the Holy Trinity of Arseholes, raising their glasses high when they spotted Nora.

"Hail the returning queen!" said Fergus.

"We hear you're back in town for a good while," said David. "What happened? Lose all your money in the stock market?"

Nora just rolled her eyes. "They never change, either, I see," she said to Aislinn.

"No, they don't."

A thick throng of people soon surrounded them, welcoming Nora warmly. Aislinn nodded her acknowledgment when they also greeted her, all so polite, their expressions a mix of pity and unease. The pity really irritated her. As for the unease, she had to admit she enjoyed that just a teeny bit. It was nice to control something— even if it was people's perception that she was fearsome.

Aislinn was dressed more formally than the last time she'd been here—not on purpose, but because she'd finished around the farm with a little time to spare. She'd pulled her hair back in a loose braid and had donned freshly pressed jeans, a simple blue V-neck T-shirt, and her Frye boots. Nora, of course, was dressed to the teeth. She looked completely out of place. She *was* completely out of place.

Nora nudged Aislinn discreetly in the ribs. "That the Yank?" she whispered, glancing at the bar.

"Who else would it be?"

"Good-looking man."

"Too bad he knows it."

"Let's go over and get a drink."

Together, the two sisters sidled through the thick, boisterous crowd. The musicians were already playing by the roaring fire, well into "The Foggy Dew." By the time they got to "The Wind That Shakes the Barley," there wouldn't be a dry eye in the house. Aislinn herself felt the prick of hot tears at the corners of her eyes just thinking about it; it had been one of her father's favorite tunes.

Aislinn reached the bar first, trying to ignore Liam's penetrating stare. Because she was cursed, she found herself next to Teague Daly.

"Evening, McCafferty."

Aislinn didn't look at him. "Evening, Daly."

She felt him looking her up and down. "You look halfway decent tonight. Maybe havin' the sister in town has roused your competitive spark, eh?"

"You're a baboon's ass."

"She still married?" Teague asked in a quiet voice.

"Yeah. But I'm sure she'd divorce her rich stockbroker husband to marry you and live on your mam and dad's couch for the rest of her born days."

"Feck off," Teague snarled.

"Nora! Darlin'!" Old Jack was beaming as he reached across the bar to clasp Nora's hand heartily. "We'd heard you're back. Is it for good, then?"

"Oh, no, no," said Nora quickly.

"Too bad." He looked at Aislinn. "The usual?" Aislinn nodded. "And for you, Nora?"

"A mojito, please."

Jack's face went blank. "A moji—wha?"

*Bloody Jesus,* thought Aislinn. *What kind of a fool orders a drink like that in a small village pub?*

"It's a drink that's popular in the States, and I guess in London, too," explained Liam, coming to the rescue. He smiled apologetically at Nora. "Sorry, I've got rum and club soda, but no lime, mint, or sugar syrup. Is there something else we can get you?"

Nora looked put out. "Can you do a gin and tonic?"

"Of course."

"Mojito," Aislinn heard Old Jack repeat to himself as he went to get her whiskey, as if it was some newfangled expression he had to wrestle with.

Aislinn regarded her sister with disbelief as Liam went to fix Nora's drink. "Earth to Nora. Did you really think you could get a mojito *here*? At the Oak?"

"They're very popular!" Nora protested.

"You're in Ballycraig, remember? According to you, we don't even have a proper supermarket nearby! What made you think you'd be able to get some exotic drink?"

Nora ignored the question. Her eyes followed Liam. "He's hot."

"So are the flames of hell," said Aislinn, taking her whiskey shot from Jack and putting money down on the bar to pay for both their drinks as Jack gave her a refill. "Thanks."

Liam appeared a moment later, handing Nora her gin and tonic. "There you go."

"Ta." Nora extended her hand to him. "I don't believe we've met. I'm Nora McCafferty, Aislinn's sister."

"Liam O'Brien."

"Nice to meet you." Nora looked coy as she took a sip of her drink. "I've heard you're a big, bad, dangerous New York outlaw."

Liam grinned. "Guilty as charged."

"C'mon, let's go get a table," Aislinn urged, tugging her sister away from the bar. "What the hell was that about?" she snapped as soon as they were out of earshot.

"What?" Nora asked innocently.

"Flirting with the Yank!"

Nora sniffed. "What's it to you?"

"Might I remind you, you're married?"

"I know. I just wanted to see if you'd get jealous. And you did."

"You sure you didn't steal a few nips back at the house?" Aislinn scoffed. "Seems to me you're imagining things."

"You fancy him," Nora declared with certainty. Her eyes scanned the low-lit, back room of the pub. "Nowhere to sit."

"Never is unless you get here at noon and want to hold your seat till nightfall."

Aislinn noticed two turf farmers she knew as passing acquaintances motioning her and Nora over. She hesitated. Surely they didn't want her and Nora to *join* them. Unfortunately, Nora saw them, too.

"We're being summoned."

"I'd rather not," said Aislinn.

"Why not?"

"I can't do small talk, Nora," Aislinn said desperately. "And I don't think you'd enjoy it much, either, unless you've a hankering to chat about the peat business."

"Nonsense. I'm sure we could have a nice conversation. How about this: I'll talk, and you can just sit there and glower?"

"Fine. Suit yourself."

The two men, both in their mid-fifties and slightly hunched from a lifetime of digging in bogs and sod carrying, rose politely when she and Nora reached the table. "Can't have two pretty ladies like you standing all night. Here, take our seats."

"Oh, no, you don't have to do that, the last thing we want to do is to turn you out of your seats," Aislinn protested.

"Not a problem," said the taller of the two.

"Are you sure?" Aislinn asked again. She hated the thought of taking advantage of their good natures.

"More than sure. Please."

"Thank you sooo much," Nora said graciously. "It's grand to know chivalry isn't dead." The two men looked pleased as they headed toward the bar. "They seem nice," she added, watching them go.

" 'Grand to know chivalry isn't dead.' Good one, that. You're quite the flirt tonight. I suppose that was a test, too, to see if I'd get jealous over one of them?"

"Just having fun," Nora said lightly. "Something I sense *you* are in dire need of." She took a sip of her drink.

"Turf farmers, huh? Did you know I've hated the smell of burning peat ever since I was a little girl?"

"No, I didn't know that," said Aislinn, though she wasn't surprised. It was an earthy smell that could sometimes border on acrid. "I don't mind it." She tilted her head in the direction of the roaring fire. "That bothering you, then?"

"A bit. But I'll live."

"That's a relief," Aislinn teased.

Nora smiled at her. "I enjoyed walking the property with you today."

"Yes, that was nice," Aislinn agreed, sipping her whiskey.

They chatted on for a while. Aislinn was actually enjoying it, until she caught sight of the Yank coming toward them.

"Shite," she said under her breath.

Nora turned to see what she was cursing about, then looked back at Aislinn. "Time for me to make myself scarce," she said with a sly grin.

"Don't you dare," Aislinn hissed.

"Hey," said Liam when he reached their table. "Mind if I join you? I'm on break."

"Yes," said Aislinn.

Nora shot her a "Don't be rude" look as she stood. "Actually, there are a couple of my old friends from school I'm itching to talk to. See you two later."

"Yup." Liam sat down. "How's it going?"

"Would you mind being a bit more specific?" Aislinn could feel all eyes in the room turning to look at them; she could imagine what they were thinking. *What's the Yank doing talking to Aislinn McCafferty? He must be touched in the head.*

"Did you finish mending your fences?"

"I did."

"And how's it going with your sister?"

"You're a real nosy parker. Anyone ever tell you that?"

Liam laughed. "My mother uses that expression all the time."

"Well, you are."

"Just making casual conversation." He took a sip of his pint. "The Oak reminds me of the pub my parents own, the Wild Hart."

"Oh?" Aislinn tried to look disinterested.

Liam looked sentimental. "Yeah. It has a real close-knit, family feel."

"Miss it, then, do you?"

"Of course I do," Liam said quietly. "It's home."

Aislinn's gaze was steady as she looked at him over her whiskey glass. "What did you do that made you leave a home you miss so much?"

"Who's the nosy parker now?" Liam asked with an amused smile.

"Sorry. I suppose I am."

"No, it's okay," Liam assured her. "It's not what I did—it's what a friend did to me. Let's just say he betrayed me."

*I know all about that*, Aislinn thought bitterly. "Betrayed you how?"

Liam hesitated. "He got me involved in something illegal. When I wouldn't keep quiet, my friend's boss threatened me. So here I am."

"For how long?"

Liam looked pained. "I don't know."

"You must be bored senseless in these parts." *What are you asking him questions for?* she chided herself. *He's going to think you care, when all you're trying to do is be polite.*

Liam's gaze pinned her. "No. There are things here that hold my attention."

Aislinn stared back at him. "Fascinating."

"Your sister seems nice. A lot different than you, though. She older or younger?"

"I don't really want to talk about Nora." His curiosity regarding her sister was irksome.

"Nope, not fair. You asked me questions; now I get to ask you some."

"Fine," Aislinn said in a bored voice. "Fire away."

"How long has she been away?"

"Ten years or so. Hopped it over to England the minute she got the chance."

"Didn't want to be a shepherd, huh?"

Aislinn snorted. "Nora, a shepherd—that's a good one. No, she's a professor at a university in London."

"What's she doing here?"

"Ask her yourself. Three questions are all you get."

"I like even numbers. Let's make it four."

"You don't let up, do you?"

"Let's just say I'm used to getting what I want," Liam murmured seductively.

Aislinn stared at him a second, then burst out laughing. "Has that line actually gotten you into womens' knickers? What movie did you steal *that* from?"

"I didn't steal it from any movie," Liam replied, looking offended. "It's the truth."

"Well, how nice for you, then, getting what you want. For the rest of us mortals, it's hit or miss."

"Do I get one more question or not?"

"Since I know you'll continue to be a royal pain in my arse if I don't accommodate you, fine, ask your final question."

"Will you go to the *céilí* with me next Saturday?"

Aislinn peered hard at him across the table. "Is this some kind of joke?"

"Why would I be kidding?"

Aislinn thought this over and could come up with no good answer.

"Well?"

"Thanks, but no thanks," she said politely.

"Why not?"

"It's none of your business why not!"

Liam took a slug of beer. "I disagree. I think the least you can do is tell me why you can't go."

"Hmm, let's see," said Aislinn, tapping her chin with her index finger thoughtfully. "I have to wash my hair that night."

"Try again."

"Final answer."

"You want to know why I think you're turning me down?"

Aislinn yawned. "Not particularly."

"I think you like me."

"If I liked you, I'd be going with you, wouldn't I?" Aislinn shot back.

"Not if you're afraid of being vulnerable, you wouldn't."

"Vulnerable to what?" Aislinn scoffed. "Your pathetic macho come-on lines?"

"To *feeling*."

Aislinn stiffened, indignant. "How dare you say I don't feel?"

"I'm sorry. Bad choice of words. What I meant was—"

She stood up. "I don't much care what you meant."

"Come to the dance," said Liam. "Come on. You don't have to come as my date. Just come. It'll be fun."

"Some of us have to get up before dawn, you know."

"You can't stay for an hour? Come on."

"Excuse me; I have to go make sure Padraig doesn't get drunk. He's of no use to me when he's hungover."

She headed back to the bar, feeling Liam's eyes on her the whole way. Well, let him stare. Arrogant gobaloon. *I'm used to getting what I want.* Giving her sloe eyes, like he was some sort of romantic hero. Handsome and mildly interesting he might be, but Liam O'Brien wasn't going to get what he wanted this time.

# 5

*"I can't believe* I let you talk me into this. Truly."

Aislinn was sitting on the closed lid of the toilet while Nora sat across from her on the lip of the tub, putting makeup on her face. For a week, Nora had been haunting her about going to the *céilí. Don't be such a stick-in-the-mud. You need to get out and start doing things. We don't have to stay long. When's the last time you got out and did anything fun?*

That was a painful question. Fun? The last time she'd had fun was over a year ago, when she and Connor had packed a lunch and hiked up to the top of Murphy's Hill the day before their wedding. They'd spread a blanket on the ground, reveling in the gorgeous, endless green fields below them stretching as far as the eye could see. A warm breeze blew, gently tickling the soft grass, and the sun was in rare form, blazing bright in the cloudless sky. Aislinn had never been happier in her life. *At this time tomorrow*, she kept thinking to herself, *I'll be Connor's wife.* She remembered he seemed a bit preoccupied, but she put it down to pre-wedding jitters. Twenty-four hours later, her dream lay in tatters.

When it became clear Nora wasn't going to let up about the dance, Aislinn capitulated, justifying her submission with the excuse that the dance was for a good cause: Grace Finnegan's husband, Fintan, had been diagnosed with bone cancer, and the dance would help raise money for him to go over to England for treatment at one of the best cancer centers in the world. Even so, Aislinn told her sister, "I'll stay for one hour, and one hour only. After that, you're on your own getting a ride back here."

Of course, Aislinn's agreeing to go to the dance wasn't enough for Nora. Oh, no. She insisted on rifling through Aislinn's closet to see if she had something "appropriate to wear," and naturally, in Nora's estimation, she didn't. To get Nora off her back—again—Aislinn agreed to wear a pair of Nora's black jeans (too tight if you asked her), spiked-heel boots (it wasn't as if she'd be dancing), and a crimson scoop-neck shirt, topped with a silk scarf around her neck. She'd also agreed to wear her hair down.

"You look gorgeous," Nora declared.

"I won't look gorgeous when I'm in traction after breaking my neck wearing these ridiculous boots," Aislinn grumbled. "You sure you didn't borrow these from Catwoman?"

Nora ignored the crack. "Let's get some makeup on you," she insisted, and that's when she'd steered a simmering Aislinn into the loo and commanded her to sit down. Aislinn had opened her mouth to protest, then realized it was futile.

"I don't know why I'm succumbing to this torture," Aislinn lamented as Nora dabbed God knows what on her face. "I hate the feel of this rubbish on my skin!"

"Don't act like you've never worn it before! You had some on, on your wedding day."

"Only because the photographer said I'd look pale in the pictures if I didn't. Why can't I just go as myself?"

"You *are* going as yourself, just an enhanced version."

Aislinn looked at her sister coolly. "Oh, so I need some enhancement, aye?"

"Aislinn." Nora paused, exasperated. "You're a beautiful woman. What's wrong with capitalizing on it?"

"Because it's not me, Nora," Aislinn protested. "It never has been."

Nora sighed heavily. "Just indulge me on this, okay?"

"Seems I'm indulging you left and right these days, but fine," Aislinn muttered. "All this dressing up—it's going to cause trouble."

"Close your eyes." Nora began lining her lids. "Trouble how?"

"The Yank is going to think I've gotten all turned out just for him. I know it."

"Why would he think that?"

"He asked me to be his date."

Nora gasped. "And you said no?"

Aislinn's eyes flew open. "Of course I said no! Why in the name of God would I want to encourage that egomaniac?"

"Because he likes you. And he's nice."

"He's full of himself. You know what he had the gall to say to me at the Oak last week? That he was used to getting what he wanted. His voice went all low and sultry. As if I'd fall for a line of bull like that! What does he think I am, an eejit? He's a horse's arse, and I want no part of him."

"Methinks thou doth protest too much," Nora teased.

"Believe me, Nora, I know the type."

"Do you now?" Nora mocked. "You've only ever been with one man your whole life, and all of a sudden you're an expert on the opposite sex?"

"I've got eyes and ears, you know," Aislinn said fiercely. "I meet men like that all the time at the farmers' market. In fact, there's one fella who buys wool who thinks he's God's gift to women. Dad and I used to fall about the place laughing as soon as he'd leave."

"I think maybe the Yank was just teasing you a bit, trying to get you to lighten up."

"No, he thought he was being charming and seductive. *I* saw how he was behaving. You didn't."

"There's no reason you can't have a little fun with him," Nora suggested slyly.

Aislinn frowned. "I'm not big on toying with people's emotions, Nora."

"There's nothing wrong with flirting."

"I'll leave that to you, thank you very much."

Nora sighed. "You need to get back on the horse, Aislinn."

"Why? So I can get thrown and kicked in the head again? No thank you."

"What are you saying? You're done with men?"

Aislinn folded her arms obstinately across her chest. "That is exactly what I'm saying, yes."

"So you want to end up like Padraig."

"What the hell does that mean?" Aislinn asked, trying to keep her temper in check. Bloody Nora! Home only two weeks and already putting her two cents in where it wasn't wanted!

"Old and alone, with nothing to live for but the farm."

"Alone doesn't mean lonely, Nora."

Nora stared at her in disbelief. "That's it, then? You've built a fortress around your heart that no man can ever penetrate?"

"Bingo."

"I refuse to believe that you never want to feel a man's arms around you again. You always said you wanted children. What, you've changed your mind?"

"Maybe."

Nora seemed to soften. "You know, you're not the first person in the world who's had their heart broken. I was there when it happened, remember? I know it was awful. But you've only prolonged your own agony by turning hard."

Aislinn stiffened. "I don't know what you mean."

"You do so. You're not thick. You pushed everyone away, Aislinn. Did you ever stop to think that if you'd done the opposite, maybe you'd have healed by now?"

Aislinn began brushing her hair. "I am healed."

"A cow's arse you are."

"I don't want to talk about this anymore."

"Suit yourself. But in my opinion, hiding up here and acting the ice princess is sad. You've got so much to offer, and you're throwing it away because one arsehole did you wrong."

"All it takes is one. Now let's finish up this torture, shall we?"

\* \* \*

*Aislinn let Nora* drive her truck down into town for the *céilí,* though she hated every moment of it. She was a horrible driver, rusty after years of using public transport in London. Aislinn knew that had she driven, they could have been to the dance in half the time.

The dance, like all dances and events involving more people than could fit in the Oak, was being held at the parish hall of Saint Columba's. Wedding receptions, memorial services, political meetings, communion parties, dances—Saint Columba's had seen them all.

Aislinn felt a twinge of sentimentality as she and Nora entered the hall. She remembered the dances she and her school chums had gone to: giggly girls on one side of the room and gawky boys on the other, trying to figure out each other's ways. *Oh, Declan Taylor is looking at me! Do you suppose he's going to ask me to dance? If I give David Shiels the once-over, do you think I'm being too bold?* Aislinn herself had never gone through such agonies; she was already going out with Connor.

The donation for the dance was ten euros, but Aislinn gave twenty, since Padraig was too ill to come. A rattling, deadly cough, he'd told her. She'd tucked him up with a good, strong cup of tea before she left—tea she was sure he'd add a splash of whiskey to. Maybe it would help him drift off to sleep, poor old devil.

The place was packed; it looked like the whole town had turned out. Folding chairs lined the walls, but only the elderly were using them. Everyone else was either dancing or standing around in small groups chatting.

Aislinn recognized the band. Five local men in their fifties who'd been playing out for years. Some thirty years ago, they fancied they might one day be as big as U2. They were competent, but nothing special. And the songs they wrote themselves were dreadful. Aislinn felt a pang of pity of them. She knew what it was like to have your dream snatched from you.

Eagle eye Nora scanned the hall. "There's the Yank," she said, discreetly directing Aislinn's eyes to the far left corner of the room. "He's standing with his aunt and uncle and cousins."

"Good for him."

"Go over there and say hello," Nora urged.

"Why don't you shut your pie hole?"

"God, you're the same stubborn thing you've always been."

"And you're the same bossy boots you've always been. Give it a rest, Nora, would you, please?"

"Suit yourself. I'm going to go talk to Grace Finnegan. Donald and I actually know one of the oncologists at the cancer center. Maybe we could help Fintan get a consult sooner rather than later."

"That's a nice thing to do."

Nora headed off, and Aislinn made her way to the bar, sure she was going to break her neck in Nora's ridiculous boots. She couldn't help but notice all the surprised looks being beamed her way. *Oh, look, Aislinn McCafferty actually showed up, and all dolled up to boot.* She shouldn't have let Nora talk her into putting this goop on her face, not to mention persuading her to pour herself into pants so tight she felt like her legs were squeezed into sausage casings. God, what she wouldn't give to be home right now, curled up on the couch with Deenie, watching telly or reading a good book.

She was just being handed her whiskey and soda when she felt a warm hand on her shoulder, and she turned. It was Old Jack.

"Hello, Aislinn," he said, a big friendly smile splitting his red, craggy face. "It's lovely to see you here."

"Well, it's for a good cause," she said uncomfortably.

"True, true. And how are you and Nora getting on?"

"Fine," Aislinn said suspiciously. *Had he heard otherwise?*

"Grand, grand. You know," he said, leaning in confidentially, "Liam O'Brien is a bit sweet on you. Asks questions about you all the time."

"Is that so? Tell the coward if he wants information on me, he should ask me himself."

"That might be why the lad's making his way over here right now," Jack said with a wink as he departed.

*Shite,* thought Aislinn. *Here it comes. The swaggering thorn in my side.*

"Hey, Aislinn."

Aislinn nodded curtly. "Liam."

"You look lovely."

She wouldn't meet his eyes. "Thank you." He didn't look bad himself, truth be told. Nice jeans, a button-down shirt, even a blazer—it suited him.

"Is it me, or is this band really, really bad?"

Aislinn relaxed a bit. "They're awful," she concurred, taking a sip of her drink.

"Where's Padraig?"

"Home ill."

"Think we'll raise a lot of money tonight?"

"I think the answer is self-evident."

Jesus, he was Chatty Chatsworth. She hoped she didn't get stuck talking to him for the next hour.

His eyes were doing a slow tour of her body, and for a flickering second, she thought maybe she was right to listen to Nora. But she shoved the thought away. Who the hell did he think he was?

"You done giving me the once-over?" she asked sarcastically.

Liam chuckled. "You don't seem to mind."

"You wouldn't care if I minded or not."

"Of course I would."

"Right. Well, if you'll excuse me, I've got to—"

"I knew you'd come," Liam said smugly.

"I beg your pardon?"

"I said, I knew you'd come to the dance."

"I'm here because I want to help out the Finnegans."

"That's part of the reason. The other part is me."

Aislinn's mouth fell open. "You've gobsmacked me. Truly. You're the most arrogant jackass I've ever met. Maybe your smoky-eyed, smooth-talking rubbish works on other women, but it won't work on me."

"You're dressed up because you wanted to look good for me," Liam continued with a self-satisfied smile.

Aislinn wished she could smack his face. "I'm dressed up because I wanted Nora off my bloody back."

"Keep telling yourself that."

Aislinn's heart began to pound. *"How dare you?"*

"I'm American, remember? We don't pull any punches."

"Neither do we Irish. Now, would you ever piss off once and for all?"

Liam's eyes blazed with adoration. "God, I love that you're so fiery."

Aislinn felt heat flash through her body against her will. *He's throwing you a line of bull. Don't soften. Don't fall for it.*

"Would you excuse me? You're boring the teeth off me." Aislinn started to walk away.

"Dance with me."

She whirled around to face him. *"What?"*

"One dance, and I'll leave you alone. C'mon."

*"No."*

"What are you so afraid of," Liam challenged, "actually enjoying yourself?"

Aislinn strolled back to him, giving him a sharp poke in the chest with her finger. "You know what I dislike most about you, apart from your misplaced arrogance?" she fumed. "It's this mad notion you have that you somehow know me. You've no idea if I'm afraid of anything or not. You've no idea if I enjoy myself or not."

"You're wrong. I do know about you. I know about Connor McCarthy, and I know about your parents—"

"That's enough," Aislinn interrupted fiercely, feeling her face go hot. Of course he would know about Connor. The whole world knew about Connor.

"I'm sorry," Liam said quietly. "I didn't mean to upset you."

"You didn't," Aislinn insisted briskly. "I just don't like discussing my personal life with strangers."

Liam looked mildly stung, and she was glad of it. He needed to be put in his place.

The band finished playing a song that sounded vaguely like the Village People's "YMCA" and launched into a version of Stevie Wonder's "You Are the Sunshine of My Life," a song Aislinn happened to love.

"One dance," Liam repeated.

"Jesus God, are you sure you're not my own mother come back in the flesh, the way you nag on?" Aislinn huffed in exasperation. "Fine, one dance, and one dance only. You got that?"

"Loud and clear."

She put her drink down on the makeshift bar and let Liam lead her out onto the dance floor. Their stance was stiff and awkward, and that was fine with her, even though she could tell he was dying to pull her closer. Still . . . dancing with a man . . . it was nice, but she was not about to let it go to her head like some pathetic, moony-eyed schoolgirl.

"You're a pretty good dancer," said Liam, trying to

pull her a little closer. Aislinn shot him a look of warning, and he backed off.

"Any twit can shuffle around the floor. Even you."

Liam laughed as Aislinn craned her neck to look past his shoulder, trying to spot her sister. She was still standing with Grace Finnegan. Both women were watching her and Liam. In fact, loads of people were watching. Aislinn ignored it, holding her head high, but there was no denying it ate at her. *Ooh, look, Liam O'Brien actually persuaded the hellcat to dance. Poor thing, with that Connor business. And her mam and dad. He must be taking pity on her poor, lonely soul . . .*

Aislinn broke away from him before the song ended. "I think I might be coming down with the same bug as Padraig. Good night."

She hoofed it as fast as she could off the dance floor, heading straight for Nora.

"Couldn't you even finish the dance with him?" were the first words out of her sister's mouth.

"I'm feeling poorly."

"I'm sure it's just the opposite."

Aislinn glared at her. "I'm off for home. You coming with, or you staying?"

"Staying, of course! We've only just got here!"

"Right, then. I'm sure you'll be able to catch a ride home with someone."

*"Aislinn—"*

"Button your lip." She kissed her sister's cheek. "I'll see you in the morning."

"Be careful driving home . . . *chicken.*"

Aislinn rolled her eyes and walked out into the night. Ah, blessed freedom. *Chicken*—Nora was daft. She leaned against the wall and pulled her sister's boots off, wiggling her toes. She'd walk barefoot to the truck. Anything was better than feeling like you were going to teeter over.

She was heading for her truck when she heard Liam call her name. *Sweet Christ on a bike, would he never leave her alone?*

"What now?" she asked crossly.

He grinned as he looked down at her stocking feet. "I had a feeling you wouldn't last long in those boots."

"Yes, because you know so much about me," Aislinn replied sarcastically. "Can I help you with something?"

"I was wondering if we could spend some time together."

"We just spent some time together."

"C'mon, you know what I mean."

"All right." She suppressed a wicked smile. "How about you come with me and Padraig to the farmers' market in Omeath tomorrow?"

Oh, it was glorious, the crestfallen expression on his face. Clearly the offer wasn't what he had in mind. But the spark returned to his face just as quickly as it had left.

"Okay. What time?"

*Dammit.* She was sure he'd beg off! But no, he never let up.

"There won't be much for you to do apart from watch Padraig and me sell wool," she warned. "Though maybe I'll put you to work, fetching me the occasional coffee."

"I could do that. What time?"

"You *have got* to be kidding me."

"I told you," Liam said stubbornly. "I want to spend time with you."

"Right, then. I'll pick you up at seven sharp."

"Looking forward to it."

"I'm glad one of us is," Aislinn replied, walking away. God, if the farmers' market didn't put him off, nothing would.

*   *   *

*"Getting her to* dance? Now *that* falls under the category of *miracle*, boyo."

Old Jack stared at Liam in amazement as he reentered the parish hall. Inviting him to come with her to the farmers' market and be her coffee fetcher—Liam had to

hand it to her, it was a good one. And leaving him standing alone in the middle of the dance floor like a jackass?
Double touché. But it was obvious why she did it: he was
beginning to get to her.

Jack was standing with David, Fergus, and Teague, the
first two nursing whiskeys, the last holding a pint of Harp.
Teague's expression was bitter.

"Big deal, so you got her to dance with you to half
a song. I still think it'll be a cold day in hell before she
gives the time of day to a *Yank*."

Liam shook his head and chuckled. Night in, night
out, he was forced to listen to this lazy, bitter lump of a
man criticize America. Liam was no superpatriot, but it
was truly beginning to get on his nerves. "What the hell
have you got against Americans?"

"You all think you're better than us."

"Leave off, Teague," said Old Jack with a heavy sigh.
"You're beginning to sound pathetic."

"He's right." Fergus slapped Liam on the back. "You're
making good headway, Liam. I'd be getting nervous if I
were you, Jack."

Jack sniffed. "We'll see."

"Were her hands ice cold?" David teased Liam. "Are
your goolies shriveled to the size of marbles?"

*Actually,* Liam thought to himself, *her skin was warm
and soft.*

"She actually looked good in them boots," said Teague.
"Kinda sexy."

"Ay, she did look good overall," Fergus admitted reluctantly. "I don't think I've ever seen her with her face all
done up like that."

"On her wedding day," Jack reminded him.

"Oh, right, right," said David. They all shook their
heads sadly.

"How have you achieved such headway?" Fergus
demanded, making Liam's quest sound like a military
mission.

"Basically, by not leaving her alone. Wearing her down."

"Well, it'd have to be that, wouldn't it?" Teague said snarkily. "Because it certainly isn't your charm." He stormed off with a glare.

"Jesus, what's his problem?" Liam asked.

"A Yank woman broke his heart."

"And you *did* take a job from an Irishman," David pointed out. "He's been on the dole for ages."

Jack rose to Liam's defense. "Well, maybe if he got his fat arse off his mammy and daddy's couch, he could find himself a job and wouldn't resent others willing to do a hard day's work, Yank or not." Jack looked at Liam. "I still think you're gonna lose the bet, son," he said good-naturedly. "Do you want anything at the bar?"

"A Guinness would be fine."

Jack waddled to the bar as David and Fergus crossed the room to ask two women to dance, leaving Liam alone on the sidelines. Even though being in Ballycraig sometimes bored him senseless, he kind of liked that it was one of those Irish villages that hadn't been affected by Ireland's boom years. No designer stores, no wine bars, no five-star restaurants—Ballycraig left that to surrounding villages.

Jack returned with Liam's pint, and they touched glasses before each downed a healthy amount of liquid. It was hotter than hell in the parish hall. "Aren't you going to ask any of the other fine-looking women of the town to dance?" he asked Liam.

"In a minute." Liam glanced around the hall. There *were* quite a few good-looking women in town, and he knew for a fact many of them fancied him. But he really had no desire to ask any of them to dance or to make the effort at small talk. At least not right now.

"You got her to dance. Amazing."

Liam turned as Aislinn's sister, Nora, joined him and Jack. No one would ever guess the two were sisters: Nora was dark-haired, well-dressed, and urban. "Chalk and cheese," as his parents would say.

"Is it?" Liam asked.

"You know it is," said Nora. "I'm glad you like her. She's really wonderful. She's just—"

"A wounded, snarling animal," Jack offered helpfully.

"That's quite a *strong* way of putting it," said Nora, looking displeased by Jack's comment, "but yes. And whether she'll admit it or not, she's beginning to like you. I can tell by all the complaining she does about you."

Liam threw Jack a smug look as the older man started to look green around the gills.

"You okay?" Nora asked Jack.

"Fine. It's just hotter than the fifth circle of hell in here." He loosened his tie. "I'm going to step outside to get a breath of fresh air. Excuse me."

Nora turned to Liam. "So what's next?"

"She's allowing me to accompany her to the farmers' market tomorrow."

"Have fun," Nora said dryly.

Liam grinned. "Oh, I will, believe me."

# 6

*Aislinn was certain* that when she pulled up in front of the Oak at 7 a.m., Liam would either be nowhere in sight or would blearily come up with an excuse to beg off accompanying her to the farmers' market. But no: there he was, bright-eyed and smiling, holding a vacuum flask of freshly brewed coffee. Bastard.

She'd heard Nora come in from the *céilí* around midnight, tiptoeing past her bedroom door. Usually, Aislinn slept like a log, but not last night. Loath as she was to admit it, she was softening a bit toward the Yank, and that was kicking up quite a bit of dust in her head. Succumbing to his overtures meant once again risking heartache. Who knew how long Liam planned to stay in Ballycraig? She could hitch her wagon to his, only to have him turn around and with that unnervingly sexy twinkle in his eye say, "It's been nice, love, but I'm back to New York." And there she'd be, shattered and humiliated all over again. No; better to tamp down her feelings.

She'd try to maneuver so that Padraig would sit in the middle of the cab, but he'd jumped out to open the door for Liam to climb in before she'd even come to a full stop. Aislinn dealt with the whisper of excitement caused by his being pressed up against her by concentrating on her driving, leaving the talking to Padraig and Liam. Their discussion was wide-ranging, running the gamut from the process of cleaning and preparing fleeces to Michelle Obama to Liam waxing sentimental about his family. Padraig kept referring to her dad as if he were still alive. Each time, she corrected him gently, and he responded with a quick, "Oh, right, right," before moving on to another topic.

They arrived in Omeath around nine. Aislinn knew most of the other vendors at the market well, having grown up around them: her dad had started taking her with him when she was just six. Padraig made a point of telling Liam that their fleeces were widely considered to be the best, always fetching the highest prices. Perhaps Liam was having them both on, but he looked impressed.

She and Padraig settled themselves in their booth, while Liam excused himself to go exploring. The market had grown over the years. In the beginning, it was just local farmers selling primarily produce, wool, cheese, and milk, but now it was big business with tourists flocking to it, drawn by its "quaintness." Today there were stalls selling crafts, homemade chocolates, baked goods, organic vegetables, handmade toys, and preserves. There was even a group of musicians playing traditional music. Aislinn remembered that at first, her father had despaired of the change, worried about "the changing face of Ireland." But eventually he accepted it, especially since the market usually drew close to four thousand people, and they'd started making more and more money there.

Within minutes of opening, one of her regular customers, a hand spinner from Garra, came by and bought three unprocessed fleeces. A good omen.

After making that first sale, Padraig leaned over to Aislinn. "I like your young man very much," he said.

"He's not my young man."

"Well, he wants to be."

"You know what I say to that."

Two more regulars came by, buying two processed fleeces each.

"It's going to be a good day," Padraig predicted.

"I agree. We're going to sell out." Aislinn looked at him affectionately. "I notice your 'rattling, deadly cough' seems to have abated."

Padraig produced a cough.

"Oh, no, no, it hasn't."

"I'll stop by tonight and make you some lovely tea." Aislinn knew he just wanted a little attention, and she was more than happy to give it.

"Now where's your young man gone to?"

Aislinn took a deep breath before answering. Either he was teasing her, or he'd already forgotten she'd told him Liam *wasn't* her boyfriend.

"He's roaming about."

"Nice lad," he repeated as if he'd never said it before.

Aislinn just sighed.

"You know, your parents would have hated to see you end up alone," Padraig said casually.

Aislinn felt a knot form in her chest. "What are you talking about, you addled old thing?"

"I remember your da saying to me—after the wedding, you know, when Connor buggered off and you lost your taste for human company—that he was worried it would scar you for good, and what a shame that would be."

"Why didn't he say this to me?"

"You know your father. He was a man of few words."

It was true; her father had never been much of a talker, especially when it came to feelings. But she wished he had told her he was worried, rather than confide in Padraig.

Liam wandered back, bearing three home-baked scones. "I figured since we didn't have any breakfast . . ."

"Thank you," said Aislinn, who was ravenous. Usually she ate a big breakfast, but she'd overslept this morning and was in a rush to get up and out before Nora could interrogate her about anything.

Liam stuck his hands in the front pockets of his jeans as if he didn't know what else to with them. "Are you sure there's nothing I can do?"

"Yup," said Aislinn, glad he seemed at loose ends. He'd wanted to spend time with her? Well, he was getting his wish. Out of the corner of her eye, she spotted the guy who thought he was God's gift to women strolling their way. "Feck," she cursed softly.

"What's wrong?" Liam asked.

"Nothing."

Aislinn steeled herself as the eejit stopped at her booth, smiling. "Mornin', Aislinn." He nodded curtly at Padraig. "Padraig."

Aislinn regarded him warily. "Morning, Alfie. You going to buy anything this time, or are you just stopping off to boast about how every woman in the republic wants you?"

"Every woman but you, apparently. Though I can't understand why."

"Could be that I have a brain in my skull." She popped a hunk of scone in her mouth. "If you're not going to buy anything, move on."

Alfie chuckled. It took him a moment before he registered Liam's presence, but when he did, his gaze was mildly contemptuous. "And who might you be?"

"I'm Liam O'Brien. Aislinn's boyfriend."

Aislinn choked back a sputter. Didn't he just wish! Then again, he was doing her a service; his wishful thinking might drive Alfie off for good.

Alfie was scowling at her. "Why are you seeing a Yank when there are loads of sexy Irishmen to be had?"

"Sexy Irishmen?" Aislinn replied, making a great show of looking around. "I've yet to meet one."

Alfie frowned. "I guess I'll be getting on."

"Please do."

With a final dirty look at Liam, he turned heel and walked away.

"What an asshole," said Liam.

"Aren't you the polite one." Aislinn looked down, wiping scone crumbs off her lap. "I suppose I should thank you for driving him away with your bold-faced lie. It came in very handy."

"It's not a lie," Liam said playfully. "It's a prediction."

Aislinn glanced up at him and snorted, even though twinges of unwanted heat were assaulting her body. "In your dreams."

*    *    *

*She sold everything,* as she knew she would. The money would allow her to make some repairs to the barn and purchase a couple of new ewes. She also intended to buy a few steaks for Deenie as a reward for her good work.

It was dusk when the market closed and the vendors began packing up. "We don't have to dash home right away, do we?" Padraig asked.

"Why?"

"I want to chat with a few of my and your da's old buddies."

"Go ahead," Aislinn urged, even though she was eager to get home and away from Liam who, to her great disappointment, had been as charming and helpful as could be all day.

After Padraig left, Liam inched a bit closer and lowered his voice. "Aislinn," he said tentatively. "I noticed Padraig forgot the prices for things a few times."

"No matter," Aislinn said briskly. "I fixed it."

"You really love him, don't you?"

"I do," said Aislinn, unexpectedly choking up. "He's family, and family takes care of family. He can work with me for as long as he likes."

"So there really is a tender heart beating inside that brusque facade," Liam murmured gently.

Aislinn said nothing.

"I know all about presenting a tough face to the world as a way of protecting yourself," Liam continued. "I was the consummate bad boy at home. But a lot of it was just a way to deflect the pain I was in, since I always felt I couldn't measure up to my older brother. And—"

"What is it with you Yanks, spilling your guts without anyone asking you to, like everyone you meet is a bloody therapist?" Aislinn interrupted. She did not want to go down this road.

"Whether you like it or not, I see through your mask, Aislinn. I see the vulnerable woman beneath the hard shell. And if you'll just let me—"

Aislinn rose abruptly, desperate to get away from him. But Liam jumped up, too, and in a bloody bold move, pulled her to him and planted a good, long kiss on her lips, one to which she instantly responded. *More,* she thought, *more,* before jerking herself away.

Liam grinned sexily. "You liked that."

"Don't flatter yourself," Aislinn replied, affecting a bored tone. "It was a moment of madness we'll never speak of again. Got it?"

"I want more moments of madness with you," Liam murmured. "Haven't you figured it out yet? I'm not going to let up until I get them."

"You could have any woman in town," Aislinn pointed out sharply. "Why set your sights on me?"

"Because you're sexy, smart, independent, and headstrong. Did I mention you were sexy?"

"Yes, my barn jacket and wellies have turned many a man's head," Aislinn said dryly.

"Believe it or not, you even look sexy dressed like that."

"God, you're a hopeless thing. It's sad. Truly it is."

"Not as sad as someone who clearly craves romance but is too chicken to take a chance," Liam retorted.

Aislinn glowered at him.

"I dare you to go to dinner with me."

Aislinn squinted at him in disbelief. "You *what*?"

"You heard me. Prove you're not stuck in the past."

Aislinn felt her temper beginning to ignite. "I don't need to prove anything to you!"

"True, you don't *need* to," Liam murmured casually. "But you know you want to, if only to put me in my place."

"You don't want to know the place I think you should be in, boyo."

"Have dinner with me."

"No."

"Have dinner with me."

"Hard of hearing *and* thick. Not a good combo."

"I'm not letting up."

"And I'm not giving in."

"I'll beg if you want." Liam got down on his knees and held his hands out to her imploringly. "Please, Aislinn, please have—"

"Get up!" Aislinn hissed, horrified by the thought someone might have seen him. "I'll have dinner with you, just—get up."

Liam rose, dusting himself off. "That was easier than I thought. Any ideas as to where you'd like to dine?"

"Anywhere but the Oak," Aislinn muttered. "The last thing I need is the whole town gawping and talking, because they've nothing better to do with their lives."

"We'll go to Crosshaven."

"That suits me. But you're not paying for me. I'll pay for my own meal."

"That's not a date."

"I thought you loved my independence," Aislinn said sarcastically.

"I want to do this the traditional way."

Aislinn put a hand on her hip. "Oh, it's traditional, is it, for the woman to pick up the man in her truck?"

"I'll borrow Old Jack's car," Liam immediately countered.

"If you breathe a word of this to anyone, I'll cripple you."

"I'm sure you could. Shall we say around seven, Wednesday night? That's my night off."

*Good,* thought Aislinn. It wouldn't draw suspicion, the way it would if he asked for a night off. He could just tell Jack he wanted to go into Crosshaven, have a look round at a much bigger town.

"Wednesday will work for me," Aislinn said coolly. God, she'd never hear the end of it from Nora.

Liam grinned. "Great. I'm looking forward to it."

"Hmmm."

Aislinn turned away so he couldn't see her small smile. She was looking forward to it, too. But she'd be damned if she'd let him know it.

# 7

*Three minutes into* driving Old Jack's car, Liam realized he should have swallowed his pride and let Aislinn drive them to Crosshaven. Jack's fifteen-year-old Ford Focus was barely able to make it up and down the hills leading to her farm. The floor beneath the driver's seat had rusted out; Jack's solution had been been to cover the hole with a thin, battered piece of sheet metal, held in place with duct tape. The upholstery was split and shredded. And the interior reeked of the lily of the valley perfume Jack's wife, Bettina, loved to douse herself with.

When he'd asked Jack if he could borrow the car, the old man guessed the reason and went pale, realizing he was going to lose the bet. At the same time, it was dawning on Liam that he was a creep to have made the bet in the first place.

He really liked Aislinn. He'd spent time with lots of women, but none had ever been as fiery or fiercely independent as she, and he was surprised how attractive he found those traits. He also loved her lack of vanity, and he had been serious when he'd told her she looked great in her caked old wellies and barn coat. Aislinn truly had no idea how naturally beautiful she was.

Liam also meant it when he said he saw behind her gruff mask. Her love for Padraig, even her love for Nora, despite pretending to be annoyed by her, revealed the tenderness she tried so hard to conceal. The more time he spent with her, the more he wanted to draw her out. A fine, sharp desire had shot through him when he kissed her, made all the more exciting because she had responded without hesitation.

Liam held his breath as the car crested the final hill, spluttering and backfiring all the way. God, she was going to mock him all the way to Crosshaven.

He was surprised to find Aislinn waiting for him outside, her dog beside her. She looked tense. Liam parked the car and got out.

"My parents always told me that when you're picking up a girl for a date, you go up to the house to fetch her," he said.

"They're right, but I don't want us to be cross-examined by Nora for twenty minutes." She crouched down, kissing the top of Deenie's head. "Run along with you now. I won't be long."

Deenie licked her face and trotted off toward the house.

"I can't believe she understood what you said."

"She's a border collie. She's smarter than half the children in this town."

Liam laughed as he walked around the car to open the door for her. "You look nice," he said as she ducked inside.

"Thank you," Aislinn said stiffly.

Liam hopped back in the car, throwing it into reverse. There was a horrible grinding sound; the car didn't move.

"Don't worry, it's just temperamental," he assured Aislinn. *Shit, please let this piece of junk go in reverse.*

He shifted back into neutral, then again into reverse. The car obeyed, and they were on their way, albeit slowly.

"So," Liam said conversationally, "how has your week been so far?" He realized he was nervous and wanted to keep awkward silence between them to a minimum.

"It's been a week. You?"

"Big excitement was Fergus and David getting into a fistfight at the Oak. Something about money owed."

"They're eleven years old in the head, those two." Aislinn cracked her window open an inch. "Jesus God, the smell of lily of the valley is overpowering. I feel like I'm in a funeral parlor on wheels."

Liam laughed. She was funny, too. He liked that.

Aislinn was looking out the window. "Where are we going?"

"A place called Cronin's. The seafood is supposed to be great. Jack recommended it."

Aislinn turned to him sharply. "You didn't tell that old busybody you're out with me, did you?"

"I told you I wouldn't say anything," said Liam, feeling like a sleazeball for lying, especially when he saw the relief that crept onto her face.

"Good."

"I don't see what the big deal is," said Liam, narrowly avoiding hitting a mangy stray cat that had appeared suddenly on the pitch-black road. "Are you ashamed of going out with me?"

"I told you: I just don't like giving people gossip to chew on, that's all," Aislinn said testily. She paused. "Do you always drive like an old man?"

Liam shot her a look of annoyance. "This is as fast as the car will go."

"Should have taken the truck," Aislinn said lightly.

"Next time."

"Next time?" Aislinn chortled. "Don't think so. I'm only out with you tonight because you dared me to."

"Bullshit. You're out with me because you like me."

"You're tolerable," she allowed with a sniff.

"I'll take that as a compliment." He hit a pothole, and both their heads almost banged the roof of the car.

Aislinn smirked. "Good one."

"In case you haven't noticed, it's pitch-dark out here," Liam said defensively. He hated these rural roads, especially since he wasn't used to driving on the opposite side of the road. What was next? Crashing into a hedgerow? He was feeling like a dorky fifteen-year-old on his first date, anxious and self-conscious.

"What's Nora doing tonight?" he asked.

"Working on her article."

"Sounds boring."

Aislinn smiled. "It does, doesn't it?"

"Yup." That smile . . . Shit, it was so distracting. "You go to college?"

"Nah. Never had the desire. I always wanted to raise sheep. Keep it in the family, you know." She eyed him curiously. "Did you go to university?"

"God, no. The minute I graduated from high school I was working behind the bar at my family's pub."

They fell quiet. Liam wondered if Aislinn was thinking about how this was another thing they had in common: their devotion to family tradition.

"They must be missing you fierce," Aislinn said softly.

Liam cleared his throat uncomfortably, overcome with a sudden wash of emotion. "Yeah, I miss them, too."

*You must miss your folks, too,* he almost said, but caught himself. He sensed it was too personal a question. Push, and he'd lose what little ground he'd gained with her.

He was about to ask her more about Nora when the car suddenly began pulling to the left. *Now what?* he thought. He slowly pulled over to the side of the road, killing the engine.

"You've got a flat," Aislinn declared.

"Let me just take a look," said Liam authoritatively,

hoping she wasn't right. He'd never had a flat tire in his life.

They both got out of the car. She was right: the rear left tire was as flat as he wished the damn road was. Great.

"Uh, let me just take care of this, and we'll be on our way."

He ducked back inside the car, opening the glove compartment. No flashlight. He opened the trunk. There was a flashlight, but the batteries were dead. Liam rubbed his forehead in frustration. How the hell was he supposed to change a tire when he couldn't see what he was doing? "You wouldn't happen to have a match on you, would he?" he asked Aislinn.

She joined him in front of the open trunk. "I do," she said, rifling through her purse. She pulled out a book of matches, and lit one. Liam pulled out the spare tire and the tools. The match went out. Aislinn lit another, and another, losing the battle against the wind.

"This is just great," he muttered.

He stood in front of the flat tire. Stalling. He had no idea how to change a goddamn tire, though how hard could it be? It looked like all you needed to do was unscrew the bolts and—

"You don't know how to change a flat, do you?" Aislinn asked, sounding highly amused.

"No, I can change a tire."

Aislinn folded her arms across her chest. "Go on, then."

He glared at her, and grabbing the jack, began jacking up the car. Aislinn burst out laughing.

"What?" Liam snapped.

"Know how to change a tire, do you? First you loosen the lug nuts, and *then* you jack it up." She sighed and picked up the lug nut wrench, shooing him away. "Here, let me do it. It'll take three seconds."

"I'm not a moron, you know."

"No one said you were. But I've no desire to stand here

half the night while you try to prove you're no girly man." Smiling impishly, she put her hand over her heart. "Your secret is safe with me, I swear."

Liam frowned and let her take over. Aislinn quickly changed the tire in the dark, whistling a happy tune that Liam was sure was meant to mock him.

"There you go, city boy," she said gaily when she was done, returning the tools to the trunk.

"Appreciate it," Liam muttered. He kicked the tire gently. Wasn't that something you were supposed to do to make sure it was sound?

"Now, here's the thing," Aislinn said authoritatively. "This spare is as bald as my aunt Charlene. We're never going to make it into Crosshaven and back on this thing. So I guess we'd best turn around so you can drop me home, and we can call it a night."

"Not happening."

"I beg your pardon?"

"We're not calling it a night. We'll go back to your place and eat there instead."

Aislinn's mouth fell open. "Oh, will we, then? Cheeky bastard! I'm not cooking for you!"

"I didn't say you had to cook for me. I said we'd eat something. Then, next week we'll take your truck into Crosshaven and try this again, because eating at your house does not count as a dinner date."

"We're not eating at my house."

Liam swung the car keys around his index finger. "I'm not driving you home, then."

Aislinn shrugged. "No skin off my nose." She turned and started walking up the road.

"Goddamn it," Liam cursed under his breath. "Fine!" he yelled at her back. "You win this one! I'll drive you home, and we don't have to eat anything, even though I'm starving to death!"

Aislinn turned and walked back to him. "Starving, aye?"

"Starving."

Aislinn frowned. "I suppose you could make yourself a sandwich."

"Thanks so much," said Liam sarcastically. He truly was starving, having eaten very little in anticipation of their meal out.

"We'll see if you still thank me when Nora plies us with questions till our eyes bleed." She held out her hand for the keys. "I'll drive. I don't think my spine can take hitting another pothole."

"I don't think so. You've already emasculated me once tonight. Twice, and my ego will be in complete tatters."

Aislinn laughed. "It's a rare man who can admit such a thing."

"Yes, well, I'm a rare man," Liam murmured.

Aislinn gave a small snort and got back in the car. "Drive on."

## 8

*As Aislinn had* predicted, no sooner did they step into the kitchen than Nora appeared. *Damn*, thought Aislinn. *Here it comes. An interrogation.*

"What are you two doing here?" Nora asked, surprised. "I thought you were going out to dinner in Crosshaven."

"We got a flat, and there's no way we'd get there on the spare, so here we are," Aislinn explained. She stared at Nora hard, hoping she'd take the hint to skedaddle. She didn't.

"I take it you're eating here?"

"Just sandwiches," said Aislinn. "Then Liam will be on his way."

Liam looked down at the stone floor, suppressing a smile.

"What's so funny, you?" Aislinn asked tetchily.

Liam looked up. "Nothing," he said, his eyes quickly catching Nora's. Aislinn didn't like it, not one bit. Some chat had gone on between them behind her back. She could feel it.

"Where's Deenie?" Aislinn asked Nora.

"Asleep on your bed, I think."

"She must be tired. She put in a good, hard day."

Nora nodded dumbly. *She has no idea what I'm talking about,* Aislinn thought. *Despite growing up here, she still has no clue as to how sheep herding works.*

"Did you have Padraig up for dinner?"

Nora frowned. "No."

"Nora, you know he eats with us!"

"It slipped my mind, Aislinn, all right? I was really absorbed in my research. In fact, I wound up taking my dinner up to my room."

"So? He doesn't need to be entertained. Please, Nora, if you're ever here on your own again, don't forget to have him up. He eats badly when he's left to his own devices."

Nora sighed. "Next time you're out, I won't forget, I promise."

"Thank you." She turned to Liam. "What kind of sandwich do you want?"

"Whatever you have."

"I've got a bit of ham. Some nice cheese."

"There's more than that," Nora chided with a cluck of the tongue. "We've got focaccia, a little caviar, and some pesto spread. I actually had to order the caviar and spread from London, since the market in Moneygall—"

"Doesn't cater to rich expats," Aislinn finished for her, shooting Nora an annoyed look. A bolt of tension passed between them. *Would you ever take yourself off and get out of here?* thought Aislinn.

Liam looked uncomfortable. "Ham and cheese is fine with me."

"How about you?" Aislinn asked Nora. "Shall I make her nibs something, too?"

Nora smiled politely. "I already ate, thank you." There was an awkward pause. "Well, I'll leave you two to it. I've got a lot of reading to do." She surprised Aislinn by kissing her on the cheek. "I'll see you in the morning. Nice to see you, Liam." She started away then abruptly turned back. "Oh, I forgot to tell you, Aislinn: Donald is coming in next Thursday for a long weekend."

*Great,* thought Aislinn. *Just what I need: a weekend with a ponce who points out everything that needs to be repaired as if he knows a damn thing about it, and who drones on about how provincial and boring Ballycraig is.* Still, he seemed to adore Nora. And that's what mattered.

"Grand," she made herself say. *You two can go shopping in Moneygall and despair over the lack of artichoke dip together.*

"Night," said Nora with a small wave.

"Night," Aislinn and Liam chimed together.

Liam joined Aislinn at the counter as she started preparing their sandwiches. "Do I sense a little tension between the two of you?"

"I don't know why in the bloody name of creation she's come here to work on her article, since she and her husband have never had much use for the farm or Ballycraig. I swear to God, the day she turned eighteen she legged it out of here so fast your head would've spun."

"Maybe she needs a breather from London."

"That's what she says. But she does pluck on my nerves sometimes, truly. Doesn't help that we're chalk and cheese."

Liam smiled. "My mother always uses that expression."

"It was a favorite of my mother's, too." Mam. Aislinn swallowed hard, the image of her mother smiling flashing through her mind. She'd had a beautiful smile: soothing and kind.

Liam sauntered away, inspecting the kitchen. "This house is huge."

"My great grandfather built it. My grandfather was born here; my da, too, and his two sisters."

"It's an amazing place."

"Thank you," said Aislinn, welling with pride. "Padraig claims it's haunted by my grandfather, but I've never seen him about." She handed Liam his sandwich. "What would you like to drink? I've got milk, water, and Guinness."

"Guinness would be great."

"I agree. Sit."

Liam sat down at the long, scarred Parsons table, practically devouring his sandwich. He looked somewhat embarrassed. "I told you I was starved."

"Clearly." Aislinn took a bite of her sandwich. "Now this is my idea of a date."

Liam's gaze was unwavering as he took a sip of beer. "This isn't our date."

"I'm fulfilling my obligation to you. You dared me to have dinner with you. I agreed. And here I am, having dinner with you."

"Doesn't count," Liam insisted. "If you won't have dinner *out* with me next week, I'll tell Jack we were together tonight, and within minutes, the whole town will know."

Aislinn cocked her head quizzically. "Did you, by any chance, have to hop it here to Ireland because you were a blackmailing bastard?"

Liam laughed delightedly. "I love it when you flirt with me."

"I don't flirt," Aislinn retorted with a scowl, annoyed by how turned on she was by his laugh.

"Yes, you do, but you just won't admit it."

"Wrong."

"Or maybe you don't know you're flirting, which makes it even sexier."

Aislinn snorted. "Jesus, can you ever spin the bull. Did the women back home fall for this rubbish? Because if they did, perhaps I've been giving American women more credit than they deserve." She nodded at his plate. "Finish up, please, and be on your way."

"If we hadn't gotten a flat, we wouldn't even *be* in Crosshaven by now."

"And what does that have to do with the price of tea in China?"

"I think you can spare me a bit more of your time."

"Fine," she grumbled. *Bigheaded pain in the neck.* But he was right, of course. Had the tire not blown, they'd most likely still be in the car right now. All told, between the drive there and back and dinner, she probably would have spent about four hours with him. Well, handsome and witty as he was, she sure as hell wasn't spending four hours *here* with him.

Sandwiches finished, she took their plates over to the sink to wash.

"Ever think of getting a dishwasher?" Liam asked.

"Ever think of minding your own business?" Aislinn soaped up the plates. "It's just me and Padraig here, and now Nora. We don't generate a lot of dishes."

She could feel him coming up close behind her and held her breath for a long moment, trying to drive away the feeling of excitement inching up on her. *Oh Lord, let him wrap his arms around me. Oh Lord, don't let him touch me. Oh Lord, my mind is a muddle.*

He didn't put his arms around her but rested his chin on her shoulder playfully. "When you're done with the dishes, I'd love it if you could introduce me to your flock."

"I'm tired. I need you to go."

Liam stuck his watch in front of her face. "We'd probably *just* be getting into Crosshaven now."

Aislinn sighed in exasperation. "You really expect me to believe you give a tinker's damn about my sheep?"

"I'm curious. Seriously."

"Yeah, and my grandda's ghost haunts the paddocks." She dried her hands on a tea towel and turned from the sink. "I suppose I'll have to let you wear a pair of my dad's old wellies so you don't ruin your trainers."

Liam's gaze softened. "You've still got them?"

"Yes," Aislinn said curtly. Nora had wanted to purge the house of all their parents' things the week after they died, as if she still bloody lived here. Aislinn refused, so Nora let it go. It was only after Nora left that Aislinn realized that her sister was only looking out for her, thinking that ridding the house of their parents' things might make it easier for Aislinn to live there.

"Well, come on with you," Aislinn urged gruffly, striding

toward the mudroom, where she pulled on her boots and slipped into her faithful old barn jacket. "The sooner I show you round, the sooner I get you out of my hair."

* * *

*Her grumpiness faded* as soon as she hit the barn, where her beloved flock were sleeping in the fresh straw she'd put down for them just that morning. She inhaled deeply, loving the warmth, the smell, everything about it.

She named every ewe, ram, and lamb for Liam, hoping that if she started gabbing on about feeding them, rotating pastures, shearing season, and everything else that had to do with running a sheep farm, it would drive him off. But no; he acted like he was interested in all of it, which she was sure was an act. She could have stood there holding forth on the different varieties of termites, and he still would have stuck around. She'd give him points for tenacity, that was sure.

"Well, I've dined with you, and you've seen my flock," she finally concluded cheerily. "Good night."

Liam checked his watch. "We'd probably be getting our menus right about now."

Aislinn sighed. "Right, what's next? Shall we peek in on Padraig? Throw stones at Nora's window? I know," she said, brightening. "Maybe I can teach you to change a tire."

Liam chuckled good-naturedly. "Actually, what I'd really love to do right now is just sit in one of the meadows and look up at the stars."

"Who's stopping you?"

"I didn't mean *alone*."

Aislinn's heart gave a small, painful lurch; stargazing was something she and Connor used to do all the time on clear nights. In fact, it was something she often did on her own.

She looked at him, at his dark, broody handsomeness and playful eyes, and decided to risk it.

"Fine," she muttered, trying to appear put-upon. "I'll get the blanket I keep in the truck."

* * *

*She led him* up to her favorite pasture, spreading the small, plaid blanket out on the grass. She could see the lights of Ballycraig twinkling down below; Padraig was still up, too, dim light emanating from his front window and smoke curling from his chimney. If he was still awake when Liam left, she'd pay him a visit.

Aislinn sat down first on the blanket, secretly thrilled when Liam sat so close their shoulders were practically touching.

"God, look at that sky," he said rapturously. "You don't see skies like that in the city. The buildings are too tall, and there's too much light pollution."

"I couldn't bear to live in the city."

"A true country girl, huh?"

"Yes."

Liam looked at her. "Chalk and cheese."

Aislinn smiled shyly. "Yes, chalk and cheese."

Liam casually snaked his arm around her shoulder as his gaze returned upward. "I guess I could understand not wanting to give this up," he said after a considerable pause.

Aislinn swallowed. The feel of his arm around her shoulder . . . it was wonderful, making her feel warm and safe. She hadn't realized how much she missed being touched by a man until now. And yet, her first impulse was to stiffen up. Liam noticed.

"Why so nervous?"

"I'm not." What an idiot she was, denying the obvious. "Look, I'm not good at this," she admitted lamely.

Liam drew her a little bit closer. "Good at what?"

"Being comfortable with a man. Not after what happened." She looked him square in the eye. "I don't quite trust you."

Liam glanced away for a moment. "I don't blame you. Not after what happened with Connor McCarthy."

She shook her head ruefully. "What kind of eejit can't tell her man is gay?"

"You shouldn't beat yourself up."

"I suppose not." Aislinn felt tears coming and clenched her jaw. Thinking about what happened still angered and humiliated her.

"That must have been hard, being jilted and losing your folks in the same year."

"It was. But I've dealt with it."

"Have you?" Liam asked softly.

She burst into tears. For a year, she'd bitten back the pain, pushed it down, not letting anyone get near her for fear of looking weak. She hated that the whole town pitied her because of what happened with Connor. The only ones she'd let comfort her had been her parents, and they, too, were soon gone. All she had was Nora, who lived in another country and with whom she'd never been particularly close. In order to go on, she'd had to toughen herself, inside and out. If that made people think she was a hard bitch, so be it. Let them walk a mile in her shoes and see how *they'd* cope.

Liam held her tight. "It's okay," he whispered. "Let it go."

And so she did, sobbing into his shoulder as if her heart were breaking all over again. Liam rocked her quietly, stroking her hair. Finally, when she was all cried out, she pulled away from him abruptly, swiping at her eyes, hard. "Sorry about that."

"No need to be sorry."

"I must look a sight."

"You look fine," Liam assured her.

"Ha! Now there you're lying. My nose gets all red when I cry, and my face goes blotchy." She swiped hard at her cheeks. "I feel like an idiot."

"Why? Because you dropped your defenses?"

"I don't enjoy being an object of pity."

"You're not an object of pity."

Aislinn laughed bitterly. "Not to you, maybe. But to the rest of Ballycraig I am."

"There's a difference between pity and feeling bad for

someone who was deceived and humiliated by the person they love."

"I suppose." She hesitated, then kissed his cheek. "Thank you for letting me soak your shirt with my pathetic tears."

"My pleasure." Liam ran his index finger softly down her cheek. "I'd like more than a chaste kiss on the cheek, please."

"Liam—"

He took what he wanted, and she let him. The kiss was sweet at first, but it quickly turned into something dark and thrilling as Liam crushed her to him. Aislinn felt a blast of heat and longing rock her body. It had been so long, so long. She was frightened but eager. *Let it happen,* she told herself as her body burned. *Let go.*

Her mind was reeling as vibrant colors swirled behind her eyes, and the feeling of being fully and gloriously alive came back to her. It was something she'd been certain she'd never feel again.

The kiss kept on, dizzying and sublime. Liam gently took her by the shoulders and laid her down on the blanket, stretching out beside her. Aislinn could see the desire in his eyes as they resumed their fevered kissing. A low moan came from her throat, and for a split second, she was embarrassed. But the longer Liam kissed her, the more she sensed his abandon, and the less inhibited she herself became. She could feel him melting against her, moonbeams kissing her skin as one of his hands slid down to cup her breast. The conflagration inside her was building. And yet . . .

Aislinn gently removed his hand and sat up, trying to steady her breathing as she cleared her mind. Liam sat up, too, his expression dazed yet distressed.

"Did I do something wrong, Aislinn?"

"No, no, of course not. It's me. I'm just—I'm not ready to go there yet. I want to, but I can't."

"It's okay."

"Is it? I would hate for you to think I'm just toying with you."

Pain flickered across Liam's face. "I would never think that."

"Or that I'm frigid. I'm not. I'm just gun-shy."

Liam cupped her chin in his hand. "We can take this as fast or slow as you want."

"And what would 'this' be?"

"You know what."

"Yes, I suppose I do." Aislinn blew out a breath of relief. "Thank you." *He's a good man,* she thought. *A wiseass, an egomaniac, a pushy Yank, but still and all, a good man.* She told him so.

Liam feigned being wounded. "Is that the best you can come up with?"

"You're a good kisser, too; I'll give you that."

Liam grinned cockily. "The best."

"I'm not sure if *that's* true."

"Have you had better?"

Aislinn chuckled. "No, come to think of it."

She was glad the heavy part of the conversation seemed to be done for now. "I suppose I have to have dinner with you next week."

"I suppose so."

She took his hand, nervously trailing an index finger back and forth across his knuckles. "I'd still prefer we keep this to ourselves for now."

Liam looked unhappy. "Sure."

Aislinn tensed. In the space of a second, she felt like the mood had changed from one of good-natured ribbing to one of discomfort. He was changing his mind about them already. She put her heart in lockdown mode.

"Is something wrong?"

"No," Liam hastily assured her. He pressed his lips to her forehead. "I just realized I'm tired, too."

Aislinn relaxed. "I'll bet. Watching a woman change a tire can really take it out of a man."

"Wiseass," Liam said affectionately. He rose, extending a hand to her, and together they walked to Old Jack's car.

"You have a cell phone, I hope, so you can call me if this old rattletrap doesn't get you back to town and I have to rescue you?" Aislinn asked.

"Of course." He put his arms around her. "Thank you for a great night."

Aislinn swallowed. "Yes, I had a good time, too."

Liam kissed her softly and got into the car.

"See you next week."

"Maybe," Aislinn said coolly.

Liam chuckled. "I'll pick you up at the same time next Wednesday."

He waved, and then he was off. Aislinn watched his car snake down the winding road, until finally his taillights disappeared. She turned and walked back toward the house. She knew she'd set something in motion, and it both frightened and exhilarated her. Still, she was willing to see where it led.

# 9

*He couldn't go* through with the bet. No way. That's all Liam could think as he slowly drove back to Ballycraig. When Aislinn said she didn't trust him, he found it hard to look her in the eye. This was a real person with real feelings; a real person for whom *he* had feelings—which complicated things immensely. His plan had been to hop on the next plane the minute he heard from Quinn that it was safe for him to go back to New York. Hell, that had been part of the reason he'd gone for the bet: not only was he confident of his skills with women, but if he won and Jack had to double his wages, he'd return home with a nice chunk of change.

Kissing Aislinn had been magical. He'd always laughed at people who said things like that, but it was the only way to describe it. It wasn't just the need and vulnerability she displayed; it was the feeling that there was a tightly coiled passion deep within her that was ready to explode. He wanted to be the one to unleash it.

He parked Jack's car behind the Royal Oak, avoiding the pub as he went directly upstairs to his apartment. He knew that the minute the clock struck twelve thirty, Jack would be knocking on his door. He was right.

"Come in," Liam called wearily. Jack looked anxious as he slipped inside.

"What happened with the McCafferty? You're back early."

"That's because your piece of shit car got a flat. No way could we make it into Crosshaven on that spare—speaking of which, you might want to get a real spare to stash in the trunk."

"Yes, right, sure," said Jack impatiently. "So you never got to wine and dine her. What did you do instead?"

"Had sandwiches at her house."

"Oh, that's dead romantic," Jack said dryly, but he looked pleased. "Not making much progress, are you, boyo?"

"Actually, I am."

"Eatin' sandwiches? I don't know how things work in New York, but let me assure you, here in Ireland we'd file that under *Pathetic*."

Liam took a deep breath, then blew it out. "I want to call off the bet."

Jack thrust his head forward. *"What?"*

"I want to call off the bet," Liam repeated. "The more I think about it, the more I realize it's a cruel thing to do."

"Don't hand me a line of cow shite, son. I know what's really going on here."

Liam was baffled. "I don't understand."

"You're losing, so you want to call it off."

"You're wrong."

"I'm right," Jack insisted, thrusting his chin out. "You can't bear the thought of Fergus, David, and Teague crowing about how Mr. Big Shot Yank failed, and it's beginning to dawn on you that not getting paid for a year will mean you'll have to move in with your relatives, and it'll leave you with no pocket money to boot."

Liam scrubbed his hands over his face. "Jesus. You're not getting this, are you? It's about compassion. It's about not being cruel. I didn't think through what would happen when I'd won the bet, how she'd feel being used that way. Hasn't she had to deal with enough humiliation?"

"Oh, I see how it is. You're losing, so all of a sudden you grow a conscience," Jack scoffed. "Convenient, that is."

Liam shrugged diffidently. "You believe what you want to believe."

"You're a coward."

Now it was Liam's turn for incredulity. "What the hell did you just say?"

"You're a coward. Only a coward reneges on a wager."

Liam gritted his teeth. He was a lot of things, but a coward wasn't one of them. "Call me that again and—"

"What? What?" Jack goaded. "Hit an old man?"

Liam took a deep breath, trying to control his temper. It had been a long time since someone had pushed his buttons like this, and he could feel the old rage and darkness churning inside him.

"Well?"

"Fine, the bet's still on," Liam snapped. "You're a fool, Jack. I just gave you a chance to save yourself a lot of money, and you turned it down."

"Perhaps. But as I said, only a coward reneges on a wager. And besides, I'm still confident you're going to be the one eating crow, not me. Night, now."

He winked and turned, closing the door to Liam's apartment behind him.

*Shit,* thought Liam. For someone who claimed to be confident, all it had taken was an old fool calling him a coward for him to feel a challenge to his masculinity, and bam! The bet was back on.

He stretched out on his bed, racking his brains about how he might be able to make this work. Finally it came to him: he'd continue seeing Aislinn, and one night, when the romance between them was firmly established, they'd come in to the pub together; Old Jack and the three ass-holes would have to concede he'd won the bet. But then, he'd simply keep on seeing her. It was so simple, he laughed out loud.

He turned out the light, smiling to himself.

# 10

*"Did you and* Liam enjoy your sandwiches?"

Aislinn tried not to frown at unexpectedly being confronted by Nora as she went into the kitchen to fetch the vacuum flasks of tea she'd forgotten for herself and Padraig that morning. If forgetting such a crucial part of their morning ritual wasn't testament to what a pleasant muddle her head was in, she didn't know what was.

"I'm surprised you're up," said Aislinn.

Nora, drinking her own tea, fiddled distractedly with her teaspoon. "I couldn't sleep."

"Something troubling you?"

"This and that," Nora said vaguely.

"You sure everything is okay between you and Donald?" Aislinn was genuinely concerned. The last thing she wanted was for Nora to also have a man shred her heart to bits.

"We're fine," Nora assured her with a faint smile. "Though I do miss him."

"He's coming next week, is he not? And there's nothing stopping you going back home to London."

"True." Her eyes tracked Aislinn as she walked across

to the cupboard to get some biscuits to bring to Padraig. "I'm sorry I'm getting on your nerves."

"You're not," Aislinn lied.

Nora just laughed.

Aislinn turned around. "Okay, you are," she confessed.

Nora looked slightly wounded. "What on earth am I doing?"

Aislinn furrowed her brow. "Well, you leave wet towels on the bathroom floor, for one, and you never remember to turn the lights out, and you put things in the wrong place in the cupboard . . . I guess it's just that I have my own ways. I feel like you've invaded my space, do you know what I mean?"

"It's not just your space," Nora pointed out. "They left the farm to both of us, you know."

Aislinn was taken aback. "Yes, and you've spent so much time here over the years because you love it here so much," she shot back. She put a box of biscuits in her pocket. "This is my *home*, Nora. It's where I've made my life. Yes, it's half yours. But that doesn't mean you can waltz in here and start giving me love advice and your opinion on Padraig and all the rest of it."

Nora gave a frustrated sigh. "I was just trying to connect with you, Aislinn. I worry about you being so isolated." She smiled slyly. "That's why I think it's great you're seeing Liam O'Brien."

"We're not seeing each other."

"Right. Did he kiss you?"

Aislinn blushed against her will.

"He did!" Nora looked delighted. "Was it good?"

"Very good," Aislinn admitted. She glanced up at the clock above the sink. Padraig could wait a moment or two. She wished she and Nora had been this close growing up.

"Are you seeing him again?"

"We're going to go into Crosshaven on Wednesday for dinner the way we'd originally planned."

"I can help you get ready," Nora said excitedly. "Do your makeup, like I did before the dance. Lend you some clothes."

"We're just going to a seafood place, Nora. And I know how to do my own makeup."

"Then why weren't you wearing any last night?"

"Because I wasn't in the mood," Aislinn said grouchily. "He's seen me with and without, and it doesn't seem to make any difference to him. I think he likes me natural. And that's how I like myself. That's the way I'm most comfortable."

"Suit yourself."

"I will." Aislinn slid into the chair next to her sister. "Come on, tell me: what 'things' are eating at you?"

"It's this article," Nora confessed. "I hate that you have to 'publish or perish' in academia if you want to get tenure. Sometimes I wonder if I chose the right career."

Aislinn was surprised. "I thought you liked teaching."

"I do, but I hate the interdepartmental politics; people stab each other in the back a lot. And the dean of my department is a dinosaur! He really thinks women are somewhat inferior to men in the classroom. Sometimes I envy you. You don't have to answer to anyone. I'd love to be my own boss."

Aislinn was shocked to hear this. "I still have pressures on me, you know."

"I know, but it's different, isn't it? You have so much more control over your life than I do."

"I guess I never thought of it that way." She looked at Nora sympathetically. "Is there anything I can do to help you feel better?"

"No, I'm all right. Really. I've gone out to walk the pastures a few times. It helps clear my head. I never realized how much land there was!"

"Aye, about thirty acres."

"That's a lot." She paused. "And it's really not too much for you and Padraig to handle?"

Aislinn rolled her eyes. "Jesus God, we're fine."

"Are you?" She touched Aislinn's hand. "Ever think you might need some kind of sabbatical of your own? Take a holiday?"

"*Me?* You must be joking. I don't have time for a holiday. The farm can't run itself, you know."

"You and Connor planned to go on a honeymoon, didn't you? Obviously you thought the farm would run fine without you."

"That was because da was still here with Padraig, so there were two of them," said Aislinn, starting to feel defensive. "If I were to go on holiday—which I have no desire to do, by the way—that would leave Padraig all alone. It would be too much for him."

"Couldn't you hire a temporary hand to help him?"

Aislinn eyed Nora suspiciously. "Why are you so eager for me to take a holiday?"

"I'm not eager for you to do anything. I just worry about you not taking any time for yourself. Aren't you worried you're going to burn out?"

"Listen to us: the worry sisters," Aislinn noted with amusement. "Here's the thing: I love what I do, Nora; I've no yen to take a break from it. Besides, what would I do, go on holiday alone? That'd be loads of fun."

"You could go with—"

Aislinn held up a hand to silence her. "Best not go there if you know what's good for you."

"Just a thought."

"Besides, he's only just gotten here," Aislinn continued, more to herself than to her sister. "It's doubtful Old Jack would let him go gallivanting off so soon into his working at the pub."

Nora narrowed her eyes. "Ah, so the thought of going away with him does appeal to you."

"Maybe," Aislinn said cagily. "Maybe not." She changed the subject. "Will we need to go pick Donald up in Cork City?"

"No, he's renting a car and driving up."

"That's good." Aislinn was glad. She hated when Donald criticized her truck.

"He's really looking forward to coming. Talk about someone who's completely stressed! It doesn't help that he hates what he does for a living."

"He does?" Another surprise.

"Oh yeah. Just did it to please his father. Of course, now he's in a 'golden handcuffs' situation: the money is just too good for him to walk away from, even though he sometimes talks about just packing it all in one day and disappearing." Nora sighed. "Being here will do him a world of good. We can relax, take walks, go into Ballycraig . . ."

Aislinn just nodded, completely baffled. The few times Nora and Donald had visited the farm, she'd never known them to take walks. Usually, they drove to Moneygall or took day trips down to Cork. In the evening, they'd go into Crosshaven. Nora had taken Donald into Ballycraig once when they'd first gotten together, and he had done nothing to hide how unimpressed he was. Aislinn couldn't forget his saying he'd blow his brains out if he had to live here. Thankfully, Donald hadn't said it in front of their father, who'd never warmed to his son-in-law. But the fact he'd said it at all pissed her off. What kind of an arse insulted someone to their face about where they lived? *Donald really has to be stressed if he's coming here for four days,* she thought. Maybe he just missed Nora.

Aislinn stood, buttoning up her barn jacket. "Right. I'm off."

"Can I borrow your truck if you're not using it today?" Nora asked hesitantly. "I wanted to go into Moneygall and pick up a few more groceries."

"Not a problem."

"I'd like to cook dinner tonight, if that's okay."

"It's more than okay," said Aislinn eagerly. She'd give Nora that: she was a great cook. "Just remember not to make anything too spicy, or Padraig will have none of it. It bothers his stomach."

Nora looked dismayed. "Right. Padraig."

"He's part of the family, Nora. I don't know why you don't like having him around."

"He's never liked me."

"What? That's not true."

"Yes, it is! He's always thought I was a snob and needled me about it. He's the one who started calling me the Queen of Sheba, remember?"

"It didn't help that you told anyone who would listen that you couldn't wait to get out of here as soon as you went to university. It was kind of insulting, Nora."

"I guess," Nora muttered.

She took another sip of tea. "He's very lucky to have you, Aislinn."

"Other way round: I'm lucky to have him." She waved to Nora as she headed back outside. "Drive safe. See you later."

\* \* \*

*"That was a* lovely meal."

Aislinn was behind the wheel of her truck, driving herself and Liam back from their dinner in Crosshaven. Cronin's was all it was cracked up to be; she'd had a wonderful dinner of fresh mussels cooked in wine, cream, and herbs, and though she hated to admit it, their soda bread rivaled her mother's. The place had a nice, low-key atmosphere, too, the walls covered with pictures of the area and old advert signs, shelves lined with miniature antique bottles of all shapes and colors. Somewhere around nine, a band of musicians came strolling in to play traditional music. Everyone joined in the singing, even Liam, which surprised her, until he told her he'd grown up hearing his parents sing the very same tunes.

Chat flowed easily, at least from Liam. Aislinn enjoyed hearing about him growing up in Manhattan, though it was hard to ignore the wistfulness that stole into his eyes when he talked about his family. He did pep up a bit when he told her stories about the regulars at his parents' pub, and whether he knew it or not, the tales of his juvenile delinquency were intriguing. Aislinn could imagine him hot-wiring cars and committing petty crimes; there was still a touch of the bad boy in him, made all the more real by his being on the lam. *Outlaw Liam,* she thought amusedly. *Sexy Liam.* The problem was, he knew it, which was why she got a kick out of taking him down a peg here and there; the man could use a little humility.

For Aislinn, opening up didn't come quite so easily. Her life felt simple and mundane compared to his, and there was still a small part of her that was holding back, fearful of trusting only to get kicked in the teeth once again. If Liam sensed her hesitancy, he didn't push, for which she was grateful.

"Dinner was worth risking my life," Liam announced.

"Excuse me?"

"Jesus, Aislinn. Drive any faster, and we'll be going at the speed of sound."

"I don't know what you're talking about. There's nothing wrong with my driving. I could drive these roads blindfolded and get us home fine."

Liam cleared his throat nervously. "Speaking of home . . . were you planning to just drop me off at the Oak or—?"

Aislinn felt a blast of heat rock her body. What a twit. She hadn't even thought about that.

Liam tucked a stray piece of her hair behind her ear. "I think I can guess your answer from your hesitation. You Catholic girls," he teased.

"It's not that. I just—I'm not interested in spending the night."

"I wasn't assuming that. I thought we could just go up to my flat, have a cup of tea, maybe make out." Liam grinned.

Aislinn turned to smile at him. "You mean snogging?"

"Yeah, snogging."

"I suppose that's all right," she said carefully, "as long as no one sees us."

Liam looked confused. "What?"

"How many times do I have to tell you, Liam? I hate the way the tongues wag in this town, and I don't want any of them knowing my business. They'll make assumptions if they see me going up to your place."

"Who the hell cares? Let them think what they want."

"And where does Jack think you are tonight?"

"In Crosshaven with my cousin Brian," Liam murmured uneasily.

"And what if Brian turned up at the Oak tonight? Jack'd know you were lying."

"Brian's working tonight." Liam squeezed her knee affectionately. "Would you stop being so paranoid?"

"Can't help it."

"You can help it. And you're making me feel like you're ashamed to be with me."

"God, no, it's not that at all," Aislinn swore fiercely.

"Then come up to my flat."

"All right."

Aislinn had to admit, she did feel a wee bit silly as she crept up the back stairs to Liam's place above the pub. It was well past closing time at the Oak, and thankfully, Ballycraig was one of those towns where the streets rolled up the minute the pub closed. There was no one about, not even Jack, who was sometimes known to stay on past closing to reminisce with the old-timers.

"Well, here it is," said Liam, unlocking the door and flipping on the light switch. "My humble abode."

*Humble is the operative word,* thought Aislinn. The sitting room/kitchenette was tiny; the only pieces of furniture were a small table with two chairs, a couch, and a coffee table, upon which sat a laptop and a photograph of his family.

She picked it up as Liam put his arm around her shoulder, pointing everyone out to her: his parents, his brother, Quinn, and his sisters, Maggie and Sinead.

Aislinn studied the picture. "Your sister Maggie is gorgeous, with that long red hair. And your brother is very handsome." She brought the photo closer to her face. "Your sister Sinead looks dead sad, though."

"Her marriage was beginning to disintegrate. They're divorced now."

"I'm sorry to hear it."

"Don't be. They should never have gotten together."

Aislinn smiled as she gazed at the image of Liam's father. "He looks just like your uncle Paul."

"I know. It's creepy."

"Your mum looks so sweet."

"She is, as long as you keep out of her kitchen."

"And look at you, Mr. Dark and Broody, trying to look all dangerous," she teased.

Liam hooded his eyes. "I *am* dangerous."

"Trust me: there's no danger to a man who can't change a flat."

Liam shook his head, chuckling. "You're never going to let me forget that, are you?"

"Not if I can help it." She put the photo back down on the coffee table. "Quite a good-looking family."

"I suppose. I never really thought about it."

"They must miss you fierce," Aislinn said quietly.

"They do, and I miss them, too." Liam shrugged philosophically. "But it is what it is. And it's not like I never talk to them: my siblings and I e-mail each other all the time, and I speak with my folks at least once a week."

"I'm not big on the e-mail. I only use my computer for business things, really. Financials. That sort of thing."

"I'm surprised you even have one."

"Yes, that's right, I write on parchment with a quill. Honestly! Just because I run a farm doesn't mean I don't own a computer!"

"You're right. My bad."

Aislinn twisted her hands together nervously. "So . . ."

"Sit," said Liam, gesturing at the couch. "I'll make us some coffee—unless you want tea."

"No, coffee is lovely, thanks."

Aislinn sat down, watching him prepare their coffee in the kitchen. She felt restless. No, that wasn't the right word; she felt anxious. She got up, walking over to one of the windows looking down on the street.

"Careful: someone might see you," Liam warned.

"Don't be a wise arse."

It was starting to rain, making the wide pavement below glisten. Aislinn wasn't fond of being out in the rain, but she did like the sound it made when it gently hit the windowpane. When she was little and it rained at night, her mother used to tell her it was the fairies tapping at the window, wanting to come inside. Aislinn always wondered why they didn't just go in the barn, but still, she loved the image of a wee band of them huddled around the big fireplace in the kitchen, warming themselves.

"My brother-in-law gets in tomorrow," said Aislinn, wanting to keep conversation going. It was a way to keep her nerves at bay. She was worried that if they fell into silence, Liam would be able to hear the drumbeat of her heart growing ever louder.

"Nora must be happy."

"Yes." She hesitated. "He can be a bit of a snob, that one. All proper and highfalutin. I'm shocked he's coming, to be honest. He hates it here." She paused. "Do you like it here?" she asked shyly.

"Of course I do."

"But it's no Manhattan, is it?"

Liam looked at her. "I'm not going anywhere any time soon, Aislinn," he said gently.

*Yes, but you'll probably be going eventually,* she thought. She elbowed the thought out of the way with one more mundane, thinking about how she and Padraig planned to trim the flocks' hooves tomorrow.

She turned back to look at the rain, which was coming

down harder now, the sound more insistent. She toyed with the idea of using it as an excuse to leave—the rain, the dark, the twisting roads—then stifled a self-deprecating laugh as she realized how completely transparent that would be.

Coffee brewed, Liam set the two mugs down on the coffee table and patted the empty space on the couch beside him. "Care to join me, or were you planning to climb out the window?"

"Now why would I ever climb out the window?"

"You tell me."

"I'm not *that* skittish," Aislinn maintained, sitting down beside him. She picked up her coffee and took a sip. "Not bad."

"I'll take that as high praise, coming from you."

"You know," Aislinn mused as a sudden thought struck her, "I've told you all about my romantic past, but I know nothing of yours."

Liam looked wary. "There isn't much to tell."

"Well, surely there must be something."

"Basically, I've been a serial dater. I've never really had a long-term relationship. It always seemed like too much of a hassle to me."

Aislinn looked down into her mug. "I see."

Liam brushed a hand across the nape of her neck. "That was before I met you."

Aislinn slowly lifted her head to look into his eyes. "And what's so different about me?" she asked uncertainly.

"Everything. The way your hair gleams in the sun. The beautiful lilt of your voice. The way you hold yourself like a queen. The love you have of the farm. Your loyalty and kindness to Padraig. Your dry sense of humor. Your fiery personality. You've got it all, Aislinn."

Aislinn was speechless. No one had ever said anything like this to her before. Ever. She searched Liam's face for a trace of insincerity, worried that maybe he was simply being a silver-tongued devil and feeding her a line of bull.

But sincerity shone in the deep, dark, alluring pools of his eyes. Sincerity and tenderness.

He leaned close to her, their mouths practically touching. "Kiss me."

Aislinn hesitated a second before letting her eyes drift shut and putting her lips to his softly. She could taste a trace of the wine he'd had at dinner, its sweetness.

"Kiss me harder," he commanded.

Lightning streaked through her veins as she pressed her mouth against his harder, the world around them burning away until there was nothing but her and Liam and the rhythm of the rain outside. Heat was juddering through her, but she didn't want to rush. She wanted to prolong the pleasure, perhaps even tease a little. She'd forgotten she could do that: tease a man, make him want her. She scraped her teeth lightly across his lower lip, thrilled when he responded with a low groan. It spurred her on; tracing his upper lip with her tongue, she dipped inside.

Her heart was pounding now, drowning out the beating of the rain. Greed was multiplying inside her, emboldening her. She crushed Liam to her, thrilling at the feel of his hard chest and the all-enveloping warmth of his body. She could sense the struggle within him to hold back the dark passion threatening to erupt. Aislinn pulled back, reading his eyes. Want. Need. Lust. It was all there, and he was waiting for her to release it.

She crushed her mouth back to his for a split second before she found herself clinging to him, her hand fisted in his hair, her mouth hot and demanding. Liam responded as she knew he would, with equal fire. The roaring in her head grew louder, rendering her deaf to all but the sound of his panting breaths. She wanted. She *needed*—and he knew it. His hands began roaming her body, curious yet expert. Aislinn felt as though she were flying down a long, flashing tunnel, the sounds of her own panting turning to low animal moans, spurring Liam on even further. A magnificent ache had taken possession of her body, frustrating yet at the same time electrifying.

Liam's touch tantalized; a featherlight stroke here, a long, firm press there. Eventually, his fingers brushed against her collarbone before one hand crept lower, cupping her breast. Aislinn pushed her chest against his hand, telegraphing her need. Liam understood: one by one, he began undoing the buttons of her shirt, until her blouse was wide open. For a split second she wished she were the kind of woman who owned sexy, lacy undergarments. But Liam didn't seem to notice or care, as he reached around to unsnap her simple white bra and free her.

"God, your skin," he whispered, as his fingers nimbly toyed with her nipples. Aislinn felt as though she were tumbling through the looking glass, body taut and vibrating with anticipation as Liam took his time kneading, stroking, caressing. By the time he lowered his mouth to suckle, Aislinn felt half mad. She wanted him to ravage her, to pound inside her until any last barrier between them disintegrated and they were pure spirit, nothing but holy ether.

She was riding the moment, riding the currents of electricity flying through her body, when Liam lifted his head. "Tell me you want me," he said, nipping at her neck.

"I do," Aislinn confessed breathlessly, her stomach trembling. There was a sense of relief in saying it, along with a growing sense of desperation.

Liam's gaze on her was steady. "Good. Because if I don't have you now, I might lose my mind."

"What little mind you possess."

Liam laughed, shrugging off his shirt. Jesus, he was a sight to see. Muscular but not overly sculpted, a lovely thatch of brown hair on his chest. Aislinn leaned over, kissing his shoulder.

"You're gorgeous," she breathed.

How could a man look so sexy, just standing to take off his socks, jeans, and briefs? Aislinn knew right then she would never tire looking at him: the handsome face, broad shoulders, the hard, muscular thighs. She struggled not to gape. She'd only ever been with Connor, and though he'd been handsome, his body was thin and freckled, as well as pale like everyone else's in this country, herself included.

Liam sat back down, gently tugged off her shirt, and slipped her bra over her shoulders, leaving her shuddering with delight. He reached out, his thumb tracing a trail down her jawline. Aislinn closed her eyes, sinking into the tenderness of it, small murmurs of pleasure coming from her mouth. She loved the way he touched her, the way he seemed to know how she wanted to be touched. "I've been thinking about this all night," he confessed.

Aislinn was too overcome to speak. Hands shaking, she unbuttoned her jeans and shimmied out of them. Liam folded to his knees, pressing his face against her belly, his tongue teasing as it ran along the top of her panties. Aislinn gave a small gasp as he reached around and, hands on her buttocks, pulled her closer to him.

"I want to taste you," he said huskily. "All of you."

His kisses grew fevered then as he tugged down her panties, and she stepped out of them. Wave after wave of pure shock pounded through her as she dug her nails into his back, pushing her hips against him. When he sank even lower and began flicking his tongue between her legs, joy flooded through her, unabashed, wanton.

Liam paused. "I want you to come for me," he whispered.

Aislinn gasped as his tongue circled her and licked, slow at first, then harder, demanding. And then it happened: she lost control, soaring as vibration after beautiful vibration shook her body. Liam looked up at her, his eyes stormy.

"Lie down with me."

Aislinn nodded, lying down on the couch. Her skin was burning, her breath still fast and hot. Eyes closed, she could hear the sound of Liam reaching into the pocket of his jeans, followed by the tearing of foil. And then he gently positioned himself on top of her, burying his face in her hair.

Aislinn pushed her hips up against him. Liam's eyes, dark with arousal, pinned her as he rubbed himself against her, his manhood hot and hard, driving her insane.

"Please." The word slipped out of her mouth, half plead, half sob.

She opened to him, crying out as he slowly slipped inside her. Liam groaned as he began to move. "God, you feel so good."

Aislinn bit her lip to stifle the screams already threatening to erupt from her lips as he began to slowly thrust inside her. She wrapped herself around him, wanting to feel him as deeply and fully as she could. Liam looked ecstatic, head thrown back, the animal noises coming from him so devastatingly male. Aislinn felt desire building in her again as he rode her faster and faster, his dominance all she needed to feel herself falling again into the molten abyss. He laced his fingers through hers, and then he was the one falling, pushing deep inside her again and again, his eyes bright and sharp. Finally, there came one hard, fierce stroke as he said her name and he gave himself over to ultimate pleasure.

# 11

"*That was . . .*"

Returning to the real world, Aislinn tried to find the right words to describe what had just happened. *Perfect* and *blissful* felt inadequate; *sacred* came closer to the mark but still fell short. Finally it dawned on her: *transcendent*. That was what it had been making love with Liam: utterly transcendent.

Lying together in the blissful afterglow, they shifted position so that she was atop him, her head resting on his chest while he tenderly stroked her hair. "That was what?" he prodded.

"Glorious," she answered, afraid that if she sighed "transcendent," he might laugh at her, sounding all soft and poetic.

Liam kissed the top of her head. "I'd have to agree."

"I really didn't think that would happen tonight."

"Neither did I, actually."

"Was I all right?" Aislinn asked, too nervous to lift her head and ask him to his face. She'd only ever been with Connor.

"How can you even ask that? Couldn't you tell how much I was enjoying myself?"

"Men enjoy themselves regardless."

"That's a myth. Men do not enjoy themselves when women lie beneath them stiff as a corpse or are too inhibited to move or make noises."

Aislinn was pleased she wasn't guilty of either.

"You're so beautiful, Aislinn."

She lifted her head to stare at him. "Go on with yourself," she scoffed.

"Why can't you just accept a compliment?"

Aislinn flushed. "I don't know. I've just never thought of myself that way."

"Connor never told you were beautiful?"

"Yes, but he was lying, wasn't he?" Aislinn said bitterly. "No more talk of him, please."

"Agreed."

Aislinn laid her head back down on his chest, loving the feel of his hands still roaming over her naked body. She closed her eyes, reveling in how easy it was to be here with him this way. And yet . . .

She took a deep breath. "There's something I've got to tell you," she murmured uneasily.

"What's that?"

"I don't take sex lightly. Maybe this is just a one-night stand for you. If it is, let me know now."

"Of course it's not."

Aislinn said a small prayer of thanks inside her head. "I'm glad."

"We're together now," Liam said.

She lifted her head again, her gaze serious. "A couple who are taking it slow *and* keeping their relationship to themselves."

"Aislinn, if we're together, I want everyone to know."

"In time. But right now, let me savor us having a little secret, please, before the news spreads like wildfire and we get no peace?"

"All right, all right."

She was guarding herself from pain. She couldn't bear it if she let the world know she was with Liam, and soon afterward, he decided to dump her. She wanted to wait until she was absolutely sure they would be together forever.

Liam searched her face. "You're really not going to tell anyone?"

"Just Nora," Aislinn said after a pause. "She's good at keeping things to herself."

"Is she going to tease the hell out of you for spending the night with me?"

"I'm not spending the night with you. I'm going to spend a few more minutes cuddling with you, and then I'm off home to catch a few hours' sleep before Padraig and I start our day."

"What time do you get up?"

"Around four thirty."

Liam looked at her as if she were daft. "Are you kidding me?"

She poked him in the chest affectionately. "Obviously you know nothing about sheep farms and shepherding, city boy."

"Four thirty," he repeated to himself in disbelief. "Back home that was the time I was usually going to bed." He brushed his knuckles against her cheek. "Stay. I'll set the alarm. You'll get back in time."

"No. Padraig will know something is up if I come rumbling up the drive at that hour. He's usually up at four."

"Sounds like my dad. The older he gets, the more trouble he has sleeping, despite putting in long, exhausting days."

"Happens to a lot of older people. My dad was the same way, too. Worried about the farm, worried about this or that."

"But you have no trouble sleeping?"

Aislinn laughed loudly. "Me? No. I sleep the sleep of

the dead. I'm exhausted by the end of the day. Plus the country air helps."

They lay there a few more minutes, chatting about everything and nothing at all. Finally, Aislinn forced herself to get up and started getting dressed.

Liam propped himself up on his elbow, watching her. "You should wear your hair down all the time."

"Can't. Not while I'm working. Last thing I need is the wind blowing it about in my face."

"I mean when you're out with me."

"If you'd like," Aislinn said shyly. She chuckled at the sight of him stretched out there on his couch, naked. "You look like a centerfold."

Liam peered down at himself with amusement. "I don't think so." His expression turned mischievous. "How do you know about male centerfolds, miss?"

"I've heard tell of them," Aislinn said coyly.

"I'll bet."

Liam rose, too, slipping on his briefs and jeans. "Next time you'll stay the night?"

Aislinn shook her head. "You'll have to stay at my house. You can sleep in while I get up to do my chores."

"Sounds romantic. Maybe I'll help you and we'll send Padraig out with the flock and we'll have sex in the barn after you've sent him out into some far field."

Aislinn eyed him skeptically. "If that's a fantasy of yours, I'd prefer you keep it to yourself for now."

Liam took her in his arms. "I wish you didn't have to go."

Aislinn sighed heavily. "I wish I didn't, either. But I've got work to do."

"When will I see you again?"

Aislinn hesitated. It was early days yet; she didn't want to rush things. Besides, if he came up to the house during the day, he'd wind up getting underfoot like Nora—*and* it would also rouse suspicion in Padraig. Perhaps she was being childish and silly wanting to be all hush-hush about it, but it felt as if the universe had given her a gift, and she wanted to keep it all to herself for just a little while.

"Tell you what," said Liam. "Call me tomorrow, and we'll figure out when we'll see each other next. How's that?"

"That sounds grand." A contentedness she hadn't felt in more than a year overtook her. "Thank you for a wonderful evening."

"My pleasure," said Liam, walking her down to her truck. He checked his watch. "I'm not tired. I think I'll e-mail my brother, see what's kicking." He kissed her nose. "Don't work too hard."

"We're trimming hooves today."

"Sounds exciting."

"Don't lie. It doesn't suit you." She hopped up into the cab of her truck, started the engine, and leaned out the window for a final quick kiss.

"Talk to you tomorrow, Yank."

Liam smiled, and with a small wave, he disappeared round the back of the building where the steps to his flat were. Aislinn made a conscious effort not to let the adrenaline flying through her dictate how wildly she drove back to her farm.

The house was dark when she finally slipped into her bed, the sheets lovely and cool. Despite her elation, it was a sense of contentment that prevailed. She and Liam O'Brien . . .

Nothing she could dream could ever be more wonderful.

# 12

*Don't lie. It doesn't suit you.*

Aislinn's words haunted Liam as he turned on his laptop. He was wired, thoughts ricocheting inside his skull like bullets. He should have told Jack he didn't care if he thought him a coward; the bet was off. He would have caught a lot of grief for it, but who the hell cared? At least he wouldn't be deceiving Aislinn, the woman he was falling in love with. The woman who thought he was something he was not: honest.

He checked his mailbox; there was an e-mail from Quinn giving him all the latest news. He was shocked to read that Quinn had taken a buyout at the newspaper, which was about to go under. Quinn had started his own website, the O'Brien File, where he blogged about NYC politics. He was also freelancing, and wrote there was a chance he might be on assignment in Dublin in a few weeks. Natalie's mother had died, and they were thinking of buying an apartment with the money she'd left Nat; their parents were well, though their father was still refusing to get his bad back looked at; their pain-in-the-ass uncle was still working behind the bar; their sister

Maggie and her husband Brendan were considering moving out of the city because they didn't want to the raise the baby there; last but not least, their sister Sinead was contemplating dating again after her painful, protracted divorce.

Despite the possibility of seeing his brother in a few weeks, homesickness still gripped Liam. He longed to be in New York with all of them. He wanted to be behind the bar at the Wild Hart, hanging out with the regulars, one of whom, PJ Leary, had a book coming out soon, which he'd supposedly sold for over one hundred thousand dollars. Liam couldn't believe it; whenever PJ read excerpts from the book at the Hart, it had taken all Liam's strength not to tell him to put a sock in it. Leprechauns battling talking salmon, fairy kings and queens—it was a Celtic nightmare. But obviously, there was a market for it.

Quinn had concluded the e-mail by telling him that he hadn't yet gotten the word from his friend in the FBI that it was safe for him to come home. Liam's heart sank for a moment before his mind clouded with confusion. If he got the okay to come home right now, would he? He honestly couldn't answer.

He e-mailed Quinn back, not telling him that he'd met someone. He knew if he did, there would an onslaught of phone calls from his parents and his sisters. His folks would want to hop the next plane to Dublin to come over and meet Aislinn. An Irish girl from their hometown— talk about their dream come true! Better to wait and see what happened. He wasn't totally clueless; he knew there was still a small part of Aislinn that was holding back. If there weren't, she'd have no problem with their relationship going public. She'd also have wanted to see him again as soon as possible; there would have been no hesitation.

He surfed the 'net for awhile, checking to see how his hometown hockey team, the New York Blades, were doing, then shut down his computer, hoping to catch some mindless TV, forgetting there were no programs on in Ireland past 1 a.m. if you didn't have cable. Restless, he went to bed, willing himself to sleep. Instead, he found himself staring at the low, slanted ceiling, thinking about Aislinn.

He never thought he'd feel this way about a woman—a cliché, but it was true. Wit, beauty, intelligence, tenderness, passion—she had it all. On a certain level, he was proud that he was the one who'd been able to crack the hard shell she'd created to protect herself. Okay, it had started off as an exercise of pure ego, but that motivation soon melted when he caught the first glimpse of the soft, sensitive, wounded woman inside—one who would tear him limb from limb if she ever found out the origin of his pursuit of her.

He closed his eyes, replaying the passion of earlier in the evening. He'd slept with a lot of women, but now he finally understood the difference between sex for the sake of pleasure and sex as an expression of something deeper. There had been a profound emotional connection between him and Aislinn that he'd never experienced before. It was as if he'd finally come home to himself.

He relaxed, picturing Aislinn's smile and hearing the soft lilt of her voice in his head. She was the one. And when the time was right, he'd tell her.

* * *

*"Padraig, when was* the last time you checked Demelza's hooves?"

It was 7 a.m., and Aislinn and Padraig were on their knees in the barn, trimming the flock's hooves. It was going swimmingly until Aislinn got to Demelza, her eldest ewe.

Grabbing her right front hoof, Aislinn saw immediately that the skin between Demelza's claws was red and swollen. *Hoof rot. Shite.* There was no way Aislinn could or would leave this unchecked, as it could run rampant through her entire flock. She waited for Padraig to answer. It was his job to check the flock's hooves every three days, just as her father had once done.

Padraig make a great show of looking thoughtful. "Let me see now . . ."

Aislinn bit back her exasperation, trying not to sound accusatory. "You don't remember, do you?"

"Ehm . . ."

"It's okay," she assured him, praying that the other sheep she hadn't seen yet weren't infected. As it was, she was going to have to use a different knife on the rest of the flock, burn Demelza's hoof trimmings, administer a vaccination, and give the whole flock a zinc sulfate foot-bath just to be safe.

"Padraig?" she prompted gently.

"I could have sworn I checked their hooves yesterday, darlin', truly. But maybe I forgot Demelza?" he offered lamely.

"Maybe." She patted his arm. "It's all right. We can handle it."

Aislinn wiped away the perspiration beading on her forehead, remembering her vow to keep Padraig on unless his forgetfulness became a liability. Perhaps she should take him to the local clinic and have them run some tests. There were pills now that could help with forgetfulness, weren't there? She glanced at the old man, who was gazing down at Demelza affectionately, and she felt a catch in her throat. Telling Padraig he had to retire . . . no, she couldn't bear to think of it.

She stifled a yawn as she got back to the business of hoof clipping. Ironically, after telling Liam she was a great one for sleep, she'd barely caught a wink. Contentedness had lost to elation; she was too fired up. The way he'd touched her . . . transcendent. Connor had never touched her that way. Of course, in retrospect that made sense, but being with Liam made her realize how much she'd been missing.

"Someone was out dead late last night," Padraig said with a sly chuckle.

"And what were you doing up at that hour?" Aislinn demanded.

"Listening to the radio. You know I can't sleep sometimes."

"You'll nap today at lunch, and that's an order."

"Take it you were out paradin' with that Yank."

"Paradin'?"

"You know what I mean."

"We had a nice dinner, then stayed up late talking." She looked away, suppressing a smile. One look in her eyes, and Padraig would know she was full of it.

"I like him," Padraig declared. "He's polite, and from what I hear from Jack, he's a hard worker. And I've always liked his people."

"Yes, the O'Briens are a very nice family." Aislinn didn't really know them that well, though Erin was always nice to her when they were in school together, and she could tell Erin liked the way Aislinn was fearless in taking on the Holy Trinity of Arseholes. The Holy Trinity. Ha! Just wait till they found out she and Liam were a couple. That'd shut their gobs but good. Old Jack, too.

They finished with the hooves at about eleven. Aislinn sent Padraig outside to burn Demelza's hoof trimmings while she gave the ewe a shot and prepared the footbath for the flock. A few minutes later, Padraig stuck his head in the barn door.

"You won't ever believe what I just saw."

"What?"

"Your sister and her jackeen of a husband roaming around outside. That's a new one, eh? How long has that British toff been coming here, and never caring one bit about the farm?"

"They're both very stressed-out in their jobs," Aislinn offered, though she agreed with Padraig that it was unusual.

"Anyroad, he's tramping around out there in your dad's wellies," Padraig harrumphed. "If you ask me, he's not fit to wear 'em, especially with the way he always treated your da."

"Too true."

It used to drive Aislinn crazy, the way Donald would talk down to her father like he was an idiot just because he was shepherd. But her father never returned fire. "I won't stoop to his level," was what he'd say when Aislinn and her mother would implore him to blast Donald with both barrels. At least Nora had had the good sense to be embarrassed about it. The few times over the years Nora and Donald had graced them with their presence, Aislinn sometimes heard her chiding Donald after a family meal.

They finished with the footbath, and Aislinn sent Padraig up to the house for his lunch and a lie down. When she came out of the barn, Nora and Donald were inspecting Padraig's cottage. Aislinn's chest tightened as she, with Deenie trotting beside her, went to join them.

"Hello, Donald," she said politely, kissing her brother-in-law on the cheek.

"Hello."

"How was your drive up from Cork City?"

"Same as always."

*Whatever that means.*

Nora's face was disapproving as her eyes roamed over Padraig's cottage. "He's really let this place fall into disrepair. It used to be so beautiful. Like something from a postcard."

"It just needs a new paint job, and the windows could use a good wash. That's all."

"It's bigger than I thought," Donald murmured.

Aislinn's gut tightened. *Please, dear God, don't let them suggest moving Padraig up to the house so that they can turn it into a guest cottage for themselves, now that they inexplicably seem to want to spend time at the farm.* She'd go mad on both counts. She would.

"How is Padraig doing today?" Nora asked with concern.

"He's fine."

"Is he really?"

"What do you care?" Aislinn found herself snapping.

"You never gave a tinker's damn before; now all of a sudden you're concerned about someone you think hates you? You're a mystery, Nora, I'll give you that."

Donald was practically baring his teeth at her. "There's no need to get nasty."

Aislinn bared hers right back. "Begging your pardon, but I'm just not used to you two showing much interest in what goes on here."

"And I feel bad about that," Nora shot back. There was a moment of tense silence until Nora's expression finally softened. "I'm trying to make amends, Aislinn. Trying to reconnect. Mum and Dad's death made me realize how important family really is. You're all I've got now. Can't you give me a chance?"

Aislinn paused to rub away the tension that was making her forehead begin to pound. "I'm sorry. It's been a bit of a morning. Demelza has hoof rot, and it's a bit alarming."

"Hoof rot?" Donald looked revolted. "Sounds charming."

*God, I wish you'd just disappear in a puff of smoke, you ponce.*

"You *name* your sheep?" he continued.

"Of course we name the sheep," Aislinn returned scornfully. "How else do you think we'd tell them apart?"

"Ah. Good point."

*Eejit.*

Perhaps sensing Aislinn's growing impatience with her husband, Nora slipped an arm through hers and started walking her away. "Listen," she said as they strolled in the direction of the house while Donald continued circling Padraig's cottage, "Donald and I are going down to the Oak tonight for a drink. Join us. That way I can show him your boyfriend."

Aislinn fought to keep a stunned expression off her face. *Nora and Donald at the pub? Together? Oh shite, they do want to turn Padraig's cottage into their second home. They want to become part of our "quaint" community.* She felt bad suspecting her sister of some kind of strategic plan, but she couldn't help it.

"I was planning to go down to the pub anyway."

Nora looked shocked. "Alone?"

"Nora, I go alone all the time."

"Well, tonight you'll go with Donald and me."

"Fine," Aislinn agreed, feeling like a cranky bitch in the face of Nora's cheerful insistence. "We'll have to drive separately, though, if Padraig wants to come."

Nora was silent. Chances were Padraig would pass, given that he'd slept so little, but you never knew. She almost told Nora, "Don't worry, he won't sit with us," but realized it was antagonistic thing to say.

"Donald looks good," said Aislinn, steering off the topic of Padraig.

"Good but tired," Nora agreed.

"He must be thrilled to see you."

Nora was beaming. "He is. And I'm thrilled to see him, too. I guess distance really does make the heart grow fonder."

"Mmm." Aislinn took a dog treat out of her pocket and fed it to Deenie, who'd been nosing her in the butt.

"How old is Deenie now?" Nora asked.

Aislinn had to think a minute. "Nine." *Now what, you're going to act like you give a rat's arse about Deenie? Don't even.*

"She seems younger."

"I think it's because she's so active."

"I'd like a dog, but Donald thinks it would tie us down too much. We like to travel."

"Yeah, I remember that Venetian glass vase you sent Mum and Dad from Italy. Mum was quite taken by it."

"I'm sure she would have preferred a grandchild," Nora said dryly. It had always made their mother sad that Nora had chosen not to have kids.

"Of course she would have," said Aislinn, surprised by Nora's bluntness. "But Connor and I planned—"

She stopped herself.

"How did it go with Liam last night?"

Aislinn looked down at the ground, suddenly feeling shy. "It went well."

"Meaning—?"

Aislinn's face went hot. "You know . . ."

"Oh my God!" Nora was wide-eyed. "You slept with him?"

"Yes, and what of it?" Aislinn asked, feeling defensive in the face of Nora's shocked tone and expression.

"I'm not judging you *or* questioning your judgment. I think it's great."

"Why's that?"

"Because you make a great couple, that's why."

"You've only seen us together a few times, and for a few minutes at that."

"Yeah, and the chemistry is unbelievable."

"Really?"

"Yes, *really.*"

Aislinn smiled, pleased.

"So, is he good?" Nora prodded playfully.

"I don't kiss and tell."

Nora playfully smacked her arm. "I'm your older sister! You have an obligation to tell me all!"

Aislinn laughed. "It was wonderful." She felt as though she were going to burst out of her skin with pure joy. She paused. "*He's* wonderful."

"You're falling in love with him."

"I am, yes," Aislinn admitted, "and it scares the hell out of me."

"Why's that?"

"Because what if it doesn't work out?"

"Why are you writing the script?"

"Can't help it."

"Okay: why are you writing a negative script rather than a positive one?"

"Perhaps because the only man I've ever loved before kicked me in the teeth?"

"Liam isn't Connor, Aislinn. Connor was lying to you. Liam isn't."

"I know, I know. It's just . . ." Aislinn halted, sticking her hands in the pockets of her coat. "I'm happy, but I hate being vulnerable. I always have."

"You can't love someone and not be vulnerable. Goes with the territory."

"I know that, too. But that doesn't mean I have to like it."

"True." Nora stroked the top of Deenie's head. "Is he in love with you?"

"I don't know," Aislinn answered honestly. "Obviously he's got feelings for me, but we've not said 'I love you' or anything like that. It's early days yet. I don't want to push anything or make assumptions."

"I understand."

"Listen, Nora, would you keep all this under your hat? I don't want anyone else to know about it yet."

Nora looked baffled. "Why not?"

"Honestly? Because I want to savor it, and because I want to be sure we're really going to be together. It'd kill me if he gave me the big brush-off, and I had to deal with half the town regarding me as some pitiful creature."

Nora shrugged easily. "Okay. Can I at least tell Donald?"

"I suppose." Since they were having a heart-to-heart, Aislinn decided to speak her mind. "Why were you and Donald inspecting Padraig's cottage, Nora?"

"I was just remembering the way it used to be, and it made me sad."

"Mmm."

"You sound suspicious."

"Not suspicious, just curious. I mean, his cottage has needed some work for a while. But you never noticed it before. And your sudden interest in the health of Padraig is unusual, you have to admit."

"I'm trying to make up for lost time. As you know, sometimes when people die—like parents—you start reassessing things."

They'd reached the mudroom. "Will you be having lunch with me?" Aislinn asked.

Nora checked her watch. "Isn't it a bit early?"

"Not when your day starts at four thirty."

"I hadn't thought about that. No, I'll wait for Donald. We'll probably go into Moneygall for lunch."

"Pick up some pesto for me, will you?" Aislinn teased. "Some caviar as well."

"I think it's a very good sign that your sense of humor has returned," said Nora.

"I think so, too." *I've returned,* Aislinn thought. Finally.

# 13

*As Aislinn suspected,* Padraig was too tired to go to the pub that night. She'd left him up at the house watching telly, knowing that by the time she got back, he'd be fast asleep on the couch, his snoring loud enough to rattle the windows. She'd do what she always did: cover him with a blanket and leave him be. She had to admit, sometimes it was nice when Padraig fell asleep in the house, because she'd wake the next morning to the lovely smell of bacon and eggs frying. He could do a good fry-up, could Padraig. He could also brew the perfect cuppa.

She, Nora, and Donald could have easily fit in the cab of her truck, but Donald was having none of it. "It smells like wet sheep and hay," he sniffed. "Besides, Nora and I might want to leave earlier than you."

"Suit yourself," Aislinn told him with a diffident shrug. Truth be told, she enjoyed trundling into town by herself: she could blast the radio as loud as she pleased or enjoy the blessed silence of the country.

Unsurprisingly, since Donald drove like an eighty-year-old man, Aislinn beat them into Ballycraig and waited outside the Oak for them, so she and Nora could

walk in together. Just like the last time Nora came to the
pub, she was greeted warmly. But there was no mistaking everyone's bafflement when they laid eyes on Donald. *Of course they're baffled,* thought Aislinn. *The man
hasn't set foot in the Oak in ten years.* He looked stiff and
uncomfortable, completely out of his element. Which he
was.

Aislinn could feel Liam zeroing in on her the minute
she stepped over the threshold, but she refused to look at
him, not wanting to give anything away, especially since
the Holy Trinity were also giving her the hairy eyeball.

"Long time, no see, McCafferty," said Teague with a
smirk as Aislinn made her way to the bar. "Where you
been hiding yourself?"

"Some of us work for a living, you know. You might
want to try it sometime."

Nora tapped Aislinn on the shoulder. "We're going to
order, and then I think I'll bring Donald round and re-
introduce him to people."

"Right," said Aislinn. God, what she wouldn't give to
be able to read their minds. First off, he was English—
that was a big black mark right there in some people's
books. Secondly, everyone in the room had a long memory, a particular affliction of the Irish. Aislinn was certain they were all aware Donald hadn't set foot in the pub
since he and Nora had gotten together, and like her, they
had to be wondering why he'd suddenly decided to grace
them with his presence. Of course, they'd all be polite as
pie to his face, but the minute he moved out of earshot,
they'd be flapping their gums with speculation.

"Aislinn," said Jack with his trademark warm smile.
"Nice to see you."

"You, too, Jack."

"Where've you been?"

"Working the farm, as I told this lummox here," she
replied, jerking her thumb at Teague.

"Sure you must be doing something else besides minding the sheep," he said slyly.

Aislinn narrowed her eyes, immediately suspicious. "And what would that be?" She'd kill Liam if he'd said anything to Jack. Truly she would.

"Spending time with your sister, I imagine."

Aislinn relaxed. "Yes, I have been doing a bit of that."

"Where's the old man?"

"Tucked up at the house. He's exhausted."

Jack looked uncomfortable. "Aislinn, darlin', about Padraig."

Aislinn stiffened. "Yes?"

"Grace Finnegan told me he came into her shop and forgot what he was there for."

"I forgot to send him with a list. That's all."

"But surely—"

"Can I have my whiskey, please?"

She saw Jack exchange glances with the trio of arse-holes. *The poor McCafferty* is what they were probably thinking. *Blind again. Can't see what's right in front of her face.*

"I'm on it, all right?" she assured Jack quietly while he poured her whiskey.

"Good girl," said Jack.

"I'm glad about that," said David. "If you weren't, he could go baaaa-listic."

The threesome laughed. Sheep jokes. Aislinn rolled her eyes.

Jack put her whiskey down in front of her. "Here you go, love."

"Thanks."

"How's it going, Aislinn?"

It was Liam, sounding as friendly as could be. If she could, she'd shoot darts at him with her eyes. No, she was overreacting. He was a bartender. It was his job to be friendly.

"Fine," she replied briskly, all business. "Yourself?"

"Pretty good."

"I'm glad for you." She put her money down on the bar. "I'm off now to join my sister—"

"And the imperialist swine," Fergus finished for her.

"There he goes, getting his Irish up," said Jack with a long-suffering sigh. "Correct me if I'm wrong, but didn't your dad work in England for a good long time, doing construction, faithfully sending money back here to your mother?"

"He had to work there," Fergus spat. "There were no feckin' jobs here."

"Well, it's not Nora's husband's fault, you twit," Jack rejoined. "It's not 1916, you know. Let it go."

"Oh, go soak your head," Fergus muttered.

Aislinn picked up her whiskey. "Night," she said to Jack.

"I assume you'll be back for a refill?"

"Of course."

"See you," Liam said.

"Night," Aislinn said. She glared at the Trinity. "You three keep your lips buttoned. I'm in no mood for your chicanery."

With that, she went to join Nora and Donald.

*  *  *

*Liam knew that* the minute Aislinn, Nora, and Donald left the pub, Jack and the Trinity would be on him, and he was right.

"Go on," Jack jeered. "Tell us again how she's all hot and bothered over you now. The she-devil could give a rat's ass you're even breathing."

"It's an act," Liam insisted. "She wants to keep things quiet."

"Oh, that's a good one, it is," David snorted. "Though I guess I could see that. If I were spreadin' my legs for a Yank, I'd want to keep it quiet, too."

Liam reached across the bar and grabbed him by the collar. "Who the fuck do you think you are? Don't you ever, *ever* talk about her like that." He released him with a shove.

"Christ on a splintered cross," Fergus marveled, his

mouth dropping open. "You've fallen for the hellcat, haven't you?"

"Don't call her that," Liam said with a glare. "And yeah, maybe I have."

"Fat lot of good it's gonna do you, by the look of it," Teague chortled.

"Face it, Liam: I'm not going to have to pay you for a year," Jack crowed. "You've gotten nowhere with her."

"Wrong," said Liam, wiping down the bar.

"Why would she want to keep things quiet?" asked Fergus. "Doesn't make sense. Usually they want the whole world to know: 'Look who I've roped and tied!' Then they get pregnant and trap you for life."

Liam frowned. "Nice attitude."

"It's true," Fergus insisted.

"How the hell would you know?" Teague challenged. "You've not had a woman look at you in ten years."

"His woman is his left hand," David added.

"Piss off, the lot of you," said Fergus, storming out of the pub.

"Back to the McCafferty," said Old Jack, pulling a Guinness for himself. "We've seen no evidence at all you're together, none at all. Until you walk through the door with her making goo-goo eyes at you, I'll not believe it."

"Just you wait," said Liam smugly.

\* \* \*

*"I hear you* wanted to call off the bet with Jack because you know you can't win."

There was no mistaking the mischievous glint in Uncle Paul's eye as he refilled Liam's coffee mug. It was Sunday morning, and Liam was there for his weekly catching up with his relatives. As always, his cousin Erin was there, but his cousin Brian was, shockingly, in church with his new girlfriend and their quaintly devout family. "Must be love," his aunt Bridget mused. "The last time that one was in church, Bono was still in short pants."

Liam regarded his uncle. "I wanted to call the bet off because the more I thought about it, the more I realized it was a cruel thing to do to someone."

"You're right," Erin piped up. "I wouldn't want it done to me."

"See?"

"Be that as it may," said Uncle Paul, "you *didn't* call it off."

"Jack called me a coward," Liam said testily. "No one calls me a coward, okay?"

Aunt Bridget sighed. "Still quick to anger, I see. Your mother used to talk about it all the time. Got you into a world of trouble during your teen years, as I recall."

Liam bristled. "That was a long time ago. I've worked all that out."

"Still, Jack was able to get your goat in three seconds flat," his uncle pointed out.

"He could get a dead man's goat in three seconds flat, the irksome old thing," Erin said with a snort.

"Thank you," Liam said, pleased that his cousin had come to his defense.

"So you're gonna continue with the bet," said his uncle, helping himself to a healthy portion of bacon. He reminded Liam so much of his father it was amazing; they could both eat like horses. "All because Jack called you a coward."

"No, because it'll be nice to have twice the wages. And because I'm not a coward. I don't back out of bets. Besides, I've already won."

His uncle raised an eyebrow. "Have you now?"

Liam took a big gulp of coffee. "Yep."

"Where's the evidence?"

"It's coming."

"Believe it when I see it," said Uncle Paul in a garbled voice, his mouth stuffed with food.

Erin looked confused. "What about thinking it's a mean thing to do?"

"Well," Liam said, leaning over to her confidingly, "as

it happens, things are not going to end the way everyone thinks."

Erin looked at him a second, then her face lit up. "You like her!"

"Yep."

His uncle choked. "You like her?"

"Da, you know she's nice!" Erin chided. "She only got hard when Connor did her wrong! But before that, she was fine!"

"True, true," Uncle Paul conceded. "Are you two a couple, then?"

Liam grinned. "Yep."

"What are you, John Wayne with all those *yeps*?" his aunt teased. "Come on, then! Spit it out!"

"Well, I started wooing her and soon realized that I really liked her. So, after we go public, we'll just stay together."

"Oh, God, your parents are going to be thrilled. *Thrilled*."

"Do *not* say anything yet," Liam warned. "You know them: they'll be on the next plane over here. I'll tell them when I'm good and ready."

His aunt looked crestfallen. "If you say so."

His uncle shook his head in wonderment. "You and the McCafferty—who'd have ever thought?"

*No kidding,* Liam thought, sharing his sense of amazement. The last thing he ever expected was to hide out in Ballycraig and fall for someone. He did feel a twinge of hypocrisy over not telling his family back home about her. How was that any different than her asking him to keep things mum for now? *Well,* he thought, to quote his mother, *It will all come out in the wash.* Soon, everyone would know. But before they did, he had a surprise for her.

# 14

*Aislinn was in* one of the far meadows with Deenie, rotating the sheep into a new pasture. Deenie had done a superb job herding them, but as always, there were a few stragglers. Aislinn raised a hand, giving her the "look back" command. Deenie turned around and went back for the stray sheep, directing them where they needed to go.

Aislinn followed, reveling in the clear, cool morning. She'd left Padraig in the barn laying down some fresh straw and filling the water troughs before waiting for some weavers who'd rung to say they were coming by to buy some wool. Though Padraig knew the prices by heart, she'd carefully written them out for him just in case. He looked insulted, but Aislinn pretended not to notice.

She'd spent most of Sunday alone, riding her bike far into the country when her first round of chores were done. Liam rang in the early evening, asking if it was all right if he stopped by today. Of course it was, she told him. Their conversation was short and sweet; Aislinn had never been one for chatting on the phone. She preferred talking face-to-face.

Her flock where it should be, the wind in her hair, the

sun on her face, a tentative but improving relationship
with her sister, a man who she was falling in love with—
life was perfect. Her only sadness was that her parents
weren't here to witness her happiness. But then again,
perhaps they were; for all Padraig's talk of ghosts, Aislinn had never been able to decide whether she believed
in life beyond the grave. But maybe there was something
to it.

Donald had left early that morning to go back to London. He and Nora had spent Sunday morning in Cork and
the afternoon exploring more of the property. It annoyed
Aislinn just to witness it. It was her land. Her home. Nora
had wanted nothing to do with it for *years*. Aislinn took a
deep breath. Maybe Nora wasn't planning to build a second home for her and Donald here. She hoped so.

Deenie returned to her side, calmly leaning against her
the way she always did. From her vantage point high on
the hill, Aislinn could see Liam cycling up the road from
town. The sight of him made her all fuzzy inside. *Oh,
you're a sad one,* she told herself, *acting like a moony
schoolgirl.*

She watched as Liam walked the bike up the rutted
drive, resting it against the wall of the small shed. Padraig came out to greet him, then pointed up to the pasture
where Aislinn was. Liam looked up at her, smiling and
waving. She waved back, waiting for him to join her.

He was huffing and puffing by the time he reached her,
his face slightly red. "Jesus," he panted, leaning in for a
kiss. "I'm in worse shape than I thought."

"I thought you were big on jogging."

"I've been lazy about it lately. Obviously I need to get
back into it. I thought my heart was going to explode on
some of those hills."

"Whose bike is that?"

"My cousin Brian's."

"Good thing you didn't take Jack's car, or I'd be tow-
ing you out of a ditch right about now."

"Sadly, I think you're right." Liam crouched down

so he was eye level with Deenie. "Hey, girl. How's your workday going?"

"She's perfect, as always. My dad trained her well."

"Man's best friend."

"You have a dog back in America?"

"Nah. My folks didn't want one, living in the city. It was bad enough when we were kids, with the six of us crammed into the apartment above the pub." Liam grinned. "I had some goldfish once. They died within a couple of days. We gave them a funeral at sea."

Aislinn looked at him questioningly.

"Flushed 'em."

"Ah."

Liam rose. "Nice job at the pub Saturday night, acting like you couldn't care less about me. Very convincing."

Aislinn took a small bow. "Thank you."

Liam looked perturbed. "How much longer are we going to keep this up? I don't like it."

"Just a little while longer. Please." She brushed the back of her hand across his cheek. "It's so lovely having you all to myself."

Liam's shoulders sank a little. "All right. But since you told Nora, I think I should be able to tell one other person, too."

"And who would that be?"

"My brother, Quinn."

"The journo?"

"Yeah." Liam's face lit up. "He's going to be in Dublin next weekend, working on a piece about Irish illegal immigrants in New York. I'm going to go up and meet him."

"That's great!"

"I want you to come with me."

Aislinn blinked. "What?"

"I want him to meet you," Liam repeated firmly.

"Why isn't he coming here?"

"He'll only be in for a long weekend, so he doesn't

have time. As it is, he'll probably only have time to meet us for dinner."

"Liam, I can't just run off and leave the running of the farm to Padraig! He can't manage alone. Besides," she mumbled, "I'm not big on cities. I visited Nora in London once, and it wasn't my cup of tea."

"Have you ever been to Dublin?"

Aislinn squirmed. "Well, no, but—"

"Then how do you know you won't like it?"

"I'm not saying I won't like it," she backpedaled. "I'm just saying, I'll feel like a fish out of water. And the Padraig issue—"

"Aislinn, come on. Who worked the farm the day of your parents' funeral?"

Aislinn felt trapped. "Ehm . . . two brothers I know from the farmers' market. Jake and Alec Fry."

"Couldn't they work it again? Just for a weekend?"

"I suppose." Aislinn licked her lips nervously. "I don't know about this, Liam. Truly. They'd be working with Padraig. He might be insulted. I'm sure in his mind he thinks he can do it alone."

"But he can't. And besides, you're full of it. Padraig is just an excuse."

"For what?"

"You're afraid to go away with me."

"That's not it at all," Aislinn insisted fiercely.

"Then what?"

"Meeting family means things truly are—"

"Serious?"

"Yes."

"Are you telling me they're not?"

"Are you telling me they are?" Aislinn shot back. *You haven't told me you loved me yet,* she thought.

"I told you the night we made love that we're a couple now."

"True." She rubbed her temples. "I'm having a hard time thinking straight here."

"All you need to think about is hiring those two guys to help Padraig run the farm. I'll take care of the rest."

"Everyone will know we've gone away together," she murmured more to herself than him. "They'll figure it out."

"So? It'll be great! Tongues will wag like crazy while we're away, and when we come back, we'll come into the Oak together, and that will be that."

"They'll all think you've lost your mind!"

"I don't care what they think." He wrapped his arms around her. "All I care about is you."

She leaned her forehead against his. "What makes you so sure Jack is going to give you the time off?"

"It's my brother, Aislinn. He can have his son Neil come up from Cork for the weekend to help him out."

"Right. Neil." Aislinn had forgotten about him. He'd been at school with her, a timid thing, as different from his blowhard of a father as chalk and cheese. He'd worked at the Royal Oak during summer holidays, and sometimes, when he was back in town for Christmas and the like, he helped his father out, even though he had no talent for the small talk needed at the bar. All she knew about him was that he was an accountant.

"Won't your family be offended Quinn won't be seeing them?" she asked suddenly.

"They'll understand. Look, like I said, he'll barely have time for us. But I really, really want him to meet you, even if it's just for a little while."

Aislinn envied Liam's excitement. She couldn't remember ever being that enthused about seeing Nora.

"C'mon," Liam teased, playfully nipping the tip of her nose. "You know you want to."

"Only if I can get Jake and Alec for the weekend. Otherwise, no." She pulled back a bit. "And while we're at it," she said, giving Liam a small poke in the chest, "if I'm to meet your brother, then once we're 'out,' it would be nice if you'd take me round so your relatives here could meet me properly. I'm sure they all think of me as the mad

McCafferty, up here on the sheep farm with no one but crazy oul Padraig to call a friend."

"I'm sure they don't."

"Well, be that as it may, it would be nice to have a meal with them sometime. I remember your cousin Erin from school, and she was lovely."

"Still is."

"I'm sure."

"So we're all set," Liam said definitively.

"Did you not hear what I said? We're set if I can get Jake and Alec here. Otherwise, you're toddling up to Dub on your own."

"They'll be here if I have to wave fistfuls of euros in their faces myself."

Aislinn bristled. "Leave farm business to me. You sort things out with Jack." She shook her head affectionately. "Dublin. With you, yet."

Liam feigned offense. "What's that supposed to mean? I've been there three times. I know my way around pretty well."

"Yes, I'm sure you know all the best watering holes," Aislinn teased.

"Well, yeah—but I know all the good tourist spots as well."

"I've no interest in the sites, really, apart from Saint Stephen's Green and having a cup of coffee at Bewley's on Grafton Street." Her aunt Charlene had gone up to Dublin frequently over the years and always raved about the famous Bewley's Oriental Café, and how gorgeous their coffee tasted. Aislinn wanted to find out for herself if it were true.

"You don't want to go to the Guinness Storehouse and get a tour of the brewery?" Liam joshed.

"Oh, that's top of my list, surely," Aislinn dead-panned.

"Well, I'm definitely taking you to Burdock's Fish and Chips. It's the best chip shop in Dublin, and it hasn't been discovered yet by the vacationing hordes."

"Now that sounds more my speed."

She stroked the top of Deenie's head, her faithful girl concentrating hard as she kept watch on the herd across the pasture, on the alert for any unusual movement or worse, predators.

Taking her cue from Deenie, she turned to Liam. "I should really get back to work," she said reluctantly. She wished she had the kind of job where you could call in sick every once in awhile and take a mental health day—or in her case, a "spend time with your man" day.

"Want company?"

"No." Aislinn looked at him with amusement. "Don't you have anything better to do with yourself than hang about a sheep farm?"

"I suppose I should go back into town and help Jack balance the books. He hasn't done it in five years!"

"I thought Neil was an accountant."

"Neil wants nothing to do with it," Liam said grimly. "Apparently whenever he tries to help Jack, they come close to fisticuffs."

"I could see that. The sad part is, Jack could beat his own son with both hands tied behind his back."

"True. Well, here's hoping I don't wind up with a black eye myself." He gathered her up in his arms again, for a slow, sweet, sumptuous kiss.

"You're quite good at that, you know," Aislinn noted wryly.

"I've had a lot of practice."

"I must confess, I'm glad I'm the beneficiary of it." Reluctant though she was, she broke the embrace. "I'll ring you when I know what's going on with the Fry brothers."

Liam laughed. "God, don't look so nervous! We're going on an adventure, Aislinn! It'll be fun!" He gave her a quick peck on the cheek. "Are you coming in tonight?"

"Depends."

"Well, we'll talk soon then."

He winked at her and was off down the hill. Aislinn watched him cycle away until he was nothing but a speck in the distance that eventually disappeared altogether. Dublin. With Liam O'Brien. An adventure indeed.

## 15

*Padraig's memory might* be going, but his eyes were as sharp as ever. He pierced Aislinn with a good glare when, two nights after her discussion with Nora, she came down to his place to tell him she'd be going to Dublin, and the Fry brothers would be helping him.

"I can manage on my own," he insisted stubbornly, brewing them some tea.

"You most certainly cannot, and you know it," said Aislinn, tossing a chunk of peat onto the fire, thinking about how Nora hated the smell. "Don't you remember they took over for us the day of Mum and Da's funeral? And they did a fine job."

"We needed them then because I wasn't available."

"We needed them then because it takes at least two people to run this place."

"Many is the time I managed here on my own when your da had errands to run and whatnot."

"He was never away for a whole weekend, Padraig. Admit it."

The old man muttered something under his breath as he stood by the stove, watching the kettle.

"Don't think I don't know what's going on here."

Aislinn sighed heavily. "What's that?"

"You and your sister, plotting to get me out."

*"What?"*

"You think I didn't see Nora and that toff husband of hers sniffing around my home?"

"I had nothing to do with that. I swear on my parents' graves."

"She hates me, that one. Always has."

"She thinks you hate her."

"Hate that she's always thought she was too good for this place. Miss High and Mighty, with her books and computer and all, writing about God knows what. She'll not have my house. She'll not."

Aislinn went to him, patting his shoulder. "I would never let that happen," she assured him. The defiance in his voice was tinged with fear, and it broke her heart. He also sounded paranoid, which wasn't good. Aislinn had done research on her computer and learned that paranoia could be one of the symptoms of dementia. She was definitely going to make an appointment for him with a doctor as soon as she got back from Dublin. She'd lie if she had to, telling him she was going for a physical herself and it might not be a bad idea if he had one as well.

Padraig poured their tea and put out his usual array of stale tea biscuits on the plate. "You've got to branch out," Aislinn teased him. "You've been buying the same biscuits for as long as I can remember."

"Why would I want to change things up now? They're fine."

Aislinn bit into a biscuit. "The Frys will be here after breakfast Friday morning."

"How much are you paying them?"

Aislinn named the price, and Padraig's eyes practically popped from his wizened face. "Jaysus, woman, they'll be able to dine out on that for years."

"They're helping me out on very short notice, Padraig. They deserve it."

He looked defiant. "I hope they don't think they're gonna be the boss of me."

"Of course not. You're going to be the boss of them," said Aislinn, feeling guilty. She'd asked Alec and Jake to keep an eye on him so they could let her know if he bollixed anything up.

"And Nora?" he continued.

"What about her?"

"Is she going to be hanging about?"

"She'll be up at the house working as usual. I already told her you and the Frys have free rein of the kitchen to eat whatever you want whenever you want."

Padraig snorted. "Oh, she must be loving that."

"She doesn't have a choice." Aislinn paused. "You could eat dinner with her, if you wanted. You know she's a good cook. She'd probably welcome the company."

"Pull the other one," Padraig scoffed.

"Well, the option is there."

Padraig harrumphed, his expression suspicious. "The Frys—are they going to be sleeping here at the farm Friday and Saturday night?"

"No. They prefer to go home to their own place."

"Well, thank God for small miracles," he said, clearly relieved.

His mood improved, and a mischievous twinkle appeared in his eye. "Going away with the Yank to Dublin for the weekend, eh?"

"How do you know that?"

"I'm not an eejit, you know."

"I know." There was no way the whole town wouldn't know now. Padraig would tell everyone in the pub; Jack's bland son Neil would be filling in for Liam—so much for keeping their romance a delicious secret.

"So, the Yank—?"

To her surprise, Aislinn found herself blushing. "Yes, we're off to Dublin. His brother is in from New York."

"The journo?"

"Liam wants me to meet him."

"And he's bypassing Ballycraig?" Padraig looked mildly offended. "His people are here."

"He doesn't have time. He's on assignment."

"You think you'll wind up marrying him or what?" Padraig asked bluntly.

"Padraig!"

"Well, you're going away with him!"

"So?"

"Only cheap girls would do such a thing casually," Padraig announced.

Aislinn patted his hand reassuringly. "It's not a casual fling."

"I figured. You're not that kind of girl."

"Thank you. As for marriage, let's not put the cart before the horse."

"It's nice to see you smiling again, Aislinn."

"I don't think I've ever been this happy. Truly."

"I don't think so, either." He leaned in to her. "Now, about Dublin."

"Yes?"

"You've got to be very careful there," he warned. "It's awash with pickpockets and con men who'd as soon rob you blind as look at you."

Aislinn raised her eyebrows. "Is it now? When were you last there?"

Padraig squinted his eyes, thinking hard. "Sixty-two, I think. Yes, that would be it. My brother Derek, may he rest in peace, was marrying a girl from North Dub. Tough old boot, she was. She wore the pants in that house, I can tell you."

"I have a feeling the city might have changed a bit since then," Aislinn said kindly. "But I'll keep your advice in mind."

Padraig nodded approvingly. "Good girl. You've always had a sensible head on your shoulders."

"I suppose that's a compliment, though it does make me sound a bit dull."

"You? Dull? Bah! Never."

Aislinn leaned forward, planting a kiss on the old man's grizzled cheek. "You're sweet." She stood. "I'd best hit the hay, and you should, too."

"Oh! Before you go, there was one thing I've been meaning to talk to you about. Will we be entering Deenie in the sheepdog trials this year?"

Aislinn swallowed. "Padraig, that's your job, and the deadline passed months ago, remember?" she reminded him gently. "I'm sure it's too late for you two to enter now."

"Oh." He looked crestfallen for a split second, then scrambled to cover it with an expression of diffidence. "Oh, well, no mind. I guess it just slipped my mind, since we've been so busy round here—you know, you and me gettin' used to running the place without your da."

"I'm sure that's what happened."

"There's always next year. I just hope Deenie isn't too disappointed."

Aislinn chuckled to herself, amused by how they all thought of Deenie as a person and not a dog. "I think she'll live. By the way, I'm sure she'll want to sleep down here with you while I'm away."

"Grand. She can lie across the bottom of my bed and keep my feet warm."

"All right, then. See you in the morning."

* * *

*"Admit it: you* like Dublin already."

Aislinn shot Liam a dirty look as they sat down on a bench inside Saint Stephen's Green, Dublin's most famous park. They'd strolled much of the lush, green grounds, pausing at one point to sit on the edge of the fountain in the center of it all just to soak it all in. She hadn't much interest in the statue of James Joyce, but she thought she should see it anyway, since everyone said he was Ireland's greatest writer.

Aislinn loved that a place so calm and peaceful existed in the middle of the city. It was a great place for people watching, too. She could spot the tourists a mile away, clumped in groups with their maps and sensible shoes. There were local people sprawled out on the grass reading in the sunshine, eating their lunch, or chattering away. Old men thinking no one could see them stealing a smoke in public. Buskers strumming their guitars, their battered old guitar cases open at their feet so people could toss coins in.

They'd driven up from Ballycraig in a car Liam had rented, which she thought was madness, since a bus ran every few hours from Moneygall. But Liam insisted on it, and it didn't seem worth arguing about. On the drive, listening to the radio, she learned he had awful taste in music. She'd been positive that once they got into Dublin proper, he'd become a nervous wreck behind the wheel, but he was as calm as could be, saying that nerve-racking as it was driving on the wrong side of the road, it was nothing compared to driving in Manhattan.

They were staying at the same hotel as his brother, a moderately posh place called Kelly's located right near Trinity College. Aislinn didn't see why they couldn't make do with a nice, small B and B, but again, Liam was insistent, assuring her he had the money to pay for it. She didn't want to admit to him that she'd never stayed in a hotel.

He playfully nudged her shoulder with his. "You haven't admitted you like it yet."

"We've only been here a few hours!"

"So?"

"Yes, I like it," she admitted. "It's smaller than I imagined. And everyone seems so friendly."

Liam looked surprised. "You expected people to be unfriendly? Here? In Ireland?"

Aislinn laughed. "I guess we do have a reputation."

"Slightly." He took her hand. "Want to go to Bewley's for lunch?"

"Oh, I would love that! My aunt used to go when she was younger. She said the coffee was lovely."

Liam looked at her quizzically. "Do you still have extended family around Ballycraig?"

"Not anymore. They've all died or gone. It's not easy to make a living if you don't farm, and even then—"

"I can help you out if—"

"I most certainly do not need help!"

Liam raised his hands in a gesture of surrender.

Aislinn grabbed one of his hands and kissed it. "I'm sorry. I didn't mean to bite your head off. What I was going to say before you cut me off was that I've never been dependent on anyone for anything, and I'm not about to start now. I'm one of the lucky ones; I make a good living selling my wool," she continued proudly, "enough to turn a profit, *and* I'm able to pay Padraig a decent wage. That's more than enough."

Liam looked at her admiringly. "It doesn't take much to make you happy, does it?"

"I guess not. Why? Does it take a lot to make you happy?"

Liam furrowed his brows. "I don't know. I was unhappy for a really long time, mainly with myself. Totally had my head up my ass. But now . . ."

"Now what?" Aislinn pressed softly.

"Things are changing." He paused. "*I'm* changing."

"I didn't know you before, so I've no way to gauge that."

"Be glad you didn't know me before. I was a surly bastard."

"I find that very hard to believe."

"Ask Quinn at dinner. He'll tell you."

"I will." She snuggled closer to him. "Where is he right now?"

"Interviewing someone for his article. He wants to meet us at six thirty at this Indian place called Jaipur. It's right up the street from the hotel. He says it's great."

"I've never had Indian food," Aislinn admitted reluctantly. "Unless you count curry on my chips."

"Doesn't count."

Aislinn suddenly felt self-conscious. "God, what a bumpkin you must think I am."

"Why would I think that?"

"Never been to Dublin, only been to London once . . ." She looked down at her hands. "I've always been happy just being in Ballycraig."

"There's nothing wrong with that. Apart from Manhattan, I've only ever been here and in Ballycraig."

Aislinn slowly lifted her head, smiling. "Really?"

"My parents own a *bar*, Aislinn. They've never made much money, so we didn't travel much. And working as a bartender, I've never made much, either. But it didn't matter, because I loved my job. I still love it."

"If you've never made much money, then how are we affording that posh hotel?" she asked fretfully. "And the car?"

"I did have *some* money saved up."

"For something special—?"

"A motorcycle."

"You could buy one here."

Liam looked up, shielding his eyes against the sun. "Mmm."

His lack of a definitive answer filled Aislinn with a creeping sense of unease. *He doesn't want to buy a motorcycle here, because he doesn't plan to stay in Ireland. Well, no use getting your knickers in a twist over it right now. Just take it as it comes.*

"I'm feeling a bit peckish," Aislinn declared.

"Yeah, I could eat." Liam stood and extended a hand to her. "To Bewley's."

"To Bewley's."

\* \* \*

*Her aunt Charlene* had been right: Bewley's did do a lovely cup of coffee, and their sticky buns were heaven. Not the most nutritious lunch, Aislinn had to admit, but she didn't care: she was on holiday and could eat what she pleased. The café was on Grafton Street, a wide pedestrian

shopping common. It was another great place to watch
people, but she disliked the crowds. There weren't any
stores there she cared to shop in, so she was glad when
they walked down to Wellington Quay and spent some
time just strolling hand in hand along the Liffey. Massive,
silent cranes towered over the skyline, a reminder of the
building boom that had stopped dead in its tracks when
the economy bottomed out. Even so, the views along the
river were spectacular. They decided to join all the other
tourists and cross the Ha'penny Bridge.

Aislinn noticed that Liam got a bit broody as the afternoon wore on. She tried to pay it no mind; perhaps the
impending dinner with his brother was prompting a small
bout of homesickness.

She did fret a bit over what to wear to dinner when
they got back to the hotel room. Aislinn had borrowed a
nice, camel colored cashmere (cashmere!) jumper from
Nora, and had brought along a pair of tight black jeans.
Nora tried to talk her into borrowing those ridiculous
spiked boots, but Aislinn would have none of it. The last
thing she needed was to turn an ankle and come home on
crutches! Plus, they were dead uncomfortable. No: black
flats were fine.

Aislinn even brought some makeup with her but ulti-
mately decided not to wear it. It wasn't who she was. Even
the jumper made her feel a little bit like a poser, until
Nora reminded her that Liam might want to go out to
dinner somewhere nice, and wearing one of her old flannel shirts or pilled, woolly jumpers wouldn't do. Aislinn
capitulated.

They arrived at Jaipur at six thirty on the dot. "Quinn's
going to be late," Liam told her. "He's always late. He
runs on Quinn time."

Liam was right. At ten minutes to seven, a well-built,
slightly disheveled man with salt-and-pepper hair came
flying through the door of the restaurant, his eyes scan-
ning the room. The minute he spotted Liam, he broke

into a wide grin, which Liam returned. Aislinn's stomach gave a small tickle as they rose to meet him.

Quinn grabbed his brother up into a big bear hug. "There he is." He pulled back, looking Liam up and down. "You look great, you bastard."

"So do you," said Liam. He pointed to Quinn's tie. "Wow. No stains."

"Bite me," Quinn said affectionately. He turned his gaze to Aislinn as he held out his hand. "Hi, Aislinn. I'm Quinn." He paused. "Ah, screw the formality." With that, he hugged Aislinn, too. She was delighted.

The three of them sat down. "You order yet?" Quinn asked.

"No, we were polite and waited for you," said Liam. "How did your interviews go?"

"The one in the morning was a tight-lipped, tight-assed SOB who wasted my time. The one this afternoon was like hitting pay dirt, especially since I greased the wheels with a few pints."

"My brother isn't shy about using colorful language," Liam informed Aislinn.

"Of course he isn't. He's got Irish blood running through his veins, hasn't he?"

"I like you," Quinn said with an easy smile. He cracked open his menu. "I can make some recommendations, if you like. I know what's good here. Believe me, this is real Indian food. None of that watered-down chicken vindaloo crap like we have at home."

"Order away," said Liam.

Aislinn couldn't believe the boatload of food that eventually arrived, all of it delicious. And Quinn was everything Liam had said he was: smart, opinionated, and curious; she felt comfortable with him right away. She sensed the two brothers were doing their best to try to minimize talking about home so that she didn't feel left out, though it wasn't necessary. She wanted to gobble up every tidbit she could about her man, and she told

Quinn so. He seemed to take great enjoyment in embarrassing Liam, and Liam had no problem embarrassing Quinn right back. Aislinn loved the way the two of them hurled affectionate insults at one another. There was so much fondness, she found it hard to believe that there was a time he couldn't stand the sight of Quinn because Liam felt inadequate. Liam O'Brien, feeling inadequate! Now *that* was sidesplitting.

She excused herself to go to the loo, wondering if they'd talk about her while she was gone. *Go on with yourself, you egomaniac. The world doesn't revolve around you.* Though sometimes, Liam made her feel like it did, and she loved that.

*    *    *

*"She's great, Li,"* Quinn said the minute Aislinn disappeared into the bathroom.

Liam's shoulders slumped. "I know."

"What the hell is your problem?"

"I'm in love with her."

"Yeah, that's a real problem, being in love with a gorgeous, witty woman," Quinn mocked.

"It *is* a problem."

"Oh, let me guess: you don't know how to be happy. Or no, wait: you don't deserve to be happy."

"Shut up for a minute, will you?" Liam replied, irritated. He took a long sip of water to cool his burning tongue that had been singed by the spicy Indian food. "What am I going to do when I get the green light to come home? She'll never give up her farm."

"Are you sure about that? Or are you just assuming it?"

"I'm sure."

"Have you told her you love her?"

Liam felt sheepish. "Well, no."

"Just tell her you love her, and see how it goes." Quinn took a sip of water. "Does she know you want to go home?"

"I assume so."

"But you haven't actually said anything."

Liam felt like he was being grilled, but he knew it was just what the situation required. Even though it had made him chafe in the past, Quinn was good at giving advice. "No, because if I tell her, she might want to end things, and I don't want them to end."

"If you love her, you should tell her."

"She probably knows."

"Does she love you?"

"I think so, yeah. Probably. I mean, I assume so."

Quinn rolled his eyes. "Quit assuming stuff, will ya? *Tell her.*"

"I will, okay? When the time is right." Liam was starting to feel testy, so he changed the subject to PJ Leary, the writer and Wild Hart regular who'd finally sold the epic Celtic fantasy he'd been writing for twenty years as the follow-up to his first book. "Incredible," said Quinn, shaking his head. "The publisher is pouring money into marketing. They might even send him out on a book tour."

"You envious?"

"Nah. I'm glad for him. The guy's been toiling in obscurity so long, he deserves a break. Mom and Dad might throw him a small book party."

Liam felt a small pang in his gut and looked away.

"Sorry," said Quinn. "That's just the type of stuff you don't want to hear."

"It is what it is," Liam replied numbly, though his brother was right.

"Mom and Dad would love her, you know."

Liam fiddled with his fork. "Yeah, I know."

"I think Dad might have gone to school with her father. I'll have to check." Quinn checked his watch. "Aunt Bridget and Uncle Paul pissed I didn't come down?"

"I didn't tell them you were in."

"I'm sure they know anyway."

"Of course they do."

"What do they think of you and Aislinn?"

"They think it's good," Liam hedged. He didn't want to tell Quinn about the bet. After years of trying to convince himself he didn't give a rat's ass what his older brother thought of him, now that they were reconciled, he found he did care. Deeply.

"Look, don't say anything about it to Mom and Dad yet, okay?"

"Sure, whatever—though if Aunt Bridget and Uncle Paul know, I'm sure they've told Mom and Dad."

"Well, if they have, Mom is sure keeping uncharacteristically quiet about it," Liam said sardonically. "She hasn't said a word to me."

"That's because you're a bad son who hardly calls her," Quinn ribbed.

Liam groaned. Out of the corner of his eye, he saw Aislinn walking back to the table. He wasn't surprised when he noticed other men's heads turning; she was gorgeous, and that proud bearing of hers telegraphed a sense of power and self-confidence that was all but impossible to ignore. He smiled proudly.

"Perfect timing," he said, standing to pull her chair out for her. "We just finished talking about you."

Aislinn laughed. "That'd explain why my ears were burning in the loo."

Quinn checked his watch again. "I hate to eat and run, but I have to eat and run."

"Another interview?" asked Liam.

"Yeah, and then I want to get back to the hotel early to type up my notes." He signaled for the bill and plucked it from the center of the table before Liam had a chance to grab it. "On me."

Liam protested unsuccessfully.

Bill paid, they walked outside. The night air was cool, bordering on chilly. Liam felt a lump form in his throat as he and Quinn looked at one another, neither of them knowing how long it would be until they saw each other again.

"Soon," Quinn said, hugging Liam tight before moving on to hug Aislinn. "Keep him out of trouble, will ya?"

Aislinn slipped her hand in Liam's and squeezed it. "I'll try my best."

"Call me when you get back to New York, okay?" Liam said to his brother.

"You sound like Mom."

"Don't bust my chops. Just do it."

"Done." Quinn straightened his tie. "Bye now."

"Bye," Liam and Aislinn called after him. She could sense Liam's pain as they watched Quinn disappear around the corner and out of sight. Liam puffed up his cheeks and blew out some air. "Well, that's that."

"He's lovely."

"Yeah, he's a good guy."

"What would you like to do now? I'm up for anything, anything at all."

Liam put his arm around her shoulder. "I just want to walk. Walk around the city."

"Great idea."

## 16

*Aislinn thought Liam's* mood much improved the next day. Perhaps their making love at the hotel that morning had helped banish the pain of parting from his brother and missing his family.

Unable to stop herself, she called the Fry brothers as she and Liam walked to the chippie for lunch. Alec assured her all was well. The Frys were highly amused by Padraig's alternating between barking orders and ignoring them. "As long as it isn't getting in the way of you two doing what needs to be done, please let it pass," Aislinn entreated them. "Course we will," Alec promised. She finished by asking after Nora; they'd seen no trace of her, apart from dishes left in the sink. "Hiding from us, she is," Alec said with a chuckle.

"Probably," Aislinn agreed.

"Here it is," Liam announced just as she was folding closed her mobile.

Liam gestured at a small, forest green storefront with the words "Leo Burdock's Traditional Fish & Chips" in white and gold lettering above the door. A line was snaking out down the narrow pavement, the delicious aroma of frying fish and sizzling chips permeating the air. Aislinn flashed back to a memory of being a little girl and driving down into Ballycraig with her da to pick up fish and chips for the family at Dooney's, the local chippie. She remembered the feel of holding the meals wrapped in newspapers on her lap, the intoxicating smell of it, the fun of unwrapping the dinners at the table and drenching the fish in malt vinegar, licking salt off her fingers, everyone chattering and laughing. Such a small memory, yet so powerful.

Liam took hold of her hand as they took their place in line. "I know the perfect place to sit," he said.

"Where?"

"You'll see."

Once inside, the heat from the fryers hit her in the face. There were no tables; it was strictly a takeaway operation. They each ordered a single portion of cod and chips, and Liam insisted on paying. Aislinn disliked his paying for everything and told him so, announcing that she'd be paying for dinner that night. "We'll see," Liam murmured. She shook her head, knowing that meant, *No, I don't think so.* She could hear Nora's voice in her head: *Just let him do it, for God's sake. Let him pamper you. Heaven knows, you've no idea how to pamper yourself.* Perhaps Nora was right.

Back outside, Liam pointed across the street at Christ Church Cathedral. "They've got a really nice garden there. Lots of people go there and just sit on the grass and eat. C'mon."

She followed him across the road. Aislinn thought maybe she'd suggest going inside the church after lunch to have a look round. She'd never been inside a cathedral before.

"Jesus God, I'll never be able to eat all this," said Aislinn as they settled down on a thick, green patch of grass and she saw how big their portions were. *Whatever I don't eat,* she thought, *I'll wrap up and bring back to the hotel.* There was a microwave in the room; she could zap it to have as a late-night snack if she wanted. She wondered, though: was that unsophisticated? It probably was, but she hated the idea of wasting food. It had been drummed into her by both her parents that it was a sin.

She near swooned as she popped the first chip into her mouth. "Gorgeous."

"I agree," said Liam, spearing a big hunk of fish with a plastic fork.

"So you've eaten in the garden before?"

"Yeah, with my folks. I've visited Dublin with them a few times. The whole family never came over together; my folks couldn't afford it. They'd take two of the four kids at a time, and the other two the next time." He chuckled, lost in reminiscence. "The last time I was here was when I was fifteen and my sister Maggie was seventeen. We thought our parents were such idiots we wouldn't even walk down the street with them!"

Aislinn laughed. "I remember walking ten paces in front of my mother when we'd go into Moneygall to shop for clothing. Oh, the humiliation of being seen with her!" She paused, thoughtful. "I was never embarrassed to be seen out with my dad, though. Odd, isn't it?"

"That's because you worshipped him."

"I suppose I did."

"Still enjoying Dublin?"

"Can't you tell?"

She looked around at the flowers in full bloom, the branches of the trees waving hello at her. She'd loved strolling around the city with him, letting the sights and sounds and smells sink in.

"Are you enjoying it? Being back in a city and all?" she asked, pushing her hair off her face. Bloody pain in the neck it was, blowing all around. She'd wanted to put it back in a braid the way she usually did, but since Liam liked it tumbling down around her shoulders, she let it be. She found she liked looking attractive for him.

"Totally."

"But you're homesick."

"A little. But not enough to interfere with being here with you." He pulled a digital camera out of his backpack, aiming it at her. Aislinn's hands immediately flew to cover her face as she groaned.

"I hate having my picture taken."

"Indulge me. Just one."

She lowered her hands. "Only if it's one of us together."

"Fine." Liam jumped to his feet, asking a man sitting nearby to take a snap of them. The man happily obliged as Liam sat back down and Aislinn rested her head on his shoulder while Liam snaked his arm around her. *I'm so happy,* she thought. *So, so happy.*

The man handed the camera back to Liam, and he stuffed it into his backpack. "I'll download it when we get home and e-mail it to you."

Joy sparked inside her. He'd called Ballycraig home.

They chatted easily, eating their lunch. Aislinn filled him in on Nora and Donald's sudden interest in the farm and how alarming it was to her and Padraig.

"I can understand that," Liam said carefully, "but look at it this way: even if they did build a place for themselves somewhere on the property, they wouldn't be there all the time."

"True," Aislinn agreed, but it was still not what she wanted to hear. She tried to picture where the cottage would be. Far from the house, probably. Which meant they'd have to clear a road on the property. When they weren't using it, they'd probably let their rich London friends borrow it. Aislinn frowned, trying to disperse the dark cloud forming in her head. *You're being a right nasty bitch,* she told herself. *Nora told you she had no designs at all on the property. Stop spinning negative tales.*

Liam turned to her, dangling a chip in front of her mouth. "Open up," he said playfully. Aislinn complied. "I love you, you know."

Aislinn halted mid-chew. "Pardon?"

"I love you," Liam repeated, his eyes shining with unabashed ardor.

Aislinn forced herself to finish chewing the chip and swallowed. "And you thought now might be the perfect time to tell me, when I've a chip in my mouth?"

"The urge was there, and I just had to go with it," Liam declared.

"Dead smooth, you are."

His shoulders slumped. "I'm an idiot."

"You're not, you're not, you're not," she rushed to assure him. "I just wasn't expecting it, was all. And no one could ever argue that it wasn't memorable."

Liam laughed, clearly relieved. Inside, Aislinn's heart was knocking against her ribs, desperate to burst out and take happy flight. She was giddy, and it was lovely.

She cut a piece of fish, holding it aloft on its plastic fork.

"Open wide," she said mischievously. Liam chuckled, then complied.

"I love *you*," she told him.

Unlike her, Liam looked nowhere near choking. In fact, the smile on his face was adorable. He swallowed, washing down his food with a sip of cola, and then leaned in to her, one hand reaching around to cup the back of her neck as he pressed his mouth to hers in a sizzling kiss. Aislinn felt paralyzed by her own desire, unable to move, not really wanting to, as the kiss burned on and on. She'd never been comfortable with doing things in public that she believed were best meant to be done in private, but right now, she didn't care. They were a couple in love, and there was no reason not to glory in it. A fantasy of the future shimmered its way into her thoughts: she saw herself in the big kitchen at the house preparing dinner, talking to a little girl with Liam's dark, tousled curls and stormy gray eyes who sat swinging her legs at the big Parsons table. "And then, would you ever believe, your da asked me to marry him as he stuffed a chip in my mouth!" The little girl laughed delightedly, begging for more details.

Liam eventually lifted his mouth from hers. "I've never said that to anyone before," he admitted.

"How does it feel?"

"Great." He paused. "And scary."

"It is scary; I agree." She took one of his hands and pressed her lips to his open palm. "But worth it."

"Definitely worth it," he agreed. He gestured at his lunch. "No way I can finish that."

Aislinn put a hand to her belly. "I'm relieved to hear you say that."

"We can wrap it and bring it back to the hotel."

"I'm relieved to hear you say that, too! I was thinking the same, but I was afraid you'd think me uncultured. Trashy, as you Yanks say."

"No. My parents always said wasting food was a sin."

"I like your parents," Aislinn said softly. She wished her parents were alive to meet him; that they'd never know him was the one pain in her heart amid all this joy.

"They'd like you, too," Liam returned quietly. Broodiness was returning; she could sense it. He missed them fiercely, a sentiment she understood all too well.

Aislinn began wrapping up their lunches. "Would you mind if we went inside the cathedral?" she asked. "I'd love to have a look round."

"Dublin is at your feet, milady," said Liam. "Whatever you want to do is fine with me."

"I'd like to just see where the day takes us. Walk around."

"Sounds great." He helped her to her feet. "This is turning out to be the best weekend of my life."

"Mine as well." She twined her fingers through his. "Truly."

\* \* \*

*The next night,* they rolled into Ballycraig at close to midnight, having left Dublin later than expected so they could milk another day out of being in the city. Aislinn was exhausted; she'd be dragging her sorry arse when it was time to get up with Padraig in four hours' time to begin her day. She was glad to see the lights of his cottage were out as she drove her truck up the long drive leading to the house; the old man wasn't having one of his bad insomnia nights.

The first thing she did was head into the barn to check the flock. They were all fast asleep on the straw that had been put down fresh that morning. Mad as it was, she'd missed them.

She tiptoed into the kitchen. Nora had never been a heavy sleeper, and Aislinn wanted to be sure not to wake her. There was a note for her on the table from Alec Fry; all had gone well, save for one incident where Padraig wanted to herd the flock into one of the pastures that had already been heavily grazed. They'd reasoned with him and in the end he capitulated, but he wasn't pleased. Aislinn's heart sank just a little. She knew she was going to get an earful about "those Fry boys" from the old devil. She also knew that she'd be calling the local medico on her lunch break to arrange an appointment for him.

She crept up the stairs, wincing as the third step from the top landing creaked loudly. Sure enough, Nora appeared in the doorway of her bedroom not ten seconds after Aislinn switched the light on.

"Hey," Nora said sleepily.

"Hey yourself," said Aislinn. "What are you doing up? Let me guess: the step."

"I was only half-asleep anyway."

"Insomnia again?"

"Yeah. Worried about my article. I'm stuck."

"I know you: you'll come unstuck."

Nora sat down on her bed, watching Aislinn as she undressed. Aislinn noticed she was wearing sweatpants, a sweatshirt, and thick wool socks. "Is that what you sleep in? No wonder you're awake. You must be boiling like a shrimp in a pot."

"It's freezing in this house, Aislinn," Nora replied,

rubbing her shoulders briskly. "Ever think of installing central heating?"

"The heating system suits me fine," Aislinn said, slipping an oversized old T-shirt of Connor's over her head.

"Gas fires in individual rooms? I feel like I'm in a Dickens novel."

"You can install central heating if you want. Feel free." *After all, it is half yours, right?* she was tempted to add. Exhaustion was giving way to crabbiness. She held her tongue.

"You look tired," Nora noted.

"I'm totally banjaxed," Aislinn admitted with a yawn. "We left late so we could get another day in Dublin."

"Did you like it? I do," Nora asked excitedly. "I mean, it's no London, but it does have a certain charm."

"It does," Aislinn agreed.

Nora pelted her with questions. Did she go see the Book of Kells at Trinity College? Did she go to the Writers Museum? Dublin Castle? The General Post Office on O'Connell Street, where you could still see the bullet holes in the pillars from the Easter Rising of 1916?

"No, no, and no," Aislinn said. She gave her sister a curious look. "I'd no idea you'd spent so much time in Dublin."

"See? There's something *you* didn't know about *me*. You missed a lot. Guess you'll just have to go back," Nora teased.

"I'm in no rush."

"What did you do, then?"

Aislinn filled her in on her glorious weekend, taking lots of time to tell her all about meeting Quinn.

"Did seeing his brother make Liam homesick?" Nora asked carefully.

"Yes."

"Are you worried?"

"Why should I be worried?" Aislinn replied, smiling confidently. She practically danced over to where Nora was sitting. "He told me loved me!" she gushed. "And I said it back!"

Nora bounced on the bed like a little girl. "Oh my God! That's so great!"

"I know." Aislinn sat down beside her. "Can you believe it? I mean, can you?"

"Yes, I can." She walked over to Aislinn's dresser, returning with the thick, horsehair brush Aislinn had had since she was a little girl. She sat back down on the bed to brush Aislinn's hair. Aislinn closed her eyes, reveling in the feeling; no one had done this for her since she was small, and Nora's strokes were so tender.

"Oh, I love that man so, Nora," she continued exuberantly. "It's positively dizzying."

Nora laughed. "Isn't it the best feeling? I remember when I realized I loved Donald. I felt like I was suffering from vertigo for days."

"I could leap in the air." Aislinn blushed. "I sound like an eejit."

"No, you sound like a woman in love. I'm so glad you let him in, Aislinn. I was so worried you'd never meet anyone."

Nora put down the brush and began braiding Aislinn's hair. "I was always jealous when mum would braid your hair, you know that?"

Aislinn was surprised. "No, I didn't know."

"She was always going on about how thick and wavy it was. And there was me with the stick-straight hair."

"But you were the beauty."

"You've never been able to see how gorgeous you are, have you? With that hair and those long legs of yours . . ." Nora shook her head.

"I hear you hid in the house while I was away," Aislinn said, eager to change the subject.

"I was not hiding!" Nora protested. "I was working on my article!"

"And avoiding Padraig."

"Can you blame me?"

"Honestly, the two of you need to let it go. It's ridiculous."

Aislinn rose, giving a big stretch. "I hate to be rude, but if I don't try to catch a bit of kip, I'll be dead on my feet by lunch tomorrow."

"I understand." Nora stood. "I wanted to tell you: I'm going back to London on Tuesday for a few days to do some research."

*A few days.* Which meant she intended to come back.

"When will you be back?"

"I'll ring you and let you know."

"Fair enough."

"I'm so happy for you, Aislinn." Nora gave her a big hug. "It's too bad Mum and Da—"

"I know." Aislinn kissed her cheek. "I'll see you in the morning."

Nora quietly closed the door behind her, and Aislinn slipped into bed. For the first time ever, it felt too big, as well as lonely. She missed Liam's body wrapped around her, keeping her warm and making her feel cherished. *Ah, well, soon enough,* she thought, drifting off to sleep. The days of hiding were over. She planned to go down to the Oak tomorrow night and let the world see she and Liam were together. She closed her eyes and slept.

# 17

*"Be prepared to* eat a big, heaping dish of crow, Jack."

Old Jack shot Liam a dirty look as he set down three pints of Guinness before Fergus, Teague, and David, who were also glaring at him. In about half an hour, Aislinn was going to walk through that door, and she was going to plant a passionate kiss on his mouth. Liam was going to announce they were a couple, and that all drinks were on him. After all, he could afford it: Jack would be paying him double starting tomorrow.

He preferred not to think about the bet that had started it all, focusing instead on the amazing weekend he'd had with Aislinn in Dublin. He'd loved that she delighted in seeing new things, having new experiences. Seeing Dublin through her eyes gave him a new appreciation for it and for Ireland.

He especially loved that she was into taking things as they came. The only time he sensed her discomfort was when they were on Grafton Street, which was packed. He could feel her longing to get back home to open air and quiet. Seeing her face crease with stress, a thought had flashed through his mind: if Grafton Street made her tense, she could never deal with New York. The thought winked out as quickly as it came. There was no point trying to predict the future.

He'd always imagined if he fell in love, he'd go the whole nine yards to set the scene to say the words: dinner by candlelight in some nice restaurant, a romantic walk through Central Park. Instead, he'd playfully popped a French fry in Aislinn's mouth and declared his heart as matter-of-factly as someone asking a buddy how her day was going. Real smooth. Yet it felt right, and, as he'd confessed to her, scary as hell. He'd never made that kind of emotional commitment before. Then again, he'd never felt this way before.

He'd known Aislinn and Quinn would get along. But spending time with his brother and then having to say good-bye to him, not knowing when they'd see each other again, had messed with his head for a while. He couldn't believe what an idiot he'd been, letting his friend Tommy pull him into the web of the Irish Mob.

Chatting with everyone who sidled up to the bar and effortlessly filling orders, Liam resisted the urge to check every time the pub door opened. After what felt like forever, Aislinn finally walked in, looking not unlike the way she did the first time he set eyes on her: faded jeans, wellies caked with mud, the well-worn barn jacket. The only differences were that her hair was tied back in a braid, not in a wild, auburn tangle around her head, and this time, she wasn't scowling. In fact, she was beaming at him as if he was the only person in the room.

"Hello, Jack," she called cheerily from the door, shucking her jacket and hanging it on a peg. "Hello Fergus, Teague, and David. A whiskey for me please, Jack."

She slipped behind the bar as if it were the most natural thing in the world. "Hello, darlin'," she said to Liam, giving him an eye-popping kiss. There was a swell of whispers, and then a hush fell over the room.

"There's my girl," said Liam. He put down the bar rag in his hand, snaking an arm around her waist to draw her

close to him. "Listen up, everyone." Liam looked at the
patrons' faces and held back a laugh. They were listening, all right—listening and looking at him and Aislinn
as if they'd never seen a man and woman together in their
lives. "I want everyone here to know I love this woman.
Madly. And if what she's told me is the truth, she loves
me, too."

"The lot of you have known me my whole life," Aislinn added, "so you know I never lie. It's true: I love the
Yank."

"I'd love for you all to share in our happiness, so drinks
are on me tonight," Liam finished.

The pub began buzzing. Fergus was staring at them,
openmouthed.

"And what might be wrong with you, Fergus Purcell?"
Aislinn asked, hands on hips. "Cat got your tongue?"

"Envy, more like," said David with a frown. He reluctantly held a hand out to Liam to shake. "Well played. I
never thought—"

"Thank you," Liam said curtly. Christ, he hoped the
three idiots didn't start talking about the bet.

"God forbid you give your heart to an Irishman,"
Teague sneered at Aislinn.

"You may recall that I did once."

"I mean a real one. Not one who was, you know, *that*
way."

"All the specimens in this town are pitiful," said Aislinn.

"So now what?" Fergus sniffed, smirking at Liam.
"You're going to become a shepherd?"

"Or maybe she'll go back to New York with him and
become a wool merchant," said Teague. The three of
them laughed. Liam stiffened. Leave it to these assholes
to bring up the one possible monkey wrench in his and
Aislinn's future.

"Oh, listen to the three hyenas entertaining themselves," Aislinn said scornfully. She drew herself up in

that imperious way that had so left an impression on Liam the first night he saw her. "There's nothing you can do or say that can put a damper on this night or on the future, so don't waste your sad, sorry breath." She turned away from them, kissing Liam softly on the mouth. "I best get out of your way."

Liam put his mouth to her ear and whispered, "Will I be coming home with you tonight?"

"Would you be upset if we waited until tomorrow night?" Aislinn whispered back apologetically. "I've still not caught up on my sleep."

"No problem at all," Liam murmured, discreetly nipping her earlobe. "I like you all energetic."

Aislinn blushed as she picked up her whiskey. "I'm off to chat with Grace Finnegan and find out how her husband is getting on at that cancer center in London." She slid out from behind the bar, raising her glass at the Holy Trinity as she sauntered past. "See you, boys."

None of them had a thing to say.

*     *     *

*"How does that* crow taste?"

The minute the bar closed for the night, Liam started on Old Jack. The old man had let the Trinity stay on past closing time because they'd been in on the bet from the first.

"You lost the bet," Liam continued. "The sooner you cop to it, the better."

Jack sighed. "Fine. I lost."

"Don't look so pleased with yourself just yet, Yank," said Teague. "You might have won her, but she's still going to tear you limb to limb when you dump her."

"I'm not going to dump her. I love her."

Teague turned to Fergus. "Will you ever listen to this one? 'I love her.' Pull the other one, mate."

"It's true."

"It makes no difference," Teague countered with a

malicious smile. "She'll still mount your balls on the wall as a trophy when she hears about the bet."

"Why would she hear about it?" Liam snapped. "Are you that cruel? She's happy. Why would you want to take that away from her?"

"It's true," Jack agreed. "It would be a rotten thing to do, especially after what the poor girl went through."

"If the bet was so rotten," David challenged Liam, "why didn't you call it off?"

"You know damn well why," Jack said. "Only a coward backs out of a bet."

"True, true," David muttered. He looked at Liam with begrudging respect. "I have to hand it to you, Yank: I truly thought it couldn't be done." He drained his glass.

"You know," said Fergus, "It's kind of nice to have the old McCafferty back again, even though she does enjoy giving us a good tongue-lashing."

"You lot deserve it," said Jack.

"Yeah, we did give her an awful time at school, didn't we?" David said guiltily. "Maybe we should apologize."

"After all these years? Don't be an arse," Teague spat. "We've an image to uphold. Besides, I'd miss the tongue-lashings; she's the only woman who ever talks to us."

"Whose fault is that," asked Jack, "with the three of you sittin' here on your arses night after night, in your cups by the time you stagger out the door?"

"Better single than spending my life with the likes of your Bettina," said Teague.

"You watch yourself," Jack growled, "or you'll never darken this doorstep again. Am I clear?"

"Yeah, yeah, clear as day," Teague muttered, hunching his shoulders.

Jack looked at Liam. "Well done."

"Thank you."

"I wish you every happiness."

"Thank you again."

"So, eh, how long you think you're gonna be in Ballycraig?"

David laughed loudly. "Ha-ha, he's afraid he'll go bankrupt paying you double for God knows how long!"

"Shut your gob," Jack snapped, turning his attention back to Liam. "Any idea?"

"None."

"Your brother had nothing to say about it?"

"Nothing apart from the fact the Major says it's still not safe."

"All right, then," Jack conceded with a sigh. "Possible bankruptcy it is."

"What a bunch of bull," said Liam. "You make a mint in here."

Old Jack scowled at him. "You've no idea what my overhead is, boyo. It'd put the likes of that rich bastard Sir Paul McCartney in a foul mood, believe me."

"Be that as it may, a bet is a bet," said Liam.

"It is, and I'm a man of my word. Starting tomorrow night, double wages for you. Now let's get this place cleaned up so this old, soon-to-be-poor man can go to bed."

# 18

*Aislinn couldn't hide* her anxiety as she sat in Dr. Laurie's examining room, waiting to hear what he had to say about Padraig. As she'd vowed, she made the appointment the day she returned from Dublin. Padraig gave her a hard time about going until Aislinn told him that she herself was going for a checkup, which was a lie, but she could live with it because it was a small one. Dr. Laurie, a short, serious-looking man in his mid-sixties, had examined Padraig first. Now he was with Aislinn, but it was for a consultation about the old man, not an examination.

The doctor's brows furrowed worriedly. "His heartbeat is a wee bit erratic, and he has a little bit of rattling in his lungs. You know, I've no records of him here."

"He's never been to a doctor in his life. Says a whiskey a night and a good smoke is medicine enough for him."

Dr. Laurie gave a small wince. "Does he smoke a lot?"

"Yes." Aislinn grew nervous. "Why?"

"Well, years of smoking could be what I hear in his chest. It could also cause hardening of the arteries, which might explain the forgetfulness you mentioned to me on the phone."

"So you noticed it?"

"When I asked him a few questions, yes. But you needn't worry about Alzheimer's or anything else like that, Aislinn. It's just the type of forgetfulness that's to be expected at his age."

"Will it get worse?"

"Probably. Is he aware he's forgetting?"

"When it's pointed out to him. Then he tries to cover."

"He seems a proud man. It must be hard on him."

"How's his blood pressure?"

"Very good. He's in good shape for a man his age."

Aislinn was relieved. "That's good to hear."

"I take it you wanted me to check on the forgetfulness because it's starting to affect his work on the farm?"

"Yes," said Aislinn, feeling guilty. "Nothing major has happened yet, but I'm afraid it will."

"Could you limit his chores?"

"I have been. I think he's getting resentful. I mean, how do you tell a man like Padraig that he's slowing down? He doesn't think of himself as old, and until he started to become forgetful, neither did I."

"Has he never mentioned retiring?"

Aislinn burst out laughing. "Are you kidding? He's going to die with his wellies on, that one."

"Perhaps you could mention it casually."

"And what would he do with himself?"

"I hear there's a nice retirement community right outside of Moneygall."

"He'd die of boredom in a month. That's not who he is. The farm is all he knows."

"Then as far as I can see, the only option you've only got is what I suggested before: limiting what he does around the farm."

Aislinn bit her lip. "He did light the wrong burner on his stove once, making tea."

"I've done that once or twice when I've been overtired," said Dr. Laurie with a smile.

"I'm glad to hear that," Aislinn said with relief.

"If he starts forgetting the words for simple things, or does something like putting his keys in the freezer or daft things like that, then there's need to worry. But for now, I think his forgetfulness is just your garden variety getting old stuff."

"Good, good."

"While you're here, I may as well give you the once-over. C'mon: let's take your blood pressure."

Aislinn complied with Dr. Laurie's pokes and prods, knowing they were a waste of time. She was right: her blood pressure was perfect, her weight was right on the mark, her heartbeat was strong, and her lungs were clear.

"Fit as a fiddle," Dr. Laurie declared, "with a glow about you as well."

"I'm in love," Aislinn confessed. It was wonderful to say it aloud. Wonderful that people could see it, too, after that horrible year of just wanting to snarl at the world and be left alone.

"Lovely," said Dr. Laurie, looking genuinely delighted. "Being in love is good for your health, you know. Strengthens the immune system. Should I be expecting my invite to the wedding soon?"

"That's truly putting the cart before the horse," Aislinn said with chuckle. "We'll see how it goes."

Dr. Laurie patted her shoulder. "Right—off with you then. Like I said, just keep an eye on Padraig."

"I'll do that. Thank you very much for fitting us in, Dr. Laurie."

"My pleasure. Have a lovely day."

\* \* \*

*"Fit as a* fiddle," Padraig crowed triumphantly. "I told you I would be."

"The doctor said your heartbeat was a wee bit erratic and your lungs rattled a bit."

Padraig thrust his lower lip out defiantly. "He didn't say a word about that to me."

"Because he knew it would go in one ear and out the other. He also said you should cut back on the smoking a bit."

Padraig snorted. "I will not. It relaxes me."

"Just a bit," Aislinn urged, her ulterior motive being that maybe, if he smoked less, it might slow the hardening of his arteries.

"Since your heartbeat was a wee bit erratic," Aislinn continued carefully, "I think maybe we'll lessen your chore load."

Padraig glared at her.

"Just for a little while," she amended.

"I don't think so," Padraig replied stubbornly.

Aislinn resisted the urge to look skyward and plead with the heavens to help her out here. "I said, just for a little while."

"And then what? You're going to drag me back here for another checkup to make sure the ticker is back to its old self? I don't think so."

"You think I want to be responsible if you keel over dead in one of the pastures?" Aislinn shot back.

"Can't think of a better way to go," Padraig countered. His expression turned bitter. "Those Fry boys filled your head with a load of bollocks, didn't they? Fibbing about me. Trying to push me out."

Paranoid. Why had Aislinn forgotten to mention to Dr. Laurie he was paranoid sometimes? Then she realized: it wasn't paranoia, it was fear. Of being useless. Of no longer being needed.

"Why would they push you out? They've got their own farm to tend to."

"Yet they were able to take time to tend to yours."

"There are three other brothers who help them work theirs. And just for the record, they didn't have one bad word to say about you, apart from the fact you'd sometimes make a great show of ignoring them or else treating them like lackeys."

"Did you or did you not say I was in charge?" Padraig challenged.

"Yes, I did, but there was no call to be rude to them, especially since they were helping us out."

"Could have done it myself," Padraig muttered.

"Button it," Aislinn warned.

"Do I sense a bit of the McCafferty temper coming on?"

"The McCafferty exasperation, more like." Aislinn patted his arm. "I need you on the farm, old man. You know that. But I also want you to listen to me. Tell me: if it was my father asking you to cut back a bit on the fags and the chores, you'd do it, wouldn't you?"

"He wouldn't ask me to do such a thing."

Aislinn was ready to scream. "*Pretend* he would."

"Then I might," Padraig allowed reluctantly. "For a bit."

"Then do it for me for a bit, all right?"

"All right." They were walking up the high street. "Where we off to now?"

"You're going to go to the truck to wait for me while I run into the grocer's to get a few things. Do you need anything?"

"Couple of packs of fags," said Padraig with an impish grin.

"One pack. That's it."

"You're a cruel mistress."

"I try."

\* \* \*

*Aislinn was satisfied* she'd made at least a little bit of headway with Padraig as she headed into Finnegan's Greengrocer. Grace was at her usual perch behind the counter, gossiping with Teague's mother, Beth, and Jack's refrigerator-sized wife, Bettina. They said their hellos as Aislinn picked up a small basket to shop.

"Poor thing," Aislinn heard Bettina murmur as Aislinn headed down the nearest aisle.

Puzzled, Aislinn hovered nearby, pretending to peruse the biscuit selection. Obviously they had no idea she could hear them.

"Why's that?" Teague's mother asked.

"Did you not hear about the bet?" replied Bettina. "When the Yank first came to town, he bet my Jack he could tame the McCafferty. He's been wooing her like mad; even took her up to Dub. Well, she fell for it, didn't she? The Yank won, and now my Jack has to pay him double for as long as he's here."

"I wonder how he did it," Grace said wonderingly.

"God only knows, but he did," said Bettina. "Well, he is handsome, and a bit of a smooth talker. Any woman could find herself falling for that eventually, even Aislinn McCafferty."

"I like his accent as well," said Beth. "He could get my juices flowing." The three of them cackled.

"What'll happen now, I wonder," Grace mused.

"He won the wager. I imagine he'll break up with her now," said Bettina.

Beth shivered. "Oh Christ, I don't want to be there when that happens. She'll be leavin' him a bloody heap on the floor."

"Poor thing," Bettina repeated. "After what happened with Connor and all."

"Still, she's always been a bit odd, hasn't she?" Beth mused. "I never understood why she wouldn't give my Teague the time of day."

Grace and Bettina were silent.

"Well, at least her sister is around now to help ease the pain," said Bettina.

"She's up to something, that one," said Grace with a sniff. "I can't stand that la-di-da husband of hers, with his nose so high up in the air I can see his bloody tonsils."

They laughed again. Aislinn couldn't move. Her throat had closed up to the size of a pinhole, and she was finding it hard to breathe. She was convinced she was going to die of suffocation or worse, a heart attack, if the relentless, crushing pain in her chest was any indication.

*You have to move. You have to get out of here without letting them know you heard them, without your expression giving any hint of what you're feeling inside.* Feeling as though she were mired in cement, she forced herself to pick up a packet of biscuits and put it in the small plastic basket in her hand. She started moving up and down the aisles mechanically, throwing random items in the basket, not caring if she needed them or not. Through sheer force of will, she finally made herself go up to the counter.

"Will that be all, love?" Grace asked kindly.

"Pack of Benson & Hedges, please," Aislinn said with a smile. Beth Daly and Bettina were smiling at her, too, the hypocritical old biddies. *I heard what you said,* Aislinn longed to lash out. *And I don't need or want your bloody pity. I might have been played for a fool, but at least I could never be like you, standing by and doing nothing while an innocent person got hurt. The lot of you can go to hell.*

She paid her bill and walked out of the shop, feeling their eyes on her back. Liam. That lying bastard. She should have known it was too good to be true. Her mind combed through a catalogue of memories: meeting him, teaching him to change a tire, the first time they'd made love, their weekend in Dublin . . . all of it bullshit. The whole town was in on it, laughing at her behind her back, the stupid, desperate, blind McCafferty making a sorry arse of herself.

Nausea rose in her throat, bitter and swift. She pushed it back down. Humiliation and heartache—well, she was an old pro at dealing with those twins, wasn't she? Time again to wall off her heart. But first, there was a certain Mr. Liam O'Brien who was going to feel her wrath later this evening at the Royal Oak. She just hoped Old Jack had a first aid kit.

## 19

*It took every* ounce of Aislinn's concentration to keep her mind on the road: all she wanted to do was pull over and pound the steering wheel of her truck, screaming out the rage and hurt inside her. Padraig seemed oblivious to her mood, chattering away about God knows what, his words like the annoying buzz of an insect in her ear.

As soon as they got home, she sent Padraig to put down fresh straw in the barn, while she went out with Deenie to rotate the flock to a new meadow. Faithful Deenie. How sad was it that the only ones in the world she trusted to never let her down were her dog and Padraig, and possibly Nora? She thought about how the whole town knew about the bet, and yet no one had tipped her off. Was she that disliked? She knew she'd scorned their sympathy and had deliberately chosen to remove herself from their company. She knew she'd been gruff, perhaps even a bit curmudgeonly. But still: didn't any of them have brains enough to see that she was acting that way because she was in pain? Was there no one, *anyone*, who'd thought to themselves, "Dear God, what the Yank is doing to Aislinn is downright cruel; I would be devastated if someone did that to me"?

Tears threatened as she thought about Liam's treachery, but she forced them back. She knew she shouldn't have trusted that smug, overconfident bastard. Anger alternated with devastation. How could he toy with her affections that way, as if she were some kind of plaything, not a human being with feelings? What kind of a man would do such a thing?

Well, she'd give him one thing: he was one hell of an actor. She'd believed every silver-tongued word that had come out of his lying mouth. How pathetic. All of Ballycraig must have thought it a testament to how lonely she was. She pounded her temples with her fists, trying to drive the thought from her mind. She couldn't bear the thought of them sniggering behind her back about the poor, pathetic, desperate McCafferty.

Liam wouldn't be the only one who she'd be laying into tonight. Every one of the villagers deserved to be exposed for what they truly were: cruel and heartless. This was it: she was done with men, and she was done with the lot of them as well. She had her farm, Padraig, and Nora. She had Deenie, who loved her unconditionally. Never again, she vowed. Never again.

\* \* \*

*She waited until* around eight to go to the Oak, when she knew the pub would be packed. When she walked through the door and Liam spotted her, he broke into that sexy, curving smile of his that usually made her go all soft inside. *Judas. Wanker.* She smiled back, refusing to make eye contact with anyone else. *Screw all of you*, she thought.

"Hey babe," said Liam, pouring out her usual whiskey.

"Hey yourself," Aislinn said, still smiling at him. Liam leaned across the bar and kissed her; she made herself kiss him back.

And then she slapped him across the face as hard as she could.

Liam stared at her, stunned, as the pub immediately fell quiet.

"How dare you?" she hissed. "How dare you use me for your own amusement?"

Eyes locked on hers, Liam slowly slipped out from behind the bar.

"Don't you dare come near me," she growled.

"Just hear me out," Liam implored, moving toward her cautiously as if she were some sort of rabid animal who might lunge at him if he approached too quickly.

"Hear you out?" Aislinn echoed bitterly. "What's to hear? That you tricked me into falling in love with you for your own amusement?" Aislinn cocked her head quizzically. "Tell me: did you think it was funny to use me that way?"

"Aislinn—"

"Shut up. You don't get to say a word, do you understand? *Not a word.*"

Liam glanced away, unable to look at her.

"Who are you?" she continued. "I mean truly: who the hell *are you*? Only the worst kind of scum would do what you did to me. You do realize that, don't you?"

Liam looked down at the floor.

"It was a cruel, insensitive thing to do. But you did it anyway, and what for?" She gestured at the Holy Trinity. "Because you wanted to impress this pathetic pack of bastards into accepting you?" She turned her disgust on Old Jack. "Because this cheap gobshite doesn't pay you enough?" Jack's gaze darted away. "What's wrong, Jack? Can't bear to look me in the eye? Can't bear to hear the truth?"

She heard a few snickers coming from behind her and wheeled around furiously. "You lot think you're any better? You think I don't know you all knew about this? I'm not going to deny that I've spent the past year keeping to myself, or that it was wrong of me to reject the kindnesses you tried to show me after Connor broke my heart and my parents died. But did my behavior really merit this kind of cruelty? Was I so awful to you all that you felt I deserved this? How would you feel if someone did this to you? Chew on that for a few seconds, you heartless bastards."

Guilty silence reigned. "You're pathetic, every last one of you," she spat, trying to keep her voice level as tears threatened. "All I can hope is that one day, someone does something as awful to you as you've done to me, so you can see what it feels like. I don't know how you can live with yourselves."

She whirled back to Liam, her blood pounding so loudly in her ears she could barely hear herself think. "As for you, *Yank*, I hope you don't have the balls to call yourself a man, because that's the last thing you are. No real man would ever, *ever* do what you did to me. Rot in hell."

She stormed out of the pub, slamming the door behind her. Her body was taut as a bowstring, quivering with rage. She paused a moment to take a deep breath and collect herself before continuing on. After a few seconds, she realized she was stomping up the street like some kind of crazed soldier and deliberately tried to slow her pace, but it was no good. She was being propelled forward by an unstoppable wave of anger. She heard the pub door open behind her and curled her fists at her side. It had better not—

"Aislinn!"

She quickened her pace, her anger ratcheting up a notch. Did the eejit expect her to stop and turn around? Did he think she'd even want to *talk* to him?

"Aislinn!"

Liam raced to stand in front of her. Aislinn simply walked around him, looking through him as if he wasn't even there.

He tried to stand before her again. "Aislinn, please."

"Get out of my way before I shove you out of the way," she threatened through clenched teeth.

Liam fell into step beside her. "I wasn't lying when I said I loved you. I do. Yeah, things started out as a bet, but as soon as I started spending time with you, I knew you were the one for me."

Aislinn ignored him.

"Did you hear—"

"Piss off, Liam. Please."

"I wanted to call it off," he insisted.

Aislinn laughed bitterly. "Oh, God, would you listen to him, trying to backpedal?" She shot him a venomous, sideways glance. "Don't you understand? The fact that you even made such a wager in the first place tells me you're not fit to lick my boots."

"It was a mistake, Aislinn. A really, really stupid mistake."

"Did you think I'd never find out about it?" she railed. "Did you think, even if you eventually told me about it yourself, that I'd forgive you for making a fool of me in front of the whole town? How much of a pushover do you think I am?" She pushed a tangle of her hair off her face roughly. "I want to know how much I owe you for the trip to Dublin."

"Aislinn—"

"I don't want to be in debt to the likes of you for *any-thing*. Now leave me the hell alone. *I mean it*."

"I'll do anything you want if you just let me explain and give me another chance," Liam pleaded. "Anything."

"The only thing I want you to do is get out of my sight. D'you hear?"

"Aislinn, look at me. *Please*."

She stopped dead, glaring at him. "Are you thick? How many times do I have to tell you?" she shouted. "I want you to leave me alone! I never want to speak with you again! Got it?"

"Got it," Liam said quietly.

"Good. Now go back to your stupid, gutless friends and make fun of me, or pity me, or whatever it is you losers do for a laugh."

She left him standing there on the sidewalk, watching her walk away. She should have spit in his face; he deserved so much more than the slap she'd given him in the pub. She never thought she could hate anyone as much as she hated Liam O'Brien right now. *God, please, let him get the green light to go back home soon.* The idea of his being here for months, maybe even years, was torture.

She climbed up into the cab of her truck, gunned the engine, and headed for home.

*        *        *

*Liam wasn't sure* how long he stood out on the sidewalk in a daze, watching Aislinn storm away. He knew he deserved the slap and everything she'd said to him. He'd made a choice to make the bet. He'd made a choice not to call it off. He'd made a choice to believe he could have his cake and eat it, too, stupid enough to think she would never find out about the wager. She was right: who *was* he?

He wished to hell he didn't have to go back inside and face everyone in the pub. The Oak was still silent when he'd run out after her, the air thick with shame. Aislinn was right: they were all complicit. But the thought offered no comfort at all. How could it? He was the main culprit, the scum who had messed with her affections when she was the most vulnerable she'd ever been in her life, and for what? To prove he was better than the three jackasses who resented his presence in Ballycraig? To demonstrate how he'd always been able to charm the pants off any woman he'd ever wanted? What a fucking loser. Because of his ego, he'd lost the only woman he had ever loved.

He steeled himself and walked back into the pub. People were hunched over their drinks, looking remorseful, no one quite meeting his eye. He couldn't say he blamed them. He wouldn't want to look at himself, either, the despicable Yank who'd turned them all into objects of contempt.

Jack's eyes filled with pity as Liam slipped back behind the bar. "Well?" he asked tentatively.

"Well what?" Liam snapped. "She basically told me to go fuck myself."

"I suspected as much," said Jack. "Here." He poured Liam a whiskey and pushed it toward him. Liam threw the shot back, and Jack poured him another one.

"I shouldn't have called you a coward when you wanted to call off the bet," said Jack quietly. "I should have let it go."

"No one here is to blame but me," said Liam. "I *was* a coward: I should have had the guts to tell you I didn't care what you thought." He threw the second shot down his throat.

"I told you she'd nail your balls to the wall no matter what," Teague crowed triumphantly.

"Fuck you."

"Did you really think that once she found out, she'd be all right with it?" Teague sneered. "You're charming, but you're not that charming, Yank."

"Enough!" Jack yelled. "I'm in no mood for fisticuffs, you hear? Which is where this is headed if I'm not mistaken."

"I wonder how the hell she found out," said Liam. He eyed the Trinity contemptuously. "One of you assholes told her, didn't you?"

"I feckin' didn't!" David protested.

"Nor did I!" said Fergus.

Liam turned his gaze to Teague.

"Don't look at me, mate," Teague snorted. "I might be a wanker, but I'm not that big of a one."

"Maybe no one told her," Fergus offered. "Maybe she overheard someone talking about it. I don't think anyone in this town would be so cruel as to tell her."

"No, but we were all cruel enough to keep our mouths shut," Liam countered miserably. His fist crashed down on the bar. "Fuck!"

Old Jack patted his shoulder. "That's it, Liam. You get it out."

"What the hell am I going to do, Jack?" Liam asked plaintively. "She hates me. She'll never take me back."

"True," said Teague, looking pleased.

"I told you to shut your gob!" said Jack with a glare. He poured Liam another shot. Liam had every intention of getting shit faced: anything to numb the pain and self-loathing.

"Maybe after she cools down, she'll realize she loves you, too, and she'll forgive you," said Jack.

"Yeah, and maybe Santa Claus is real," Liam jeered. He downed his third shot. "Would you forgive me if you were her? I wouldn't."

"Now, now, our Lord forgave those who nailed him to the cross," Jack reflected. "I'm sure she could forgive you. You've just got to give her time to lick her wounds and all that."

"I'm a moron," Liam said to no one in particular.

"Would a song cheer you up?" Jack offered.

Liam gave him a withering glance. "No thank you."

"Just trying to help," Jack muttered.

"I know," Liam said miserably, pouring himself another shot. "I know Aislinn: she's not going to stop coming in here. She'll come in for her whiskey when she's in the mood, and she'll just sneer at me like the asshole I am. *Shit.*"

"Talk to Nora," Jack's wife, Bettina, suggested. She'd been stacking glasses behind the bar, listening in on the conversation. "She might put in a good word for you."

Liam rallied a bit. "That's not a bad idea. She seemed happy when Aislinn and I got together."

"There you go. I'm sure she'd be willing to plead your case when the McCaf—when Aislinn is ready to hear it." Bettina colored, turning away to fold napkins.

"I want you to keep paying me my regular wages," Liam told Jack. "Fuck winning the bet. I don't want the money now."

"I would," said Teague.

"That's because you're a jackass," said Fergus. He looked at Liam. "If there's anything I can do to help you win her back—*anything*—you let me know."

"Me, too," said David. "It's the least we can do."

Teague said nothing.

Liam thanked them, but he knew it was a lost cause.

## 20

*Aislinn drove home* from the pub slower than usual, trying to appreciate the beautiful stars standing out in the inky sky, but it didn't work. The whole world had been stripped of its beauty, thanks to that New York arsehole.

God, the gall of him, asking her for another chance, as if she'd ever trust the likes of him again! Who the hell did he think he was? As for her fellow Ballycraigers, well, this time she had every right in the world to rebuff them if they came round trying to make amends. In some ways, their being in on the bet hurt even more than Liam's duplicity. She'd known these people all her life, or thought she had. Now she felt herself surrounded by strangers.

The light in Padraig's cottage was still on. Aislinn resisted the urge to check on him. She was in no mood for idle chat; plus, she was afraid that when she told him about the bet, he'd get all worked up and threaten to go into town and blacken Liam's eye, as if he were still a twenty-year-old with a mean left hook. It had happened when Connor had betrayed her: Padraig (and her father, too, come to think of it) had gone mental, threatening to break his bones if he dared ever show his face in

Ballycraig again. She decided she'd let Padraig hear about what happened through the grapevine; she had enough on her plate right now without worrying about him fancying himself Barry McGuigan.

She'd forgotten to leave the light on in the mudroom, and so she entered a completely dark house, the perfect match for her mood. It felt as though the house's silence was mocking her. *Did you really think things would ever work out for you?* it jeered. *You're a loner, just like your da. Always have been, always will be. Just accept your damn fate and get on with it.*

"Cut the self-pity," she chided herself brusquely, slipping out of her boots and jacket. "It doesn't suit you."

She went upstairs, stopping off in the loo to brush her teeth and wash her face. She studied her face in the mirror, remembering Liam telling her she was beautiful. She couldn't bear it. He hadn't meant a word of it. Not a word.

She padded into her room, not wanting to wake Deenie, who was fast asleep on her bed. The steady rhythm of the old dog's breathing was a comfort. She slipped into the oversized T-shirt she'd bought years ago at the Galway Festival and climbed into bed. When Connor had wrecked her life, she'd thought she'd never recover from the pain. But the pain she was in now, all-encompassing and pressing down on her like a boulder, felt ten times worse. She turned on her side and curled up in a fetal position, drawing her covers tightly around her. When she was little, she sometimes used to think, *Nothing can upset me when I'm in the big bed, with its warmth and safety and promise of sleep.* She wished she could still believe that.

\* \* \*

*The next morning,* Nora called Aislinn to let her know she was coming back from London. Aislinn's heart sank, not only because she was worried Nora's presence would grate on her nerves, but also because she'd have to tell Nora about what Liam had done to her, and she hated the thought of her sister pitying her. She didn't want Nora's pity or anyone else's. She just wanted to get on with her life.

Nora arrived at around eleven p.m. Aislinn waited up for her, even though she was bone-tired after a day of work and deworming the sheep, one of her least favorite things to do. Padraig's strength came in handy: he was good at holding them down and tipping their heads back at just the right angle so the fluid she had to squirt down their throats didn't spill on the ground or worse, get into their lungs.

"Aislinn?" Nora called out from the kitchen. Aislinn switched off the TV in the sitting room and went to join her sister.

"Here I am." Aislinn gave her sister a kiss. "You're much later than I expected."

Nora looked rueful as she put down her bags. "I wanted to squeeze in as much time with Donald as I could, though he'll probably be coming over in a couple of weeks for a long weekend." *Jesus wept,* thought Aislinn. *Would you just admit you want to build a house here and get it over with?*

Aislinn just nodded. "How did your research go?"

"Well, I think. We'll see."

"You must be famished. There's some mashed potatoes and boiled ham in the fridge. I could zap it in the microwave if you'd like."

Nora yawned. "That would be lovely." She sat down wearily at the table, watching Aislinn as she moved from the fridge to the microwave. "What's wrong?"

"What are you talking about?" How on earth could her sister tell anything was wrong?

"You seem tense. Is it because I'm back?"

"Don't be daft."

"What, then?"

"I had a tough day, is all."

Nora scrutinized her face. "You're lying. You look awful. You've been crying."

It was true: she had been crying before Nora came in, which she *hated*. Tears made her feel weak.

"Just feeling blue," Aislinn replied, working to sound blasé. "PMS. You know how it goes."

Nora chuckled, shaking her head. "You've always been a terrible liar, Aislinn. Just like Dad. Everything shows on your face and in your body language. Did something happen between you and Liam?"

"We split up," Aislinn said bitterly.

Nora looked shocked. "Already? What happened?"

"What happened is he's a lying bastard of the first degree. You told me to let my guard down and let him in. Well, I did, didn't I? And guess what? He put the boot in. Humiliated me." She pressed the heels of her hands into her eye sockets, determined not to let loose the flood of tears threatening to have their way. "I don't want to talk about it."

"Aislinn." Nora's voice was gentle as she went to Aislinn's side. "Please tell me what happened. Maybe I can help."

"You? The prodigal sister, returned home and thinking we'll be close instantly? I don't think so."

Aislinn regretted the words the minute they slipped off her tongue. "I'm sorry," she said in a quavering voice, holding back a sob. "I'm not thinking straight. I just want to lash out, and you're the only one here. I'm sorry."

"Sshh, sshh." Nora gathered her up in arms. "It's all right. People say and do things when they're in a right state, which you are. Talk to me."

Aislinn burst into tears, holding Nora tight. "It's too awful. God, I hate him! I hate them all!"

She proceeded to tell Nora about the bet through hiccupping sobs. Just retelling it made her feel humiliated all over again. Nora rocked her, wiping her tears away. Finally, Aislinn broke contact.

"I'm pathetic," she said vehemently.

"You're not pathetic."

"Never again," Aislinn vowed, swiping her tears away.

"I mean it. Twice now I've fallen for liars; do you realize that? Twice now I've been kicked in the teeth and turned into someone to be pitied. Obviously the universe is trying to tell me something."

"And what would that be?" Nora asked gently.

"Maybe I'm one of those people not meant to be part of a pair. Some people aren't, Nora. Some are perfectly content being on their own, like Padraig. And me."

"I don't buy that for a minute."

"That's easy for you to say! You're happily married!"

"Look," Nora said carefully, taking her steaming dinner out of the microwave. "There's no denying that what Liam did to you was awful. But clearly he regrets it."

"Why are you defending him?" Aislinn cried.

"I'm not. All I'm saying is, people make mistakes, and sometimes, if you truly love someone, you forgive them."

"Again: easy for you to say."

"Actually, it's not," Nora murmured quietly. "Three years ago Donald had an affair with one of his coworkers."

Aislinn's jaw dropped. "And you forgave him? I would have kicked the bastard out on his arse!"

"Believe me, that was my first impulse. I was devastated. But he genuinely seemed to regret it. We went to couples counseling. It took us a long time to rebuild things, but we did, and I'm glad I didn't throw seven years of marriage away because he'd made one mistake, no matter how awful."

Aislinn was silent, trying to wrap her head around this. "And you trust him?" she asked incredulously. "Alone in London without you? *You trust him?*"

"I have to. Without trust, there's no point in having a relationship."

"Well, I bloody wouldn't trust him," Aislinn sputtered. "And I'll certainly never trust that Yank again."

"I wouldn't expect you to, feeling the way you do right now. The wound is too fresh. But—"

"Never," Aislinn hissed. "I wish to God I didn't have to set eyes on his lying face ever again."

"That shouldn't be hard to do."

"Yes, it will, because I'm not going out of my way to avoid him. He's the outsider in this town, not me. I will not change my routine for fear of running into him. Let him squirm like the worm he is when I go into the Royal Oak. Let them all squirm. I'll not let him drive me into hiding up here on the farm."

"You're right." Nora wrapped Aislinn in a hug. "I'm so sorry, love. But trust me: you *will* get over this, and eventually, you'll be ready to get back on the horse. Until then, there's no need for you to suffer alone. I'm here." She touched Aislinn's cheek. "I hate the thought of you growing old here alone. I truly do."

"Well, I don't," Aislinn said dismissively. "It suits me fine." She patted Nora's arm. "Now eat your dinner before it gets cold."

* * *

*As was his* usual routine, Liam went over to his aunt and uncle's house for Sunday breakfast the next morning, though God knows he wanted to bail. His hangover was so bad it felt like someone was shooting a nail gun into his skull. He downed two paracetamol and then plodded the half mile to their house, eyes barely open. Coffee. He needed a big mug of coffee filled with a small mountain of sugar.

As soon as he let himself in, he could tell his family already knew what happened. They were staring at him with worried expressions on their faces. He kissed his aunt, then gestured toward the kitchen. "Can I go grab some coffee?"

"I'll grab it," she said. "You go sit."

"Thanks. Five teaspoons of sugar."

"You got it."

Liam convened with his cousins and uncle at the dining room table. The sun was blazing through the windows, making the room supernaturally bright. Liam moaned. "Can I close the blinds?"

"Headache that bad, eh?" His uncle patted his shoulder sympathetically. "Course we can draw them. I've been there meself."

Liam slid into the chair next to his newly devout cousin, Brian. "Let me guess: what happened last night was all the talk after church and as soon as you got home, you told the family."

"Yep," said Brian, who was already helping himself to some sausages.

Liam got defensive. "And the whole town thinks I'm an asshole, right?"

"Actually, everyone is feeling guilty, especially since the Mc—Aislinn asked them how they'd feel if it was done to them."

"I told you it was a mean thing to do," said Erin disdainfully.

Aunt Bridget came out of the kitchen bearing not one but two mugs of coffee. "I thought you might need more than one," she said. She wrapped her arms around Liam's neck from behind, giving him a loving hug. "We're so sorry about what happened between you and the McCaf—Aislinn," she murmured sympathetically.

"Don't feel sorry for him!" said Erin. She looked at Liam with dismay. "I hate to say this, but I've no sympathy for you. I know you love her, but I'm glad she gave you a good telling off and dumped you. You deserve it."

"You think I don't know that?" Liam replied miserably.

Aunt Bridget looked sad. "I wonder if the poor girl will go all hard again."

"Wouldn't blame her if she did," said Erin, glaring at Liam.

Liam chugged down his first mug of coffee, avoiding his cousin's gaze. He knew it was psychological, but he felt marginally better. Coffee, the great American cure-all.

"She really walloped you badly, huh?" Uncle Paul asked.

"Put it this way: if words were punches, I'd be in intensive care right now."

Uncle Paul winced. "She doesn't hold back when she gets going, that one."

Brian looked at him curiously. "Does she love you?"

Liam snorted. "Not anymore, obviously."

Uncle Paul speared a piece of sausage, pointing at Liam with the fork. "Give her time to cool down," he advised. "Then go back to her on your knees and plead for another chance."

Erin frowned. "He's got to do more than that."

"What would I have to do?" Liam asked nervously.

"Woo her. Prove to her that you want her so badly you'll do whatever it takes."

"In other words, wear her down," Brian added unhelpfully. "If she loves you, she'll succumb eventually."

"How would you know?" Erin jeered. "You've only ever had two girlfriends in your life, the first when you were eleven."

"Shut up, Erin."

"I'm just saying. Don't go trying to give love advice when you don't know a damn thing."

Liam closed his eyes. The sharp tenor of their bickering felt like another nail being shot into his skull. He was beginning to wonder how he was going to make it through the day.

"Erin's right," mused Uncle Paul, proffering a plate of eggs to Liam, which made his stomach do nauseating flips. "Woo her relentlessly . . . yes. It could work."

Liam waved the plate away. "And if it doesn't?"

"Then you'll have learned a hard lesson," Aunt Bridget said with a sigh of resignation.

*Wear her down.* Liam mulled this over as he reached for his second sickeningly sweet cup of coffee. It had worked the first time, hadn't it? Perhaps coupling it with the right wooing and telling her he wasn't going to give up would, indeed, win her back? Yeah, right. If he even set foot on the farm, she'd probably blow his head off. What he needed were some allies.

He looked around the table at his extended family. "Maybe you could help me."

"How?" his aunt Bridget asked eagerly.

"Put in a good word for me if you see her. I don't know."

"Bit obvious, isn't it, your family singing your praises?" Erin pointed out.

Liam's shoulders sank defeatedly. "True."

"Do what I told you," she continued with irritation. "Woo her. Properly. Relentlessly."

"Hmm."

Liam didn't want to admit it, but part of his hesitation regarding this course of action was that he'd never had to woo anyone before. Egotistical as it sounded, until he met Aislinn, his good looks and ability to smooth talk had done all the work for him: all he had to do was express interest in a woman, and she was all over him.

"Maybe you should talk to her sister," said Uncle Paul.

"That's what Bettina said last night."

"What's the story with that Nora?" Aunt Bridget sniffed. "For ten years she could barely bring herself to come home, and now all of a sudden she's installed herself up at the farm like the Queen of bloody Sheba?"

"I think she really wants to reconnect with Aislinn," Liam explained. "She realized how important family is once their parents died."

"Never liked her," Aunt Bridget continued. "Highfalutin."

Liam sprang to Nora's defense. "She's really nice. And she loves Aislinn."

"If you say so," Aunt Bridget said dubiously.

"Get her on your side first," said Erin.

"But like I said, give the McCaf—Aislinn some time to cool down a bit," added Uncle Paul.

Liam took a long slug of coffee. "How long?"

"A few weeks?" said Uncle Paul, looking to Aunt Bridget for confirmation. "Isn't that how long it took you to stop being hotheaded when you gave me the heave-ho?"

Erin's eyes popped. "You two split up once?"

"About six months before we were married," said Uncle Paul. "She was mad I didn't want to wear a tux for our wedding."

"What the hell did you want to wear?" Brian asked.

"His lucky jacket," Aunt Bridget said contemptuously. "A right rag it was, frayed bare with holes. I would have looked like I was marrying a tramp. But no, he was insistent. So I told him to take a hike."

"I gave her a few weeks to cool off, and then I came round and told her I'd wear the bloody tux." He leaned in to Liam confidentially. "Pick and choose your battles, son. Some just aren't worth winning."

"Watch yourself," Aunt Bridget warned him. She turned to Liam, patting his hand. "If you love that girl, then do what you have to do."

# 21

*Three days after* the "revenge of the McCafferty," as everyone in town had taken to calling Liam and Aislinn's breakup at the Oak, Aislinn strolled into the pub. Shame flashed through Liam, discomfort following quickly on its heels as she calmly ordered her usual whiskey from Jack. Liam girded himself for her glare, but it never came. Instead, she looked through him like he wasn't even there, which was worse.

*He* might not have been surprised to see her, but everyone else clearly was. There was a split second of abrupt silence when she entered before people went back to their conversations, looking somewhat sheepish. No one approached her. There was a distinct aura of coolness around her, an unmistakable vibe that the last thing she wanted to do was talk to any of them.

Still, Old Jack did try. "Here you go, darlin'," he said, handing her drink.

"Thank you," Aislinn said politely.

Jack cleared his throat nervously. "How's Padraig doing?"

"Well."

"And Nora?"

"Also well."

"Tell her I asked after her."

"I will."

Jack nodded, out of words. Liam glanced at the Holy Trinity, wondering if they would try to make things as normal as possible by teasing her. But even they were quiet. Aislinn noticed.

"What's wrong, boys?"

"Nothing," Fergus mumbled, looking nervous.

"I'm not going to bite you," Aislinn said derisively.

Teague came to life. "Maybe not us," he said with relish, "but I wouldn't mind seeing you sink your teeth into the Yank and drawing some blood."

"He's not worth the effort."

*Could you please stop talking about me as if I'm not even here?* Liam thought, peeved. If he could, he'd take Teague outside after closing time and punch his lights out. The guy was a prick. He remembered his aunt's words to him a few months back: *Still quick to anger, I see. Your mother used to talk about it all the time. Got you into a world of trouble during your teen years, as I recall.* Well, he wasn't a teenager punching his way through life anymore. He'd keep his rage in check, even if it killed him.

*He's not worth the effort. Ouch.* Liam knew Aislinn wouldn't give him the time of the day, but he couldn't help himself: he had to say something. Maybe she didn't want to acknowledge his presence, but he needed to acknowledge hers.

"Hey," said Liam.

Aislinn turned to him slowly. Liam wanted to cringe when he saw the contempt in her eyes. "Did I or did I not tell you I never wanted to speak to you again?"

Liam caught Teague smirking into his beer and took a deep breath to stop himself from reaching across the bar and grabbing him by the throat. He hated this guy. *Hated him.*

"I thought we could at least be civil to each other," said Liam quietly.

"Civility isn't my strong suit," Aislinn shot back, "at least not with the likes of you. *Leave me alone.*"

Liam faked a diffident shrug and turned his back to the bar, pretending to busy himself with straightening the bottles of booze along the back wall. Wear her down? Woo her? The woman could barely stand the sight of him.

Even so, he knew he wouldn't be able to live with himself if he proved to be a coward of a different stripe, one who gave up the fight before he'd even begun. No one could turn their emotions on and off like a faucet; furious as she was at him, he knew that deep down, she still loved him. But whether he could get her to believe he truly loved her and was sorry for what he had done was another story.

* * *

*He waited until* Wednesday, when Aislinn was at the farmers' market in Omeath, to go talk to Nora. The flock was grazing in the field across the road from the house, all of them halting to stare him down as he walked up the hill. He knew it was crazy, but he swore they knew what had happened. That made it easy to avoid making direct eye contact with any of them. Aislinn told him they interpreted this as threatening, unless they knew you well. Liam had a sudden vision of the flock amassing themselves into a woolly army and leaping over the low stone wall to attack him as payback for what he'd done to their mistress. Death by sheep. Fitting.

Liam headed around the back of the house to go in through the mudroom, stopping short before he pulled the door open. He wasn't Aislinn's boyfriend anymore; he couldn't just stroll in as he pleased. He'd have to go around and knock on the front door as if he were any other visitor.

He felt slightly furtive as he walked back around and

rang the doorbell, sending Deenie into a paroxysm of barking on the other side of the door. He half hoped Nora wasn't home: odds were high she'd rip into him for what he'd done to her sister. He started preparing himself for the possibility she'd tell him to take a hike.

"Deenie! Quiet!"

Liam squared his shoulders as Nora opened the door. She looked surprised to see him, but not unpleasantly so. Deenie, recognizing him, calmed down immediately and began wagging her tail, lifting Liam's spirits just a tiny bit.

Liam leaned against the doorframe, shoving his hands in the back pocket of his jeans, feeling somewhat sheepish. "Hey."

"She's not here," Nora said coolly.

"Actually, I'm here to talk to you."

"Ah." Nora hesitated, and for a moment, Liam thought she was going to turn him away. But she opened the door wider. "Come in."

Liam followed Nora into the kitchen. "Coffee?" she offered. "I brought some good stuff over from London. Organic."

"No, thanks." He pulled out a kitchen chair. "Okay if I sit?"

"Of course."

He hadn't anticipated feeling this uncomfortable. Clearly the onus of conversation was on him, but he was pretty sure he'd look like a jerk if he started begging her for help right off the bat. He needed to ease into it.

"How was London?" he asked conversationally.

"Fine," said Nora. "I needed to do some research."

"What's the subject of your article again?"

"Economic development in South Africa."

"Wow, that's—"

"Boring?" Nora finished for him dryly. "I'm beginning to think so, too. In fact, I'm beginning to wonder what the hell I'm doing in academia at all." She sighed. "Still, I started it, so I'm going to finish it."

"The peace and quiet here must make it easy to write," Liam offered.

"It does. Plus I get to spend some time with Aislinn."

"Yeah, she had mentioned—"

"Mentioned what?" Nora cut in.

"You're big on interrupting, aren't you?"

"Sorry. You were saying?"

"Aislinn had mentioned you haven't been home much in the past few years," Liam proceeded carefully. "I think she's enjoying you being here."

"I wouldn't go that far," said Nora with a curt laugh. "Believe me, I know my sister."

Liam paused. "How's she doing?" he murmured.

"How do you think she's doing?" Nora shot back. "You've decimated her."

Liam fought a flinch. "You must hate me."

"Hate's a very strong word," said Nora. "Let's just say that if I could chop off your bollocks and put them in a meat grinder right now, I would."

"Right," Liam said grimly. Just thinking about it made his balls retract.

"You wanted to talk to me?" asked Nora, frowning as the ancient coffeemaker spluttered to life. "We need a new one," Liam heard her mutter under her breath.

Liam kneaded the back of his neck. He was going to speak plainly, though for a split second, he wished he possessed his brother's eloquence with words. "I know you're going to laugh your ass off when I tell you this, but I love your sister."

Nora looked dubious as she folded her arms across her chest. "Uh-huh."

"I know the bet was a shitty thing to do. I should have called it off the minute I started having feelings for your sister."

"But you didn't," Nora pointed out coldly.

"No, I didn't," Liam admitted, feeling ashamed.

"Why?"

"Because I'm a macho asshole, not to mention delusional. I actually thought I'd be able to have my cake and eat it, too: you know, win the bet and keep on seeing Aislinn. I figured once everyone saw how happy we were, who'd be mean enough to tell her about the bet?"

"This isn't New York. It would have gotten back to her eventually. There are no secrets in a village this small. None. So perhaps it's better she found out what a bastard you are when things were still in the early stages."

Liam swallowed. "Did she tell you she loved me?"

"Of course she did. And it was hard for her to admit it, too. You think she would open her heart to just anyone after what happened with Connor? She doesn't date casually. Never has."

"And up until I met her, that's all *I've* ever done."

Nora pursed her lips, looking him up and down critically.

"Mmm, you seem the type."

"Why's that?" Liam asked defensively.

"Handsome. Charming. You play the moody Byronic role quite well, from what I hear. "

Nora was right: there were no secrets in this place. He wondered if Aislinn had told her that, or if Jack had mentioned his occasional dark moods to someone in town. *Get a life, people,* he thought.

Liam heaved a sigh of impatience. "Fine: so we've established I'm an asshole."

"Understatement of the year."

"I love her," Liam declared. "And I want her back."

Nora cocked her head inquisitively. "May I ask you a question?"

"You can ask me almost anything."

"Why on earth should she give you the time of day?"

"Because she loves me," Liam shot back fiercely. "Because I'm the man she's meant to be with."

Nora grabbed a mug out of the cabinet, filling it with coffee. "My, we *are* sure of ourselves, aren't we?"

"When it comes to me and Aislinn being together, then yeah, I am. In fact, our being together is the only thing in my messed-up life I *am* sure of."

Nora took a sip of coffee. "Your intensity is impressive."

"I'm not trying to impress you. I'm just stating simple fact." Liam jiggled his left leg impatiently. "Look, I know I have no right to ask you this, and if you tell me to go to hell, I will totally understand. But I need your help trying to win your sister back."

"I'm not going to tell you to go to hell."

"Well, that's—"

"The truth is," Nora interrupted, "you made my sister happier than I've ever seen her."

Liam felt a twinge of hope. "Thank you for—"

"But don't expect her to forgive you right away," Nora cut in again. "She's going to need time. And if she does decide to forgive you, she's not going to make it easy for you."

"No kidding."

"You need to prove you're worthy of her."

"And how do I do that?"

*Please don't say "Woo her."*

"Woo her."

*Shit.*

"Show her you're not going to give up, no matter what."

Liam felt an uptick in confidence.

"Now." Nora splayed her hands on the table in front of her. "I'm willing to help you by pointing out to her that people do make mistakes. In fact, I've done that already."

"Really?" Liam was surprised.

"Yes. But she's so devastated right now she can't really hear me. I'll keep trying."

"I appreciate that. But I need more help than that. I need suggestions. She's not like other women. I don't think flowers and lingerie will do the trick."

"You're an idiot," Nora said without animus. "She *is* like other women. Of course she'd like flowers and lingerie, though God knows she'd never admit it. Be creative."

"Could you be more specific?"

"No."

"Right," Liam said despondently. Creativity was Quinn's strong suit, not his. Maybe he'd e-mail his brother and ask him for a few suggestions. Of course, that would entail telling Quinn about the bet. He could hear Quinn's voice yelling in his head: *What are you, a fucking idiot?* Answer: yes.

Liam stood. "I appreciate you taking the time to talk to me."

"I'm doing it for Aislinn, not you."

Liam nodded his understanding. "I can show myself out."

He was almost out the door when Nora called out to him, "Woo her creatively."

*I'm doomed*, thought Liam bleakly as he quietly closed the door behind him. The pressure was on.

# 22

*Aislinn was in* a foul mood as she and Padraig came inside for lunch. It was pissing down rain, turning the fields to mud and Padraig into a first-class grumbler.

It had been a month since she'd parted ways with Liam O'Brien. As she'd told her sister, she in no way altered her actions because of what had happened, though she noticed other people had. Every time she came into the Oak, Fergus and David were solicitous, chatting her up. Maybe they'd returned to the delusion that she might go out with one of them. Fat chance. She had no use for them and for men in general.

As for the Yank, he was giving her a wide berth, and she was glad of it. She hated the way the sight of him still made excitement flash through her body. It felt like a betrayal. She couldn't believe how exhausting trying to hate someone could be. Bastard. At least she'd stopped crying at the drop of a hat.

"I'm starved," Padraig declared, sitting down on the mudroom bench to pull off his boots.

"When aren't you?" Aislinn teased.

"A man my age needs sustenance."

"Beyond whiskey and cigarettes? Glad to hear it."

Padraig shot her a dirty look as he hung his raincoat on one of the pegs on the wall. "Don't get lippy with me, girl. I was there with your da when you learned to walk."

Aislinn laughed, hanging her coat beside his. Deenie sat by her side, dutifully lifting each of her front paws so Aislinn could wipe off the mud.

Padraig rubbed his hands together in anticipation. "Good grub today?"

"Nora made some potato leek soup last night."

Aislinn and Padraig walked into the kitchen, surprised to find Nora typing away on her laptop. She closed it, looking up at them. "I was getting bored writing in my room. Thought a change of place might do me good."

Padraig heaved himself into a chair. "Your soup smells good," he told Nora begrudgingly.

"Thank you."

"It does," Aislinn agreed. She fetched three bowls and filled them, then cut up the loaf of brown bread she'd bought in town the day before, putting it in a basket before bringing it all to the table. Padraig was big on dipping bread into his soup.

Nora asked them how their morning had been. Aislinn knew she didn't really care, but she appreciated the attempt, anyway. Aislinn returned the gesture, asking after Nora's article. Padraig commented that the article sounded like a "load of buggery bollocks," thus erasing the seeming détente of a few minutes before. Aislinn hated the tension between them. She wasn't surprised when Padraig legged it back outside as soon as he could.

Nora came up behind her as she washed the dishes when they were done eating. "There's a package for you in the sitting room. It came in the post this morning."

Aislinn was puzzled. "A package?"

"Yes. I had to sign for it. Whoever sent it wanted to make sure you got it."

"Hmm."

Aislinn finished washing up, then went to the sitting

room to check out the mysterious package sitting on the coffee table. It was wrapped in plain brown paper, post-marked Ballycraig.

She sat down on the couch, opening it slowly. Inside was a bottle of perfume called Love by someone named Nina Ricci. There was a small card attached that read, "Subtle, Sexy, and Classic—just like you. Please give me another chance. Liam."

Aislinn stared at the bottle. Did the twit not know her at all? She'd never worn perfume in her life! Still . . . she discreetly spritzed some on her wrist. It was nice. But still, not her cup of tea. Not one bit.

Nora popped her head in. "What did you get?"

"You'll never believe it when I tell you," said Aislinn, putting the perfume back in the box.

"What?"

"Perfume from Liam, with a little note attached telling me he wants me back. I'm tempted to send one back saying, 'How does it feel to want?'" She shook her head in disbelief. "He's unbelievable."

"He's romancing you," Nora said softly. "Trying to win you back."

"He can romance me till the cows come home. I'll have none of it."

Nora came closer and sniffed the air. "Tried some, I see. Isn't that Love? It's a lovely scent, and he's trying to send you a message."

"Well, I've got a message for him: go to bloody hell."

*　*　*

*What a stupid* fucking idea it was to buy Aislinn perfume. That was the first thing Liam thought when she walked into the pub that night, heading straight for him with a stony expression on her face.

"We need to talk," she said curtly.

"Let me get you your whiskey first."

"Suit yourself."

Liam poured her whiskey, feeling the Trinity's eyes

on him all the while. He didn't need to look at Teague to know the bastard was smirking, while his new allies Fergus and David were trying to not betray their concern. They said "Hello," to Aislinn, who politely returned their greetings. Liam poured himself a double before handing Aislinn her drink.

She was scowling at him, not blinking once as she downed her shot. For the first time, Liam understood how she earned her nickname. She was formidable, downright intimidating. *Don't be a pussy,* he chided himself. *You of all people know it's a defense against pain.*

He gestured at her glass. "Another?"

"I don't think you'd like that very much."

"Why's that?"

"Another might loosen my tongue, and I'll say all the nasty things about you swirling in my head."

Teague laughed darkly. "Do it, McCafferty. We haven't had a good laugh in here for a while."

"You want a laugh, Teague Daly? Go look in the mirror."

Teague tried to laugh off the put-down. "She's back, all right, and in top form, too."

"Go chase yourself," said Aislinn with a glare.

"He can't," Fergus wisecracked. "Moves too slow. He'd catch himself."

Everyone at the bar laughed.

"Go feck yourselves, the lot of you," snapped Teague, turning his eyes to the sports pages of the *Irish Times* lying open in front of him.

Aislinn's eyes zeroed back in on Liam's face. He threw *his* shot of whiskey down, then poured himself another. "What's up?" he asked, trying to ignore his heartbeat picking up speed in his chest.

"I got your gift," she told him coldly.

"Did you like it?" he asked stupidly.

"You shouldn't have wasted your money. For one thing, I don't wear the stuff, but then again, you'd know that, wouldn't you, if you'd ever truly given a toss about me. For another, you're soft in the head if you think I'd ever forgive you."

"Then why aren't you returning it to me?" Liam challenged.

"I gave it to Nora."

"Liar."

*"Pardon?"*

"You're lying. You kept it because you care."

*"How dare you?"*

Liam loved that he was getting to her. The vehemence of her reaction said more than words ever could. She cared, all right.

"Give it back to me, then. I kept the receipt. Just in case."

"I just told you: I gave it to Nora."

"I'm sure she'd understand."

"You want it back?" Aislinn asked contemptuously. "Ask her for it yourself."

"I will."

"Next time she comes in *here*. I don't want you anywhere near my house."

"The road passing your house is public. If I want to take a walk, and it happens to take me past the farm, there's not much you can do about it."

"Except pity you for the pathetic creature you are." She reached into the front pocket of her jeans, putting money down on the counter. "For the whiskey. I'd tip you, but I'm a bit low on cash. Sorry."

"I wouldn't fret over it," said Teague, still looking down at the paper. "He's rich now with them double wages of his."

*Moron.*

"That's all I have to say to you," Aislinn concluded, buttoning up her barn jacket and heading for the door.

Liam watched her go, smiling to himself. It was going to be a struggle, and she'd make him pay a steep price, but in the end, he knew he'd win her back.

* * *

*"Well, you played* that cool," said Jack, impressed, "which is amazing, considering the stupid gift you gave her."

"Perfume isn't stupid. Everyone's been telling me to woo her. So I'm wooing."

"That's how you woo a girly girl," said Jack. "The McCa—Aislinn is most certainly not one of those."

"Look, I've seen a side of her none of you have, all right? And believe me, there's a part of her that is totally girly girl."

He made a point of smiling boastfully at Teague, whose fat, waxy face was contorting with envy. He was exaggerating, of course. There was a feminine side to Aislinn, but characterizing it as *girly girl* was definitely pushing the edge of the envelope.

He'd known she'd probably scoff at the perfume, but he was trying to be creative, the way Nora had advised. Four days ago, he'd dragged his cousin Erin into Crosshaven to act as his guinea pig. It had been she who'd selected the perfume, declaring it "Subtle, sexy, yet classic," whatever the hell that meant. But it sounded good to him—so good he decided to steal the phrase and write it on the card inside the package. Aislinn probably laughed her head off when she read it, but that was okay. He was hoping that by showing her he was willing to make a total jackass of himself, if would soften her feelings toward him.

"She didn't give the perfume to Nora," Liam said confidently.

"How do you know?" David asked.

"If you were Nora, would you take a gift meant for your sister? Of course you wouldn't. You'd tell her to return it. I think Aislinn kept it for herself. If she really didn't want it, she'd have brought it here and thrown it in my face."

"You're probably right," Jack concurred.

"Still, I don't think you're her favorite person quite yet," David put in uneasily.

"The fearsome glare is back," said Fergus with a shudder.

"It's all bluster," said Liam.

"I don't care what you call it," Fergus returned. "It's effin' scary."

Aislinn scary—the idea amused Liam immensely. She was a lot of things, but scary wasn't one of them.

"What have you got up your sleeve next?" Jack asked.

"I'm just going to keep bombarding her until she gives in."

"You should try singing under her window," David advised. "That's considered romantic."

"I'll keep that in mind," Liam said dryly.

*    *    *

*"I've got to* tell you something."

Jack sounded grave as he locked up the Oak and sat down on the barstool beside Liam, rolling a pint between his hands. Bettina was there, too, rearranging glasses beneath the counter and lining up the bottles of booze. She looked uneasy.

"What's up?" Liam asked, wiping a small bead of sweat from his forehead. Spring had arrived, and when the pub was packed, all those bodies generated a helluva lot of heat, and Jack had no air-conditioning. He'd have to shower before he went to bed. It would help relax him.

"There was a guy came in here today, asking questions about you."

"Oh yeah?"

"Yeah." Jack looked grim. "Wanted to know if there was an American working here, how long you'd been here, where you lived."

Liam's mouth went dry. "And what did you tell him?"

"I lied to him, of course. Told him I had no idea what he was on about."

"Good."

"He looked very unsavory. Big scar across his right cheek."

"Bear of a man," Bettina added.

"Shit."

Jack looked disturbed. "I think the Mob might have tracked you down, son."

Liam head's began to swim. The Major had told him to leave New York for his own safety, but the bottom line was, whether Whitey was rotting in jail in the States or not, that didn't mean his reach didn't extend beyond New York. It didn't make sense, though. Liam's transgression had been relatively minor in terms of screwing Whitey over. But Liam knew that tracking him and doing Christ knows what to him would enable them to finally exact revenge on Quinn. *Shit*.

Liam began to brood. "I don't think there's much I can do about it, apart from leave town."

"We could hide you," Bettina suggested.

*"What?"*

"Clearly he doesn't know what you look like," Bettina reasoned.

"So?"

"Well, if he comes sniffing around here again when you're here, we can just hustle you out to the back or send you up to your flat till he leaves."

"Good idea," said Jack.

"But what if he's asking about me around town?"

"This is a small village, and we don't like outsiders threatening one of us. You may be a Yank, but you're our Yank. Besides, everyone loves your mam and da."

"Maybe I should go to Dublin," Liam thought aloud. "Lay low for awhile."

"It's easier to hide where you've got people to hide you than where no one knows you."

Jack patted his shoulder reassuringly. "It'll be fine. We've all got your back. You just concentrate on wooing Aislinn."

## 23

*"Hello, Aislinn."*

Aislinn smiled at Alec Fry as he paused by her stall at the farmers' market. It was a gorgeous morning, one that made her wish she didn't have to work seven days a week. She'd give anything for long, leisurely bike ride in the country, followed by a lovely lie-down on a blanket, where she could bask in the sun.

"How are you today, Alec?"

"Well. Yourself?"

"Very well."

"Hello, Padraig," Alec said with a sly wink at Aislinn.

Padraig nodded curtly. "Alec." He stood, making a point of turning his back to him as he addressed Aislinn. "I need to stretch my legs a bit."

"Go on. Bring me a scone or something on your way back."

Padraig nodded, throwing Alec a dirty look as he walked away.

"Well, he showed me." Alec chuckled.

"Ah, you know how he is. He's convinced you're after his job."

"I am."

Aislinn gawped at him. "What?"

"Here's the thing: I need part-time work. Our farm is not near as big as yours, and as you know, there are five of us working it. We're falling over each other. There's not enough for me to do, and it's driving me mad. So I thought maybe you could take me on part-time. You and I both know that Padraig is slowing down a bit, and he's not as—"

"I know," Aislinn cut in. She took a deep breath, exhaling heavily. "I'm sorry. It's just hard for me to talk about Padraig sometimes." She drummed her fingers restlessly on the table in front of her. "You've put me on the spot here, Alec."

"I know," he replied, looking apologetic. "I should have rung you."

"I'm not a great one for the phone," Aislinn confessed.

Alec looked amused. "Yeah, I noticed that when you rang from Dub to check in: on and off as fast as you could."

*That was because I couldn't wait to get back to Liam,* thought Aislinn, feeling a painful twist in her chest. Some days, it felt like all that happened a million years ago; on other days, it was as if it had happened just yesterday. Either way, every little detail remained vivid in her mind . . . and excruciatingly painful.

Aislinn forced a smile. "Guilty as charged." She took another sip of coffee. "Let me think about this a bit, will you?"

"Of course."

"Thanks."

Alec turned to go, then pivoted back to her. "Maybe we could grab a bite sometime, talk about farming and other things?"

"That sounds grand," Aislinn lied, as she tried to cover her shock. Alec Fry, asking her out? Why now? Suspicion flashed in her mind: *He wants to woo me and marry me, and then my farm will be his.* Christ, she was getting as paranoid as Padraig. Still, it was odd. They'd known each other for donkey's years, and he'd never so much as asked her for the time of day. Then again, maybe he just wanted to be friends. She'd think about it. But not right now.

*  *  *

*Aislinn woke the* next morning in a decent mood, attributing it to her success the day before at the farmers' market. Though she had arrived home exhausted, she'd sold every fleece, making a tidy sum. If things kept on this way, she'd definitely attend the next livestock auction in Omeath and buy two or three new ewes with an eye toward breeding them.

Dawn was just beginning to break when she joined Padraig in the smaller of the outbuildings beside the barn, the sky a lovely muted pink above the horizon. Spring was her favorite time of the year. But this year, like last, the pleasure she took in the turning of the seasons was gone, stolen by heartbreak and betrayal. She wondered if she'd ever enjoy anything again. She heard her mother's voice in her head: *Time heals all wounds. My arse,* Aislinn thought.

"Morning," she said to Padraig, handing him his thermos.

Padraig was silent, his expression sour.

"What's the matter?" Aislinn asked, stifling a yawn. No matter what her mood, it was still hard sometimes to drag herself out of bed at this hour. "Didn't you sleep well?"

Padraig glared at her. "Oh, I slept well enough, my girl. But I don't know if that will be the case from now on."

Aislinn sighed. "Look, I'm in no mood for guessing games at this hour. Tell me what's giving you such a nervo."

Padraig marched over to one of the workbenches and with a dramatic flourish picked up a brand-new, state-of-the-art variable-speed clipper for shearing sheep. "Think I can't do my job anymore, eh?" he accused, walking back to shake the clipper in Aislinn's face. "Think I need one of these fancy clippers or else I'll bollix things up?"

"Calm down." Aislinn grabbed the clipper from him, turning it over in her hands. "Where did you get this?"

Padraig narrowed his eyes accusingly. "You know where."

"No, I don't know where," Aislinn answered through gritted teeth. "Show me."

Padraig pointed at a plain cardboard box atop the battered old worktable in the corner. Aislinn went to inspect the box, rooting around inside. That's when she came upon a small white envelope that Padraig had missed. She was tempted to just leave it there, but curiosity got the better of her. She pulled it out.

"What's that?" Padraig asked.

"It's for me."

She opened it. Inside was a card Liam had obviously made himself on his computer, featuring the picture of the two of them in the Christ Church Cathedral garden in Dublin, the picture they'd politely asked a man to take of them with Liam's camera. Inside was written, "Look how happy we were. I love you. Please forgive me. Liam."

Aislinn stared at the picture as a lump formed in her throat. They *were* happy that day; anyone looking at the picture could see how mad they were about each other. Or rather, how mad she was about him and how good an actor he was. She made herself stop looking at it and put the shears—which had to cost at least two hundred euros—back in the box. She noticed it hadn't been sent through the post. Liam must have come up here to the house and left it.

Oh, she'd kill Nora for this, truly she would. Letting him come onto the property when she'd explicitly told him she didn't want him here. She tucked the card into the pocket of her jacket.

"Well? What's the big mystery?" Padraig wanted to know.

"The clippers were a present for me."

"A present? From who?" He narrowed his eyes suspiciously. "One of those Fry lads, isn't it? Trying to butter you up, get you to fire me."

"Everything's not always about you, you know!" Aislinn snapped. "As it so happens, they're a gift from Liam."

Padraig looked befuddled. "Liam?"

"Yes, Liam."

"Whatever for?"

Aislinn hesitated. "It's his way of, you know, trying to win me back."

Padraig hooted with laugher. "Oh, he's a real romantic, that one." His expression darkened. "I hope you're not going to take him back. Not after the treacherous thing he did. Worse than Connor if you—"

"Leave it out, will you, please?" Aislinn snapped.

"Sorry." Padraig eyed the box. "Well, now that we've got them, I guess we might as well use them," he murmured.

"In your dreams."

"You can't let a gorgeous piece of equipment like that go to waste!"

"I thought they were too fancy for your taste."

"I'd be willing to try them out," Padraig replied nonchalantly. "On a trial basis, of course."

Aislinn shook her head, more with affection than disbelief. "You're some piece of work, you know that? Fine, we'll keep them. Now, let's get to work."

Clippers. What was next? A bloody vacuum cleaner? Well, it didn't matter; it wasn't going to work. She was going to go into town later to tell Liam that if he trespassed again, she'd call the garda. But first, she was going to give her sister a piece of her mind at lunch for letting him set foot on the property in the first place.

* * *

*Aislinn waited until* Padraig had finished his lunch and was back outside before bringing up the subject of Liam to Nora.

"So," Aislinn began casually, carrying the lunch plates over to the sink, "let's talk about Liam."

Nora's eyes sparked with hope. "What about him?"

"What do you mean, 'What about him?' You know what."

Nora's face was a blank. "Aislinn, I have no idea what you're taking about."

Aislinn frowned. "You let him come up here and leave a present for me in the small outbuilding! Why didn't you tell him to take his bloody box and just piss off?"

"I had no idea he came up here!"

Aislinn could tell Nora wasn't lying.

"He's not going to give up, Aislinn."

"More fool him," said Aislinn, sudsing the plates.

"What did he give you this time?" Nora asked curiously.

"Clippers."

There was a stunned silence. "Clippers?"

"To trim the flock."

More silence. "Actually, I think that's kind of cute," Nora said eventually.

Aislinn turned away from the sink to face her. *"What?"*

"You can't accuse him of not knowing who you are," Nora pointed out.

"He made the safe choice," Aislinn countered dismissively.

Nora looked highly amused. "You do realize that you wouldn't be getting all worked up about this if you didn't care about him, right?"

Aislinn turned back to the sink. All morning long, a storm had been brewing inside her. Should she give Liam a second chance? Or would she be an idiot to open herself up again to someone who had no compunction about playing such a cruel trick on another human being, not to mention someone who might hightail it back to the States at the drop of a hat? She was so inside her own head that Padraig had to remind *her* when to give Deenie the proper command to drive the sheep down a steep bank to an ungrazed pasture.

"He's wasting his time," Aislinn muttered.

"Suit yourself. What are you going to do with the clippers?"

"Padraig wants them, even though I do most of the shearing."

"The way dad always did," Nora said quietly.

"Yes."

"I miss them."

Aislinn stilled. "So do I."

"Listen, I wanted to talk to you about something," Nora said carefully.

"What's that?"

"I spent the morning going through Mum and Da's things."

Aislinn slowly put down the sponge in her hand and turned back around to face her sister. "You did *what?*"

"It's time, Aislinn. I know you: you'd never get around to."

"You had no right, Nora. *You* should have told me, and we could have done it together."

Nora ignored her. "I've put together some bags for the Salvation Army."

"Then un-put them together. If you're after giving Dad's clothes away, I want Padraig to have first crack at them."

"Oh. I didn't even think of that."

"Of course you didn't."

Nora glowered at her. "I was trying to *help*."

"You want to help? Leave things as they are. This is my home, Nora. *Mine*."

"It's half mine," said Nora, staring Aislinn down.

"You know what? You're right. So from now on, how about we split the monthly expenses round here right down the middle. Sound fair?"

Nora's mouth twitched.

"And maybe I can teach you about the flock as well. I mean, they're half yours, too, right?"

Nora frowned. "I'm working on my article, Aislinn. And I have no interest."

"But the flock is where the money comes from to pay the household expenses, Nora," Aislinn replied sweetly. "It's only right that you know how to run the house, too."

"Point taken," Nora mumbled.

"Good." Aislinn took a step toward her sister. "Because if you say one more time that this farm is half yours after not giving a tinker's damn about it for ten years, then I will send you packing back to London so fast you won't know what hit you, so help me God I will."

Nora opened her mouth to say something, then clearly thought better of it. "Fine," she said in a clipped voice.

"Glad we agree. I meant what I said about Padraig having first crack at Dad's clothes. And if you put Dad's wellies in one of the bags, then take them out and return them to the mudroom, please," Aislinn said coldly. "They might not mean anything to you, but they have great sentimental value to me."

"I'd like his walking stick, if you don't mind. For Donald."

"I gave it to Padraig when Da died."

Nora frowned. "I thought you might have."

"Why would Donald want a walking stick, anyway?"

"For when we take walks here," Nora said defensively. "I told you: he enjoys it."

"Oh. Right. His sudden interest in walking the property. Well, it's Padraig's now, so I suppose you'll have to find something else of Dad's to give to him."

Aislinn bit down on her tongue to keep herself from

yelling, *Do you think I'm blind? Or stupid? Or both? Do you think I haven't figured out yet what you're planning? God, the gall of it.* Every time she began to feel close to Nora, Nora would up and do something that would remind Aislinn of how self-absorbed and insensitive she could sometimes be. Was it possible to love and hate someone at the same time? Because that's what she was beginning to feel toward her sister.

"I best get back to work," Aislinn announced briskly.

"Me, too," said Nora, who couldn't quite look at her. "Need anything in town?"

"No, I'm fine."

"See you later, then."

She pulled on her boots, grabbed her barn jacket, and headed out the mudroom door. Between Padraig, Nora, and Liam, she'd be lucky if her sanity remained intact. *Thank God for Deenie,* she thought. *Deenie and work.* At least those two things were constant.

Clippers. She shook her head, and headed out for the north meadow.

# 24

*Christ, I hate this place*, Liam thought to himself as he walked up Ballycraig's high street to the market. He was in a dark mood. Everything sucked, and anyone who tried to suggest otherwise was a moron. If he were back in New York, he could try to lose himself by hitting an afternoon matinee; but there was no movie theater in Ballycraig. He supposed he could browse the 'net, but he'd go nuts if he was cooped up inside.

A light rain was falling. It was always goddamn raining here. He could take the bus into Moneygall. But what the hell would he do in Moneygall? Hit the mega market? No thanks.

He entered Finnegan's, pulling his crumpled shopping list from the back pocket of his jeans. Beth Daly was there, sitting on a stool behind the counter with Grace, but Bettina, the third musketeer, was nowhere in sight. As soon as they spotted him, they motioned him over, their eyes sharp with worry.

"What's up?"

"There was a fella in here about an hour ago asking after you," Grace said in a voice a little above a whisper, even though there was no one in the shop but the three of them.

Liam tensed. "Asking what?"

"Did we know someone named Liam O'Brien, and if so, where did he work and live, and how long has he been here."

*Fuck.* "What did you tell him?"

"Not a thing," said Beth proudly. "We all know you're on the lam."

"He must be after you," Grace said, sounding slightly excited. "Tracked you down."

*This is my life,* Liam wanted to tell her, *not some goddamn thriller.*

"What did he look like?"

Grace scrunched up her nose. "I can't really recall. I was too nervous."

"Was he big? With a scar across his cheek?"

"Yes," said Beth.

"No," said Grace, looking at her friend disdainfully. "The one thing I'm quite sure of was that he didn't have a scar."

"Maybe it was the way the sun was shining in on his face," Beth mumbled.

Liam pinched the bridge of his nose. Did the guy have a scar or not? Was he a bear of a man like Bettina said or not? Why couldn't you ever get a simple, straightforward answer from anyone in this goddamn town?

*Calm down,* he told himself. *You're just flipping out because Whitey has found you, though how is a mystery.* He had to call Quinn and ask if he'd heard anything, and have Quinn talk to the Major. He'd been under the impression he'd be safe as long he stayed here. Obviously he was wrong.

"Don't worry about it," he told the two older women.

They looked at him dubiously, then went back to gossiping.

Liam strolled the narrow aisles, throwing items into

his basket: fruit, a few frozen dinners, coffee, brown bread, butter.

"Look, if this guy comes snooping around again, make sure you tell me," Liam told Grace and Beth when he paid for his groceries.

"Of course we will," said Grace, as if it were self-evident. "No one here would ever let anything happen to you."

"Thank you," said Liam, kissing her powdery cheek. Beth looked put out, so he kissed hers, too. Grace's words helped buoy his mood a bit.

That is, until he walked out into the street and saw Aislinn walking toward him.

He watched her for a moment, her braid flying behind her, her stride purposeful. She seemed lost in thought until she spotted him; then a thundercloud overtook her beautiful face.

"Just the man I wanted to see," she said in a voice tinged with sarcasm.

"Of course I am," said Liam with a charming smile. "What woman doesn't want to see the man she loves?"

"Feeling a bit delusional today, are we?" Aislinn replied tartly. "Listen: I need to get a few things in Finnegan's, and then you and I are going to have a little chat. Don't you move."

"Come to my flat when you're done. I'm not going to stand out here on the rainy sidewalk like your obedient little puppy dog."

"Well, well." Aislinn looked somewhat impressed. "Look who's bossy now."

"Fight fire with fire is what I always say."

"Is it now? I could have sworn your motto was, 'I don't care who I hurt.'"

Liam ignored the dig, knowing that not responding would drive her nuts. "See you in a few," he said, walking away.

Their exchange left him feeling somewhat exhilarated.

They'd started their "relationship" sparring verbally; he took it as a good sign they were sparring again. Of course, it was entirely possible he was pathetically grasping at straws. But he'd take what he could get.

*   *   *

*Liam tossed his* groceries in his small fridge and tidied up his flat a bit. He half expected Aislinn to change her mind and not show up, just to show him who was boss. But no; five minutes after they'd talked on the sidewalk, she was knocking on his door.

"Come in."

Aislinn breezed past him, putting her bag of groceries down on the small kitchen table.

"Coffee?" he offered.

Aislinn frowned. "Of course not. I'll be gone before you even have a chance to put the water up."

Liam just chuckled, which seemed to irk her.

"What's so damn funny, O'Brien?"

"Nothing," Liam replied innocently.

"Out with it!"

"You're so transparent. I know you still love me."

Aislinn's face twisted in indignation, but before she could say anything, Liam impulsively grabbed her up in his arms, kissing her. She struggled, but there was no denying the heat between them. He could tell she liked it even as she shoved him away.

"How dare you?" she sputtered.

"You loved it."

"You're losing your mind!"

"Am I?"

"Listen, you." She came so close they were practically nose to nose. "Don't you ever set foot on my land again, do you hear me?"

Liam just smiled.

*"Do you hear me?"*

Liam took a step back. "Did you like the shears?"

"Yeah, they made me want to fly back into your arms and forgive you," she replied sarcastically.

Liam was undeterred. "You can't claim I don't know you."

The comment seemed to have a strange effect on her. She made a frustrated, strangulated noise that was accompanied by a look of sheer murderousness.

"Nora enjoying the perfume?" he asked casually. God, this was fun.

"Loves it," Aislinn retorted.

"Glad to hear it." Liam lifted his eyebrows questioningly. "Ready to forgive me yet?"

"Are you thick as a bag of hammers or what? That's never going to happen."

"Yes, it will," Liam said confidently.

Aislinn clutched her head. "You are the most maddening man on earth."

"And you're the most maddening woman on earth, which is why we belong together." He folded his arms across his chest, amused. "You do realize I'm not going to give up, right?"

"Do what you please. It's of no difference to me."

"You were raised Christian. Don't you believe in forgiveness?"

"If Jesus had had to deal with the likes of you, he would have changed his tune, believe me."

Liam took a step toward her. "God, I miss your sense of humor."

Aislinn held up a hand of warning. "One step closer, and you'll feel it in your goolies, so help me God you will."

"You're all talk."

"And you're thick as a plank. Stop the gifts. Now. You're wasting your time. And mine."

"Where are the clippers?"

"Padraig is using them."

"Convenient, the excuses you have for hanging on to my gifts," Liam noted.

Aislinn stamped her foot. "God in heaven, you are *maddening*! You want your stupid gifts back? Right! I'll bring them down to the pub on Friday night! How's that?"

"Keep them, so you're reminded of how much I love you and how I'll do anything I have to, to get you back."

Aislinn picked up her groceries. "Remember what I said: if you set foot on my property again, you'll feel my wrath. If I have to, I'm even willing to resort to unloading some buckshot into your backside."

"A sheep farmer with firearms," Liam murmured, hooding his eyes. "Sexy."

Aislinn ignored him and walked out the door. She was weakening. He could tell. He was going to keep being tenacious, never giving up until he got what he wanted.

That is, if he wasn't killed by Whitey first.

## 25

*Liam was shocked* when, two nights later, Nora walked into the Royal Oak. As far as he knew, the only transportation up at the farm was Aislinn's truck. She had to be delirious if she let Nora take it into town.

"Hello, Nora dear," said Old Jack, ever bright as a publican should be. "What can I do you for?"

"Hmm. Got Pimms and lemonade?"

"We do," said Jack, going to make it.

"Hello, Nora," said David. "What brings you into town solo?"

"A Mercedes, probably," Fergus cracked.

Nora ignored him. "I needed to get out of the house."

"The McCafferty driving you mad?" Teague asked.

"Excuse me, what?" Nora asked uncomprehendingly.

"The McCaf—never mind," Teague covered hastily.

Nora looked angry. "I better not ever hear you call her that again. Got it?"

"Right, right," Teague grumbled. "No need to bite my head off like a bloody praying mantis."

David looked at him with pity. "Ever notice you're always putting your foot in it with the ladies?"

"That's about all he'll ever put in the ladies, I'm thinkin'," cracked Fergus.

Everyone at the bar laughed loudly, especially Liam.

"You know," said Teague, glaring at David and Fergus as he gave Liam the two-fingered salute, "for two people who are supposed to be my mates, you treat me like shite."

David clapped him on the back affectionately. "Lighten up. It's all in good fun."

Teague muttered something into his drink, while David turned his attention back Nora. "So what brings you into town?"

"I told you: I needed to get out of the house. I've been cooped up for hours in front of a computer, and I need a break."

"I can't believe she let you take the truck," Liam marveled.

"I know. She must really want me out of her hair. That truck is on its last legs, if you ask me. She needs to buy a new one."

"Well, you're rich, aren't you?" said Teague snidely. "Why don't you buy a new one for her?"

Nora ignored him as Jack handed her her drink. "One Pimm's and lemonade for the lovely Nora O'Brien."

"Thank you." She put her money down on the bar. "Can I borrow Liam for a minute, Jack?"

"Sure, but just for a minute. It'll be getting busy soon."

Puzzled, Liam went to stand with Nora at the counter lining the opposite wall, resting his foot on the brass railing.

"What's up?"

"Two things," said Nora, taking a sip of her drink. "Not bad. It's better with fizzy lemonade, though."

"Then you should have asked for fizzy lemonade."

"I just assumed—"

"We're bartenders," said Liam wearily, "not mind readers."

Liam could see why she sometimes got on Aislinn's

nerves. One minute she was down-to-earth, the next judgmental and imperious.

"What do you want to talk about, Nora?"

"Your stupidity."

"That could take hours."

"What the hell were you thinking, coming up to the farm when she told you not to? She thought I gave you permission! I got quite the tongue-lashing!"

Liam winced. "Sorry. I just figured that if I sent something through the mail again, she might send it back unopened." He paused. "Can I ask you a question?"

"Certainly."

"Did she give you the perfume I bought for her?"

Nora stared at him like he was nuts. "Of course she didn't."

Liam slapped the edge of the counter, smiling triumphantly. "I knew it!"

Nora looked astonished. "What, she told you that?"

"Yup."

"I guess I shouldn't be surprised. She'd never let on that she kept it—or liked it. She sprayed some on her wrists, you know. I could smell it when I went into the sitting room to see what she'd gotten. I've no doubt she's put it away in her dresser somewhere. But what were you *thinking*, giving her a pair of shears?"

"You told me to be creative!"

"There's creative, and then there's stupid. That was stupid!"

"But I thought it would show that I knew who she was. That I *cared* who she was." He leaned closer to her. "She kept the clippers, too, by the way," he confided happily.

"I know that. She gave them to Padraig."

"So she says."

"In this case, I believe it."

Liam was mildly crestfallen. "The point is, she's keeping my gifts. That's got to be a good sign, right?"

"Might be. I don't know."

Liam glanced behind him. The bar was indeed beginning to fill up; Jack needed him. "What should I do next?
Any suggestions?"

"For God's sake, think *romance*," Nora urged. "Look,
I know she still loves you. That's why I'm here: to tell you
not to give up and to be patient. You know Aislinn: she's
going to make you crawl across broken glass before she
takes you back."

"I'll do whatever it takes."

"Just don't come near the house."

Liam just smiled. "There are other ways for me to see
her."

*   *   *

*The following week* at the farmers' market, Aislinn sent
Padraig off on an errand as soon as Alec Fry stopped by
her booth. She'd thought long and hard about his invita-
tion to grab a bite to eat sometime and decided there was
no harm in it.

"Mornin', Aislinn."

"Alec."

"I see you've got your usual array of gorgeous fleeces
and wool. You're gonna drive the rest of us out of business."

"You do all right for yourselves," Aislinn observed.

"Yeah, but you do more than all right. What's your
secret?"

Aislinn grinned. "Can't tell you that. If I did, it
wouldn't be a secret." Alec smiled back at her; then they
lapsed into an awkward silence.

"Listen, Alec, about taking you on part-time. I've no
need of you for steady work right now, I'm sorry to say.
Padraig and I are doing fine."

Alec's face fell. "I thought you might say that. Maybe I
could just lend a hand during shearing season? You'd get
it done that much faster with three of us."

"That's true." She hadn't thought about that. She was
about to tell him she'd definitely hire him for shearing

and maybe mending the odd fence or two when out of the corner of her eye, she saw Liam striding toward her like the cock of the walk, a big, confident smile plastered on his puss. *Oh, Jesus, God, no.* He had to be kidding.

"Hey, you," he said.

"Liam," Aislinn said sourly. "Alec, this is Liam O'Brien. Liam, Alec Fry."

Liam looked from Aislinn to Alec. "Nice to meet you," he said politely.

"You're the Yank," said Alec, looking him up and down disdainfully. "I've heard all about you."

"Interesting, because I've never heard about you," Liam said churlishly.

*Christ,* thought Aislinn, *this is all I need, a bout of "my willy's bigger than your willy," and in the middle of the market, too. If this conversation falls on the wrong ears, it'll be all over the county.*

"Alec and his brothers own a sheep farm about two miles from me," Aislinn explained. "They were the ones who helped Padraig when I—we—went to Dublin, remember?"

"Oh, right. Guess you two must have a lot in common, then," Liam said, mildly sarcastic.

"Guess we do," said Alec with a cold stare. He turned to Aislinn. "Have you thought about the other thing we discussed?"

He was bringing it up in front of Liam on purpose; any twit could see it. *Well, let Liam twist a little,* Aislinn thought. Egotistical bastard, always so pleased with himself, with his silly gifts. Let him see that she really didn't give a rat's arse about him. She was moving on.

"I have," Aislinn said cheerily. "How about Friday night?"

"Grand," said Alec with a big smile. "I'll fetch you around eight, then." He winked at Liam. "Nice to meet you, Yank." With that, he walked away.

Liam looked beside himself. "What the hell was that all about?" he demanded. "Do you have a date with him or something?"

"None of your business."

"It is my damn business."

"No, it is *not*," Aislinn fumed. "You've no claim on me, Liam O'Brien! You gave that up when you kicked me in the teeth and made me the laughingstock of the town!"

"Oh, I get it," Liam said smugly, rocking on his heels. "It's spite time. You want to get back at me."

"That's right; you're the be all and end all of mankind," Aislinn said with scorn. "How could any woman possibly want to spend time with anyone else? It's one of the great mysteries of the universe."

"A fucking sheep farmer. You've got to be kidding me."

"I'm a 'fucking sheep farmer,' or have you forgotten that?" Aislinn snapped.

"Yeah, it's perfect. You two can get married and combine farms and live happily ever after."

"You couldn't stand that, could you?" Aislinn taunted.

"It would be pitiful," Liam retorted. "Especially since you love me. You know, I actually feel a little sorry for the guy, being used on the rebound."

Aislinn felt fury begin to percolate inside her. "I'm not the one at this table who uses people. Enjoying getting double wages at the pub, are you?"

"I'm not. I told Jack I didn't want them."

"Aren't you noble," Aislinn mocked. "If you're not going to buy anything, then please move on."

Liam dug into his back pocket and pulled out his wallet. "I'd like some fleece, please."

"I sell it in half-pound bags, a minimum of four bags."

"Fine."

Aislinn could feel Liam positively steaming behind her as she turned from him to weigh the fleece and put it into the bags. "Forty euros," she said when she was done, shoving the bags across the counter at him and holding out her hand for the money. "Knit yourself a new girlfriend with it."

Liam carefully laid the money in her palm, his gray eyes pinning her. "I don't want a new girlfriend. I want my old girlfriend, and I'm not giving up until I get her back," he said stubbornly. "I don't care if Alec"—he spat the name contemptuously—"has decided you're the shepherdess of his dreams. You and I both know there's still a spark between us, Aislinn. Why can't you just forgive me?"

"Why can't you get it through your thick Yankee skull that's never going to happen?"

"Oh, it's gonna happen, all right, even if it takes me years."

"Yeah, good luck with that." Aislinn craned to look past him at a slight woman waiting behind Liam to talk to her. "Now, if you'll excuse me, I seem to have a customer."

\* \* \*

*Don't do it,* Liam told himself, trying to quell fury inside him as he went in search of Alec Fry. He knew he had no right to bother the guy. But he couldn't help himself.

He found Mr. Sheep Farmer at a booth at the far end of the market, chatting with two men who were obviously his brothers, since they were tall and blond like he was. Spotting Liam, Alec's upper lip curled in a sneer as he lightly elbowed one of them in the ribs.

"This is the Yank I was telling you about."

"The one who did Aislinn McCafferty wrong?" asked the one with a weathered face who was wearing, ironically, a New York, New York sweatshirt.

"Yup," said Alec. He gestured at the bags of wool in Liam's left hand. "Come to comparison shop, have you?" The brothers sniggered.

"I've come to have a word with you."

Alec turned up his palm, sweeping his hand in front of him. "Speak away."

"In private."

Alec chuckled, smirking at his brothers. "Won't be a mo."

He followed Liam out into the parking lot. Liam took a deep breath, trying to compose himself as the anger beating inside the walls of his head threatened to explode. He wanted to grab this guy by the throat and throw him against a car, warn him that if he made a move on Aislinn, he'd be dead meat. But somehow, something entirely different happened.

"What is it you want?" Alec asked, making a great show of checking his watch.

"It's about Aislinn."

"I've figured that much out."

"Look, you seem like a nice guy. I just wanted to let you know that if you're planning to make a move on her, you're wasting your time."

Alec raised an eyebrow. "Is that so?"

"Yeah. She still loves me."

"You Americans," Alex sneered. "You're all so big-headed."

"I'm only bigheaded where she's concerned."

"Did you ever stop to think that maybe—just maybe—she's tired of eejits like you? That she's ready for a good man who will treat her right?"

"I am a good man. I just fucked up, and now I'm trying to fix things. Seriously, pal, don't waste your time. You're not going to get anywhere."

"I should punch your feckin' face in," Alec growled.

Liam shrugged. "If that's what you need to do to prove what a man you are, go for it."

"*Feck you.*"

"Yeah, fuck me, whatever," Liam said, bored. "Have fun on your date. But don't say I didn't warn you."

## 26

*God in heaven,* Aislinn prayed, *I swear to you I will never think ill of another person or be waspish with one of your creatures if you just make Alec Fry shut his gob.* All the way into Crosshaven, she'd listened to Alec rattle on about his bloody tool shed. His favorite pliers. His nail puller. His fence stretcher. She'd smiled and nodded and tried to look interested, but by the time they got to town, it was taking every ounce of strength to keep her eyes from rolling back in her head.

Impossible as it was to believe, dinner was worse. Aislinn thought the expression "a bite to eat," implied something casual: a café, maybe, where they could have sandwiches or a decent hamburger. But no; he'd steered her inside an elegant, dimly lit place called Le Something or Other, where the waiter looked her up and down as if she were a piece of rubbish just blown in from the street because she was underdressed.

"I thought we were going somewhere a little more informal," she said to Alec under her breath as they were seated.

"I wanted to surprise you," Alec replied. "You're worth splashing out for."

Aislinn smiled weakly.

Christ, he was boring as sin. She was starting to understand why Alec hadn't a wife by now, the way his brothers did: no woman could deal with someone so endlessly tedious. On and on he went about his prize ewe and the pros and cons of electric fencing. At least she could join in this talk, but who wanted to jaw on about work all night? Still, it kept them from talking about personal things, and she was glad of that.

Aislinn could see he was affronted when she insisted on splitting the check, but she didn't care; she didn't want to owe him anything. Which reminded her: she was going to write a check as soon as she got home for half the cost of the Dublin trip and give it to that jackass, Liam O'Brien. If he didn't want to cash it, that was his business. But she didn't want to be indebted to that one for anything, either.

Driving back to Ballycraig, Alec was still yakking away, forcing Aislinn to stifle several yawns. She couldn't wait to get home and go out for a late-night walk with Deenie in blessed *silence.* Finally, after what felt like an eternity in hell, he drove up her pitted drive, pulling right up to the front door.

"Well," he said as a sense of expectancy filled the car. *Shite,* thought Aislinn. *Time to make my good-byes and get out of here.*

She turned to him, smiling graciously. "Thank you for a lovely night, Alec. The food was delicious."

"As was the company."

Aislinn went to get out of the car, but Alec touched her shoulder. "Can't a fella get a nightcap or a cup of tea to finish off the night?" He chuckled.

"Normally I would," Aislinn fibbed, "but I'm really knackered. You know what it's like, getting up that early in the morning . . ."

"I do," he conceded. "But maybe we could just sit

here a minute or two and keep talking before we call it a night?"

Aislinn felt guilty. "All right."

Silence.

"What do you want to talk about?" she asked.

"Oh, anything," Alec said casually, putting a hand on her knee.

Aislinn firmly removed it. "I know what we can talk about."

"What's that?" asked Alec, now trying to put his arm around her, the clueless twit. Aislinn leaned out of range.

"Let's talk about how we're friends, and nothing more."

"It doesn't have to be that way," Alec murmured, trying for what Aislinn thought was a smoldering look. Either that or dinner was repeating on him.

"But it *is*." Aislinn struggled to find the right words. "Look, I think you're a lovely man," she said sincerely. *Boring as a tick, but lovely.* "But I'm not looking for any romance in my life right now."

"But—"

"No buts. I've no interest."

Alec's shoulders slumped. "It's the Yank, isn't it?"

"What?"

Alec sighed forlornly. "He told me at the farmers' market that you were still in love with him, and I'd be wasting my time if I tried to get something going with you."

"Oh, he said that, did he?"

"He did."

"Well I'm here to tell you, it's nothing to do with that bighead."

"Then what?" Alec asked, looking pitiful.

"It's me, all right?" She was trying to keep her exasperation in check. They could go round and round on this issue forever. "I'm content on my own." She searched his face. "You understand that, right?"

Alec nodded sadly. "Yes. But if you ever—"

"Don't go down that road, Alec, please. It makes me very uncomfortable."

"I'm sorry, Aislinn." He ran his hands nervously along the sides of the steering wheel. "This talk we just had . . . my trying to . . . isn't going to affect our friendship, is it?"

"As long as I don't catch you giving me moony calf eyes, we'll be fine," she half joked.

Alec looked relieved. "I won't. I promise."

"Then we're square, so."

Aislinn opened the car door. "I'll see you at the market on Wednesday?"

"As always."

"Night, then."

"Night."

She gave a friendly wave as he backed his truck down the long drive and went on his way. *Well, that was awkward, but at least I nipped it in the bud.* As for Liam, her first impulse was to collar him and tell him to keep his nose out of her business, but then a thought struck her: He *wanted* a reaction from her. It was a way to get her to interact with him. Well, she wasn't going to give it to him. Let him sit there and torture himself as he wondered what she might be getting up to with Alec Fry. In fact, she was going to stay away from the Oak for a while, so he'd have no opportunity to see her at all unless he dragged his sorry arse to the farmers' market again. She went inside, feeling quite pleased with herself. For the first time since the split, she felt like she was in the driver's seat.

\* \* \*

*Eleven days. That's* how long it had been since Aislinn had been in the pub. Eleven days of Liam's imagination running wild, picturing her laughing with Alec Fry, making out with Alec Fry, making love with Alex Fry. Imagining her saying: *God, you've been right under my nose all along! I know it's early days yet, but I think I'm falling in love with you*. Obviously she was staying away from the pub for a reason, and the reason had to be Alec Fry.

Naturally, it had affected his mood considerably. The last thing he wanted to do was chat or make small talk, but it was part of his job. It didn't help that Teague remarked on Aislinn's absence.

"Seems to me she can't stand the sight of you," he said more than once. "I'd not be surprised if she waits till you're back in America to start coming in here again, though maybe that Mob fella who's been sniffing around here might wind up killing you first." Jack saw the fury in Liam's eyes and told him if he lost his temper and hit Teague, he'd have to fire him. The threat of no income at all was the only thing standing between his fist and Teague's face.

In addition to his bleak, tortured imagination, Liam had to deal with constantly looking over his shoulder, worried that one day he'd be walking down the street and some man would walk up to him, say, "This is from Whitey," and blow his head off.

He told Quinn about the guy; Quinn in turn had talked to the Major, since he'd been the one who had recommended Liam hightail it here in the first place. The Major told Quinn he doubted Whitey's reach extended to Ireland, but that Liam should be careful. *Great,* thought Liam grimly. *I tore myself away from my family for nothing.*

He was so deep in his thoughts he startled when Jack tapped him on the shoulder, pointing to the far end of the bar at Ned Sykes, Ballycraig's sole mechanic. "He's asked you twice for a bottle of Harp, Liam."

"Sorry." Liam hustled to get the Harp and handed it to Ned, who was seventy if he was a day. "It's on me," he told him.

"Ah, no need," said Ned. "We all know you've a broken heart and you might be gunned down in the street at any minute. Anyone in your situation would be distracted."

"For feck's sake, Ned!" Jack said sharply. "That's a terrible thing to say to him!"

Ned looked sheepish. "Sorry."

"Thanks," Liam muttered. He moved to the other end of the bar, where Bettina was gazing at him sympathetically.

"How many days has it been, love?"

"Eleven," Liam said glumly.

"It's possible she's just been dead busy at the farm what with Padraig starting to go doolally and all."

"I think she probably just can't stand the sight of ya," said Teague.

"Button it, you," Bettina warned.

Liam moved to the small alcove to the left of the bar, where some supplies were stored, motioning for Bettina to follow him.

"What's up?" Bettina asked.

"She went on a date with Alec Fry about two weeks ago."

"Alec Fry!" Bettina exclaimed loudly.

"Jesus, will you keep your voice down?" Liam peered behind him to see if anyone had heard Bettina's none too subtle exclamation. Thankfully, it looked like no one had.

"Do you think she's going out with him?" Liam asked bleakly.

"Alec Fry? Are you mad? He's a nice enough man, but dear Christ, he's as boring as a sack of spuds. I'd be shocked if she was spending time with him. *Shocked.* Not only that, but if she was dating Alec Fry, don't you think she'd be in here parading it under your nose?"

"I don't know."

"Well, I would if it were me. Do you want my expert opinion?"

"Obviously."

"I think she's keeping her distance because she wants to drive you mad with worry, thinking she's off with Alec Fry."

"Well, it's working."

"She'll be back in eventually. This is her local, after all. If you're worried, why don't you try to get the scoop from her high-and-mighty sister?"

"Hmm." It was a thought, though he hated relying on Nora for everything. He was kicking himself for not running out and getting Aislinn something romantic the day after Nora had come in to the pub.

"C'mere." Bettina led Liam back out to the bar.

"Listen up, everyone!" Bettina bellowed. The entire Oak fell quiet. "We all know about the bet and how it broke Aislinn McCafferty's heart. And we all know we're partially to blame for wounding the poor creature because we were in on it. Now, Liam here wants her back. So I think we should all put our heads together and think of ways to help him. If the whole town pleads his case, she'll have to give in eventually. So hop to it."

Heads nodded, then everyone went back to their business.

"There you go," Bettina said to Liam, looking pleased with herself. "Alec Fry or no, with the whole town singing your praises, she'd have to have a heart of stone to resist."

"Thanks," Liam said, striving to sound grateful. He appreciated the gesture, but it worried him. Who knew what the hell some of them would come up with? Then again, beggars can't be choosers, and at this point, he was willing to get on his knees and beg her to take him back. Maybe Bettina was right; maybe with all of Ballycraig rooting him on, she'd let down her guard and let him back in. He'd just have to wait and see.

\* \* \*

*Another fence to* mend, another day on her knees in the grass with pliers and wires. Aislinn couldn't believe she'd missed this one. Then she remembered: this was one of the fences she'd sent Padraig out to mend. Obviously he'd forgotten, or else his mind had bumped along to something else.

It had been twelve days since she'd crossed the doorstep of the Royal Oak. She wondered: was it juvenile of her to derive pleasure imagining Liam picturing her with Alec Fry? Because she certainly was deriving pleasure from it, even though she was also depriving herself of her usual whiskey at the pub. She'd never admit it, but she even missed trading insults with the Trinity. She missed Jack's smiling face, the turf fire, and the music. She even missed the cacophony of voices of all those bastards who'd betrayed her. Clearly she was going soft.

Fence mended, she rose, wiping the dirt on her hands off on her jeans and turning up the collar of her barn jacket against a slightly chilly spring breeze. She'd trusted Padraig to take the flock across the road to the uppermost northern meadow. Though it was long passed, he was still all broody about missing the sheep dog trials. She could see him practicing his commands up on the hill with Deenie, who loved it. She made a mental note to make sure *she* entered them next year.

She was about to check the next length of fence when she caught sight of a man walking up the drive. She squinted; it was no one she recognized. Assuming it was someone who'd come to buy some wool, she hurried down to the barn.

"Hello," she said cheerfully. "I'm Aislinn McCafferty."

She paused, waiting for the man to tell her his name, but he didn't. Odd. He was a twiglet, so thin it looked like a good wind would blow him right over. Unsmiling, too, with a bony face.

"Are you here for some wool?" Aislinn continued pleasantly.

"Actually, I'm not. I was wondering: do you know if there's someone named Liam O'Brien, lives in Ballycraig?"

Aislinn's heart began to pound. "The name isn't familiar, no." Her mind flashed to all the whispered excitement around Liam's arrival when he first arrived in town. *On the lam.*

The man looked perplexed. "Are you sure? I heard he might work at the pub."

"Have you checked there?"

The man frowned. "They say they've never heard of him."

"Well, there's your answer, then."

"Not quite. I've been told otherwise."

"Then someone must be having you on. There's no Liam O'Brien around here that I know of. By the way, why are you asking?"

"Curious."

"Because—?"

"I'm not at liberty to say."

"I see." Aislinn tucked her ponytail up under her baseball cap. "Well, sorry I couldn't be of more help to you."

The man nodded curtly and started back down the drive to where his car sat idling. *Please, God, don't let him go across the road and question Padraig,* Aislinn thought desperately. The old man was so guileless he'd tell everything. She held her breath, not releasing it until the man drove away. As soon as he was out of sight, she ran across the road and up the steep hill.

"Padraig," she said breathlessly as she reached the old man, who had just successfully commanded Deenie to drive the herd into a shedding ring.

"Come to check on me, have you?" he asked sardonically.

"No need to check on you. You've got it all under control."

"It can't be lunchtime already."

"It's not. I need to talk to you about something that's not related to the farm."

Padraig rested his chin on the top of his staff. "What would that be?"

"Has anyone come sniffing around here, asking you questions about Liam?"

"Not that I can remember."

"You're sure about that?"

"I'm not an eejit, you know!" Padraig barked.

"No, but you do forget things sometimes!" Aislinn shot back without thinking. *Feck.* "I'm sorry. I know you wouldn't forget something like that."

"Oh, ta very much for the compliment," Padraig sniffed. He put two fingers in his mouth, gave three short whistles, and Deenie came scampering to his side. "Why is someone asking about the Yank? Is this to do with his troubles in America?"

"I'm not sure yet. Just promise me something, will you?"

"What's that?"

"If anyone does ask you, tell them you've never heard of Liam." She made a mental note to tell Nora the same thing.

Padraig clucked his tongue. "Still sweet on him. It breaks my heart."

"I'm not sweet on him," Aislinn said tartly. "I just hate to think of anyone seriously hurting him. I mean, no man deserves that, not even a low-down dog like Liam."

"True. Well, if anyone comes nosing around asking questions, I promise to keep the old lips zipped up tight."

"Good man." Aislinn tilted her head in the direction of the farm. "I'm going back over to see if anything else needs fixing."

"We should be thinking about cutting some hay soon."

"I know, I know." Aislinn sighed. "One thing at a time."

"Off with you, then."

"See you at lunch."

She walked slowly across the road, filled with a short-lived sense of relief. She decided that out of basic human decency, she'd make a quick visit to the pub tonight to let Liam know that someone was snooping around asking questions about him. As she'd told Padraig, even the likes of Liam didn't deserve what this mystery man might do to him if he was somehow connected to what happened in America. She yanked the thought from her mind and went back to work.

## 27

*"Aislinn! Good to see you!"*

Aislinn acknowledged Old Jack's over-cheery greeting with a small smile as she entered the pub. As usual, the Oak was packed, and she had to wade through a small sea of people, all of whom she knew, as she made her way up to the bar. The musicians, not one of them a day under sixty-five, looked to be getting ready to play. Saturday night in Ballycraig, the same old routine for decades. There was comfort in that.

"The usual?" Jack asked. It was just him and Bettina behind the bar.

"Yes, please."

She tapped her foot impatiently on the footrail as she waited for her shot, noticing out of the corner of her eye that Fergus was grinning at her like an idiot.

"What are you flashing your gums at, Fergus Purcell?" she asked, pleased to be needling him.

"We've missed you round here."

"Give over."

"Well, a certain *someone* has missed you," David put in, wiggling his eyebrows. "Even pining, I'd say."

Aislinn frowned. "Right." She discreetly scoured the pub for Liam, wondering where he was. Sick? Hiding from the nosy bastard tracking his whereabouts? The latter thought made her nervous.

She returned her gaze to the bar to find Bettina looking at her, a wry smile on her face. "Looking for someone in particular, are we?"

Aislinn picked up her shot glass. "Not in particular, no," she said coolly.

"He's in the basement," said Bettina with a wink. "I'll go get him."

Before Aislinn could protest, she was bustling off. God, did no one have lives of their own to tend to here?

She took a drink of whiskey, remembering the first time she'd ever tried some, stealing a sip from her father's glass when she was fourteen. Jameson, it was, and she thought it the most vile-tasting thing on earth. "An acquired taste," her father told her when she was old enough to drink legally. She worshipped him so much she decided to emulate him, and gradually, she did acquire an appreciation for it. She silently toasted him in her head: *Miss you, Dad.* She was missing him a lot lately, what with Padraig getting a bit soft. But she knew what her father would do, and she was doing the same: keeping an eye on the faithful old soul while letting him continue doing the work he loved for as long as humanly possible.

Teague, hunched possessively over a pint as if he half expected someone to snatch it from his fat fingers, interrupted her reverie. "Left Her Royal Highness at home, have you?"

"Don't call my sister that if you value the teeth in your head," Aislinn threatened.

"Will you listen to it?" said Teague, nudging David in the ribs. "The oul McCafferty is back, and in fightin' form."

"None of that," Jack scolded. "She's got a name, and a lovely one it is, too."

*What the hell is going on here?* Aislinn thought. Jack had never said anything like that to her in her life.

She took another sip of whiskey, pushing some hair off her face as Jack asked when she planned on shearing her flock.

"Padraig and I will be pulling out the old clippers next week," she told him. She thought about the top-of-the-line shears Liam had bought her in an effort to win her back and suppressed a laugh. *King of Romance, that one is. Hopeless is more like it.*

Bettina reappeared, Liam behind her. "Here's your boy," she said to Aislinn with a big smile.

Aislinn snorted. "He wishes."

Liam gestured for her to wait a minute so he could make sure everyone at the bar had everything they needed before he gave her his attention. "What's up?"

"We need to talk," said Aislinn. She could see Teague straining to hear what she was saying. Were he a cartoon, his ears would be three times the size of his head.

She stared at Teague pointedly. "I think we best go where we can have some privacy," she said to Liam.

"Sure."

Liam looked apprehensive as he followed her outside, where the streetlamp cast a ghostly yellow halo on the glistening pavement. He shoved his hands deep in the front pockets of his jeans, peering nervously up and down the street. Very few people were out; most were inside the Oak.

"I know why you're as nervous as a cat around water," said Aislinn.

"Do you?"

"Yes, unfortunately." She paused uneasily. "A man came up to the farm yesterday asking all sorts of questions about you."

Alarm streaked across his handsome face. "What did you tell him?"

"Not a damn thing. And I told Padraig to keep his yap shut if he comes sniffing again."

"I appreciate that." Liam ran his hand back and forth across his mouth. "I'm screwed, Aislinn," he said in a voice cracking with emotion. "They've figured out where I am."

Aislinn took him by the shoulders. "You're not screwed," she replied fiercely while at the same time trying to erase an image in her mind of the man swaggering into the Oak and shooting Liam point-blank in the chest. "No one here will let anything happen to you."

"Even you?"

"Christ, I'm not that much of a bitch, am I?"

"Of course you're not."

"Thank you." Aislinn dropped her hands from his shoulders, suddenly feeling tongue-tied and emotional. If anything happened to him . . . no, she was right, nothing would. He was one of their own.

Liam looked sad as he began walking back toward the pub. "Well, thanks for letting me know. I appreciate it."

"One more thing." Aislinn pulled a check out of the back pocket of her jeans. "For Dublin."

Liam's face fell. "Aislinn—"

"Maybe it's too much, maybe it's too little, I don't know," she said hurriedly, wanting this awkward moment to be over. "All I know is we're even now. I don't owe you anything."

Liam looked pained. "Dublin was my present to you. Can you please at least . . ."

"All right," Aislinn said softly, putting the check back in her jeans as she followed him back into the pub. She hated to admit it, but his anguish felt like an arrow to *her* heart. She reminded herself that he had no one but himself to blame. But still . . .

\* \* \*

*Inside, the musicians* were playing one of her favorite tunes, "Star of the County Down," when all of a sudden, their red-faced, roly-poly lead singer, Chuck Clayton, abruptly motioned for the band to halt. Looking as solemn as a judge, he whispered something in the ear of each musician, to which all of them nodded in agreement. When he was done, he addressed the pub at large.

"We'd like to play a little tune for Aislinn McCafferty and Liam O'Brien, who as we all know are meant to be together. It's a song by an American duo called Peaches & Herbert—"

"Herb, you eejit!" someone called out.

"Herbie, called 'Reunited,'" Chuck finished, looking right at Aislinn.

Too stunned to speak, all Aislinn could do was glare at Liam while the old men launched into the most pitiful version of the song she'd ever heard.

"Don't look at me!" Liam protested. "I don't have anything to do with it!"

"Get all that out of your mouth."

"I'm not lying!" Liam insisted vehemently.

"Oh, so they decided to do this of their own volition, did they?" Aislinn scoffed.

"Apparently so. Maybe you should take the hint."

"And what hint would that be, pray tell?"

"To give me another chance. To reunite with me, 'cause 'it feels so good,'" Liam said playfully, laughing as he quoted the song.

Aislinn was incredulous. "You're a real piece of work, you know that?"

"All the more reason to love me. Wouldn't you rather be with a piece of work than a snooze like Alec Fry?"

Aha! She knew she'd been right to avoid the pub for the past twelve days and leave him twisting in the wind, torturing himself over Alec Fry.

"I'm not discussing Alec Fry with you."

She longed to flash him a final glare and leave but found herself unable to move, pinned to the spot by the hopeful look in the eyes of all her fellow Ballycraigers. *Take him back,* their gazes said. *You know you love him. Go on.* She looked down at the floor, hating every moment of their scrutiny. She'd always felt uncomfortable being the center of attention, and this was no exception.

The song seemed to go on for an excruciatingly long time, especially since the poor old boys were massacring it. Liam must have asked them to learn it and play it the next time she came to the Oak. She had to give him points for creativity, but the fact the band was up there blatantly shilling for him—well, it was sad.

The song ended, an expectant silence hanging over the room. Aislinn could feel everyone's gaze still fixed on her, waiting, watching. She raised her head slowly. "Good night," she said politely, and walked out of the pub.

\* \* \*

*"Well, that went* over like a fart in church." Jack sighed sadly once Aislinn was out the door.

Liam had been mortified when the band started playing the song. He knew they meant well, and he more than appreciated the effort, but what they'd done was not going to aid his cause. Still, he thanked the musicians profusely. "We tried, son," said Chuck, picking up a pint for himself at the bar to assuage his "powerful thirst."

"I know you did, and I appreciate it." Liam waited until Chuck went back to play traditional tunes with the band before regarding Bettina.

"I think it might be better if I tried winning her back on my own."

"Nonsense," she declared. "That was just the first blow."

"You're right there: they did indeed blow," Fergus agreed.

"Peaches & Herb," Jack mused. "I always did like them."

Bettina squeezed Liam's arm affectionately. "Don't worry. She'll come round. We've all of us just got to keep at it."

"Maybe you all should tell me what you plan to do so I can let you know whether it's a good idea or not," Liam said carefully. "I mean, I'd hate for you all to waste your time."

"I'll make a mention of it at coffee after church tomorrow," said Bettina.

"Thanks," said Liam, mildly relieved. He got back to work, but it was hard to be affable as he struggled not to drown in the darkness inside his head. He hated that Whitey's guy in Ireland had talked to Aislinn. Jack must have noticed how preoccupied he was, because he pulled him aside during a rare lull.

"Talk to me, boyo. You've got your head up your arse by the look of it."

"Some guy was up at the Aislinn's farm asking about me," he said miserably. "It's just a matter of time." He laughed bitterly. "It's ironic. I mean, if I'm gonna be killed, why not just go home and let them do it there? At least I'd be with my family."

"You are not going to be killed."

"If I get killed here," Liam mused, ignoring Jack's reassurance, "it means coming here was a waste of time. I could have been home all along."

"But you wouldn't have met Aislinn," Jack pointed out.

"Didn't think of that."

"Obviously."

Aislinn. Something dawned on him. "You know, if we get back together, I could be putting her in danger."

Jack rolled his eyes. "For feck's sake, will you stop writing a gangster movie in your head and just concentrate on getting that girl back?"

"That's not likely to happen after tonight."

"Don't worry: I'll tell Chuck and the boys to stick to the old songs. We can't have them playing the likes of 'Sexual Healing' the next time she comes in here. That'd put the nail in your coffin for sure."

Liam laughed. "Thanks for making me feel better, Jack."

"Ah, it's nothing," Jack deflected. "Now get back to work."

Liam returned to the bar with a lighter heart, his head somewhat cleared. Aislinn had to be softening *a little*, didn't she?

# 28

*"Unbelievable."*

Aislinn shook her head as she signed for the package the postman had just delivered to her front door. It had to be from Liam. Had to be. This was the second time anything had ever been delivered to the farm that had to be signed for. Unbelievable.

She ran up to her bedroom to stash the package before returning to the kitchen to finish up lunch with Padraig. Nora had taken the truck into Moneygall for her weekly run to buy gourmet tidbits for herself. Ironically, Padraig seemed to be developing a taste for the organic, gourmet coffee Nora insisted on buying, even though it really cheesed her off when one of the three bags she'd brought home one week went mysteriously missing. Aislinn offered to pay for it, though she did feel compelled to point out to Nora there were worse things on earth than aging, coffee poaching shepherds.

Things had been slightly tense between them since their row about Nora's sorting through their parents' things without Aislinn. There had been a lot of late-night phone calls to Donald in London. Aislinn was just waiting for Nora to drop the bomb about building the guesthouse.

Padraig's eyes tracked her as she sat down across from him at the table. "Who was that?" he asked, taking a big sip of coffee.

"None of your beeswax, you nosy parker."

Padraig shrugged. "No need to tell me. I know it was the postman. Recognized his voice."

"Then why did you ask?"

"Just making conversation."

"Mmm." Aislinn took a few bites of her ham sandwich, stalling. She needed to talk to Padraig about shearing day, and she was dreading it, but she knew she couldn't avoid it any longer.

"I wanted to talk to you about Friday."

"I'm looking forward to testing out those fancy clippers the Yank gave you."

"I'm sure." Aislinn folded her napkin neatly on the table. "The thing is, I've asked Alec and his brother to help us." Her hand shot out quickly to cover his. "You know the two of us can't do it alone. We need at least one other person, and with Dad gone . . ." She cleared her throat as she started to get choked up. "So Alec and Jake are going to help."

Padraig's gaze was hard. "Your father and I used to do it alone, you know, before you joined us."

"Yes, and it took you forever!" Aislinn countered. "With four of us, think how fast it will go: Alec can secure each animal to be shorn, I can gather up the wool and fleece from the shearing area, Jake can mind the gates and do general cleanup, and you can shear."

Padraig was silent.

"Say something."

"I don't like this one bit."

"It's going to save us a lot of time, Padraig," she repeated.

"I'm not surprised you've asked your new boyfriend to join us."

"My what?"

"Don't think I don't know you went to Crosshaven with Alec Fry."

"We had dinner together. That's all. Not that it's any of your business."

"He's angling to marry you so he can take over the farm, and then he can get rid of me."

"Jesus God, help me," Aislinn said under her breath. "You sound crazy when you say things like that, you know that?"

"It's clear as day," Padraig maintained stubbornly.

"If you don't stop saying mad, paranoid things, I'm going to call the doctor and tell him you're going soft in the head!" Aislinn snapped.

"Is that what you think?" Padraig shot back. "That I'm a crazy old man?"

"Oh, dear God." Aislinn cradled her head in her hands. "Right now, I do think that, yes, when you talk out your arse. The faster we shear, the faster we can clean the wool, and the faster we can sell it and *make money* to keep the damn farm going!"

Padraig just harrumphed.

"Did you not catch that I said you're doing the shearing? I wouldn't dream of having anyone else."

"Really?"

"Jesus, are you going deaf as well? *Yes*."

Padraig leaned back in his chair, a satisfied look on his face as he crossed his arms over his chest. "I've always been a dab hand at it, if I say so myself." He chugged down some coffee. "How much are you paying them?"

"You let me worry about that."

"And Nora? Are you thinking of giving her a job as well?"

"Oh, right," Aislinn chortled. "She'd love that." She paused thoughtfully. "Actually, maybe I can ask her to take care of lunch and dinner. That would be helpful."

"She's not fond of them Frys, you know. Hid in her

room the whole time they were 'helping me out' when
you skipped off to Dublin."

"You make it sound like I abandoned the farm. I went
away for a weekend. As for Nora, well . . ." Aislinn just
shrugged. She wasn't about to make excuses for her sister.
"Anyway, I'm sure she'd be willing to help out, at least in
the kitchen."

"That article of hers—what, is she rewriting the Bible?
You'd think she was back here for good, it's taking her
so long."

Aislinn felt the same way but held her tongue, trying
to remind herself that she'd never had to write anything
longer than a shopping list, so she had no idea whether the
research required was as time intensive as Nora claimed
it to be. She seemed tired at the end of the day, that much
was certain, though Aislinn did sometimes hear her rumbling around at night. Well, she couldn't worry about
Nora right now. She had other concerns, like her workday
and the package waiting upstairs in her bedroom.

*   *   *

*Aislinn sat on* the edge of her bed, eyeing the plain brown
package as she brushed her hair. She'd been thinking
about it all day, wondering what could be in it, hating
herself for even caring. *Maybe I'll send it back unopened*,
she mused. Her gaze moved slowly to the bottle of perfume on her dresser, the only scent she'd ever owned.
That's the only reason she'd kept it; it had nothing to do
with Liam. She figured that in case she ever did meet a
man worthy of her, it might be nice to wear some scent
occasionally, but not too much, like Bettina. Nora wore
perfume every day. Aislinn didn't see the point; who was
there to smell it, besides herself and Padraig? Nora said
it made her feel feminine. *Liam made me feel feminine*,
she thought. She shook out her hair as she shook away
the thought.

Despite his balking, Padraig had taken the news of the
Fry brothers helping out better than she'd imagined. The

key, of course, was letting him do the shearing, which was the most important job. Nora had been more than amenable about preparing a hearty lunch and dinner for them all on shearing day. Perhaps, in her way, she was trying to make peace.

Aislinn braided her hair, then padded into the bathroom to put some moisturizer on her face. Vain thing, she chided herself. But she did work outside all day, and coming up on thirty in a few years as she was, she didn't really want to look weathered before her time. The moisturizer made her think of her mother, who'd once told her, "There are two things a woman should do every night before turning in: tell her man she loves him, and put some cream on her face to keep a youthful glow." Aislinn chuckled to herself; only her mother would use a term like *youthful glow*. But evidently there was something in it: her mother's skin had been gorgeous. The memory made Aislinn nostalgic, but strangely, not sad. Perhaps she was truly beginning to move past the sting of her parents' deaths.

She returned from the bathroom and sat cross-legged on her bed, pulling the package onto her lap. Now there came memories of Christmas, she and Nora always so careful when opening their presents; no mad ripping of paper in the McCafferty household, since their mother liked to save it for use again the next year. She tore at the plain brown paper as quietly as she could; the last thing she wanted was for Nora to hear. Inside the plain brown paper was a box with the La Senza logo across the top, tied up prettily with a pink bow. Aislinn remembered what a big deal it had been when a La Senza shop opened in Moneygall, the scandal of it among some of the older women of Ballycraig. Heat rushed to her face as she clumsily opened the box and held up the gift nestled in the pale blue tissue paper inside: a short, sheer, blush pink nightie with white lace trim. Aislinn stared at it a long time, not even needing to read the card to know it was from Liam. Her mind flew back to their weekend in

Dublin, how he'd whispered sexily in her ear one night about how he'd love to see her in some lingerie, even though he swore she was gorgeous in nothing but a man's oversized T-shirt. The memory of his words kindled a warmth inside her that was overpowering.

Aislinn chewed on her bottom lip. Surely there was no harm in trying it on just once before sending it back to him. She stood up, pulling her T-shirt off over her head, and shimmied into the nightie. It felt gorgeous against her skin, silky and lovely. She went to look at herself in her full-length mirror, loosening her braid and playing with her hair so it fell about her shoulders. She looked . . . sexy. She held her hair up, pulling down a few soft tendrils around her face and the nape of her neck. Not bad. She swallowed. She did look beautiful. Never in her life did she think she'd see herself that way.

Her eyes were drawn to the bottle of perfume on her dresser. No harm in putting a little spritz of that on her wrists, just to complete the picture. Smelling lovely, looking gorgeous, she walked back to her bed to pluck out the small card nestled at the bottom of the tissue paper. No harm in reading it. The card had two red foil hearts entwined on the front. Inside, Liam had written, "I really hope I have the thrill of seeing you in this one day, even though you're beautiful no matter what you wear. I love you, Liam."

Aislinn felt herself melting. *God, look at you, going all gooey inside*. She quickly shimmied out of the nightie, folding it carefully and putting it away in a dresser drawer, the card atop it. She decided she'd toy with him by keeping it. If he asked if she'd gotten anything in the mail recently, she'd tell him no. Maybe it was mean, but she was mean, wasn't she? She had a reputation to uphold. After all, she was the McCafferty.

# 29

*"I could shear* them twice as fast, you know."

Aislinn tried to pretend she didn't hear the comment Alec had just made under his breath as the two of them, along with Alec's brother Jake and Padraig, took a small coffee break after three hours of shearing. Aislinn's heart sank when daylight revealed dark gray skies; if it rained, they'd have to reschedule the shearing for another day. Luckily, the clouds gave way to generous sunshine.

She'd felt slightly awkward when the Fry brothers showed up, since she hadn't seen Alec since the night she'd had to set him straight. But he seemed himself, raring to go. It was a lucky break that he and Jake were already well-acquainted with her farm and her flock, since it meant they'd save even more time performing the tasks ahead. Or so she thought.

Things had started off well, but Padraig seemed to slow down a little as he clipped each member of the flock in turn. A few times, he seemed to be having a hard time holding down the larger ewes and rams, which had never happened before. When Aislinn gently offered to help, she was met with a snarl. She cursed herself for asking. She was sure that in Padraig's mind, she'd just given the Fry brothers more ammunition to use against him in their imaginary plot. Still, Alec was right: he probably could get the job done in half the time.

"Let's leave him be for now," she said to him quietly.

"Aislinn—"

"Alec, please." Her tone bordered on pleading. "So what if he's a bit slow? It'll all get done."

"You're too kind to him by half. You know that, don't you?"

"He's family," Aislinn said softly, looking at Padraig, who sat brooding on one of the bales of straw across the barn.

"Well, if you ever decide you need permanent help, I'm still available," said Alec.

Aislinn just sighed and went over to Padraig to try to assuage his mood.

"Looks like someone's got his knickers in a twist," she teased gently.

"And whose fault is that, offering me help I didn't need in front of those bigheaded Frys, who I'm sure think they can do a better job than me."

"You did need help," Aislinn maintained quietly.

"Don't tell me how to do my job, Aislinn McCafferty," Padraig scolded. "I've been shearing sheep since before you were born."

"I know that. But some of the larger ones seemed to be giving you a bit of trouble."

Padraig waved his hand in the air. "All in your head."

Aislinn felt the beginnings of a headache coming on and began rubbing her temples. "You've got to be more careful about nicking them, too."

"There's always a few nicks here and there. You know that."

*Yes, but you're nicking them more than usual.* She decided to stop banging her head against the wall.

"See how much faster it's going with the Frys helping us?" she offered, hoping he'd at least admit to *something* positive.

"Doesn't seem any faster to me," Padraig muttered.

"Suit yourself." Aislinn sighed, tired of trying to appease him. She went back to talk to Alec. Boring as he was, it was better than dealing with the stubborn old man and his nonstop glares.

\* \* \*

*She let Padraig* keep shearing for as long as she could, even though she could tell it was driving Alec mad. But when she saw him grab three different sheep and pull them by their wool, she called a halt to everything.

"What are you doing?" Padraig asked.

"What am *I* doing?" Aislinn flared. "What are *you* doing? You know better than to grab and pull them like that! You're hurting them! And you can damage the wool!"

"Lower your voice!" Padraig growled. "I don't want them Frys—"

"Give me the shears," Aislinn commanded, well past caring about Padraig and his paranoia.

"I will not."

"Give me the damn shears, old man!" Aislinn bellowed.

"So that's how it is, aye? Betrayer! Judas!" Padraig threw the clippers to the ground. "Fuck the lot o' you!" he shouted, storming out of the barn.

Shaken, Aislinn watched him go. They'd never, ever had a blowup before, and it made her feel sick inside. She hated that she'd lost her temper with him in front of Alec and Jake, but she'd reached the end of her tether with him. Truly.

Her first impulse was to chase after him, but she squelched it. She'd not go scampering after him begging to be forgiven, when what he'd been doing was wrong and could have hurt some of the flock. Christ, she wished her father were here. He'd have known the right way to handle him.

Alec walked over to her, bending down to pick up the shears. "You did the right thing."

"I shouldn't have lost my temper with him," Aislinn replied, troubled.

"Anyone in your shoes would have done the same thing."

Aislinn felt tears prick at the corners of her eyes. "Shite, Alec. I really do think he's really starting to lose it, more than I've been willing to admit."

"Do you want to shear, or should I?" he asked kindly.

"You do it," said Aislinn, resolutely getting hold of herself. "I'm sure you can do it faster than I can, and I want to get this day over with as soon as possible, if you don't mind."

He patted her shoulder. "Understood."

*  *  *

*"I had no* idea Padraig was so stubborn."

Dinner finished, Aislinn and Nora were doing the dishes. It was a warmish night, so Aislinn cracked the window open a bit, allowing a lovely, crisp breeze to sweep the room. Nora, of course, insisted it was freezing.

As Aislinn knew would be the case, Padraig hadn't returned to finish up the shearing with them, nor had he come up to the house for his dinner. He was punishing her. Aislinn knew she'd have to be the one to make the first move, but right now, she hadn't the energy after the exhausting day she'd put in. If he wasn't up at the house at the crack of dawn as was their usual routine, she'd go down and fetch him. *Stubborn old bastard,* she thought. She needed this kind of aggravation like she needed a hole in her head.

She handed Nora a rinsed plate to dry. "He was born stubborn, and no doubt he'll go to his grave that way."

Nora tossed aside the wet dishrag, reaching for a dry one. "We should really look into getting a dishwasher."

"We?" Aislinn returned sardonically.

Nora pressed her lips into a thin, hard line. "You."

"I don't need one."

"But look how many dishes were generated tonight!"

"There were only four of us! We'll be done with this in no time."

"Whatever," Nora muttered. "Alec Fry likes you."

Aislinn sighed heavily. "Yes, I know. But I've straightened him out on that score."

"Told him you plan to live the rest of your life like a cloistered nun, did you?"

"Very funny."

"I don't blame you for not wanting to get involved with him," said Nora. "He was boring the teeth off me at dinner."

Aislinn laughed.

"I saw Liam last week," Nora continued casually.

"Did you?" Aislinn replied, affecting nonchalance. "And where was that?"

"At the pub. I walked into town the other day. It's a very pleasant walk."

"Yes, it is." Aislinn eyed her sister curiously. "*You* went into the pub on your own?"

Nora looked defensive. "What's so surprising about that? I was in town. I thought I'd just pop in and say hello to everyone."

*Oh, that's right, because all of a sudden you want to be thought of again as a Ballycraiger.*

"So you were saying? The Yank?"

"Yes, I saw Liam. He was asking about you."

"Expected me to fly back into his arms after getting the shears, did he?"

It was on the tip of her tongue to tell Nora about the lingerie she'd received, but she decided against it.

"I've told you before: he's not going to give up." Nora picked up another plate to dry. "Yes, he did an awful thing, but everyone deserves a second chance, don't you think?"

"Seems to me we've had this conversation before."

"I'm sure we'll keep having it until you stop being so bullheaded and just admit you love him."

Aislinn stared out the window. "We'll see."

*   *   *

*No Padraig the* next morning. Aislinn was cheesed off: he knew there was no way she could work the farm without him. She tramped down to his cottage in the dew-covered grass with his thermos of tea in hand, preparing her apology in her head.

She knocked then entered, expecting to find him sitting at his kitchen table, listening to the news on Radio Éireann. But he wasn't there. In fact, there was no fire going in his fireplace, which was unusual.

"Padraig?" she called out. "Come on, you old bastard, show yourself. I'm fully prepared to grovel for the privilege of your company."

No answer.

A sick feeling began to form in the pit of her stomach as she slowly walked across the small room to the closed door of his bedroom. Aislinn closed her eyes a moment. *Please, God, let him be all right.*

She slowly opened the bedroom door. Padraig was lying beneath the thick wool blankets of his single bed, his eyes closed. *Sleeping,* Aislinn told herself, pushing herself over the threshold. *Must have tied one on last night in his fury. God, please.*

She forced herself to his bedside. His eyes were closed, a still, soft look on his old face, his very dead old face with its blue lips.

And all she could think was: I've killed him.

# 30

*Leaving Padraig's cottage,* Aislinn walked back up to the house slowly, her body so heavy it felt as if she were hauling pounds and pounds of wet sand on her back. She called Dr. Laurie's office, got the answering service, and left a message. Then, despite the early hour, she woke Nora. She didn't want to be alone.

The next few hours unfolded as if in a numbing dream: Dr. Laurie coming to the house and issuing the death certificate. Calling the funeral director to come fetch Padraig's body, then going to the funeral home with Nora to pick out a casket. Nora was appalled that he was going to be laid out in their living room in the manner of old Irish wakes, but it was what Padraig wanted, and truth be told, Aislinn found a measure of comfort in it. He wanted to be cremated, too, and have his ashes scattered among his two favorite meadows. He didn't want a Mass, but he once told Aislinn he wouldn't mind Father Bill saying a few kind words about him.

Nora was a godsend. It was she who called the Frys and asked them to come work the farm for a few days, and she who called around Ballycraig, telling everyone what the funeral plans were. There would be a one-day wake, followed by a short memorial service the next morning. Aislinn knew Padraig wouldn't have wanted a fuss, and truly, a one-day wake was all she could bear.

Aislinn kept her emotions in check until after supper. Dinner was difficult; it was as if she had forgotten how to have a proper conversation. Thankfully, Nora didn't push. They sat together in the kitchen, Aislinn painfully aware of the old man's absence, and of the heavy stillness that comes to a house when someone has passed on. When they finished doing the dishes, Aislinn went up to her room, pleading exhaustion.

That's when she fell to pieces.

Padraig's death was her fault. She knew it as sure as she knew her own name. There was no stopping the tears now that they decided to come. She lay down on her bed, curled up into a little ball, and began weeping.

Nora slipped into the room so quietly Aislinn almost didn't hear her. Aislinn almost asked her to go, but she'd learned her lesson the hard way after her parents' death and the incident with Connor: *Don't push people away when you're in pain. Let them in. It doesn't mean you're weak. It means you're human.*

Nora sat down on the bed, taking Aislinn's head in her lap while she tenderly stroked Aislinn's hair. "It's all right," she whispered over and over. "Let it out." Aislinn cried as though her heart was breaking, because it *was* breaking.

Finally, she looked up at her sister through watery eyes. "It's my fault he's dead," she choked out.

"What on earth are you talking about?"

"I made him feel useless. This farm is all he's had his whole life, and I made him feel useless. He went home and died of a broken heart."

"That's madness."

"No, it's not, it's true," Aislinn insisted, sniffling. "I embarrassed him in front of the Frys by taking his clippers away, making him feel old and incompetent. I shouldn't have done it, Nora. I should have kept my mouth shut." Her lower lip trembled. "The last thing he told me—told all of us—was to go feck ourselves. And now I'll never get to apologize and make it up to him, because he's dead," she sobbed.

"Aislinn, listen to me," Nora said firmly. "You did not kill Padraig. He was an old man. Dr. Laurie says it's likely he had a heart attack or just passed on in his sleep."

"If he had a heart attack, it's because he was so worked up over my embarrassing him and our row!" Aislinn cried.

"Nonsense! The man's been a heavy smoker for years! I bet his arteries were clogged from here to kingdom come." Nora continued stroking Aislinn's hair. "Maybe it was just his time, love."

"I hate that the last words between us were harsh," Aislinn choked out. "It kills me."

"He knows how much you loved him."

Aislinn sat up, rubbing her eyes, which felt like someone had dragged sandpaper across them. "Oh, God, Nora what am I going to do without him?"

"You're going to hire Alec Fry, for starters."

Aislinn sighed heavily. "I know, I know. I'm going to talk to him about it tomorrow morning. Or at the wake."

The wake. She hoped no one expected her to get up and say anything. She wasn't good in those situations. If anyone else wanted to speak, that would be fine. But she would not. Could not.

The one thing she did intend to do as a tribute to Padraig was to put together a collage of photos of him to display. There were loads of photos of him on the farm, in town, in the pub; pictures both old and new, chronicling his life. She'd bought a big piece of oaktag for the backing when she and Nora were in town earlier in the day.

Aislinn pulled a tissue out of the front pocket of her jeans, blowing her nose. "I've got to go sort through the photos."

"You can do it in the morning."

"I have to work in the morning, remember? I took today off, and I'll be taking all day Sunday and Monday off, too. If I don't do some work tomorrow, I'll go mad."

"All right. I'll help you with the pictures, if you want."

"That'd be great."

"It's no problem."

Nora started to rise from the bed when Aislinn impulsively grabbed her hand. "I'm so glad you're here."

"Now there's five words I never thought I'd hear," Nora quipped. She squeezed Aislinn's hand tight. "I'm glad, too."

* * *

*Liam felt self-conscious* as he walked through Aislinn's front door with his family. He hadn't brought a suit with him to Ireland, and as a result, he had to borrow one from his cousin Brian. It was too tight on him, but he had no choice: there'd been no time to go out and buy one. The same held true for shoes: he'd had to borrow a pair from Jack; otherwise, he would have been forced to wear the suit with his hiking boots or running shoes, which would have made him look like a total idiot.

News of Padraig's death had shocked everyone, including his parents, whom he'd called immediately. Toast after toast was hoisted in his honor at the Oak, and the band played many of his favorite old tunes: "Whiskey in a Jar," "Danny Boy," "I'll Take You Home Again, Kathleen" . . . The songs made Liam homesick, as memories of his parents and other relatives singing them at family gatherings overwhelmed him.

When he heard about the old man's death, Liam's first thoughts were of Aislinn. Nora had told Jack that Aislinn was the one who'd found Padraig dead in his bed. It had to be awful. Liam knew how much she loved the old man, no matter how much she complained about him being a royal pain in her neck. And with his death happening less than a year after the death of her parents—Jesus, it had to be ripping the scab off that painful wound, big time.

The house was packed with familiar faces. People were speaking in hushed tones, but Liam knew that once night fell, those who stayed late would relax and have a few drinks, and anecdotes would be told, accompanied by quiet laugher. He remembered Aislinn calling him a plastic Paddy the first time they met, and right now, that's what he felt like: he'd never been to a wake where someone was laid out in the house before. He was morbidly curious.

His cousin Brian elbowed him discreetly in the ribs, tilting his head left in the direction of the living room as they stood in the foyer. "There's the old devil."

Liam glanced left. Sure enough, there was Padraig's coffin laid out upon a tabletop. It was surreal to him, but of course everyone around him was unfazed.

"We should go pay our respects," he said.

Liam led his cousin into the room, his aunt and uncle right behind him. His gaze quickly swept the space: no Aislinn. She had to be in the kitchen. He hoped it wasn't that she was too distraught to leave her room. The thought killed him.

A mild sense of uneasiness overtook him as he watched his aunt go over to the casket, make the sign of the cross, and kneel before it. He'd seen this before at countless wakes, and it had always freaked him out a little bit. An image of himself laid out in a coffin suddenly blazed through his mind, and he forced himself to make it go away. *That guy asking questions about you all over town, whoever he is, is not going to kill you. Not only that, but what the hell are you doing thinking about yourself? It's Aislinn you should be concerned with.*

His aunt finished her prayer and returned to where he and his cousins stood. "Mr. Stanley did a beautiful job on him. He looks very handsome."

"That's good," said Liam, not knowing what else to say.

His cousins headed toward the casket, kneeling down like their mother before them. Where was Aislinn? Liam was relieved when Nora came into the room.

"Nora."

She waded through the crowd toward him, squeezing his hand when she got to him.

"Sorry about Padraig," Liam said.

Nora looked guilty. "Thank you." Liam knew she didn't care about the old man the way the Aislinn did.

"Where's Aislinn?" he asked.

Nora snorted quietly. "Where do you think she is? In the barn checking in with Alec Fry! And she's all dressed up, not that she cares!"

Liam smiled to himself. That was Aislinn.

"How's she holding up?" he asked with concern.

Nora leaned in closer. "Truthfully? She's a wreck. It's hit her very, very hard. Not that she's going to let anyone here see that."

"Everyone here probably knows it, whether she shows it or not." Liam paused. "Do you think she'll be upset I'm here?"

"No, I think she'll be glad—again, not that she'll show it. But you never know."

*   *   *

*Aislinn came into* the mudroom, sitting down on the long bench to pull off her wellies. Even though Alec knew her farm as well as his own, slipping outside to "check on him" gave her a chance to catch a breath of fresh air, which she desperately needed.

The house was spilling over with people. Padraig would have been pleased. Aislinn had bought some whiskey for those who wanted to stay on past the official end of the wake to chat and reminisce. Two of the musicians from the pub, Simon Bothy, the bodhran player, and George Terkle, the fiddle player, said they wanted to stay on as well to play some music. "We'll send him off good and proper," George told Aislinn. It made her happy;

between the whiskey and the music, the odds of things turning morose were small. Padraig would have hated it if they all sat around moaning over the loss of him. They were gathering to celebrate his life, not his death.

She wondered if people would notice she was wearing the same dress she'd worn at her parents' wake and funeral. It was the only proper dress she had. Simple and emerald green, Nora said it made her look gorgeous, since it played so well off her red hair. Looking gorgeous didn't concern her at all; looking respectful did, though the devilish thought did streak through her mind that since Padraig knew her best in her barn coat and wellies, he would have gotten a real kick out of it if she wore that. *Sorry, old man,* she thought. *I've got to bow to decorum for a few days.*

She walked into the kitchen, where a sizable number of people were milling around, many of whom had coming bearing casseroles and had yet to offer condolences. This time around, Aislinn let them comfort her. She didn't shut down or push them away emotionally the way she had when her parents died. When tears started to flow, she let them come. She let Liam's aunt wrap her in a hug and Old Jack fetch her a glass of water. It made them feel useful, and it felt good to be cared about.

Eventually, she excused herself to go into the living room. It still gave Aislinn a small jolt every time she saw Padraig lying there in the pine box on the table. Thank God she'd stopped Nora from giving their father's clothing to the Salvation Army; had she done so, there would have been nothing to lay him out in. He was wearing an old but well-kept suit of their father's, his hands at his sides. Aislinn had nearly burst out laughing when the funeral director, Mr. Stanley, asked if she wanted him to twine a set of rosary beads through Padraig's fingers. Oh, Padraig would have loved that, all right! She was tempted to ask if he could put a pair of shears in his hands instead, but she had the feeling Mr. Stanley would find it highly inappropriate. She did, however, place a picture of

Padraig and her father, taken in the pub when they were young, in the one of the breast pockets of the suit. They'd been best friends since childhood.

"Hey."

Aislinn turned around to find Liam standing directly behind her. She hadn't seen him since the night she'd come down to the pub to tell him about the mystery man asking questions about him. He looked handsome in the suit he was wearing, even though it was clear it wasn't his.

"Hey," she returned.

He hesitated a minute, then pressed one of her hands in his. "I'm really, really sorry about Padraig."

"Well, it was bound to happen sometime," she returned, trying to sound brave. "But thank you."

Aislinn closed her eyes for a moment. She wished she could ask him to hold her tight, right here and now. But she couldn't. It would send the wrong message to him, and it would open a door she wasn't sure she was ready to open.

She changed the subject. "Did you see the collage I made? Here, I'll show you."

She steered him over to the large collage of pictures on display at the foot of the casket. She and Nora had been up half the night working on it, and in her opinion, they'd done a great job, even though they did tear up numerous times as they sorted through pictures of Padraig with their parents.

Liam studied the collage. "Wow," he said, impressed. "This is amazing."

"Thank you."

He pointed to a picture of her as a little girl sitting on a tractor with Padraig. "That's you?"

"Of course it's me; look at the hair color. Not only that, but do you think Nora would ever have been caught dead on a tractor?"

Liam laughed, leaning in closer to study the picture. "You were gorgeous even then."

Aislinn swallowed. "Don't."

"It's hard not to." He looked back at her, a small, wry smile on his face. "You smell nice. I guess Nora let you borrow some of the perfume you gave her, huh?"

Aislinn's face felt hot as it turned red. She'd completely forgotten he'd be here. "She's quite generous about those things, yes," was all she could manage.

"You're a terrible liar," Liam whispered in her ear. "It's one of the things I love best about you."

"This isn't the time or place for this, Yank."

"You're right. I'm sorry."

"Apology accepted."

"Can I tell you just one more thing, and then I'll leave you alone?"

"What's that?"

Liam leaned in for another whisper. "You don't have any shoes on your feet."

Aislinn looked down. He was right; when she'd taken her wellies off, she'd forgotten to slip back into her flats.

"Oh, God," she said, mortified, glancing around. "Everyone here must think I'm a flaming eejit."

"I'm sure they realize you have a lot on your plate right now."

"I better go put them on before Nora accuses me of being some kind of wild woman."

"You are a wild woman."

"Enough now. I mean it." She hesitated. "Will you be staying on after?"

His eyes searched hers. "If you want me to."

"If you want to."

Liam shook his head, chuckling. "I'll stay. But if you want, we can pretend you didn't ask me." He kissed her cheek softly. "Hang in there."

# 31

*"Do you remember* the time he was repairing the roof of the church, and the windows were open and he heard Father Bill bellow to the congregation, 'I hear the voice of the Lord!' and he hollered down, 'You're a liar! I'm up higher than you, and I don't hear a damn thing!' " Old Jack swiped at his eyes, he was laughing so hard. "That was brilliant. Brilliant."

Aislinn laughed, taking a sip of her whiskey. It was close to ten, but per tradition, a number of people stayed on past the wake to swap memories of Padraig. The youngest ones there were her and Liam. Nora had gone to bed shortly after they'd cleaned up the kitchen, saying she was bone tired. Aislinn had to admit, that bothered her slightly. It would have been nice if Nora stayed for just one drink, seeing as she'd known Padraig her whole life. She had to have at least one good memory she could share.

"I forgot about that," said Grace Finnegan, reaching for the whiskey bottle to pour herself another glass. Aislinn wondered if she'd wind up in her cups, and Jack would have to take her home. Well, that would be all right. Her Fintan's cancer treatment in London wasn't going very well. If memories of Padraig and a few drams of Jameson helped her forget, even if it was for just a little while, then it was worth it.

"C'mon, Aislinn, girl," urged Simon Bothy, his bodhran drum at his feet. "You've only shared a few stories. You must have loads."

"Well, he was softhearted, though he tried to pretend otherwise. Anytime we lost a lamb in birthing, he'd cry like a baby." Her eyes filled up, but it was a good, happy memory, not painful. "And God knows he loved going to the sheepdog trials."

"Had a winning streak going there for about five years in a row, if I remember correctly," said George Terkle.

"Six," Aislinn corrected. "In the late nineties with Cilla, the dog we had before Deenie."

"Sad that he never married," said Grace.

"Truth be told?" said Jack, dropping his voice as if Padraig could hear him. "I think he was always sweet on your mother. Adored her. I don't think any woman could even come close in his estimation."

"I always thought that, too," Aislinn agreed softly.

"If your dad knew, he never let on." Jack shook his head sadly. "Terrible, the three of them gone now."

"Come now, let's have no mournful talk," said Simon, picking up his drum as George picked us his fiddle. "Any requests?"

* * *

*Chat, music, and* memories stretched on until 1 a.m. Eventually, one by one, everyone headed back to Ballycraig, until finally it was just Aislinn and Liam left. She was regretting her impulse earlier in the day of asking him to stay on past the wake. It was done in a moment of weakness, but there was no way to take it back.

"Do you want me to turn out the lights in the living room?" Liam asked, interrupting her reverie as he walked into the kitchen. The whiskey had been put away, the glasses washed, the whole room tidy.

Aislinn considered the question. "I know I'm going to sound soft in the head, but I'd like to keep one lamp burning in there all night."

Liam looked moved. "You don't sound soft."

"I remember my father once telling me that in the old days, someone would stay up all night with the body. Can you imagine?"

"Would you like me to stay with him?" Liam asked quietly. "It'd be no problem."

Aislinn choked up. "No, no, don't be daft. I mean, he's dead, after all." Dead. Really and truly. She'd never see him again, never eat his stale biscuits, witness his pride in having trained Deenie, never bring him coffee in the morning, none of it. "Oh, God."

She turned away from Liam, covering her face with her hands as she began to cry.

"C'mere. It's okay."

Liam drew her into his strong, protective embrace. Her first impulse was to resist so as not to appear weak. But he was right; he *knew* her, and so there was no hiding her grief from him. No *need* to hide it.

She let the pain consume her, Liam holding her tight. "I'm here," he whispered over and over. "And I'm not going anywhere. Ever."

She sobbed freely, her anguish tearing her apart. She realized she wasn't just crying over the loss of Padraig; she was crying over the loss of her parents and the knowledge that things would never, ever be the same on the farm again. Her rational side knew that life was constantly changing: up, down, joy, sorrow. But the vulnerable part of her was overwhelmed by it all. She wished she could go back in time with the magical power to erase Connor, bring her parents and Padraig back to life, make it so Liam had never made that bet with Old Jack.

"Hey." Liam tilted her chin up, tenderly swiping away the tears pouring down her face. "Everything's going to be okay."

"Is it?"

"Yes."

He looked deep into her eyes, then slowly covered her mouth with his. Aislinn had neither the will nor the inclination to resist. She wanted to lose herself in him—lose herself, period. She wanted to be enveloped in joy, not sorrow. She twined her arms around his neck, returning his ardor, near swooning when the tip of his tongue slid between her lips. Dizzy, dizzy, so wonderfully dizzy. So wonderfully alive. Liam's mouth moved from her lips to her earlobe, nipping, his heated breath sending quivers through her body. "Do you know how much I'm dying to make love to you?" he whispered into her ear huskily.

Aislinn nodded silently, and taking him by the hand, slowly led him upstairs to her bedroom. She realized she'd never had a man in her room before; since she'd always lived on the farm, she'd always respected her parents' rules pertaining to "romancing" under their roof.

For a split second she wished she had a small candle to light to make things feel a bit more romantic. But then she saw that she needn't worry: moonlight was pouring through the windows, bathing the room in a radiant pearl glow. And there was something else that could heighten the mood.

She steered Liam to sit down on the bed, playfully nipping his bottom lip. "Can you excuse me one minute?"

Liam, sloe eyed, ran his index finger over her lips. "Of course. Take your time."

Aislinn went to her dresser drawer, pulled out the lingerie he'd given her, and headed for the bathroom. Anticipation tumbled through her as she stripped off her clothing as quickly as she could and shimmied into the sheer pink nightie. The silk against her skin felt almost decadent. She loosened her braid, letting her hair fall free around her shoulders, tousling it for good measure. Then she returned to the bedroom.

Liam was stretched out on the bed with his back against the headboard. He'd stripped down to his briefs, and the moonlight shining in on his bare chest made him look even sexier to her than usual, like some kind of nocturnal god waiting for her to come to him so he could show her what heaven was really like. The desire smoldering in his eyes when he caught sight of her caused a bolt of heat through Aislinn's body so strong, she felt giddy.

"God, you look beautiful in that," he murmured, drinking her in. "I knew you would."

Aislinn approached the bed slowly, taking the hand he held out to her. She lay down beside him, reveling in the slide of his skin against hers as he took her in his arms. They lay there a few moments, just drinking each other in. He was breathtaking: Those stormy gray eyes of his, already making love to her with just a look. His dark, silky, tossed hair that she so loved to run her hands through, the sexy way it looked when he let it get too long and it fell into his eyes. The sound of his voice, the one he used just for her when they were in bed: pure male growl, sensuous yet demanding. She grabbed his face in her hands, kissing him hard. Her whole body was screaming for him, his hot mouth, his hard body.

She'd shocked him. Liam's head jerked back slightly, and then he was on her, his tongue snaking in and out of her mouth in a way that was almost obscene before he tore his mouth away and began nipping and scraping at her neck. Aislinn gasped and shuddered beneath him, her whole body on fire. She could feel his hardness against her, the pulsing heat making her feel helpless.

"Take off your nightie," Liam commanded hoarsely. He sat up, his legs still straddling her, and helped her slip the nightie off over her head. She reached for his hands and put them on her breasts, watching his eyes turn darker and darker with desire as his fingers circled, pinched the nipples lightly, explored with his fingers. Aislinn closed her eyes, reveling in the feel of his burning fingertips on her flesh. But it wasn't enough. Not nearly enough. She opened her eyes, took his hands from her breasts, and leaning forward, put one of her breasts into his mouth.

Liam's groan was primitive as he laid her back, positioning himself above her again, his tongue flicking her nipples, sucking, licking. She was greedy for him, rough, desperate, pushing up against him hard, wanting him to devour her with his mouth. Delirium threatened as desperation grew. When he reached down to cup her between the legs, she exploded, screaming with pleasure and bucking wildly against him as a golden, shuddering heat poured through her.

It was more than Liam could take. In one swift motion, he tore off his briefs, his hands possessively grasping her hips. Aislinn rocked against him, conveying her need with her body as she opened herself to him. Liam growled, and then he was inside her, the rhythm hard and deep, self-assured and unhesitating. Sweet pressure began to gather inside Aislinn again, concentrated, explosive. She quickened the pace, breathless, wanting, on the edge. And that's when Liam began slamming into her with an abandon that left her mind spinning and her body roaring once again for release. It came within seconds, the amazing delirium of it catapulting her into another dimension where there was only here, now, them.

"You," she gasped, running her nails up and down his back. "Now you."

Rough, almost desperate, Liam pounded inside her wildly until he reached his own release with a final, panting shudder, and they were both complete.

# 32

*Liam woke the* next morning to find himself alone in Aislinn's bed with the mouthwatering scent of coffee, eggs, and sausages wafting up from the kitchen. He was disappointed she wasn't beside him for a morning cuddle, but he knew Aislinn: she'd probably gotten up at the crack of dawn to do some chores, even though the Fry brothers were filling in today because of Padraig's memorial.

Fingers twined behind his head, he lay on his back staring at the ceiling for a moment, reveling in memories of the night before. He'd known Aislinn would look sexy as hell in that nightie he'd bought her, and he was right. He'd also been right about why she'd held on to the gifts he'd given her: she still loved him.

Liam ran his hand along his jawline. He needed a shave. He glanced around the room. It was simple and unadorned, yet there were feminine touches here and there: the pitcher of dried lavender on her night table, the bottle of perfume he'd given her on the dresser, which made him grin. Hell yeah. He'd been right to listen to those who'd told him to romance her.

He sat up with a yawn. He wished to hell there was a

bathrobe here he could borrow; he was going to have to wear his damn clothes from yesterday. He'd ask Aislinn if he could borrow her truck after breakfast to go into town.

Liam got dressed and came downstairs, momentarily jolted by the sight of the casket in the living room out of the corner of his eye before heading for the kitchen. Aislinn was at the stove, looking surprisingly preoccupied as she scrambled eggs. He could tell from the way she was dressed, in jeans and a big flannel shirt, that he'd been right; she'd already been out working.

He came up behind her, slipping his arms around her waist. "Hey, you."

"Good morning." Her voice was quiet. "Did you sleep all right?"

"I slept great. You?"

"I did all right for myself."

"I see you've already been out to visit the flock."

"They're my job. I should be out there with Alec right now."

"I thought they were Alec's job today."

"Technically. But there was no harm going out, since I had the time."

"Where's Nora?"

"Lying in with a headache. I hope she doesn't miss the service, though I wouldn't be surprised if she did."

Liam released her with a grin, sitting down at the table. "Them sounds like fightin' words."

"They never got on. It was a bit nerve-racking. But I still think it's only proper she pay her respects." She frowned. "I'm worried now that Padraig's gone, she's going to make her move. She's been unnaturally interested in his cottage ever since she got here, and I know neither she nor His Lordship are happy in their jobs. I know it's coming; I can feel it in my bones. And you know what? I resent it. This is my home, Liam." She frowned, looking guilty. "God, I feel a right bitch saying that, especially since we've had some lovely moments together. But sometimes her sense of entitlement when it comes to this place . . ."

"Why are you thinking about this now?"

"Can't help it. My mind's flying off in a thousand different directions this morning." She filled two plates with eggs, sausage, and toast, joining him at the table.

Liam speared a piece of sausage. "What's got your mind spinning, honey?"

"The farm. Padraig." She paused. "Us."

"What about us?" Liam took a sip of coffee. God, it was good. It had to be that organic, fresh-ground stuff Nora bought that Padraig had been crazy about.

"You know," Aislinn mumbled.

"You know, for someone known for her hair-raising bluntness, you're being a little vague here. Spit it out."

"Last night . . ." She looked ill at ease, not quite meeting his eye. "It was nice, but I hope you don't think it means we're back together."

Liam just blinked.

"I wasn't thinking straight."

Liam snorted. "You seemed to be thinking pretty straight to me."

"Liam, please," Aislinn begged. "Don't make this more difficult than it already it is." She took a slow sip of coffee. "I was distraught over Padraig. I needed comfort. I—"

"So you used me."

"No, no," Aislinn said, looking distressed. "I would never do that."

"Then what?"

"It just—it shouldn't have happened. It sent the wrong signal. And I'm sorry for that."

"You want to know why it happened?" Liam countered forcefully. "Because you still love me, and you wanted to be with me. If you didn't, you would have returned my gifts by now. No one hangs on to lingerie given to her by a guy she doesn't give a damn about."

Aislinn was silent.

"Don't deny it, Aislinn."

"Fine," she capitulated. "Of course I still love you."

"Then what's the problem?"

"I feel overwhelmed," she confessed, looking on the verge of tears. "Padraig is gone, I've got to learn to work with Alec, Nora's still underfoot. I need to keep things simple, Liam, and you and I are anything but simple."

"I disagree."

Aislinn raised her eyebrows. "Oh, do you. Well, I suppose you're allowed your opinion."

"It's not an opinion; it's fact." Liam drained his coffee cup and stood. "Ball's in your court."

Aislinn's face fell. "What?"

"You heard me."

"You're angry."

Liam laughed curtly. "Believe me, Aislinn, this is nowhere near angry for me. This is frustration. This is impatience. I love you, I want you, but I'm rapidly approaching the point where I'm starting to look pathetic, and I'm not willing to do that. You know where to find me if you start feeling less overwhelmed. I just hope it's sooner rather than later."

With that, he walked out the door.

* * *

*"That was really* nice," Nora told Aislinn as they put the last of the food away following Padraig's memorial service. Aislinn was glad Nora showed up. It was the right thing to do.

The service had been simple, held outside Padraig's cottage. A few people had gotten up to speak: Old Jack; Alan Fry, Alec's father, who'd known Padraig since they were boys; Beth Daly, Teague's mother; and Grace Finnegan. Aislinn was thankful that Father Bill, who'd never quite forgiven Padraig for making an arse out of him in the roofing incident, kept his holy talk brief. Padraig had never been a great churchgoer, though he did believe in "the big fella in the sky." It saddened Aislinn that Padraig had no family alive who could be there, but she found comfort in knowing that Padraig always knew he was considered part of her family and was dearly loved by his fellow villagers.

Liam was cool toward her, and Aislinn knew she deserved it. She *was* sending him mixed messages, and it was unfair, as well as selfish and cruel. *Ball's in your court.* She vowed to get her head on straight as soon as possible.

After the service, everyone headed back to the house for coffee (Nora's gorgeous coffee—how the compliments flew) and sandwiches. There was enough food left over to feed the whole of Ballycraig, especially when you added in the collection of casseroles people had brought yesterday. But perhaps that was a good thing: it would be one less thing to worry about.

"So, you and Liam," said Nora casually. "What's up?"

"Nothing."

"I'm not an idiot. I know he spent the night."

Aislinn felt her face go red. God, had she and Liam made noise? Had Nora heard? She'd die if that were the case.

"We were both a little drunk."

Nora looked dubious. "You're saying it was just sex."

"Yes."

"The perfume, the clippers, his determination—none of it has made an impression on you at all."

"I've got a lot on my plate right now, Nora. I really don't want to talk about this."

Nora rolled her eyes, but she let it drop.

"I'm glad you came to the service," said Aislinn, wiping down the kitchen table.

"Me, too," said Nora. "Even though he's gone, it made me feel like I was letting bygones be bygones. Plus I couldn't stand the thought of everyone disliking me."

"Since when did you ever care about that?" Aislinn asked, trying to keep the sharpness out of her voice.

"People change, Aislinn. I want to be liked, especially by the people we grew up around."

"Right." Aislinn put down the sponge in her hand. "Let's just get it out on the table, shall we?"

"Get what out on the table?"

Aislinn sighed wearily. "You know what. I'm not a stupid woman, Nora. I know you've got designs on the farm. You want to build a second home here, don't you?"

"Actually, I don't."

"Oh, no? What, then? Spit it out."

Nora sat down at the kitchen table. "Only if you promise to give me a fair hearing."

"Fine. Right. Talk."

"This farm has a lot of untapped potential, Aislinn."

"What does that mean?"

"I mean we could make a lot of money from it if you were willing to make a few changes."

"Like what?"

"We could turn the house into a B and B." Nora's eyes shone with enthusiasm. "Donald and I would run it. We'd finally get to be our own bosses. Meanwhile, guests would get to have a real rural experience—you know, spend time on a working farm, go into Ballycraig at night . . . We could even turn Padraig's cottage into a sauna."

"Let me get this straight," Aislinn said slowly, pure shock a slow-moving force through her body. "You want to turn *my* house into a bed-and-breakfast."

"It's half—"

"Shut up, Nora. What's this 'working farm' rubbish you're spouting?"

"Guests could watch you and Deenie herd the sheep, and watch you shear them when it's time. Maybe they could even watch some lambs being born in the spring! We could even have hay rides and hold sheep dog trials here."

Aislinn clenched her jaw so hard it began to hurt. She fought the urge to storm upstairs, toss all Nora's things in her bloody suitcases, and call her sister a cab. Instead, she simply stared her down.

"Who do you think you are, marching in here and thinking you can just take over?"

"I'm not trying to take over. Don't you see? It's something we could do *together*."

Aislinn snorted derisively. "Right. You, me, and Donald, the three musketeers. One for all and all for one. Tell me: have you really been working on an article all this time, Nora? Or you have you just been here trying to get the lay of the land?"

"I've been working on my article," Nora insisted defensively.

"What the hell for, if your master bloody plan is to try to turn this place into a B and B?"

"I want to keep my academic career going as a backup—"

"In case what?" Aislinn snapped. "The B and B doesn't work out? Where would that leave me?"

Nora colored a little. "Actually, I hadn't thought about that."

"No, of course you hadn't, because you're a selfish cow. How dare you think you can just turn my life upside down? Worse, where do you get the gall to think I'd go along with it? *How dare you?*"

"You're being shortsighted, Aislinn," Nora insisted.

*"This is my home!"* Aislinn shouted. "You left ten years ago and never looked back! Now all of a sudden you're here because you see a business opportunity, you and that stuck-up husband of yours—who by the way, hardly seems the type to run a B and B. But let me guess: if things didn't work out, he has an out, too: he could just go back to his nice, cushy, financial job, couldn't he? Put his 'golden handcuffs' back on. How lovely for the two of you."

Nora looked guilty as she glanced away.

"Ashamed, are you?" Aislinn challenged, coming to stand right in front of her. "You damn well should be."

"Take some time to calm down and really think about this, Aislinn. This could be a very, very lucrative venture."

"As if I give a tinker's damn about money!" Aislinn shook her head in disbelief. "You're unbelievable. Did you really think I'd go along with this? Do you not *know* *me*?"

"I just thought—"

You've no respect for me and the life I've built here," Aislinn cut in angrily. "None at all."

"That's not true."

"Go back to London, where you belong," Aislinn said coldly.

"This house is half mine. I can stay as long as I like."

"Fine. Then we'll draw a chalk line down the middle, and you stick to your side, and I'll stick to mine. I'll be giving you a bill tomorrow for your half of the household expenses. You can also find your own way into Moneygall the next time you want to make a run for gourmet groceries. My truck is off-limits—unless you're going to start giving me money for petrol and repairs. Now, if you'll excuse me, I have work to do."

# 33

*"All right, spit* it out."

Liam pretended he didn't hear Bettina as he stared out the back window of her and Jack's jalopy as the three of them returned to Ballycraig after Padraig's memorial service. Liam had been in a foul mood ever since he'd walked home from Aislinn's earlier that morning.

After their fight, he'd fought not to let disappointment and anger overtake him. He could understand Aislinn being overwhelmed; what he didn't get was why she thought their being together would contribute to it. Their getting back together should have made her feel the opposite. She was stalling, and he was losing patience. Liam meant what he'd said: he loved her, but he had no intention of being one of those pathetic guys who pined for a woman for eternity, one of those guys who, it turns out in the end, was wasting his time. The ball was in her court, and if she didn't hit it back to him soon, they were done. To add to his mood, by the time he got back into town, his damn feet were covered in blisters from having to walk in Jack's too-tight shoes.

Later that day when it was time to drive back to Aislinn's for the memorial service, Jack flashed him a "you sly devil" look when they'd gotten in the car. Liam sent Jack one quick, cutting look that he hoped conveyed he was in no mood to talk about the previous night. But Bettina wasn't going to let him keep her in the dark after she'd noticed how cool Liam and Aislinn were toward one another at the service. The minute they got in the car to drive home, Bettina started prodding him.

"I know God gave you ears, so don't pretend you don't hear me," she said. Christ, she sounded like his mother's long-lost twin.

"And don't pretend you don't know what I'm talking about, either," she added.

Liam cracked the window, hoping fresh air would dissipate the overpowering scent of Bettina's lily of the valley perfume. He remembered Aislinn saying it made the car smell like a "funeral parlor on wheels" and held back a laugh. She was right.

"Things didn't work out with Aislinn the way I thought they would."

"But you slept up there last night," said Jack, unable to stay out of it.

"So?"

"Were you too drunk to do the deed?" Jack asked, catching Liam's eyes in the rearview mirror. "Is she mad that you couldn't, you know, perform?"

"I performed fine, thank you very much!"

"What then?" Bettina pushed.

"She says it shouldn't have happened. That she wasn't thinking straight because of grief."

Bettina clucked her tongue. "Poor thing. She's still frightened."

"Well, I don't know how much more of it I can take, and I told her so."

Bettina looked shocked. "You didn't."

"Good on ya, I say," Jack countered proudly. "A man

can only endure so much. It's good you laid down the law." Bettina shot him a withering look, and he hunched in the driver's seat. "Relatively speaking, I mean."

"Don't you worry: she'll come round," Bettina assured him. "She loves you; it's clear as day. I bet it's just that she's feeling she's got too much on her plate right now, what with the old man gone and trying to get in a rhythm with Alec and that bloody Nora hanging around. Did you see the way that one was swanning around after the service, making sure everyone had enough to eat and drink? Like she was the hostess. I don't trust that one."

"Neither does Aislinn," said Liam. "She's convinced Nora wants to build a second house for her and her husband on the property. Or refurbish Padraig's cottage for themselves."

Jack laughed loudly. "Over Aislinn's dead body."

"Did their parents not leave the farm entirely to Aislinn?" Bettina asked, sounding mystified. "It's been her home her whole life—and God knows the Queen of Sheba never cared about the place."

"I'm sure her parents thought leaving it to both of them was the right thing to do," said Liam. "Cutting Nora out would have been cruel."

"I'm sure that's what they thought, too," Jack concurred. "I mean, she might have legged it out of here faster than a hare being chased by a hound, but she was still their child."

"True," said Bettina. She took some lily of the valley out of her purse and spritzed her wattled neck. Liam fought a gag as he cracked his window wider.

"Did you give Aislinn a deadline?" Jack asked.

"Are you kidding me?" Liam snorted. "Give Aislinn an ultimatum? She would have told me to take the express train to hell!"

Bettina laughed. "True."

"No, I just told her I wasn't going to wait around forever."

Jack nodded approvingly. "A sensible approach."

Bettina jerked a thumb at Jack. "Will you listen to Mr. Relationship Expert over here?"

"A man's entitled to his opinion," Jack huffed.

"Keep telling yourself that." Bettina touched Jack on the shoulder. "Did you tell Liam about the phone call you got from America?"

"Thanks for reminding me. Totally slipped my mind with Padraig's death and all." Again his eyes met Liam's in the rearview mirror. "I got a call from some woman in America. Said she worked for a book publisher and that there's some big shot writer over there who's doing a book tour of Ireland and wants to do a reading at the pub. Says he knows you."

"PJ Leary?"

"Yes. That was the name."

"He's been a regular at my parents' place forever. He's been writing some Celtic fantasy novel for years. Quinn told me he sold it for megabucks. He's a nice guy."

"All right, then. I'll call the woman back and tell her it's a go."

Liam thought the villagers would probably like PJ. He was down-to-earth, and since he was capable of talking the ear off a brass monkey, he'd probably get on well with Jack.

"This doesn't mean we have to buy a copy of his book, do we?" Bettina asked apprehensively.

"Nah, he'll probably give you one for free."

"Great. I could do with a good read." There was a split second of quiet, and then Bettina gasped.

"Liam, get down! Get down!"

"What?" Liam asked, bewildered.

"That fella who's been asking after you—he's walking down the high street!" said Jack.

"But he doesn't even know what I look like!"

"Just get down, get down," Bettina hissed.

*Shit,* Liam thought, slumping down. He was just about at his wit's end with this melodrama. If the guy wanted to kill him, he'd find a way to kill him, and there was nothing he could do about it.

Jack slowed down, obeying the town speed limit. Unable to resist, Liam peeked his head over the edge of the back window. The guy was tall and thin, dressed in a suit, carrying a briefcase. Once they were past him, Liam sat back up, poking Jack in the shoulder.

"That was the guy?"

"That was him, all right."

"You told me he was beefy! And that he had a scar on his cheek and looked kind of shady!"

Jack coughed uncomfortably. "I might have, you know, exaggerated a bit in all my nervousness."

"Yeah, just a bit," Liam replied sarcastically.

"You'd think he'd have figured out by now that he'll get nowhere," snapped Bettina.

Liam grimaced. "Trust me: if the Mob sent him, he's going to keep coming back until he gets what he came for."

Bettina looked upset. "Please don't say things like that."

"It's true." Liam rolled up the window as it began to rain.

"Maybe he's just going to kneecap you or something," Bettina suggested weakly.

"Well, whatever he's going to do, I can't stop him. If he comes into the pub asking about me and I'm there, then I'm not going to run. I can't duck him forever. If he's gonna kill me, he's gonna kill me, end of story."

Bettina shuddered. "Let's stop talking about this. Please."

They drove the rest of the road in silence.

# 34

*Aislinn was tiring* of her cold war with Nora. It had been three weeks since they'd had their showdown, and they hadn't spoken a word to each other since. She'd been cranky, reluctant to talk about it with anyone, but eventually Alec coaxed the source of her bad mood out of her. Unfortunately, he then turned around and told one of his brothers, and as was always the case in Ballycraig, eventually the whole town knew about Nora's plan. Aislinn felt bad about that, but maybe, if enough people told Nora it was a mad idea, it would help her get it through her thick head that the B and B plan would never happen.

At least she and Alec were working well together. He'd kept his promise not to make calf's eyes at her and proved to be a natural salesman at the farmers' market. As she'd done with Padraig, she split all profits with him.

Aislinn hadn't yet worked up the courage to clean out Padraig's cottage. It felt too soon, as well as too sad, especially since he had no family to give his belongings to. There was only one memento she wanted to keep for herself: a photograph of her father and Padraig when they were in their early twenties, standing together smiling after herding the flock into the meadow directly across the street. They looked so handsome and happy, Padraig's arm draped congenially over her father's shoulder. Both doing the job they loved to do—a job she, too, loved.

She hadn't been down to the pub since she and Liam had had their discussion in the kitchen the morning of the memorial service. She told herself it was because she was too exhausted, but the truth was, she was nervous that she'd walk in there, and he'd tell her he'd given up on her. Aislinn knew she couldn't avoid him forever, so she resolved she'd go to the Oak that evening for her usual dram of whiskey and let the chips fall where they may.

*   *   *

*I knew she couldn't avoid me forever*, Liam thought to himself, pleased, when Aislinn came breezing into the Oak. She was immediately the center of attention when she walked through the door. Everyone felt compelled to come over to her and put their two cents in about Nora.

"How's the B and B coming along?" Fergus called to Aislinn, tongue in cheek.

"Oh, grand, grand," Aislinn replied, coming over to the bar.

"She'll get hers yet," Bettina sniffed. "The usual?"

Aislinn nodded, her gaze almost tentative as she regarded Liam. "Hello."

"Hey." Behind him, Liam sensed Bettina and Jack acting as casual as could be, but he knew they'd be listening in on every word he and Aislinn exchanged, mining it for nuance and hidden meaning.

"I heard about Nora," Liam continued.

"Everyone's heard about Nora."

Aislinn accepted her drink from Bettina with thanks. She was being friendly, conversational. Liam wasn't sure how to interpret it. Maybe she'd come to tell him she wanted to get back together and was just easing into it?

"Is it true she's still up at the house?" David asked.

Aislinn nodded.

"Surely she's got to leave sometime to go home to that toff," said Jack.

"Yes, she does—home to the toff *and* her job, when her sabbatical ends," Aislinn explained.

"And when's that?" Bettina asked.

"Not soon enough, believe me," said Aislinn.

Everyone laughed—until the pub door swung open wide and in walked the mysterious stranger. Talk came to a grinding to a halt. The man looked around the room; finally his cool, appraising stare zeroed in on the bar.

"You Liam O'Brien?" he asked.

"Yes."

Liam felt oddly calm, even though his guts were turning into ice water. All he could think was: *Please, God, don't let him blow me away in front of everyone. Let him at least have the decency to ask to talk to me outside and do it there*. He hated the thought of the people he loved, especially Aislinn, having to see his brains splattered against the back of the bar.

"Ah, so we finally meet," said the man. No one moved. No one said a word.

He hoisted his briefcase up onto the bar. Liam tensed as he opened it.

Out came a sheaf of papers. "It's been brought to my attention that you've been working in Ireland illegally."

Liam furrowed his brows. "Who are you?"

"Name's Thomas McNulty. I'm from the INIS— Irish Naturalization and Immigration Service. We were informed you were working in this country without a work permit and came to investigate."

"And you were told this by—?"

"I'm not at liberty to say."

"You are aware you can be deported for this," McNulty continued.

"Not unless you're putting him on a plane right now," Aislinn spoke up.

McNulty turned to look at her. "Pardon?"

"We're getting married tomorrow morning," she declared, "which means he'll be married to an Irish citizen, and his working here won't be an issue."

Liam stared at Aislinn. She stared back. Her face revealed nothing.

McNulty frowned. "Is that so?"

"It is," said Bettina, her hands on her hips. "That's why we're so packed in here tonight: we're all celebrating. Can I get you anything, Mr. McNulty? It's on the house."

"A whiskey, thank you." McNulty actually looked disappointed. "You might be able to work here legally as of tomorrow," he said to Liam in an authoritarian tone, "but tonight you'd best come out from behind that bar right now, unless you want to be arrested and deported."

"A night off? Sounds great." Liam whipped off his apron and came out from behind the bar, putting a friendly hand on McNulty's shoulder. "Anything else I can help you with?"

McNulty closed up his briefcase. "That will be all." He raised his glass. "Congratulations on your impending nuptials. May you have a long, happy life together."

"Thank you," Aislinn and Liam said in unison as he quickly drained his glass. "You drive safe now," Bettina called after McNulty as he left. "And while you're about it, don't let the door hit you in the arse on the way out," she muttered under her breath. When he was gone, she turned to Aislinn with a big grin. "So, what time should we be at the registry office tomorrow morning?"

\* \* \*

*As soon as* McNulty left, Liam excused himself to go to the men's room to throw up. He knew it was just his body purging itself of the terror of thinking the guy had come to kill him. *Thank God*, he thought, splashing his face with cold water as he tried to stop shaking. *Thank God, thank God, thank God.*

He ambled back out into the pub, patting Teague on the

back collegially as he pointed behind the bar. "Go on. Fill in for me tonight. That's what you were hoping for when you called the INIS, right? That I'd be deported, and the job would open up for you, the Irishman I'd robbed of employment? Go for it."

Teague gave him a dirty look.

"Yes, come on, Teague," said Jack. "Show us what a hardworking and sociable lad you really are."

"He's not coming behind this bar," Bettina snapped. "He'll be lucky if I ever let him in here again after what he did."

"I didn't do anything!" Teague insisted.

"Fat lying bastard," Bettina continued disgustedly. "I can't stand the sight of you. Get out!"

Teague scrambled off his stool faster than Liam had ever seen him move in his life. Everyone watched him go.

"He's a disgrace, that one," said Bettina. "He'd best give me a wide berth if he knows what's good for him."

"You and me both," said Liam. He walked over to Aislinn. "Can we talk?" he asked quietly.

"Of course."

"Let's go upstairs."

\* \* \*

*She'd never been* one for impulsiveness, but Aislinn knew there were times when one had to take action, and when the INIS man threatened Liam with deportation, the words "We're getting married" just flew from her mouth. She waited for the man to accuse her of just marrying Liam so he could remain in the country. But that wasn't why she had done it. She'd done it because she loved him, and because a world without Liam O'Brien in it wasn't one she wanted to live in.

She followed Liam into his flat, smiling to herself as the chatter in the pub resumed. Liam sat on the couch, looking up at her incredulously.

"What?" Aislinn asked, sitting down beside him.

"You didn't have to do that."

"I know I didn't." Aislinn took his hand. "But I wanted to. Because I love you. That was me tossing the ball back into your court, love. I couldn't bear it if you were deported."

"So we're getting married tomorrow." He sounded stunned.

"Unless you don't want to, in which case—"

"I have an idea," Liam interrupted.

"What's that?"

"How about you just shut up and let me kiss you?"

Aislinn laughed. "I think that might be allowed."

Liam wrapped his arms around her, kissing her passionately. She could feel her blood throbbing through her body, reminding her that this was how it felt to be truly alive. It was an amazing feeling, almost sacred in its intensity.

"I have another idea," Liam whispered in her ear.

"What's that?"

"How about you let me show you my gratitude by making mad, passionate love to you?"

"We can't," said Aislinn. "Not with everyone downstairs. They'll *know*."

"So?"

"I can't," Aislinn said sheepishly. She ran her index finger lightly along his jawline. "Surely you can wait until tomorrow night. It'll be our wedding night, after all."

"Yeah, after I get off work."

"I'm sure Jack will give you the night off." She shook her head in disbelief. "I'm stunned Teague would do that to you, all for a job tending bar."

Liam laughed. "It was never about the job. It was about you."

Aislinn was baffled. "What are you talking about?"

"He's got a crush on you. He's probably had it for years."

"Teague Daly? Don't be daft!"

"I'm telling you, that's what's going on," Liam insisted. "And I can see why."

"Oh yes, because I'm so desirable," Aislinn mocked.

"You are."

"Give over."

Liam put his arm around her, and Aislinn rested her head on his shoulder. "I guess we should talk about tomorrow," he said.

"Registry office opens at ten. I doubt there will be a problem. First off, it's during the week. Secondly, I know the judge. Even if he can't take us right away, I'm sure he'll fit us in somewhere."

Liam nodded. "I wish there was time for my family to come over," he murmured sadly.

Aislinn cupped his face tenderly. "We can always have a proper church wedding somewhere down the line if you want." She paused. "Maybe even in New York."

Again, Liam looked stunned. "You would do that for me? Get married again in New York?"

"Why not?"

Liam began stroking her hair. "Are you going to ask Nora to come?"

*Nora.* She hadn't thought about that. "We haven't spoken in three weeks, Liam," Aislinn said quietly. "It's been hell." She paused. "But she is my sister," she decided, snuggling closer to Liam. "Of course, she might not come."

"I doubt that."

"Don't. As we've all discovered, my sister Nora is just full of surprises."

"I guess I better go over to my aunt and uncle's house to let them know." Liam looked distressed. "What about rings? We don't have any rings."

"Oh, pssstt, that's nothing," Aislinn said dismissively. "Stop fretting like some old lady. We'll get them eventually."

"I'm gonna have to buy a car to get back and forth to town."

"You're not getting a *car*," Aislinn scoffed. "You're getting that motorcycle you were saving for."

"That's a lot of money."

"I have some money saved, too, you know."

It was the money she planned to use to buy a few new ewes, but that could wait. It was more important that her husband (her husband—how she loved the sound of that!) be able to get back and forth to work.

"I can't take money from you!"

Aislinn was amused. "Darlin', as of tomorrow, it won't be my money; it'll be our money."

"Oh. Right." Liam paused, his expression uneasy. "I have just one request."

"Yes?"

"Can we dress casually tomorrow? I had to borrow Jack's shoes for Padraig's wake, and my feet were covered in blisters. I also had to borrow my cousin's suit, which was the most uncomfortable thing I've had to wear since my first Holy Communion."

"I think a nice pair of jeans and a button-down shirt would be fine. As for me, I'll be in my wellies and flannel shirt."

Liam shrugged. "Fine with me."

Aislinn slapped his arm playfully. "Get on with yourself. I might be a sheep farmer, but I'm still a woman. I'll wear what I wore at the memorial, that green dress? Maybe fancy it up just a little bit with one of Nora's scarves. What do you think?"

"I think you're going to look like a goddess no matter what you wear, McCafferty."

Aislinn laughed loudly. "It's *the* McCafferty, thank you very much."

"No, it's the wife, and the woman I love with all my heart."

Aislinn felt her eyes begin to glisten with tears. "I love you so, you plastic Paddy."

"And I love you." He rose and held his hand out to her. "We should go back downstairs. I'm sure there are some people who'd like to hoist some drinks in our honor. Shall we?"

"My pleasure, Mr. O'Brien."

\* \* \*

*Returning from the* pub, where many drinks indeed had been hoisted in honor of her and Liam's nuptials tomorrow morning, Aislinn had a moment of hesitation before she padded upstairs and rapped lightly on Nora's door. What if she invited Nora, and she refused to go? She tossed out the thought. This was her sister.

"Come in."

Nora was sitting up in bed, reading. She looked surprised to see Aislinn as she closed her book and took off her glasses. As usual, she was bundled up to her neck in a flannel nightie as if it were the dead of winter. Aislinn bit back the temptation to call her Nanook of the North.

Aislinn pointed to the side of the bed. "Can I sit?"

"Sure."

Aislinn sat down.

"To what do I owe the pleasure of your company?" Nora asked coolly.

"I'm marrying Liam tomorrow morning. I'd like you to come."

Nora looked shocked. "What?"

"I'm marrying Liam," Aislinn repeated, "and I'd like you to come."

"What on earth happened?"

"That sneak Teague Daly ratted Liam out to the INIS and told them he was working here illegally. So we're getting married tomorrow—not just so he can stay here legally, but because I love him."

"Whose idea was that?"

"Mine."

"You asked Liam to marry you?"

"Actually, I didn't so much ask as declare it to the INIS fella."

"Very romantic."

Aislinn ignored the crack. "I'd like you to be there."

"Of course I'll be there," Nora replied. "I take it Liam will be moving in with us?"

"With *me*," Aislinn corrected politely. "Don't you have to be back at university in about a month or so?"

"I do. Unless you change your mind about the B and B idea."

"Nora, that's never going to happen. Just out of curiosity, where were you planning to get the money to turn the house into a B and B?"

"I thought we'd take out a loan."

"We being who? You and Donald, or you and me?"

"You and me."

"Oh right," Aislinn chortled. "And then what? If the place went belly-up we'd default, and our credit would be wrecked? No thank you."

Nora said nothing.

"This is nothing more than a stupid escape fantasy for you, Nora. Admit it. Have you thought about what running a B and B entails? Yes, you'd be your own boss, but do you really want to be getting up early in the morning and cooking big breakfasts for guests? You really want to spend the day doing endless rounds of laundry and making up the beds fresh every day? Keeping the house impeccably clean? Always have to be pleasant and have a smile on your face, even when you're in a foul mood? That's your dream?"

Nora pressed her lips into a thin, hard line. "You're choosing to focus on the negatives."

"No, I'm focusing on the reality."

"The reality is we could make a lot of money, Aislinn."

"I told you: I'm not interested. If you and Donald are so hell-bent on a B and B, why don't you buy one in England and see how it goes?"

"Let's not talk about this anymore," Nora said wearily, changing the subject. "Who else will be there tomorrow?"

"Liam's relatives. Jack and Bettina." She paused. "It really means a lot to me that you'll be there," Aislinn added softly.

She heard Nora swallow. "It means a lot to me, too."

"I may not like you very much," Aislinn noted dryly, "but I do love you."

"Funny, I feel the same way."

"I'm going to call Judge Taylor and see if he can fit us in at ten. We'll ride down in the truck." Aislinn grinned. "I'm bringing Deenie, too."

"Judge Taylor isn't going to let a dog into the registry office!"

"Ah, of course he is. He's an old softie. My girl has to be there; she's part of the family."

"What are you wearing?"

"My green dress. Maybe I can borrow a scarf to spruce it up with a bit?"

"Of course."

Aislinn stood. "Well, I guess that's it, then. See you in the morning."

"Yes, good night," said Nora, slipping her reading glasses back on.

Aislinn felt like she was being dismissed, then decided she was being oversensitive. What mattered was that they'd put their differences aside on what would be the happiest day of her life, and for that, she was glad.

* * *

*There was one* more thing Aislinn needed to do before she tried to go to sleep. She walked down to Padraig's cottage and made herself a cup of tea before sitting in "her" chair.

"I don't know if you can hear me, old man," she started, a knot forming in her chest. "But I want to apologize for the way we parted. I know you left this world mad at me, but I just hope that wherever you are, you can forgive me. You know how much I love you; you've always been like a second father to me, and it just won't be the same around here without you."

She sat there for a good while, sipping her tea, combing through a catalogue of memories. When she was done, she rinsed the cup and put it on the drainboard before slowly moving to the front door. She started to leave, then turned back to look at the place where the old man had lived most of his life.

"Rest in peace, Padraig," she whispered. "Rest in peace."

## 35

*"This is mayhem. Truly."*

Liam ignored Old Jack's assessment of the registry office, which was, admittedly, packed with people. He should have known half the town would turn up for the wedding: not only because they wanted to see him and Aislinn tie the knot, but because word had spread fast that his aunt and uncle were hosting a small brunch at the pub after the ceremony. Never underestimate the lure of free food, he mused.

Liam's aunt and uncle had "gone mental," as his father would have said, when he told them the news. They were sad that his immediate family wouldn't be there, and his aunt predicted his mother would be "in floods of tears," which made Liam feel awful.

Unable to sleep, he called New York at 4 a.m. his time, 10 p.m. theirs. His parents were thrilled by the unexpected call. But when he told them he was getting married in a few hours, he was greeted by a stunned silence. Then he remembered: he'd never told them about Aislinn. He gave them the condensed version of their romance (omitting the bet, of course). By the time he was done, his mother *was* indeed in "floods of tears." She wondered aloud what this meant for his future. Was he intending to spend the rest of his life in Ballycraig? Would he and his wife be moving to the States? Liam evaded both questions, because he himself didn't know the answers and he really didn't want to think about them.

It was a surreal morning. Him. Getting married. To a sheep farmer. While hiding out in rural Ireland.

Since he hadn't been able to sleep, he'd driven out to the countryside in Jack's car to collect some wildflowers for a bouquet for Aislinn, just in case she hadn't had time to do so herself. He wished to hell he had a ring to give her, but she was right: that was a minor detail that could be taken care of later.

Bettina checked her watch. "She's late."

Liam's eyes lifted to the clock on the wall. "Only ten minutes."

His cousin Erin looked worried. "I hope her truck didn't break down."

Jack nudged him playfully in the ribs. "Maybe she came to her senses and isn't going to show."

"Thanks a lot," said Liam. He loved the image of Aislinn driving herself down to her own wedding in her truck. That was his girl. He hoped Nora was with her.

Grace Finnegan came hurrying through the door. "She's here!"

"Is Cleopatra with her?" Bettina asked.

"She is. And Deenie."

"Aislinn's a damn sight nicer than I would be to that traitorous—" said Bettina.

"Now, now," Jack chided. "It's a day for happiness and generosity."

"You're right," Bettina conceded, patting his arm.

Anticipation dashed through Liam as he waited for Aislinn to walk through the door of the registry office. In fact, the whole room was thick with it as his fellow Ballycraigers, too, held their breath.

Liam felt himself unexpectedly choking up when she

finally appeared. She looked breathtaking: her hair was pinned up loosely, soft red tendrils framing her face, and she'd woven wildflowers through her hair. She truly looked like she was glowing. The fact that the happy smile on her face was meant just for him made him feel as though this was all he'd ever need in life: her loving him, him loving her back.

Murmurs of "Oh, doesn't she look lovely," came from all over the room. Nora walked in behind Aislinn, holding Deenie on a leash. Nora's gaze was also fixed on Liam, likely because she didn't want to see the dirty looks coming her way.

Finally, Aislinn was beside him. Feeling as awkward as a boy at his first school dance, Liam held out the bouquet to her. "I didn't know whether you'd have time to put one together yourself, so I picked a few."

Aislinn's eyes glistened. "They're beautiful," she murmured.

"*You're* beautiful," said Liam, twining his fingers through hers.

"And you're quite the handsome devil."

Judge Taylor came out from behind the big mahogany door at the rear of the office, sending a hush through the room. He smiled when he saw Aislinn, extending his hand for Liam to shake.

"Congratulations. You're quite a lucky man."

Liam beamed. "I know."

The judge leaned in to Aislinn. "That wool you sold my Jenny last spring? Knitted me a gorgeous, gorgeous sweater."

"I'm glad."

He clapped his hands together. "Right! Let's get you two hitched."

Since two witnesses were needed, Liam's cousin Brian was his "best man," and Nora was Aislinn's "matron of honor." Liam could feel himself grinning like an idiot through the brief ceremony; he was deliriously happy, happier than he ever thought possible.

He'd given his camera to his cousin Erin so she could take pictures that he could later download and send to his family in New York. She was snapping away like a woman possessed. He couldn't wait for everyone back home to see how beautiful Aislinn was.

Finally, the words he couldn't wait to hear: "I now pronounce you man and wife."

A loud cheer went up from the crowd, and Aislinn actually blushed as Liam kissed her.

"Aren't you supposed to throw your bouquet?" Liam whispered to her.

"I think that's after," Aislinn whispered back. She squeezed his hand tight. "I love you so much it hurts."

"Me, too." He stole another kiss. "Onward to the Oak, Mrs. O'Brien."

*   *   *

*"Jaysus, it's hotter* than the fires of hell in here."

Aislinn laughed as Old Jack cranked open all the windows of the pub and put two bricks in place to hold the pub door open wide. There was no avoiding the heat: that's what happened when bodies were packed together tighter than sardines.

"I'm tickled everyone's here," Aislinn marveled.

"Course we're all here, darlin'. We wouldn't miss it for the world."

"Thank you, Jack."

"For opening up the pub like this? It's nothing. Besides, there was no way everyone would fit up at the O'Brien place."

Aislinn nodded. She'd never been to Liam's aunt and uncle's house, though now that would change, she imagined. She hoped with all her heart that she'd soon feel part of their family, now that all she had was Nora, and God only knew how that might end up.

She looked round for her sister but didn't see her anywhere. Excusing herself, she pushed her way through the crowd and headed outside. Nora was sitting on one of the benches outside the pub, smoking a cigarette.

"Since when do you smoke?" Aislinn asked, sitting beside her.

"I'm putting on weight. Time to go back to the tried-and-true coffee and cigarette diet."

"Sounds awfully unhealthy to me." She bumped her sister's shoulder affectionately, the way they used to do when they'd sit together at the kitchen table, or when they'd be stuck in the sitting room watching some horrible, boring show on the telly with their parents, and they were trying not to burst out laughing. "Thanks for coming."

Nora sucked on her cigarette. "Thanks for inviting me."

"Don't be daft."

Nora slowly blew out a trail of smoke. "A lot of people inside think you're daft to have invited me."

"I don't care what they think and never have. You know that."

"They hate me, Aislinn." Nora actually sounded miserable. "They think I'm a bad person."

"They don't think you're bad. They think you're—" Aislinn hesitated.

"What? You can say it."

"Stuck-up," Aislinn finished quietly. "Stuck-up and selfish."

"You left out insensitive," Nora said bitterly.

*Well, that, too,* Aislinn thought, but she didn't want to add salt to the wound. She changed the subject. "I wish Mam and Da were here today."

"Me, too. They would have loved Liam."

"I wish Padraig were here, too. I can't believe how much I miss that moody old bugger."

"Well, you two were close."

"We were." Aislinn touched Nora's shoulder. "Come back inside," she urged softly.

Nora shook her head. "No. I'm going to be taking off soon."

"What are you talking about?"

"I'm actually waiting for a cab." She knocked her shoulder against Aislinn's. "You and Liam are newlyweds! You're entitled to a little privacy, don't you think? A cab will be here to pick me up in a few minutes to take me back to the house to get a small bag, and then it'll drive me to Cork so I can catch a plane back to London."

*And will you be coming back?* Aislinn was dying to ask, but she didn't want to go there, not today.

"You haven't seen Donald in a while."

"No, I haven't. I'm looking forward to it."

"Give him my regards."

"I will." Nora yanked on one of the tendrils framing Aislinn's face. "Get back inside! It's your wedding day! You're supposed to be celebrating!"

"All right, all right." She gave Nora a hug. "Talk soon?"

"Of course."

Aislinn stood. "You sure you don't want me to wait with—"

"Get inside!" Nora scolded.

"Leave a message on the answer phone when you get home so I know you arrived safe and sound."

"I will."

Aislinn leaned over, kissed her sister on the cheek, and went back inside.

*     *     *

*"I can't believe* they decorated the truck!"

Aislinn was standing naked in front of the mirror in her room, undoing her hair. What was supposed to be just brunch had turned into an all-day affair that eventually turned into a *céilí.* Aislinn was glad; you were supposed to dance on your wedding day, though she did burst out laughing when Chuck Clayton again led the band in its anemic and out-of-tune version of Peaches & Herb's "Reunited."

"I think this should be our song," Liam had whispered in her ear as they attempted to dance to it.

"I think you should have your Yank head examined," Aislinn replied.

Things finally wound down at around nine. Aislinn had been shocked when they'd said their good-byes, left the pub, and found her truck covered in white crepe paper and cardboard wedding bells, with ten soup cans tied to the back bumper, across which was a sign that read, "Just Married!"

"Who could have done that?" she'd asked Liam.

"David and Fergus, I think. Jack told me they had something planned."

"Jesus, I never thought they'd do anything nice for me in their lives. I guess this means I'll actually have to be nice to them."

Liam had laughed.

While Aislinn brushed out her hair, Liam slipped out of his clothes. She loved that he slept naked. She'd never been able to; she'd always had to have at least a T-shirt and panties on. But perhaps, now that she had that gorgeous body to snuggle up to every night, she could learn to do otherwise. Flesh touching flesh all night long; that's what she wanted.

Aislinn paused, turning around to look at him. "It was a great day," she said with a happy sigh.

"It was," Liam agreed. He stretched out on the bed, ankles crossed, his fingers laced behind his head. "My mother wants to talk to you on the phone tomorrow."

"What?" said Aislinn, panic hitting her smack in the center of her chest.

Liam looked amused. "Don't worry; she's not going to grill you! She just wants to welcome you to the family."

"I'm not good on the phone," Aislinn said uneasily.

"Just be yourself. It'll be fine."

"If you say so."

"I should probably look for my bike tomorrow."

"There's a Honda dealership in Moneygall."

"Want to come with me?"

"You know I can't," Aislinn said with a pout. "I've got work to do."

Liam sighed. "I know." He turned on his side, propping himself up on his elbow, watching her. "It's going to be weird, you getting up at five and me coming home around one. Different schedules."

"We'll make it work," Aislinn said confidently.

"Course we will." Liam's gaze was tender. "Promise me you won't ever cut your hair."

"Promise me you won't say this house is cold as an icebox."

"Cold doesn't bother me. In fact, I kind of like it. Winter is my favorite time of year back ho—back in New York."

*Back home. He was going to say back home. You're home now,* she thought.

"Perhaps we'll go over at Christmas, if we have the money."

"If it's safe for me to go back," Liam said grimly. He paused. "My family is going to love you," he continued, steering them back onto a happier topic. "I know it."

"I hope so."

Liam rolled onto his back. "Do you think we should move into your parents' room? It is a lot bigger."

Six months ago, the thought would have horrified her; it would have been like desecrating sacred space. But now it felt right. It was her and Liam's house now, and someday, hopefully, her room would belong to one of their children.

"That's a good idea. Maybe we could even get a new bed. King size."

"Living high off the hog," Liam teased.

"You bring out my decadent side," Aislinn purred, slipping beneath the covers beside him.

"Mmm, I like the sound of that," Liam murmured, turning to her. Aislinn twined her arms around his neck as Liam's arms reached round to lightly grip her back. She nuzzled his neck, the musky scent of him drugging. A small groan escaped his lips, and he pulled her tighter to him. Aislinn lifted her head and stared into his eyes. There was no need for words; she was so overwhelmed with love for this man, she wasn't sure she could form any, even if she wanted to.

"I love you," Liam finally whispered, kissing her temples softly. Aislinn let her eyes drift shut, her breathing slow, her heart belonging to him and him only. He kissed her forehead. Kissed her eyelids. Playfully nipped the tip of her nose. And then, ever so gently, almost as if he'd never done it before, he parted her lips with his tongue, kissing her slow and deep.

*So lovely, always so lovely and perfect,* she thought as her mind danced round itself. She wanted him, but she was in no rush. Tonight she wanted their love to unfurl slowly, so slowly she'd be acutely aware of every sound made and every sensation felt. She could tell that Liam felt the same way: His hands were moving up and down her back lazily, his tongue dancing around hers languid and slow.

His mouth moved to her throat, kissing sweetly, nipping lightly. "You always taste so good," he whispered. Aislinn sighed, allowing herself to sink mindlessly into his touch, loving it as his mouth trailed lower to kiss her collarbone and then her breasts. She adored the way he was leisurely exploring her body, the care he seemed to be taking to know every inch of her skin. His touch was like magic; no matter where his hands were, no matter where his mouth went, golden pleasure prevailed.

She was touching him, too, ever so lightly, her fingertips gliding over his smooth, warm skin. Up and down his back; along the sides of his muscled legs, all of it enhanced by an overwhelming sense of amazement. *This is my husband. This is the man I'm going to spend the rest of my life making love to.* Just thinking about it made her tremble with wonder and excitement.

The touching between them bedazzled, aroused, layer upon layer of pleasure slowly being uncovered and treasured. Finally, Liam lifted his head, framing her face in his hands, his look so fiercely tender it took her breath away. "I want to be inside you."

"God, yes, please."

Aislinn gently rolled onto her back, watching him as he slowly eased between her legs, shivering at the sight of pure carnal pleasure that streaked across his handsome face as he began moving inside her. They moved slowly, never taking their eyes off one another. *No need for words,* she thought again as the rhythm between them grew steadily, like a lovely, unexpected rainstorm in the dead of summer that starts off as a drizzle and builds itself into a torrent: beautiful, pounding, washing away everything but that moment.

Her husband.

## 36

*Liam couldn't stop* his jaw from dropping when a black stretch limo pulled up in front of the pub and out stepped PJ Leary. This was the guy who, a year ago, was dressed in threadbare clothing and ran up a tab at his parents' bar that Liam ignored because he knew the poor bastard couldn't afford it. Now he was a famous author: his book, *The Wee Ones of Galway*, was a worldwide bestseller. The last time Liam had called home, his brother Quinn told him PJ had sold the movie rights to Steven Spielberg for ungodly sums of money. *Good for him*, Liam thought.

PJ looked like he'd just come off the beach in the Hamptons: chinos, topsiders, a starched white oxford shirt, a pink crewneck casually tied around his neck. A pair of expensive sunglasses perched on top of his head.

"Liam!" There was a happy grin on PJ's face, and he drew Liam up into a friendly hug, clapping him on the back. "It's great to see you!"

"You, too!" He gestured to Aislinn, who stood smiling beside him. "I want you to meet my wife, Aislinn."

She'd been nervous about meeting PJ. "I've never met

someone famous before," she'd lamented. It had taken Liam showing her pictures on his computer of the down-and-out PJ of a year ago to convince her he was just a regular guy.

"Pleased to meet you," said PJ, shaking Aislinn's hand.

"You, too," said Aislinn, visibly relaxing. "I've heard a lot about you."

PJ chuckled. "Good things, I hope."

"Well, a few bad things," Aislinn teased, "but we won't mention them."

"I couldn't believe it when your parents told me you got married," he said to Liam in amazement. "Remarkable what can happen on a holiday, isn't it?"

"Guess so," said Liam, still grinning at the new PJ.

PJ looked Liam up and down, sizing him up. "You look good. Married life suits you."

"It does," Liam agreed. He and Aislinn had been married for two months, and so far, so good. They both had a tendency toward moodiness, and each had learned to give each other a wide berth when the other had a mood on. Liam liked to tease her that he was holding on to his flat above the Oak just in case she ever kicked him out in a fit of temper. He couldn't imagine that ever happening, though there were times when her mood truly did border on foul. That tended to happen on the weekends Nora showed up with Donald in tow. Liam himself had tried to talk some sense into Nora, trying to convince her there was no way Aislinn would ever turn the farm into some kind of B and B, but Nora wouldn't listen. She thought her presence would eventually wear Aislinn down. Actually, it was doing the opposite. Every time Nora showed up, Aislinn dug her heels in further, and her resentment grew. Nora was now beginning to piss Liam off, too.

Liam glanced around the sidewalk. "Where's your publicist?"

"I told her to go on ahead to Galway City, and I'd catch up with her tomorrow. She's been driving me crazy; it's like having a hyperactive, twittering bird around twenty-four/seven. I wanted to be able to relax and spend some time with you."

"Where are you staying tonight?"

"In a hotel in Crosshaven."

"You most certainly are not," declared Aislinn. "You'll stay up at the farm with us."

PJ looked touched. "That would be wonderful."

"I can drive you up to Galway City tomorrow," Liam offered.

"You've always been a good sort," said PJ affectionately, "despite your reputation."

Aislinn lifted her eyebrows questioningly. "And what reputation would that be?"

"You know, moody bad boy," said PJ with a wink.

"She knows all about that. Besides, that's when I was a teenager," Liam pointed out. "I haven't been bad in a very long time."

"Still moody, though," Aislinn noted.

Liam tugged a lock of her hair. "Look's who's talking." He glanced behind him at the limo driver, still sitting in the car. "Is this guy—?"

"Well, he's supposed to stick around and wait for me so he can drive me to Crosshaven and then Galway, but I guess I can let him go now," said PJ. He explained the situation to the driver, who got out to fetch PJ's bags from the trunk before he started carrying copies of PJ's books inside.

"You don't have to do that," PJ told him. "My friend Liam here and I can do it."

The driver looked grateful. "Thank you. I guess I'll see tomorrow in Galway, Mr. Leary."

"Call me PJ. Please. Drive safe, Timothy."

The driver nodded and got back in the car, pulling away from the curb smoothly.

"Seems like a nice guy," Liam noted.

"Very nice."

Liam bent and picked up a stack of PJ's books. "Shall

we? I think the eager hordes will be arriving soon, wanting to meet the famous writer."

"I'm still pinching myself," PJ said humbly and followed Liam inside.

* * *

*"What the feck* is he goin' on about with this army of leprechauns shite?"

Liam discreetly shushed Old Jack as he himself feigned
intense interest while PJ read from his book. Just as Liam
remembered, the book seemed to focus on a long-running
battle between a legion of leprechauns and some magical
talking salmon. Liam wasn't big on books, but PJ was a
very dramatic reader, and judging from the rapt attention of everyone in the pub, it seemed likely he might sell
every copy of his magnum opus, which were stacked high
on one of the tables near the fireplace for the book sign-
ing after the reading.

"Look, I need to talk to you about something," said
Jack, low.

Liam rolled his eyes as Jack led him into the small
alcove behind the bar. "What's up?"

"Bettina and I are going on holiday in a month."

"Oh, where?"

"Torremolinos. She's been on me for ages about it.
Anyway, we'll be gone about two weeks. Do you think
you can handle the bar on your own?"

Liam pursed his lips. "Prob . . . ably."

Jack looked irritated. "I suppose I could get in Jake
Fry to help you out, if you don't think you can man it
alone. He's got a bit of experience."

"That would be good."

"All right," Jack grumbled.

"You cheap bastard! You want me to do it alone so you
don't have to pay anyone else!"

"Of course I don't. D'ya think I'm made of money?"

"More than you let on, I know that much." He patted Jack's shoulder. "C'mon, we can talk about this some other time. I want to listen to my friend read."

"Talking fish," Liam heard Jack mutter behind him. "God help us all."

\* \* \*

*"God, I'm stuffed."*

Liam smiled as PJ patted his belly. The two of them were sitting on the bench in the mudroom, pulling on their shoes so they could take an early morning walk around the farm. Aislinn had already been up and working for a couple of hours. Liam had drifted in and out of sleep after she left their bed, but when he heard PJ moving around at about six thirty, he decided he'd get up and make his friend a big breakfast before he drove him to Galway. Liam was glad when PJ said he wanted to take a stroll before the drive. It was a gorgeous day, and he knew the pride Aislinn took in the farm. She'd be pleased to see Liam out there showing him around, especially since they hadn't been able to do it last night.

He took PJ up to the highest meadow first, the one where Aislinn had been mending fences the first time he ventured up to the house. The memory made him chuckle. She'd been so gruff and dismissive with him, and now look at them: married.

PJ did a slow, three hundred and sixty degree turn as he took in the breathtaking panorama of green stretching as far as the eye could see. "This is amazing. Is it all Aislinn's?"

"Most of it." He pointed down and to the left to an old stone wall that was so far away it looked like a thin gray ribbon. "That's where the neighbors' farm starts."

"Are they sheep farmers, too?"

"Dairy."

PJ looked entranced. "You're lucky to be surrounded by all this. You know that, don't you?"

Liam forced a pained smile.

"Homesick?" PJ guessed.

"Yeah," Liam said quietly.

"So take your bride home for a visit! Is it a money issue? Because if it is—"

"No, no, nothing like that."

"Then what?" PJ pressed.

Liam shrugged. "It's just a matter of timing," he said evasively. "I'd have to work it out far in advance with Jack, Aislinn would have to get someone to fill in for her, stuff like that. We'll get over there soon, don't worry."

"You better. Your mother's going to lose her mind if you don't. She can't wait to meet Aislinn."

"I think they'll get along, don't you?" said Liam as he began leading PJ to a neighboring pasture.

"Two headstrong Irish women? Could be trouble."

Liam laughed. "All the Irish women I know are headstrong. I think it will be fine. What about you, Mister Bestseller? You seeing anyone?"

"Not right now." He paused thoughtfully. "You know what depresses me? I couldn't get a woman to give me the time of day when I was poor. But now that I'm rich, they're flitting all around me like moths to a flame."

"They say money is the ultimate aphrodisiac, right?"

"Apparently." PJ kicked a stone. "Well, we'll see. I'm pretty content on my own. Always have been."

They made their way down to the far meadow below the house, where Padraig's cottage sat. PJ started to circle it, then stopped. "Sorry," he said apologetically. "Someone must live here."

"Unfortunately, it's empty. Padraig, the guy who used to help Aislinn's family on the farm, lived here, but he died a little while ago."

PJ stared at the cottage for a long time. "Do you think Aislinn would sell it to me?"

Liam didn't know what to say. "Uh . . ."

"One of my fantasies has always been to have a place in Ireland—not year round, just summers; a place where

I could escape for a couple of months to relax and write."
He put his hands on his waist, drawing in and blowing out
a deep breath as he surveyed the hills and pastures. "This
is perfect. The cottage is perfect, the setting is perfect."

"I—you should talk to Aislinn," Liam managed. He
felt like someone had just clocked him in the head with a
brick. This was not a conversation he ever imagined having in a million years.

"I'd pay whatever she wanted."

"Talk to Aislinn," Liam repeated.

"Now?"

"Yeah, why not? This isn't the kind of thing she'd want
to discuss over the phone." He had visions of delivering
PJ to Aislinn and then making a run for it. He did not
want to be there when PJ told her he wanted to buy some
of her precious land.

"All right," said PJ. "Let's go talk to her."

*   *   *

*No no no no.* That was Aislinn's first instinct when Liam
ambled across the road with PJ, and PJ told her he was
interested in purchasing Padraig's cottage. Actually, her
first instinct was to kill Liam. Surely he knew what her
reaction would be, but he'd brought his friend over here
anyway, and now she was going to have to tell the man
she'd no interest.

But then she began thinking about it. He'd only be
around in the summer, and it wasn't like they'd have to
entertain him, though she was sure they'd have him up
for supper sometimes.

"How much were you thinking of spending?" she
asked PJ casually. Out of the corner of her eye, she saw
the shocked expression on Liam's face. Clearly he had
thought he was bringing an innocent lamb to the slaugh-
ter, but he'd done it anyway.

"Name your price."

Aislinn pulled an outrageous figure out of the air.

"Are you sure you're not selling yourself short because I'm a friend of Liam's family?" PJ asked. "Because I wouldn't want you to do that."

Aislinn nearly choked. *Selling herself short?* She'd named such an exorbitant number she was sure PJ would just laugh and say thanks, but no thanks.

"No, I'm not selling myself short."

"All right, then," said PJ. "Sold."

Aislinn felt her stomach flip. "You know what? Would you mind if I spoke to a local estate agent and got an appraisal? Because I'd hate to overcharge you; it wouldn't be right."

"Fair enough," said PJ. "We'll be in touch, shall we? I'll be in Galway for three days."

"I'm sure we'll be able to discuss it by late tomorrow or the following morning at the latest."

PJ opened his arms wide for a hug. "It was great meeting you, Aislinn. I look forward to us being neighbors, at least in the summer."

Aislinn swallowed. "Yes." Did she really want to do this?

She kissed Liam. "Get him there in one piece, would you?"

"I'm not the lunatic driver in this family." He turned to PJ. "Shall we?"

"Onward and upward."

Aislinn watched them walk back across the street, Liam looking over his shoulder once to give her a *What the hell was that about?* look.

She smiled at him.

"Trust me," she mouthed.

## 37

*"All right, what* have you done with my wife?"

Liam was only half joking as he strode into the barn. Driving PJ up to Galway had taken longer than he thought, and he wound up speeding all the way home, not that anyone else on the road seemed to care. He told himself it was because he wanted to make sure he wasn't late for work, but really, he was itching to know what the hell was going through Aislinn's mind when she'd agreed to think about selling the cottage to PJ.

Aislinn was on her knees, giving an injection to a small lamb, who was panting heavily. "There you go," she soothed, as the animal scrambled back to its feet and made a beeline for its mother. Aislinn put the syringe back in the pocket of her barn jacket and turned around, smiling at the sound of Liam's voice.

"What did you say?"

"I said, what have you done with my wife? Clearly you're an imposter. The woman I married would never, ever entertain an offer to buy some of her land. Ever."

"The woman you married might just be a genius."

"I'm listening."

They sat down together on a big bale of straw. "After you left, I rang Carole Brown, the local estate agent, and she came over to give me an estimate for what she thought Padraig's cottage and the lower meadows would go for. My teeth almost fell out of my head when she told me." She put her arm through Liam's. "Here's my idea," she stage-whispered. "I sell the cottage and land to PJ, and then give Nora the money in return for her share of the farm." Aislinn looked excited. "It's a ton of money, Liam! More than enough for her and Donald to go buy some B and B in England or do whatever the hell they want to do. They get to pursue their dream, I get to keep my farm, everyone's happy."

"Look, I don't want to rain on your parade," Liam said carefully, "but what if she doesn't go for it?"

"Then we split the money on the sale of the cottage and the land, and she can spend the rest of her days trying to talk me into turning this place into a B and B, which is never going to happen."

Liam nodded slowly. "It could work. Is she coming in this weekend?"

"Yes, I think she's getting in tomorrow morning. Hopefully we can get this hammered out as soon as possible."

"Will His Lordship be with her?"

Aislinn chuckled. "You're getting as bad as Bettina. I'm not sure."

Liam looked round the barn, listening to the chattering of the starlings that nested in the high beams. Aislinn seemed not to notice them, but he was still struck by the sound every time he walked in here. It was part of the soundtrack of his wife's life: the sounds of the barn, the wind in the trees, the baaing of the flock . . . Nora's plan was hopeless. Aislinn would never let strangers come in here to watch her work and bombard her with questions, ruining her peace.

He regarded his wife seriously. "Are you absolutely sure you'll be able to handle PJ being around in the summer?"

"I thought about that. It's not as if he's going to be living in the house with us. He'll have his own place, and he'll be down there writing. He can walk into town or ride a bike. And it is only for the summers."

"Hypothetical: what if he decided he wanted to move here full-time?"

Aislinn bit her lower lip. "Well, again, he's in his own place, with his own land. . . ."

"I'm not saying he would," Liam was quick to assure her. "The guy's a lifelong New Yorker. But I thought it was worth mentioning."

"I guess we'll cross that bridge if we come to it." Aislinn stood, straightening out her jacket. "I'll talk to Nora when she gets in."

"Need backup?"

"I think you should make yourself scarce. Otherwise, she'll feel like we're ganging up on her."

Liam stood, checking his watch. "Shit. I'm going to be late for work. Any chance of you popping in tonight?"

"Sure thing. I have to keep an eye on you, make sure you don't flirt with the ladies, especially after PJ revealed what a bad boy you are."

"Yeah, that's me," said Liam dryly. "Bad to the bone." He kissed her nose. "See you later. Love you."

"Me, too," said Aislinn as he started out of the barn. Back outside as the sun began to set, PJ's words came back to him: *You're lucky to be surrounded by all this. You realize that, don't you?* Liam knew it rationally, but after spending the day in the car with PJ, his head was filled with images of home, remembered sights, remembered sounds, and the fear that he might never see any of it again. It could happen. It wasn't *likely*, but it could. He made the thought vanish as he ran inside to take a quick shower, then headed off for work.

\* \* \*

*Aislinn couldn't believe* she was nervous about talking to Nora. *Nora.* She didn't know what the hell she would do if her sister dug her heels in. She imagined years worth of tension . . . it would be hell.

Nora arrived midmorning. Aislinn was in the high north meadow when she saw the cab pull up, and she involuntarily held her breath, waiting to see if Donald followed her out of the back of the taxi. He didn't. Relieved, she left Alec in charge and went down to the house to talk to her sister, feeling mildly nauseous.

Nora was in the kitchen, unpacking groceries. *Hell on a stick,* thought Aislinn. *She's planning to be here awhile. Well, I can deal with it. Especially if she does the sensible thing.*

"Good morning," said Aislinn pleasantly. "How was your flight? And the ride up from Cork?"

"The flight was fine, but the cab ride was hell. The cabbie would not shut up. I got to hear his whole life story! I finally told him I had a headache, and he left me alone."

Aislinn wanted to shoot back, "Oh, that bodes well for someone who wants to run a B and B. You think the guests won't be chatty? What are you planning to do? Put up 'Don't Talk to the Hostess Unless Absolutely Necessary' signs in all the bedrooms?" But she held her tongue.

"How's Donald?" she asked.

"Stressed," Nora replied, putting two tins of caviar in the fridge. She gave Aislinn a pointed look. "In dire need of a career change."

"That could be arranged."

A look of cautious hopefulness jumped across Nora's face. "You changed your mind?"

"Nooo," Aislinn said slowly, rocking on her heels, "but a very viable alternative has presented itself that could make both of us happy."

Nora looked dubious as she put the last of the groceries away and put up some of her beloved gourmet coffee in the coffeemaker. "I'm all ears."

"You know that writer friend of Liam's? PJ? The

one who did a reading here and whose book is a big success?"

Nora scrunched up her nose. "That talking salmon book?"

"Yeah."

"What about him?"

"Li and I had him up here for dinner. Long story short, he wants to buy Padraig's cottage and the land around it. I had Carole Brown up here to give me an estimate of how much we could get. It's out of this world, Nora. Truly." She named the price, avidly watching her sister's face transform from doubtful to amazement.

"You're joking."

Aislinn put her hand over her heart. "Swear to God."

Nora slowly sat down at the kitchen table. Aislinn could practically hear the wheels spinning in her head as she stared into Aislinn's eyes. "So . . . we can split the money and—"

"I'll give you the whole thing if you drop the B and B idea."

Nora looked stunned. "What?"

"You can have it all. It's more than enough to open a B and B somewhere in England."

"And what do you get?"

"The farm. You sign over your claim to the property to me."

"And where does that leave me if you decide to sell it?"

"How many times do I have to tell you? This is my home. This is my livelihood. I have no intention of ever selling the farm." Aislinn couldn't contain her excitement. "We'd both get what we want, Nora."

Nora looked dubious. "This is so sudden."

"I know. I know. It's like it dropped right into our laps."

"You'd really be willing to let this guy live in Padraig's cottage?"

"He only wants it for the summers." Aislinn clasped her hands together imploringly. "Please tell me you'll consider it. Please."

"I need to talk to Donald about it."

"Yes, of course."

"What does Liam think?"

"He thinks it's perfect. *Perfect*."

Nora peered intently at the coffeemaker. "Does Liam know you've no intention of ever leaving here?"

Aislinn was caught off guard. "I—well, we've never talked about it, but it's pretty obvious, isn't it?" She was too impatient to think about all that right now. "Talk to Donald. ASAP if you can."

"Can I have a cup of coffee first?" Nora asked dryly, but her expression was amused.

"Sorry," Aislinn murmured.

"Go back out to work," said Nora. "We'll talk at lunch. I promise."

"Grand."

Aislinn practically danced out the door. Maybe it was nothing more than wishful thinking, but she had a good feeling about this.

# 38

*"Admit it: you'll* miss me a teeny bit."

Aislinn smiled at Nora's gentle ribbing as they strolled the farm arm in arm. They'd closed on the sale of the cottage and land that morning. Aislinn felt a huge weight lift off her back when PJ Leary's solicitor handed a bank check for the full amount to Nora. Nora then signed a document prepared by Aislinn's solicitor, giving over her half ownership of the farm to Aislinn. Things felt right between them, finally. They were both getting what they wanted.

Aislinn squeezed her sister's hand. "Of course I'll admit it."

"I owe you an apology," Nora said quietly.

Aislinn looked at her, surprised. "What's that?"

"You were right: it was selfish and insensitive of me to try to persuade you to turn this place into a B and B. This *is* your home; it was wrong of me to come over from England and try to throw my weight around."

"Thank you," said Aislinn, choking up.

"You were also right about something else, too," said

Nora, exaggeratedly sidestepping a small patch of muddy grass even though she was wearing a pair of wellies. *Nature girl you're not,* Aislinn thought to herself with amusement.

"Yes?"

"The B and B? It *is* a pure escape fantasy. Who are we kidding? Donald and I are the last two people cut out for the hospitality industry. Imagine the first time someone asked us to get up extra early to cook them breakfast because they needed to leave for some reason. We'd lose two customers right there. We'd be so resentful they'd never come back."

Aislinn laughed loudly. "I have this image of you banging plates around the kitchen, cursing to yourself."

"And Donald throwing the plates down in front of the guests, snarling, 'There you go,'" Nora joined in with a giggle.

"What happens next for you two, then?"

"We might use some of the money to live off while Donald figures out what he'd really like to do."

"And you? What do you want?"

Nora sighed heavily. "I don't know. For now, I'm going to keep on teaching. But if I get fed up, there's enough money there for me to take a break as well."

"I'm glad. Well, I have big plans, too," Aislinn boasted.

"What's that?"

"I'm going to buy two new ewes."

"That's *very* exciting," Nora teased.

"I know."

Nora slowed to a halt. "I love you, Aislinn."

The sisters embraced.

"I love you too, Nora."

Nora looked wistful as Aislinn released her. "I suppose I should pack."

"Liam will drive you down to Cork tomorrow morning."

"Are you sure? I know he gets in late."

"It was his idea, actually."

"He's a good man, Aislinn. I'm glad you found each other."

"Me, too," said Aislinn contentedly. Every time she thought of her husband, she felt a small thrill. She'd heard that the romance of the early years of marriage eventually transformed into something deeper and less passionate, but she couldn't imagine not feeling that little pinch of ardor whenever she thought of Liam. Her mother once told her that she developed a renewed crush on her father every spring, because "spring is when a young girl's fancy turned to romance, and I always feel like a young girl when I'm with your father." *Too much information,* Aislinn had thought when she was younger. Now she thought it was lovely.

She and Nora started back toward the house.

"Do you think Liam will eventually work the farm with you?" Nora asked.

"I think the Oak is more to his liking. He needs to be around people a lot more than I do. If he spends too much time alone, he gets crabby."

Nora chuckled. "The exact opposite of someone else I know."

Aislinn grinned. "Chalk and cheese, as mum used to say."

"They would have loved him."

Aislinn sighed. "I know."

"When do you think you'll meet his parents?"

Aislinn hesitated. "I don't know. There's talk of them coming over at Christmas, which would be lovely."

"And the rest of his family?"

"I'm not sure any of them have the money right now, apart from his sister Sinead, who's a lawyer. His sister Maggie just had a baby, a little boy named Charlie, named after Liam's dad. He's a gorgeous little thing. It's so nice being able to upload pictures on the computer and send them back and forth." Her mood deflated a bit. "Liam's a bit depressed right now about not being in New York. He's sad he's going to miss the baby's christening."

"It must be tough on him," Nora murmured sympathetically.

"It is. But they all e-mail back and forth and the like, and he does speak with his parents and brother at least once a week. That helps a bit. At least I hope it does."

Nora glanced at her tentatively. "Any chance of you and Liam visiting us in London?"

"Maybe," said Aislinn, even though the thought made her groan inwardly. She'd not liked London the one time she was there. Then again, it was a while ago, and Liam had never been to London.

They'd reached the house. Standing outside the mudroom, Aislinn tilted her head in the direction of the pasture across the street. "I best get back to Alec and Deenie. They've been holding down the fort all alone all morning."

Nora paused introspectively. "It's all worked out the way it was supposed to, hasn't it?"

"It has," Aislinn agreed, surprised to find herself getting a little tearful. If anyone had told her a year ago that she'd recover from her broken heart to find herself married—to a Yank, yet!—she would have told them to go chase themselves. Yet here she was, madly in love, owner of the family farm, and slowly healing her relationship with her sister despite some rough patches. She wasn't a big one for prayer, but tonight before she fell asleep, she intended to give thanks for her wonderful life.

*   *   *

*What the hell is going on?* Liam wondered as he finished up work for the night. Twice during the evening, Quinn had texted him, writing to tell him to call when he got the chance. He knew Jack would have let him take a break to make a call, but if it was bad news, he didn't want to know in the middle of his shift. Better to wait until the night was done.

It was close to 1 a.m. when he locked up the Oak and

headed out to his motorcycle. That meant it was 7 p.m. in New York. As soon as he reached the parking lot, he called Quinn, who answered on the first ring. Liam steeled himself.

"Hey. What's up?"

"You sitting down?"

"No, I'm sitting on my bike worried sick that Dad's dead."

Quinn clucked his tongue. "Why do you always assume I'm calling with bad news?"

"Gee, I don't know, maybe because I was forced to leave the country so I didn't get killed?" Liam replied acidly.

"You can come home."

Liam was silent.

"Did you hear me?"

"Yeah, I heard you."

Liam closed his eyes. He'd always thought that when he got the green light to go back to Manhattan, he'd be overjoyed. Instead, he felt sick to his stomach.

"Li?"

"I'm just trying to process this," he managed. Aislinn. What the hell was he going to tell Aislinn? What the hell were they going to do? Shit, they really should have talked about this rather than telling themselves that somehow, things would work out. The truth was, Liam had thought he wouldn't have to deal with this for years.

"What happened?" he made himself say.

"The Major got a message that you're out of danger."

"What about Whitey?"

"He's dead," Quinn said with a tinge of glee in his voice. "Had a heart attack in prison. The Major got word that since Whitey didn't have kids, and everyone in his crew is either in jail or on the outs with the rest of the Mob, you're in the clear." Quinn paused. "I know this complicates things for you."

Liam laughed bitterly. "That's putting it lightly."

"Talk to her."

"Obviously."

"Dad is really champing at the bit to have you back behind the bar. Uncle Jimmy is driving him nuts."

"You're not helping here," Liam snapped.

"Sorry. It's just the thought of having you back . . . it would be great, Li." Quinn's voice was cracking with emotion.

Liam closed his eyes. "I'm exhausted from work, Quinn. I can't even—"

"I understand. Talk to your wife, figure things out."

"Right." Liam rubbed his right temple. "Look, can you do me a favor?"

"Sure, anything."

"Ask Mom and Dad not to start bombarding me with phone calls, because you know they will, and the pressure will make me want to blow my brains out. And tell them I don't want them pressuring me through Uncle Paul and Aunt Bridget, either." He paused. "What would you do if you were me, Quinn?"

"I always go with my gut," Quinn said softly.

"My gut's a confused mess right now," Liam said miserably.

"Go home. We'll talk soon. Love you, Bro."

Liam felt his eyes fill. "Love you, too. Give my love to Nat."

"And mine to Aislinn. Bye now."

"Bye."

Liam sat on his motorcycle, unable to move. How, he wondered, could he feel numb and overwhelmed at the same time? Why now? Then he thought: *Would this happening years from now make any difference? You'd still be facing the same dilemma.* Maybe he and Aislinn shouldn't have gotten married. But the heart wants what it wants, and his wanted her. The only problem was, his heart yearned for home, too.

Liam put on his helmet and started up his bike. *If I go back to New York, I'll have to sell my motorcycle,* he thought idiotically. He took a deep breath of the cool night air, hoping it might help slow his galloping thoughts. It didn't. By the time he got home, he was still wound up. He crept up to bed. Aislinn was fast asleep. The sight of her tortured him, and rather than lying beside her, tossing and turning, waking her, he went down to the living room and curled up on the couch, praying that sleep would eventually come.

# 39

*Aislinn never needed* an alarm clock. After years of getting up at the same time—4:30 a.m.—her body instinctively knew when to wake. But since her marriage, she some-times found herself wishing she could linger between the sheets just a little while longer, so she could wrap herself around her gorgeous, sleeping husband. This morning, like all mornings, she went to give him a soft kiss on the cheek before quietly padding downstairs to make her breakfast. She was shocked to find his side of the bed empty.

He was probably sleeping at his old flat above the Oak. They'd agreed that if he stayed after closing time to hoist a few drinks, Liam wouldn't put himself—or anyone else—in peril by driving home. But she was shocked to come downstairs and find him dozing on the couch. Per-haps Deenie had been hogging the bed. Sometimes Ais-linn would find Liam clinging to the edge of the mattress while Deenie stretched out beside her in what she clearly felt was still her rightful place.

Aislinn crept across the hall into the kitchen, putting up the coffee as quietly as she could. Alec usually arrived at five thirty, giving her time to have a nice, relaxing breakfast. She was just about to crack the eggs into the pan when Liam appeared, crusty-eyed and yawning, wrapped in the mauve afghan her mother had made years ago that was kept over the back of the couch.

"I'm sorry," said Aislinn with a small wince. "I was trying to be quiet."

"You didn't wake me," Liam said sleepily. "It was the smell of the coffee brewing."

"You sure?"

"Yeah." He rubbed a hand over his face, yawning. "Is there enough there for me?"

"Of course." Aislinn smiled at him, her sexy, sleepy husband. "It'll be nice to have breakfast together."

Liam shuffled over to her and kissed her on the cheek before sitting down at the table.

"Deenie push you out of bed?" Aislinn asked with an amused smile.

"No. I was having trouble sleeping, and I didn't want to wake you up."

"You best nap today so you're not dead on your feet tonight," she advised.

"Yeah, I know." He looked at the coffee machine longingly. "How long is that going to take? God, that thing *is* ancient."

"You sound like Nora. It works fine. And besides, age has nothing to do with how fast it brews. Be patient." She threw a pat of butter into the pan, scrambling the eggs. "Why couldn't you sleep?"

Liam was silent.

Aislinn turned to him worriedly. "Liam? What's going on? Is everything all right back in America?"

"Oh yeah, everything's great back in America," he said grimly. There was a long pause. "Quinn called last night. It's safe for me to go home."

Aislinn felt her heart jerk to a halt. She knew this day would come. She just never thought it would come so soon. No, that was a lie. She had hoped it would never come.

She turned back to the stove, not knowing what to say. Behind her, she heard Liam get up and fetch two coffee mugs from the cabinet. *Don't throw up,* she told herself. She looked at the wooden spoon in her hand pushing the eggs around the pan: it was shaking. She made herself control it.

Liam appeared at her side, putting a cup of coffee down next to her on the counter.

"Thank you," Aislinn said quietly.

"Obviously we need to figure this out."

"Yes," she managed, not looking at him.

"Do you want to talk about it now, or wait till later?"

"I don't see any point in waiting." She slid the eggs onto their respective plates, then walked over to fetch the toast.

She could feel Liam's eyes on her back. "Why won't you look at me?"

"Because I need to keep a level head. I need to keep things simple in my mind: Serve eggs. Get toast. If I don't, my head is going to explode."

"I feel the same way, believe me."

"Come. Sit down. Have breakfast."

Liam joined her at the table. "Talk to me," he begged softly.

She forced her eyes to his. "No, you talk to me. Tell me what Quinn said."

Liam looked pained as he took a long sip of coffee. "The guy who wanted me killed died in prison. He's got no heirs. His crew is scattered. Quinn got word that I'm out of danger. End of story."

"Except it's not."

"No."

The smell of the eggs was making her sick. She forced herself to take a mouthful, trying not to gag as she forced the food down. She put down her fork.

"I take it you want to go home."

Liam looked pained. "Of course I do. But—us."

"We're idiots. We probably shouldn't have gotten married," Aislinn said dismissively. "Big mistake."

Liam gripped her hand. "Don't shut down on me now, Aislinn. Please."

"I'm trying not to."

"Talk to me," he begged again.

Aislinn closed her eyes, trying to put her jumbled thoughts into a coherent order. "I love you. Part of me is happy you're now free to see your family. But you married an Irishwoman who owns a sheep farm in Ireland."

"Maybe there's a way to compromise."

Aislinn opened her eyes. "And what would that be?"

Liam hesitated. "You lease your farm to Alec and Jake. We move to America, and I go back to work at my family's bar—"

"You know I've no desire to ever live in a city," Aislinn cut in.

"You didn't let me finish. We go to New York," Liam continued, "and we get a farm outside the city. You run the farm, and we see each other on weekends."

Aislinn stared at him. "You're joking me. I just sold some of my land so I can keep this farm. I *love* this farm. You know I've no desire to live or work anywhere else. That's a mad idea."

"Idea number two: we have the ultimate long-distance marriage."

"What? You move back there, and I stay here?" Aislinn asked incredulously. "We might as well divorce, then. How about this: we keep living the life we've set up here, except now, we're free to go see your family whenever we please."

Liam looked miserable. "And what am I supposed to do? Work for Jack the rest of my life?"

"What's wrong with that?"

"It's pathetic."

"Oh, but working for your father isn't," Aislinn retorted.

"It's a family business. That's different," Liam countered heatedly.

"You never said that was important to you."

"I thought it was obvious!"

"And I thought it was obvious I wanted to live in Ballycraig forever!"

Liam cradled his head in hands. "I guess it was," he said miserably. "I don't know."

"You *do* know. You just didn't want to think about it."

Liam lifted his head, glaring at her. "And you just didn't want to think about how I'd get the green light to go home one day."

Aislinn swallowed, trying to get hold of her temper so things didn't escalate. "We're both at fault here," she pointed out calmly. "This issue has always been the pink elephant in the room, and we chose to pretend it wasn't there. But it is. We should have dealt with it ages ago."

"I know." Liam grimaced. "See, part of the problem for me is Ballycraig itself."

"What's wrong with Ballycraig?"

"There's nothing to *do* here, honey."

"What is it you want to *do* that you haven't been able to?"

"Go to the movies."

Aislinn snorted derisively. "There are cinemas in both Moneygall and Crosshaven. Correct me if I'm wrong, but you've lived here almost a year and, as far as I know, you've never gone into either town even once to go see a movie."

"I didn't have a car."

"Oh, please, give over. I've got a truck. If going to the movies was crucial to your sanity, we could have gone any time. Don't deny it."

"You're right," he muttered.

"We can go to the damn movies any time you want," Aislinn continued as anger and desperation began creeping up on her. "You want a satellite dish? We'll get a satellite dish. That'll at least be something." She chugged her coffee and put her cup down on the table with a resounding thud.

"You're getting pissed."

"I am, but more at myself than you, for ignoring the obvious."

Neither said anything for a long time. Finally, Aislinn rose. "I should get to work."

"Let me ask you something," Liam said abruptly. "If you had a choice between me and the farm, which would you choose?"

Anger won. "Are you giving me an ultimatum, Liam O'Brien?"

"Of course not. It's just a hypothetical."

"Well, here's a hypothetical for you: if you had a choice between me or going home to New York, which would *you* choose? Chew on that."

She walked out, calling for Deenie from the bottom of the stairs. Deenie came trotting down, and together they walked back through the kitchen into the mudroom. The sentence, "It'll all work out" didn't exist anymore in her vocabulary. It never should have. She was out of words for now, so she left him sitting there, staring out the kitchen window into the morning darkness, brooding and silent.

\* \* \*

*Liam went into* town early. Were it a normal day, he would have awakened somewhere around midmorning, taken a run, enjoyed lunch with Aislinn and Alec, and then gone into town to help Jack sort things out at the pub before they opened. Today, however, he finished his breakfast, showered, and headed directly into Ballycraig.

Shit, what a way to start the morning. Yet on a certain level, he was glad it was out there on the table, even if their discussion did take place at the ungodly hour of 4:30 a.m. As he'd expected, the news rocked her, the same way it had rocked him the night before. Despite the ratcheting tension, the longer they talked about it, the more he saw that Aislinn was right: they were both at fault. They should have discussed this earlier. But he couldn't help wonder: would it have made a difference? They loved each other. Would they not have gotten married if they'd acknowledged that one day, a gut-wrenching decision would have to be made, one that could result in mutual heartache? Or would they have given themselves over to their feelings anyway, trying to enjoy whatever time they had together, whether it was months or years?

Stupid as it was, he was smarting over her comment about the movies. He hadn't gone once since he'd moved to Ireland. Not once. As if he went all the time when he lived in Manhattan! If he was honest with himself, his days here weren't that different from his routine at home: late nights at the bar, sleeping in, working out . . . the only difference was, in his downtime he often spent time with his family.

The Oak was dark as he unlocked the door and slipped inside. He turned on the lights, slowly taking in the pub, thinking about how every night, it was packed with friendly, familiar faces. He enjoyed working here. It was a lot like home, with one major difference: it *wasn't* home.

Remembering he still had some coffee in the fridge in his old apartment, he crept upstairs. It was close to six now. He thought he was being quiet, but apparently he wasn't. There was a knock at the door, and then Jack walked in wearing a tatty old flannel robe that he couldn't close fully because of his belly.

"Jesus God, do you have any idea what time it is?"

"Sorry," Liam mumbled.

Jack rubbed his eyes. "She throw you out?" he asked, looking amused.

"No, but she might by the end of the day."

"Ah, I detect a note of misery in my young friend's voice." He leaned against the kitchen counter. "Talk to Jack, boyo—after he gets some coffee down his gullet."

They made small talk until the coffee was done, Jack bitching and moaning about how much Bettina loved their holiday in Torremolinos, while he'd hated it. "Filled with Brits," he said sourly. "And Spaniards." She'd kept dropping hints to him about retiring there, saying that she was fed up with the Irish damp and the way it was seeping into her bones. "I don't know what the hell she's on about," said Jack. "There's no damp here."

"It does rain a lot," Liam observed.

"Oh, and I suppose it never rains in Spain?" Jack challenged. "She's a pain in my neck, that one. It's a mystery to me why we ever got married."

"Love?" Liam offered tentatively, an image of Aislinn on their wedding day stealing into his mind.

"I suppose." Jack sighed. "She was gorgeous when she was young." A look of tenderness overtook him. "I still think she's gorgeous now, truth be told. I don't see the wrinkles she says she has, nor the fat arse she's always on about. A piece of wisdom, by the way: if Aislinn ever asks you if she looks fat, always say no, even if she has an arse the size of Croagh Patrick. That's the only right answer to the question if you value your life, especially your goolies."

Liam laughed. "I'll remember that." He poured their coffee, and together they sat down at his small kitchen table.

"What's on your mind?" asked Jack, cupping his hands around the mug.

"I heard from my brother Quinn last night. Apparently, it's safe for me to go home."

Jack looked surprised. "Already?"

"What do you mean, 'Already'? I've been here almost a year."

"That's not too much time."

Liam frowned at him. "Says who? It was enough time for me to get married, wasn't it?"

"True, it was." Jack took a sip of coffee and made a face. "This is swill."

"It's all I've got."

"No wonder you're always cranky when you first come in to work, if this what your belly is filled with. It's shite."

Liam huffed with frustration. "Can we get off the topic of coffee?"

"Sure, sure." Jack pushed his cup away. "So let me guess: you told the missus, and she said go chase yourself, that she's not leaving her farm to move to New York."

"Pretty much. I mean, I tried to offer up some compromises."

"Such as?"

"We go back to New York, and she has a sheep farm outside the city, and I work at my parents' bar on the weekends and—"

Jack waved a hand in the air. "Crap idea, since she just got Nora to sign the farm over to her. Next."

"Long-distance marriage."

"Otherwise known as divorce."

"That's what she said."

Jack looked mystified. "Look, you two knew this was going to happen one day."

"I know. But we've avoided talking about it," Liam said miserably.

"You truly do have Irish blood in your veins."

"Help me out here, will you?"

Jack rubbed his chin thoughtfully. "Question one: this means you *can* go home to New York to visit whenever you please, right?"

"Yeah."

"Question two: do you love your wife?"

"That's pretty obvious, isn't it?"

"How much?"

"More than my life," said Liam, trying not to get choked up.

"Right, here's what I think. You love your wife more than anything. You've built a new life here, one that now allows you to see your family at will."

"But I want to go home," Liam said softly.

"Do you? Really? Or do you think you *should* want to go home after being away so long?"

Liam looked down at the table.

"You need to listen to your heart," Jack declared.

Liam sighed heavily, rolling his eyes. "My brother says to listen to my gut."

"Gut, heart, same thing. It's the best advice there is."

"I know," Liam said miserably.

"I don't know what else to tell you." Jack stood. "Well, I'm off back to bed."

Liam looked at him incredulously. "How can you go back to bed once you're up?"

"It's called getting on in age, and trust me, it's not for sissies. I'll see you later."

Liam nodded, rolling his coffee cup between his hands.

*Listen to your gut. Listen to heart.* Liam knew it was the only thing to do, but he felt like his heart was telling him to do one thing one minute and something completely different the next. Suppose he chose wrong?

# 40

"*It does my* heart good to see you back behind that bar," said the Mouth with a satisfied smile. The Mouth, one of the regulars at his parents' pub, wasn't the first person to express this sentiment when they walked into the Wild Hart to find Liam back at his old post. PJ, back in New York after a worldwide book tour, had said so, too, as had Mrs. Colgan (whose new parrot, Rudy II, was just as annoying as his predecessor). Even the Major, the man of few words, made a point of coming over to say he was pleased to see Liam.

Things had changed in the year he'd been away. The Wild Hart had become the unofficial hangout for the New York Blades, Manhattan's hometown hockey team, who were determined to bring the Stanley Cup to New York for a third time. There was a female bartender, Christie, who'd replaced him. Liam felt bad for her, since she'd been forced to work with his uncle Jimmy, a retired cop who lived to milk his back pain and loved to needle people. That Christie was a firefighter just made Uncle Jimmy's barbs all the more pointed.

And of course, things had changed in his family, too.

Maggie and Brendan now had baby Charlie, whom Aislinn couldn't seem to resist picking up and cuddling. Sinead was talking about dating again. Quinn's blog had become very popular. Quinn's wife Natalie was managing an extremely prestigious French restaurant. Everyone was happy and healthy, including his parents who, though they were definitely looking older, had lost none of their spunk or backbreaking work ethic.

Liam smiled at Aislinn as she slipped behind the bar and gently tugged on his apron. "We've got to leave for home soon, you know."

"I know. I just wanted to see if I can get this lot"—he gestured at the regulars— "to give me some decent tips. God knows they didn't before I left."

"*I* didn't have the money, then," PJ pointed out.

"Yeah, but you do now," said Mary Colgan in a voice tinged with envy. "So don't be a skinflint."

"It's always been my belief that money can complicate the delicate balance of friendship," said the Mouth, the bar's philosopher. "As the great—"

"Please shut up," Liam begged with a groan.

"Bet you don't miss that," Christie ribbed.

"Believe it or not, I do."

Christie looked at Aislinn. "I can't believe you're dragging him home! It's been so much fun having him here."

"Dad said he's interviewing a replacement for Jimmy, don't worry," Liam assured her.

"I hate to tell you, but he's been saying that for a year," said Christie.

"I'll put a bug in his ear before I go."

"Thank you," she said gratefully.

"Thank *you* for doing such a great job," said Liam, squeezing her arm. He turned to Aislinn. "Shall we?"

\* \* \*

*"Now, we're coming* over at Christmas. Don't forget."

Aislinn smiled indulgently as her mother-in-law reminded her of this for the third time in an hour. The whole family was standing in the small kitchen of Liam's parents' flat above the Wild Hart, all gathered round to say their good-byes before she and Liam flew back to Ireland.

She still got queasy when she thought back on how she'd been on pins and needles the whole day after she and Liam had had their "discussion." What if he came home and said he wanted to go back to America, and she could take it or leave it? He'd come in after work that night to find her waiting up for him in bed, tense and wakeful, bordering on fearful. He'd stripped off his clothes, slid between the sheets, and, tenderly pushing a few stray wisps of hair off her face, had whispered, "I love you. Our life is here."

Oh, God, the joy of it nearly propelled her through the ceiling. She thanked him for making that sacrifice for her, but he told her that in the end, it was a no-brainer. Jack had told him he had a job at the Oak for as long as he wanted, and that eventually he could buy the pub when Jack retired because, according to Jack, his son Neil would "rather drive a spike through his own head than own the Oak."

"That sealed the deal right there," said Liam. "That, and realizing the most important thing in my life is you. You're a Ballycraiger, and now I am, too."

Two weeks later, they'd flown into New York to see Liam's family, who were warmer than she ever could have imagined. His parents were affectionate and chatty and welcomed her into the fold immediately, making her feel as if she'd known them her whole life. Sinead was slightly aloof at first, until Aislinn realized that it was more shyness than anything else. Maggie was colorful and exuberant. Her even-tempered husband Brendan was clearly the anchor that kept her tethered to the earth. Quinn was as charming as he'd been in Dublin. *Talk about chalk and cheese!* The first thing Aislinn thought when she met Quinn's French wife, Natalie, was that opposites obviously attracted. She was quiet and refined, quite the contrast to Quinn's boisterousness. But it was clear that she and Quinn adored one another. Aislinn was sad to be leaving; their visit seemed to have flown by.

Aislinn reveled in the hug Liam's mother gave her. "It was lovely to meet you, darling."

"You, too, Mrs. O'Brien."

"How many times have I told you?" Liam's mother chided with a cluck of the tongue. "It's Kathleen. Or Mom, when you feel comfortable enough."

"Mom, then," Aislinn said softly.

Liam's mother cupped Aislinn's cheek. "I'm so glad he found you."

"You're a definite step up for him," said Quinn.

"I agree," said Maggie, joining in on the teasing as she looked at Liam. "You married up, Bro."

"Tell me about it." Liam regarded his father. "You have to replace Uncle Jimmy. Seriously."

"Tell me something I don't know," said his father wearily. "But it's hard. He's my brother, and he says he doesn't know what he'd do with himself if he didn't have this job, now that he's retired."

"Couldn't he set himself up as a private detective or something?" asked Aislinn.

"Oh, yeah, he's a right gumshoe, that one," said Mr. O'Brien dryly. He patted Liam's shoulder. "I'll find a replacement, I promise. I know he's driving Christie spare. I don't want to lose her."

"Good. I mean, I know no one could ever be as good as me behind the bar, but still . . ."

"Hey, truer words were never spoken," said Liam's dad. "I hope Jack realizes that."

"He does." Liam checked his watch. "We should go," he said quietly. "I'm sure our cab is downstairs waiting."

Aislinn swallowed, a lump forming in her throat as she hugged Liam's mother again. "Thank you so much. It's been a wonderful visit."

"Don't be daft."

Aislinn moved on to hug Liam's father. "You keep an

eye on him now," he said to her, a mischievous glint in his eye. "Keep him out of trouble."

"Oh, she's whipped me into shape, believe me," Liam quipped. "It's very clear who wears the Wellies in our house."

Everyone laughed as Aislinn's jaw dropped. "I beg your pardon?"

"That was a joke, McCafferty."

"It had better be."

Aislinn hugged Quinn, then Natalie, who squeezed her hand tight. "Any time you need a place to stay in New York, you're welcome to stay with us."

"Or us," said Maggie.

"And I have a pretty roomy apartment myself," said Sinead.

"I can see we're going to have to draw straws next time you're here," said Liam's dad.

Aislinn hugged Maggie warmly, then bent to kiss little Charlie's rosy cheek. "God, he's gorgeous."

"Most of the time," said Maggie. "Perhaps I'll send him over to you when he hits the terrible twos." She looked at her husband, Brendan. "What do you think?"

"I think that's a great idea," he said with a big grin. He drew Aislinn into a big bear hug. "You and Li should feel free to get in touch with my family next time you're in Dublin. They'd love it."

"That'll probably be about five years from now," said Liam, razzing Aislinn. "She's not big on cities."

His mother's face fell. "Did you not like it here in New York?" she asked Aislinn, looking disappointed.

"No, no, I liked it fine," Aislinn hurried to assure her. She'd been overwhelmed at first, and truly, it wasn't her cup of tea, but the visit was less about getting to know the city than getting to know Liam's family.

Liam put his arm around her shoulder. "She prefers the country life," he said affectionately.

"I can see that," said his mother, looking sentimental. "I do miss Ballycraig sometimes."

"You'll be back there soon enough, woman," Liam's father said.

"True," she said. She looked down at Aislinn and Liam's bags. "You've got everything?"

"Yup," said Liam.

"I packed you some soda bread for the plane just in case you get hungry," Liam's mother confided to Aislinn.

Aislinn laughed. "Thank you."

Liam picked up one of their bags, Aislinn the other. "Off we go." They started down the stairs.

"You'll ring when you get in, won't you?" his mother called after him.

"Of course we will."

"Bye," everyone called down to them. "Love you!"

"Love you, too!" Aislinn and Liam replied. Aislinn hadn't felt this loved since her parents were alive.

\* \* \*

*Downstairs in the* bar, they made a quick stop to say goodbye to the regulars, PJ especially. "I'll see you two in the summer," he said to Aislinn.

"Looking forward to it," she replied, meaning it.

"Safe trip," the Major said quietly.

"Thanks," said Liam, patting his shoulder. "For everything."

The Major nodded curtly, then returned to reading his copy of the *Irish Independent News.*

"Me 'n' Rudy here will miss you," said Mrs. Colgan, petting her parrot. She paused. "Do you have many parrots in the Emerald Isle?"

"Uh, I'll have to get back to you on that," said Liam.

The Mouth, somewhat formally, shook both Liam and Aislinn's hands. " 'Parting is such sweet sorrow'—so sayeth the immortal bard."

"Right," said Liam. He looked at Aislinn. "Let's roll, McCafferty."

"You got it, O'Brien."

*  *  *

*In the cab* on their way to the airport, Aislinn was prepared for Liam to descend into melancholy. If the visit with his family had flown by fast for her, she couldn't imagine how the time must have raced by for him.

She took his hand. "You okay?"

Liam looked perplexed. "Yeah. Why do you ask?"

"I just thought you'd be blue after saying good-bye."

"I am," he admitted. He leaned back with a sigh. "But it'll be good to get home."

Aislinn laid her head on his shoulder contently, closed her eyes, and smiled.

Home.

Go ahead. Try…

# *Just a Taste*

By *New York Times* bestselling author

# Deirdre Martin

Since his wife's untimely death, Anthony Dante has thrown himself into his cooking, making his restaurant, Dante's, a Brooklyn institution. So far, his biggest problem has been keeping his brother, the retired hockey star, out of the kitchen. But now, a mademoiselle is invading his turf.

Stunning Vivi Robitaille can't wait to showcase her taste-bud-tingling recipes in her brand new bistro, Vivi's. Her only problem is an arrogant Italian chef across the street who actually thinks he's competition.

The table is set for a culinary war—until things start getting spicy outside of the kitchen…

It's a...

# *Total Rush*

Free spirit Gemma Dante wishes her love life were going as well as her New Age business. So she casts a spell to catch her Mr. Right. But when the cosmic wires get crossed, into her life walks a clean-cut fireman who's anything but her type.

Sean Kennealy doesn't know what to make of his pretty neighbor who burns incense. He only knows that being near her sparks a fire in him that even the guys at Ladder 29, Engine 31 can't put out.

From
*New York Times* Bestselling Author

# Deirdre Martin